A LAST

Born and brought up in the south of England, the eldest girl of nine children, DEE YATES moved north to Yorkshire to study medicine. She remained there, working in well woman medicine and general practice and bringing up her three daughters. She writes historical fiction, poetry and more recently non-fiction. Occasionally she gets to compare notes with her youngest sister Sarah Flint who writes crime with blood-curdling descriptions which make Dee want to hide behind the settee.

A LAST GOODBYE

Dee Yates

For Carol
Love & Best Wishes,
Dee
x

www.ariafiction.com

First published in the United Kingdom in 2018 by Aria, an imprint of Head of Zeus Ltd

9 7 5 3 1 2 4 6 8

A CIP catalogue record for this book is available from the British Library.

ISBN (E) 9781788545112

Aria
c/o Head of Zeus
First Floor East
5–8 Hardwick Street London EC1R 4RG
www.ariafiction.com

About *A Last Goodbye*

On a remote hill farm in beautiful Scotland, Ellen and her father Duncan are enjoying a peaceful life away from the belching mills and hustle and bustle of the growing towns.

In time they're joined by rugged farmhand Tom, come to lend some muscle to Ellen's aging father, who has begun to find sheep farming hard to manage alone. Almost inevitably romance grows between Ellen and the new arrival but once married however, Ellen discovers that Tom has a brutish side to his character. As war in Europe spreads, she begins to dream of him leaving for the trenches as a way for her to escape.

Even with Tom fighting abroad however, the family cannot hide from the realities of war as a group of POWs are brought to their valley to build a reservoir. And amongst the men, sworn enemies and shunned by all the locals, Ellen finds a gentler heart that is hard to resist…

To my friends in the Camps Valley with thanks for renting me the shepherd's cottage and for teaching me as much as I know about sheep.

1

Turn of the Century

A low strangled moan halted the shepherd in his progress to the barn. His border collie Tess, sensing the hesitation, gave a staccato bark. Overhead, a near full moon dimmed the brightness of a sky full of stars. The hard ground crunched beneath the man's boots as he took one step, two, towards the noise. The floor of the valley sparkled white with frost. Before and behind him, the outline of the hills ran in black peaks and troughs into the far distance, at which point the two sides seemed to coalesce and enclose the farmhouse and its scattered buildings in a huge amphitheatre.

Duncan knew that appearances were deceptive. On a rare sunny day in summer he had taken the afternoon off and walked the track eastward with Janet. The season's lambs were growing fast and older sheep, newly shorn, grazed lazily in the warm air, the sound of tearing grass interrupted momentarily as they had taken a few startled steps away from the approaching shepherd and his wife.

In front of the couple, hills had parted slowly to allow them access, folding in behind them as they ventured further. There had been no alteration to the undulations, no diminution in the deep clefts dividing each from the next and giving birth to the water that grooved and gouged the land as it raced to the Clyde. Neither had there been any increase in the scattered farmhouses, whose owners eked out a hard living with the help or hindrance of the countryside around them. But that unspoiled day in a singularly warm summer, when he and Janet had lain together in the warm heather, was far from his thoughts as he stopped again and listened.

In the distance the cheerful gurgling of the stream caught his ear now and the shepherd felt suddenly less alone in this wide expanse of whiteness. Here and there the meandering water gleamed in the moonlight. The moan came again and, after a pause, a third time. He cursed softly under his breath. He was a mild man, not given to swearing… not given to saying much at all. But he had been looking forward to a night's uninterrupted sleep with Janet in his arms. Janet, so near her time, like most of the flock scattered across the valley floor and up the slopes around him. He had only stepped outside to check on the dogs before settling down for the night. But if he failed to respond to the cry, there could be a dead lamb or two by morning.

He saw her by the water. He saw the ripples in her

swollen abdomen, as she lay on her side. With each moan, she lifted her head and turned sorrowful eyes to the heavens. Duncan set down his lamp on the grass and slowly approached, but the sheep made off across the field. With a swift sideways swoop, he caught the ewe and brought her to the ground again. Taking hold of her by the horns, he dragged her to the protection of the sheepfold and secured the entrance. Then he went back for his lamp and set it on the wall.

She was a first-timer, a gimmer. He knew that she was well due for lambing but she had been grazing quietly when he did his last round and he had guessed wrongly that she would not go into labour during the night. Looking at her now, he could see that the lamb was dead already. Its head protruded from the birth canal but the front legs, which should have led, were absent, caught in the mother's womb. The result was suffocation. Duncan slowly inserted his arm into the warm interior of the ewe. Struggling to grip the legs, he pulled them to the outside. It was a big lamb but, once the position was correct, it delivered easily. Duncan cursed under his breath. He hated to lose a lamb unnecessarily... and he considered this an unnecessary loss.

He moved a few yards away to where he could see another ewe in labour. She was an old lady of the flock and had lambed many times before. He hesitated, guessing that she would need neither his presence nor his help. The cold air bit at his nose and fingers. He glanced across to the ewe with her dead lamb. If he left now, he would miss the opportunity to put a spare lamb to her. And if this sheep was to give birth to more than one, it made sense to put one of them to the first ewe. Years of experience told him that both lambs would stand a better chance of survival that way, especially with the weather being so cold. He caught hold of her and dragged her into the fold where the first ewe was resting.

He was right to stay. The first birth was rapid, the lamb slithering wetly into a heap on the grass. Duncan pulled away the vestiges of membrane still clinging around its head and inserted his finger into its mouth to clear the passages of blood and slime and stimulate it to breathe. Then he stood back and watched as the mother licked and nuzzled her baby until it stood swaying on bended legs and uttered a first pitiful bleat. Then she lay down and laboured again.

All around him the silence was intense. Even the stream seemed hushed. The ewe strained without a murmur, her breath, like his, forming dense clouds in the freezing air. Duncan stamped his feet in an effort to encourage some feeling back into them. He cupped his hands round his mouth and blew gently. The newborn stumbled in the grass, struggling to stay upright, its body convulsed with shivers. The shepherd frowned. What was taking the ewe so long?

At last he knelt behind her and sunk his hand and

arm into the womb, trying to make sense of the jumble of legs that he encountered. Finally, he found a head. It was bent back on the neck in such a way as to cause an obstruction. She would never lamb with it in this position. Carefully he untwisted the head and felt around for the two front legs, which he pulled to the outside. With another push, the lamb was out, lying at the side of its complaining twin.

Quickly he inserted his finger into its mouth and ran it across and round its tongue. It stirred, shook its head and bleated. The ewe turned and gently butted her lamb, encouraging it to stand. Duncan pulled on the mother's teats and the first of the twins nuzzled into her side.

The gimmer still stood by her dead lamb. Taking hold of the lifeless lamb by its legs, Duncan left the shelter of the fold and, by the light of the hurricane lamp, quickly skinned the carcass. He cut holes for the legs, returned to the fold and fitted the skin onto the back of the second twin. It was an uneven pairing and the little coat trailed behind the lamb as it struggled to walk. He picked it up by its front legs and placed it next to the childless ewe. Then he left them together and stood on the other side of the wall to watch. He had not long to wait before his action had the desired effect. The gimmer sniffed the lamb and licked it, recognising the smell of her own lamb and after several futile attempts the lamb found the warm teat and began to suckle.

Duncan gave a contented smile. The lamb's struggles

were by no means over, but it looked as if the two would bond. He would leave them together in the fold and check on them at first light. Reaching for his lamp, he began to trudge back to the cottage, feeling happier now that he had saved the life of the lamb and probably its mother.

Once inside, he unlaced and removed his boots and hung his coat on the back of the door. He stood for a moment in the quiet darkness, savouring the warmth, and then padded in stockinged feet into the kitchen. A bucket of water stood on the floor in front of the sink, a necessary precaution on nights such as these when water from the gill often froze solid in the pipes. From the draining board he took a bar of soap and washed his freezing hands and arms in the even colder water. In the parlour, the coals of the fire still glowed red. Crouching down on his haunches in front of the hearth, he tried to coax life into his numb fingers. He could imagine Janet's words if he should climb into bed and attempt to touch her with his cold hands and feet! At the thought of her warm, soft body, he stood and hastily pulled off his shirt and trousers before searching for the handle of the bedroom door.

Her gentle breathing indicated that she was asleep, but as the bedsprings creaked with his weight, she turned slowly and planted a languid kiss on his cheek.

'Is that you done the neet?' she murmured into his ear.

'Aye. While you've been lying in your bed, I've been oot delivering twins.'

'Is that so? Well, gud! That's what ah says. Ken, you need all the practice you can get.'

She turned away from him onto her side and he wrapped his body round hers and laughed softly into her hair. Within a couple of minutes her rhythmic breathing indicated that she was asleep again. Tenderly sliding his hand over the crispness of her nightdress, he took in the fullness of her breasts and his thoughts flicked briefly back to the struggles of the new lambs to find their mothers' teats. He let his hand travel downwards and come to rest on the huge roundness of her belly, feeling their child respond to his touch. Not many days now, he thought, feeling again a little nudge against his large hand, and then a more definite kick and a tensing of his wife's muscles. Not many days now.

His eyes fought against sleep as he thanked God that Janet would be able to give birth in the comfort of their cottage and not have to contend with the wild spring weather, as did his flock. The midwife would come and see to it that the birthing went smoothly and then, when all was done, he would be able to hold in his arms a little son or daughter. Their child would be born in the final year of the old century but grow up in the new, alive to all the possibilities and challenges that it would bring.

2

Sunshine in a Dark Sky

It was with a sigh of relief that the young man stepped down from the overheated carriage. He walked quickly to the guard's van at the back of the train and retrieved a small but cumbersome trunk. This he carried awkwardly to the back of the platform and placed on the ground out of the way of passengers arriving or alighting at the station. Showing his ticket to the porter, he explained that he would be back shortly to collect his luggage, and stepped out into the late afternoon sunshine.

An open wagon stood on the rutted path. In it, holding the reins loosely in her hand, sat a girl. She had the gangling, uncoordinated appearance of adolescence. Her hair was long and fair, caught behind with a ribbon and falling untidily down her back. Her pinafore, stained and less white than it should have been, covered a dress that was struggling to contain her developing figure and showing more of her legs than was the current fashion. As the man emerged from the station, he looked at the girl, turned away and gazed down the road.

'Are you Mr Thomas Fairclough?' the girl said, making him jump. She flashed him a smile, showing a set of slightly irregular but very white teeth.

'Aye, and who are you?'

'I'm Ellen… Duncan Simpson's daughter. He's away to get some more baccy for his pipe. He'll be back directly. He said to settle you and your luggage in the carriage. Do you want me to help?'

'Nay, lass. I can do it.' Turning back to the station entrance, the young man disappeared and, a few seconds later, staggered out with the trunk, which he heaved onto the back of the wagon. That done, he pulled off his jacket and threw it onto the luggage. Lastly, he drew a large handkerchief from his pocket and mopped his brow. 'I'm fair lathered,' he said, making the girl break into a fit of giggles. 'What's wrong? What are you laughing at?'

'You, of course. You speak so strange. Is that how yous talk, where you come from?'

'Happen so. I hadn't thought owt about it till now. It doesn't seem odd to me.' He grinned at her.

'Here's Father now,' the girl indicated with a nod of her head, as a man plodded unhurriedly along the path. 'He'll be glad of your help. He's tired. Do you ken all about sheep?'

'Pardon? Oh… aye. My parents have a farm in the

Dales... the Yorkshire Dales, that is. Do you "ken" where that is?'

'No.' The girl laughed. 'I've never been further than... well... here, I suppose... the railway station. I go to the market in town quite often now... with my father.' She turned to the older man as he approached and smiled. 'Have you got your messages, Father?'

'Aye. And you must be Thomas Fairclough. I'm pleased to meet you. Welcome to Scotland. You must make the most of this spot of good weather. It's not often you see the countryside in the sunshine.' He held out a large hand in greeting and the young man took it, feeling the roughness of the skin that indicated a life of hard manual work.

'They call me Tom. I'd be happy for you to do t' same.'

'Aye, I'll do that. Are you going to step into the back, Ellen, and let Tom sit up here by the side of me?'

Ellen swung her legs in a less than ladylike fashion over the seat and jumped down into the body of the wagon next to Tom's trunk. Their visitor climbed up, and the horse responded to the light flick of the reins on his back and began to make its slow way along the track and onto the road.

Tom looked around with interest. Trees in full leaf lined their way, and here and there they passed a cottage at the side of the road or dotted among the fields. The land sloped down to a river flowing northwards. On either side, rounded hills formed the horizon and, when he looked ahead, he could see higher hills grey and bare in the distance.

In all his twenty-two years he had never travelled so far from home and, although he had probably been farther afield than Ellen, he had to admit that only rarely had he ventured outside his native Yorkshire. He had never wanted to until now. His nature was very much like his appearance. He was a solid young man, medium height, and heavily built, strong enough to do most of the work on his father's farm without a murmur. His face was tanned from a life spent outside in all weathers and his hair, dark brown and unruly, flopped untidily over his forehead.

He glanced at Duncan, but the man was staring into the distance as though lost in thought and Tom didn't like to disturb him with questions of what awaited him at the farm. He knew what these shepherds were like... lone, silent men, though whether it was their chosen career that made them like this or their self-contained nature that led them into such a solitary occupation, it was impossible to say. He was himself a man of few words. He was sure he'd rub along well with this shepherd and his family.

Making their way down a steep road, they crossed a long narrow bridge that spanned the river. Their way wound on into the hills that had appeared grey in the distance but now turned green as they neared. They were speckled white with sheep, as far as the eye could see. The wagon followed the track along one side of the broad base of a valley. When Duncan turned down a smaller track, just a cart's width, that crossed the valley floor, Tom could see the farm up ahead. A copse of trees surrounded the farmhouse so only the roof was visible. Over a wooden bridge and up a slight incline, two white cottages stared out across the valley, standing sentinel as though ready to warn the occupants of the approach of inclement weather.

Duncan turned to Tom. 'This is your cottage, next to ours.' He nodded to the first of the two low dwellings. 'You'll come for your tea first. Ellen will put the kettle on, won't you, hen?' He looked round, but Ellen had already jumped down and was disappearing into the cottage. He turned back to Tom. 'Tomorrow we'll see about you getting in some supplies so you can look after yourself. I gather you'll no' be bringing a wife with you?'

'No, not yet.'

'Och! That will come soon enough. Well now, Kenneth Douglas is still at market. He'll be back soon and then I'll take you down the hill and introduce you.' Duncan swung his legs round slowly and stepped down from the wagon. 'Go on in and find Ellen. I'll join you when I've put Archie away.'

Ellen had laid the table with a clean cloth and set out crockery and cutlery. As he entered, she was cutting slices from a loaf of bread. A blackened kettle hung over a low fire. He stood at the door watching her, uncertain what to do.

Glancing up, she smiled a welcome.

'Come away in and sit down.' She indicated a chair by the fire.

'Is there owt I can do to help? After all, I've been sitting all day and I think I'd rather be standing.' He also had no wish to be too near the fire, which was pumping out yet more heat into an already stiflingly hot room.

'Aye, you can reach down three mugs from the shelf there and you'll find a jug of milk in the pantry. Oh, and there's a fruit cake in the tin... the one with the flowers on. Bring that out, will you?'

When Tom had done her bidding, his eyes took in the neat room... the floor swept clean, the row of boots inside the door, the absence of any dirty dishes cluttering up the draining board. He pondered the whereabouts of Ellen's mother, who must have made the cottage so pristine prior to his arrival.

'Is your mother not joining us?' he said, to fill the long silence that accompanied their preparations.

'I don't have a mother. Well, of course I *had* a mother, but she died giving birth to me... so I never knew her.'

Tom, taken aback, immediately wished he hadn't spoken. 'I'm sorry. I shouldn't have asked,' he stammered.

'Why not? It's only natural to ask. I'm sorry too...

sorry that she wasnae here to look after me. But it's all right. I've always had my father. Him and me get along just fine.' She wrinkled her nose. 'Father says I'm just like her, so I suppose that's nice for him. My mother was called Janet.'

At the frankness of her information, Tom was lost for words. He pondered her as she went about her jobs, trying to imagine, and failing, what it must be like to be brought up without the comfort and care of a mother. He had always been very close to his and that closeness had remained, even when his sister had been born several years later.

'Did you stay with your parents before you came up here?' Ellen asked.

He smiled at this indication of how their thoughts had proceeded along the same lines. 'Aye, I did.'

'It will be hard for you with no one to look after you. I'll come and help you sometimes if you like.'

'Oh, happen I shall manage well enough,' he said and then, because the words sounded overly blunt, added, 'But thank you for the offer.'

'That's all right. Anyway, I shall bake you a cake next time I do one for us.'

She stopped in her preparations and looked at him frankly.

'Don't you have a sweetheart in England?'

Tom felt himself blushing. This young lass was far too straightforward for comfort.

'No... no,' he said hurriedly. 'Leastways... no, not really.'

'That's a shame. It would be nice to have a lady living nearby. There's Mrs. Douglas... that's the farmer's wife. But she's a bit above the likes of us! And there's Margaret Murdie... but she's along the valley a mile or two. Do you have brothers and sisters?'

'Aye, I have one sister... Annie. She's much younger than me. I shall miss her though. We were reet close.'

Ellen filled the teapot and placed it in the middle of the table. 'I shall have to pretend to be your sister then. I sometimes think I'd have liked a brother or a sister. But then I'd have to share my dad with someone else, instead of having him all to myself.'

The object of her affections could now be heard taking off his boots in the porch and a moment later he appeared in the doorway.

Ellen ran over to him and kissed him.

'Come along, Feyther. Tea's ready. Sit yourself down.'

He responded by enveloping her in a bearlike hug. He regarded the newcomer over his daughter's head. 'She's a good girl, this one... looked after me since she was old enough to stand, she has.'

Ellen laughed, pulling away from her father's embrace and crossing to the table, where she started to pour the tea. 'I think you were looking after me for a good while first.'

'Aye well, you were my little ray of sunshine in a dark sky in those days.' His eyes misted over and then, himself again, he went on, 'Now, how about offering our visitor some of that delicious cake you made specially. He must be thinking you've only put it there for decoration!'

*

After their meal, the two men strolled down the hill to meet the farmer, who had by now returned from market.

'Did you have a good day, boss?'

'Aye, Duncan. Not bad, not bad at all. They fetched a good price, most of the lambs. I bought half a dozen good-looking hoggs to replace the ewes we lost during lambing. They're over there in the bottom field.' He turned to Tom. 'Is this the new shepherd, then?'

'Aye, this is Thomas Fairclough. Tom, meet Kenneth Douglas – your boss and mine,' Duncan smiled.

The farmer held out his hand to Tom. 'You answer to Duncan here... he'll be your boss. If he's happy with your work, that's good enough for me.'

'I reckon he'll have no cause to complain. I've always been a steady worker,' Tom offered.

'You'll find it a bit different in these hills from what you're used to. The weather comes in bad during the winter months... and it's not so good in the summer at times.' The farmer gazed into the blue sky and shook his head. 'We don't see this kind of day often, do we, Duncan?'

'We don't. If it's warm, it's usually wet with it.'

'Oh, Yorkshire weather can be pretty bad,' Tom volunteered. 'There's been plenty of times me and me dad have had to dig the ewes out of snowdrifts… and lost a few as well.'

Kenneth Douglas stared into the distance thoughtfully. 'There was plenty of talk in the market today about possible war… not that it's likely to affect us around here, I don't suppose. Is much being said about it down in England?'

'Only that, if it comes, it won't last long. It doesn't seem as though it will make any difference to us farming folk. Yorkshire's a bit like round here… away from the big cities. We only get to hear of these things at market, like you.'

'What's brought you up here, then, lad? Won't your father be missing you?'

'Aye. But I need to gain experience of different areas and different kinds of sheep. These black-faced hill sheep are new to me.'

'I think you'll take a liking to them. Canny wee creatures, they are… full of character. Anyway, you'll get to know soon enough. You best go and let Duncan show you your cottage. It's plainly furnished, but no doubt better for that, when you've no lady around to keep it clean for you. How old are you, by the way?'

'Twenty-two, sir.'

'Twenty-two! Well, you've a good set of muscles on you. Not that you won't find sheep farming uses every one of them, as you no doubt know!'

Bidding the farmer goodbye, the two shepherds made their way up the path to their adjacent cottages. Duncan pushed open the door to Tom's and they stepped inside. It was, as Kenneth Douglas had hinted, lacking in adornments. Through a scullery they entered the main room, in which were four chairs round a wooden table. Two more chairs with horsehair-stuffed cushions and wooden arms were arranged at either side of a fireplace with a built-in oven. A bookcase, containing several dusty volumes and a pile of well-thumbed farming magazines, stood along one wall and a picture of cattle on the banks of a river, with a backdrop of rugged mountains, softened the bareness of another. Through a door, Tom could see a chest of drawers and a bed decorated with a tartan rug.

He looked around in satisfaction. The spartan appearance of his quarters suited him well enough. His eyes came to rest on the fireside oven and he frowned, doubting his ability to make good use of it. Duncan followed his gaze.

'Ellen's a good girl. She'd no doubt be happy enough to give you a hand with cleaning... and cooking maybe.'

'I'll bear that in mind... thanks,' he said, regretting his earlier refusal of Ellen's offer of help. 'But hasn't she her schoolwork to do?'

Duncan smiled. 'She left school well over a year ago. A clever wee lass she is – that's what her teacher told me. Gets it from her mother, not from me.' He grunted. 'I suppose by rights she could have got a job anywhere... but there's always so much to do on the farm... and me with no wife to help keep things nice around the house... I need her here. Fifteen years me and her have been here together.'

So the girl was fifteen. Tom was surprised. She was small for her age, lacking the sophistication that some young ladies of his acquaintance began to accrue as they passed into womanhood. His own sister, a similar age to Ellen, seemed much older than Duncan's daughter.

'Right.' The shepherd's voice jerked Tom out of his reverie. 'I must do some jobs before nightfall. You get yourself moved in, and I'll see you first thing... half five, I usually start.'

*

The sun was setting behind the hills at the back of the cottages. Those strung out along the other side of the valley were topped with golden light that crept up the slopes till only the tips were lit, the rest being plunged into obscurity. It was different here, the landscape, Tom thought. Yorkshire was a land of drystone walls, dividing the fields this way and that and running up hillsides so steep that he wondered how men had ever been able to build them.

He had always marvelled how these walls stood the test of time, some of them as much as a hundred and fifty years old, and it was only when he had spent a week of instruction with an elderly farmhand, who had made it his life's work, that he understood the reason for their longevity. He could build them himself now, though neither so well nor so fast as his instructor.

There were walls here, though much less numerous. 'Dykes', Duncan called them. The stones were dark grey and much less picturesque than the limestone around his former home. He gave a slight smile. It was unlike him to wax lyrical about the appearance of the countryside. When all was said and done, a wall was there to keep sheep in or sheep out and its colour didn't matter one jot.

He thought of the parents and sister he had left behind and then his musings moved naturally to the girl he had moved to be near. Had he done the right thing in making this journey? What he had said to the farmer was the truth. He did need to get away from his parents' protection and gain experience elsewhere. But the real reason he had travelled this far from home was to be near to the girl he had loved since childhood, with an unswerving, unquestioning adoration. And she had no idea of his proximity. His mouth went dry as he wondered what she would say when he presented himself on her doorstep. He would spend a bit of time getting to know the farm and satisfying Duncan that he was a reliable and good worker... and then he would seek her out.

3

Along the Valley

The scenery of the remote area chosen by Tom as his initiation into Scottish hill farming was on a scale, the like of which he had never seen before. The entire countryside was so far above sea level that the tops of the hills were bare of trees. The growing season was short and there was a constant worry whether the grass would give sufficient nourishment to sustain the flock through the harsh months of winter. Only the knotty heather seemed resilient to the vagaries of the weather. From his viewing point on top of the hill behind the cottage, it was exhibiting its short-lived display of colour, painting with subtle shades the hills that stretched away in all directions.

Tom sighed with satisfaction. It had been a good decision to come here. He loved the wildness of the terrain and the bareness of the hills. He was used to hill country, but where he came from, there was always a homestead or two sheltering in the comparative gentleness of the next valley. Here, farms were few and far between.

Every day, Tom covered several miles or more on foot, checking the flock. Within a month of the three he had been here, he was acquainted with the geography of the hills, the natural contours of which had led to the development of the ancient system of hefting. Sheep born and raised on a particular hill developed a homing instinct for it. Tom knew that even if the sheep were brought into the in-bye for shearing or dipping, he could release them from the pen, safe in the knowledge that they would make their way back to their own hill, even if they took their time doing so. This impulse to return meant that the land belonging to the farm was grazed evenly, the rough along with the smooth, barren parts as well as more fertile areas. Tom's daily trek over the land had also enabled him to establish where the dangerous parts of the terrain were to be found, those gullies and crevices and steep drops where a sheep could get stuck or lose its footing.

Although he had already walked the hills in the early morning, Tom liked to climb the hill behind his cottage when the day's work was done, taking the steep rise at a more leisurely pace. His sheepdog Nell would bound ahead and flatten herself against the grass, long pink tongue lolling and eyes alight with the joy of it, as though he were one of the ill-behaved sheep who needed bringing into line. He had climbed most evenings in the summer, clouds of midges rising from the long grasses at his measured slow steps up the steep incline. He wouldn't stop to look until the summit was reached, and then he would stand perspiring and study the view in all directions, while he caught his breath. It was autumn now, but he was loath to curtail his evening walk, though the nights were drawing in.

Nell barked a warning and rose to her feet, tail wagging furiously. Tom followed the bounce and fall of her body as she raced across the heather. In the gloom, a figure was approaching. It was Ellen. He recognised her immediately. If anyone else had disturbed his solitude, he would have resented the intrusion. But not so with the girl. Perhaps because he was drawn to her down-to-earth nature, her habit of calling a spade a spade. Maybe it was her outlook on life, sunnier than his own, that he coveted.

'Na' then, lass,' he greeted her, as she covered the remaining space between them at a run and flopped down panting in the long grass. 'What are you doing up here? Haven't you owt to do at home?'

'Father says to ask you if I can come with you to market tomorrow.'

'Tomorrow? Happen so. But don't you have jobs to do around the house?'

'Oh, there are always jobs to do around the house. But I've some messages to fetch – some for Father and some for Mrs Murdie. And maybe, if I'm finished in time, I could creep in at the back of the market and watch the buying and selling.'

Tom looked dubious. 'That's man's work. Happen you won't be welcome there.'

'Stuff and nonsense! If I'm quiet, they won't even see me at the back. Feyther lets me. Och, go on, Tom. Let me. Surely you don't think that girls should stay at home and cook and clean and not do anything else?'

The colour of Tom's already weathered face darkened. 'No,' he said quietly. 'I don't believe that.' He grinned at her. 'All right... as long as you don't make a noise.' He became silent, gazing along the valley to where the hills folded in on one another.

'It won't look like this for much longer,' Ellen's voice broke into his thoughts.

'What? What do you mean?'

'The valley... the reservoir. Haven't you heard?'

'I've heard nowt.'

'They're going to build a reservoir along the valley. They say that the big towns north of here haven't enough water and this is the best place to collect it, the hills being so high.'

Tom stared at her. 'Are you sure about this?'

'Of course I'm sure. They've been talking about it for years. Feyther says there's men coming down this week to talk to the villagers and to the farmers as well.'

'But what about the bricks and... and everything? You can't carry enough bricks to build a reservoir along that tiny road.'

'That's all been thought of too. There were plans to build a new road but now they've decided that there's to be a railway as well.'

'A railway?'

'Yes. Isn't it exciting! It won't be for us to travel on of course, but even so....'

'Well I don't think it's exciting. All those men and all that noise and dirt... it'll ruin the valley.' Tom took a sudden step away and Nell, who had been sitting on a nearby hillock, jumped up and barked. 'Come on, Nell. Let's get back down.' He glanced at Ellen. 'And you better get to your bed,' he said with a brief smile. 'We've an early start in the morning.'

*

Tom, who was reluctant to acknowledge the advantages of what others saw as progress, was further dismayed by the words that were on everybody's lips at market the following morning. Talk of the war was everywhere. And although the general feeling was that the conflict that had started only six weeks earlier would be over in a few months, Tom's natural pessimism led him to consider what would happen if this were not so. Surely troops would be needed... more than those foolhardy individuals who had joined up the moment war had been declared. Reinforcements would have to replace those who, God forbid, did not return from the battlefields.

His fears were confirmed as the day progressed. News was filtering out from the city. Glasgow Corporation, it seemed, had asked for volunteers from the tram workers to raise two battalions of men. Over a thousand had responded. Maybe it would have been safer to stay in Yorkshire. But no! There were cities not far away from the Dales farms too. He had no doubt that these cities would be encouraging the strongest and fittest young men to enlist.

Tom took comfort in the thought that it was foolishness for farm workers to abandon their homesteads in favour of the battlefield, for food would always be necessary. Besides, Duncan Simpson and Kenneth Douglas could not be expected to manage things by themselves. Hill farming was a young man's job. It needed the strength and stamina of youth.

So he went to and fro among the farmers and shepherds at the market, Ellen skipping by his side. He heard much and said little, convinced of his arguments but with a bleakness in his soul, as he considered the future and the intended proposal that he would make to the girl in the city from which all these stories were flowing.

4

Sacrifices for the Greater Good

Sir Angus MacPherson and his committee, smartly attired in dark suits and top hats, alighted from the first-class compartment of the southbound train. A soft rain was falling as they left the station and climbed into the wagons that were to carry them into the valley. Sir Angus had suggested this form of transport in order that the committee should obtain an uninterrupted view of the countryside. He chuckled into his bushy white beard at the sight of the group, none of whom appeared to be relishing a ride in an open wagon on such a day. Even with their legs swathed in tarpaulins, the rain would soon soak their suits and dampen their enthusiasm for the trip ahead.

'What did I tell you, gentlemen? This part of the country has an average rainfall of fifty inches per annum. Where better to site the reservoir? The water quality is excellent and free from the stain of peat. The same cannot be said of much of the water in Scotland.' The blue eyes of their chairman sparkled in merriment as he viewed the already bedraggled appearance of his fellow engineers. He sat back with a smile of satisfaction and gazed around at the land through which they were passing. All the negotiations had been worthwhile, even though they had taken three years and, up to now, not a spade had been wielded, nor a stone turned.

It had taken him only six months to come to the conclusion, backed up by figures, that the existing water supply to the larger towns north of this stretch of countryside would be woefully inadequate, should there be a time of drought. An inadequacy that amounted to over two million gallons a day, no less. Not only this, but the population of these towns was increasing all the time and so was their need for a plentiful supply of clean water.

He had considered the possibilities. He could have enlarged an existing reservoir a few miles distant. He might have devised a plan to construct an upper reservoir to feed into an existing lower one several miles in the other direction. But neither of these plans guaranteed a sufficient supply now, let alone in the future. In addition, any interruption to the supply during construction work would have been catastrophic.

No, Sir Angus was a little man with a big vision. The ideal plan was the construction of a new reservoir here, at the head of the valley. He had visited several times. Its position was advantageous from an engineering perspective. That made it an economically sound proposition. It had, of course, meant planning for additional pipelines to connect to existing mains some miles away, and the diversion of some local roads to accommodate the alterations, but, even with this added cost, it was an excellent way to meet the growing need of the expanding towns.

He and his fellow engineers had visited later that year and together they had studied the lie of the land and the most efficient way of channelling the water to where it was most needed. And then came the long wait – nearly a year – until the Water Act was passed by Parliament. But it was passed in its entirety... and so was a plan of afforestation to improve the land around the newly built reservoir.

'Have we any need to worry about our scheme now that war has broken out, Sir Angus?' The question came from James McEwan, a tall thin man with sparse grey side whiskers and a perpetual drip at the end of his nose, enhanced by the dampness of the day.

'They say that it'll be over by Christmas, so I can't see it affecting our plans,' the chief engineer, Andrew Lamb, interjected.

'If anything, our scheme should be pushed forward. I hear there's talk of building munitions factories further north, so even more water will be needed in that eventuality.'

'But will we complete it within the ten years stipulated in the Act? Over a year of that has gone already and work hasn't begun yet.'

Sir Angus sighed. 'I admit that is a problem, particularly if more and more men are encouraged to enlist. But there are some things over which I have no control. Parliament will surely make allowances if the war does continue for longer than everybody expects. And, look at it this way, gentlemen, the government is hardly going to put a stop on a much-needed scheme like this, once it is nearing completion, is it?' His eyes twinkled playfully.

The two wagons pursued their bumpy course into the hills, leaving the small village behind. Even the steady rain couldn't disguise the beauty of their surroundings. Each rounded hill was painted purple with heather. Sheep grazed peacefully on every slope, their lambs almost as large as the mothers who had borne them. At scattered intervals, farmsteads interrupted the autumn colour.

'Rather them than me,' James McEwan said with a sniff, indicating the farms. 'Give me the convenience and the pleasures of a town any time.' One or two of his companions nodded in agreement, even though the speaker looked as though he derived very little pleasure from either town or countryside.

At the place where the retaining wall of the reservoir was planned, the men dismounted. A further two officials had already arrived. They formed a deputation from the Board of Agriculture for Scotland.

'Congratulations, Sir Angus. We understand you have been engaged to act as consultant for the duration of the project,' the older of the two, Dougie Strachan, said, shaking the hand of the diminutive engineer.

'Thank you, yes. I have that honour. It is an exciting prospect, is it not, gentlemen? I have invited you today to show you the area to be afforested. Obviously, we would like this area to be as scenic as possible when the project is completed.' He swept his arm from one side to the other of the valley to take in the limits of the proposed reservoir. 'The hillsides along both sides of the water are to be planted. The resulting view will be even better than it is now.'

'It will indeed. But where will you find the money to plant so many trees?'

'Ha! There the Local Authority is helping us out. It is to be given an advance to encourage planting... five pounds per acre has been suggested for this site. The Authority will pay back what it has borrowed, plus compound interest of three per cent, when the trees have matured. Everything over and above that belongs to them. A good scheme, is it not, gentlemen?'

'Yes, we see no argument with it, none at all.' Dougie Strachan looked at his colleague, a young man by the name of Allan Murdoch, who had recently been appointed to the Board of Agriculture.

'I will have to put forward the idea to the treasury. The money comes from them, you understand. But I see no reason why there should be any delay.' Sir Angus glanced at his sub-committee, who were talking among themselves, and turned back to the forestry officials. 'If you would care to accompany us, sirs, we will show you the finer points of the design.'

They rejoined the group and proceeded into the heart of the valley, where the hills appeared to meet in an unbroken amphitheatre behind the agreed position of the reservoir.

'Where we are now walking, gentlemen, will be covered with water to a depth of ninety feet. It will contain over two thousand million gallons of water. Even I find that a difficult figure to assimilate!'

'May I ask something, Sir?' said the youthful Allan Murdoch. From his fresh face, idealism glowed like a beacon among his world-weary seniors.

'Of course. What is it you wish to know?'

'What will happen to these families... this farm we are passing and the one in the distance?'

'Naturally, the farms will be sacrificed. The occupants will have to move. We will build them other houses, of course... and they will be compensated for the loss of their land and their farm, as will everyone who has land in the affected area.'

'But their families must have farmed here for years and years.'

'Of course. But these are small sacrifices for the greater good.'

Allan Murdoch shrugged in disagreement. 'My parents are farmers. The farm has belonged to my family for generations. I can't imagine how they would cope if they were ordered to leave. It would break my mother's heart.'

'Have you considered this, my friend? There are many families that at present have no water supply of their own. They draw their water from a communal tap in the street or from a well at the back of their garden. How many mothers' hearts have been broken by the death of their children from diseases carried in such polluted water?' The engineer fixed the young man with a steely stare. 'Sometimes we need a bigger perspective on things than the loss of two farms and the removal of their occupants to dry land. Such considerations must not be allowed to stand in the way of progress.'

With a nod of his head, Sir Angus stepped back to the waiting committee. The next moment he was discussing the timetable for widening and improving the existing road and laying down the lines for the railway that would carry construction materials to the site of the new reservoir. Alan Murdoch turned away with a sigh, the idealism in his face fading with Sir Angus's dismissive words.

5

Separate Paths

The latest war bulletin being echoed from most newsvendors, as Tom made his hesitant way through the streets of Glasgow, was the sinking of a German U-boat by the HMS Dreadnought. Never having heard of the battleship, the story of the ramming of the enemy submarine nevertheless sent a shiver of horror down his spine. What worse ending could there be than drowning in a metal box from which there was no hope of escape?

Tom had no liking for the sea. Twice as a child he had been to Scarborough with his parents. On the first occasion, they had taken a pleasure steamer round the bay and he had been violently and repeatedly sick. On the second occasion, the strong winds and high tide had rendered seafaring impossible. Huge waves crashed over the promenade and sent holidaymakers scurrying for safety. From the vantage point of the castle walls, he watched intrepid and foolhardy young men risking their lives as they dodged in and out between the breakers.

But his thoughts dwelled only briefly on the disaster,

returning to the purpose of his visit... his first visit... to the city. He had decided at last, after nine months at the farm, to visit Clara. She had no idea of his intention and he was anxious as to her reaction when she answered the door to him. He had written to her the previous autumn, after he had served enough time on the farm to be sure that he liked working there and that Duncan was satisfied with the quality of his work. Aware that she would be curious as to his move to the Scottish Uplands, he had explained that he needed experience in all aspects of sheep farming and that there was no better place to gain such understanding than among the native breed of those parts, the Scottish blackface sheep or 'Blackies'.

She had replied promptly, expressing surprise and pleasure at his proximity and hoping that she might see him sometime. He had heard from her again at Christmas, when she had sent a greeting from Yorkshire, where she had gone to visit her father. He thought of acquainting her with his intended visit, but something made him hold back. Perhaps it was a rejection or a postponement that he feared. Having steeled his reserve, he didn't want to have to do so a second time.

In his jacket pocket was folded the letter she had written, with the address in her neat handwriting across the top of the page. He drew it out now and stopped to ask a passing man for directions. The reply he received might have been in a foreign language, so little did Tom understand. He asked the man if he would repeat his directions and was greeted with the same incomprehensible outpouring. He nodded his thanks and went on in the direction the man had pointed. No doubt his own Yorkshire speech caused as much head-scratching as the Glaswegian tongue did to him.

Having stopped twice more to ask directions, he at last reached the address he had in his pocket. A narrow flight of steps led up to a front door painted black and a tall house of four floors, joined on both sides to similar ones, which, in their turn, were joined to others; so the whole formed a formidable row that dominated the street and blocked out every ray of sunshine. Screwing up his courage, he climbed the steps and rang the bell.

For a long time no one came, and he was about to give up when the door swung open and a middle-aged woman stood there.

'Can I help you, young man?'

'I... er... thought Clara Moxon lived here. I've called to see her.'

'And who might you be?'

'My name's Tom. I'm a friend of hers from home.'

'Are you now? Are you not aware that young ladies are not allowed gentlemen visitors... not without prior arrangement anyway?'

'Oh, I didn't know. Well, could I see her just for a minute? She does live here, doesn't she?'

'Aye. But she's no' here now. She's at the college. She has lectures during the day. Surely you must know that if you're a friend of hers.' The woman eyed him suspiciously.

He cursed himself for not having thought that she would be at her studies. Smiling uncomfortably at the woman, he continued, 'Of course. I'll go there now. It's Queen Margaret's College, isn't it?'

The woman raised her eyebrows. 'You know something then. You realise she may not be free... and you won't be allowed in, even if she is.'

'I only want a word with her. Thank you for your help.' Tom was descending the steps as he spoke, her reprimand evoking an unwelcome memory of distant schooldays.

'First left at the end of the road,' she called after him. 'Cross the main road, then ask again.'

He waved his thanks and hurried along the street, his spirits rising. It was late morning now and he was conscious that the time he had intended to spend with Clara was ebbing away.

At last he found himself in front of the college. He hesitated uncertainly at the bottom of the steps, fearing another rebuff. While he stood there, the doors were flung open and girls began to pour out of the building. Some looked at him as they passed and one nudged her neighbour and smirked. He stepped aside, so as not to interfere with their progress, and, glancing up, saw Clara emerge in the company of two other girls. She didn't notice him at first and continued to chat animatedly with her friends.

He stepped into her path and smiled… and smiled more broadly when he saw her surprise.

'Tom! What are you doing here?'

'I've come to see you, of course. I thought you might be missing me.'

Clara gave a quick glance at the two girls on either side of her and he saw her colour rise as she faced him again. 'Tom, may I introduce my friends. This is Jessica Pattison.' She indicated the small, dark-haired girl on her right. 'And this is Annabel Hunter-Henderson.' She turned to her left, to the tall girl in a beautifully cut green suit and large matching hat that accentuated her height. The girl was giving him a superior smile.

'Well, well, Clara. You are a dark horse. You haven't mentioned this young gentleman before. Is it one of your friends from the countryside?' She looked him up and down, her eyes coming to rest on his mud-stained boots.

'We were friends at school.'

Tom, sensing Clara's embarrassment and at pains to understand the reason for it, said, 'We grew up together in t' same village. We've always been friends, haven't we, Clara?'

'Yes, yes we have. Look, girls, will you give me a few minutes with Tom. I'll meet you in the library after break.'

'Of course,' began Annabel. 'We wouldn't dream of depriving you of your little tête-à-tête, would we? Come along, Jessica. Let's leave the two friends to renew their acquaintance.' She linked arms with the smaller girl and the two set off down the steps and along the pavement, leaving Clara gazing down on Tom.

Quickly, she glanced behind her and ran down the remaining steps to his side. 'We can't talk here, Tom. If any of the lecturers should see us, I will be severely reprimanded.'

'You should have told me where I could see you then.'

'Well, I didn't know you were coming,' she replied, then continued, 'Come on, let's go into the park over there. I only have twenty minutes or so before I have to be back in class.'

Tom, fighting disappointment that the meeting was not going as he had planned, took her elbow to guide her over the road. In the relative sanctuary of the trees, he stopped.

'Are you pleased to see me?'

'Of course... it's just that you took me by surprise.'

'And have you missed me?'

The colour that had suffused Clara's cheeks began to rise again. 'Of course I have.' She paused. 'We've been friends for such a long time.'

'I had hoped that we were more than just friends.'

She looked away, frowning. 'You know that's not possible, Tom. I've all my studies... and the exams at the end of them.'

'I'll wait. I'm happy in t' job. I can wait while you finish.'

'I don't know, Tom.' Her tone was evasive. 'I can't think about all that just now.'

'Happen not. I suppose your head is buzzing with all those books you have to read.'

'Aye! That's true.' She gave a small laugh. 'There's plenty to read. You'll remember from our school days how I like reading.'

'Promise me one thing,' Tom said, when they retraced their steps to the road. 'Promise me that you'll come and stay on t' farm in the holidays.'

She hesitated and looked as if about to decline the invitation. Then she nodded and smiled. 'I would like to... as long as I pass my next exams. And I won't have much time off because we all have to work on the wards.'

'A proper doctor then!'

'Hardly. It will be a long time before I'm that.'

They had reached the entrance to the college.

'Look after yourself, Tom. And take care on those hills.'

'Oh, you needn't worry on that score. I know those hills like the back of my hand.' He stood watching her as she climbed the steps and turned to wave. 'I'll see you in the summer. Let me know and I'll meet you at the station.'

She looked about to say something but a flurry of

girls surrounded her and she was carried inside with the throng. Doors swung shut behind them and he was left standing alone. Glancing at his watch, he turned abruptly and began to walk swiftly in the direction of the station. He must not miss his train. He needed to check on the ewes as soon as he reached home. Lambing time would soon be upon them. He allowed himself a rare smile. After lambing came silage making and buying and selling at the markets and then she would be there… at the end of summer.

*

'A letter for you,' the postman called across to Tom four days later. Tom let go the ewe he was examining and straightened up. He trudged across the field and took the envelope, studying the writing with a rising colour.

'Aye, thanks,' he murmured, as the older man turned to go. 'Much obliged to you.'

A smile spread slowly across his face. She must have been pleased to see him to be writing so promptly. Maybe she would say how much she was looking forward to her visit to the farm. He slid the letter into his shirt pocket. He would finish his morning's work… check on the ewes that were in the in-bye, put the feed into barrels and sweep the floor of the barn. This way he could savour the moment when he would tear open the envelope and read its contents.

The day was warm and he had stripped off his jacket and rolled up his shirtsleeves. He pulled up an old kitchen chair and sat in the sunshine to read.

Friday, 19th March.

Dear Tom,

I feel I must write to you without further delay. In an effort to avoid hurting you yesterday, I fear I did not make myself clear and wish to prevent misunderstanding.

I have always valued our friendship, but it can never be more than that... a friendship. You and I are very different people and we have our own separate paths to follow. This is as it should be, for you have always been an excellent shepherd, and I hope one day to be a good doctor.

I must moreover be perfectly honest. I do not, and never could, think of you as anything more than a dear friend. I suspect that your thoughts are otherwise, but please forgive me if I assume too much. It is better to be clear about this than to go on entertaining false hopes.

To this end, I feel it is best that I do not visit in the summer. Maybe later in the year would be preferable, when any embarrassment has blown over.

With my very best wishes for your future, Clara.

The sun had gone behind a cloud. Tom got up

abruptly and a chicken that had been pecking in the dirt at his feet clucked away in alarm. He screwed up the letter in his fist and thrust it deep into the pocket of his trousers. Then he grabbed his jacket from the fence, slung it over his shoulder and set off with huge strides up the side of the hill.

6

A Good Enough Bed

Tired and hungry after three hours' continuous walking, Tom closed the door quietly behind him, tugged off his coat and hung it on a hook in the porch. A clattering of dishes intruded on his solitude. Ellen was in the scullery. She had lit the fire, swept the room, hung clean washing on the rack to air and taken out of the oven a meat pie newly baked.

'You've no need to do all this,' he commented to her back, where she stood at the sink. Duncan's daughter was growing up fast. He watched her move round the room with an easy grace, before he turned to warm himself at the fire. 'I'm quite able to look after myself, tha' knows,' he added more kindly over his shoulder.

'I ken that – I only thought you'd welcome a bit of help, especially with lambing so near.'

'I do, lass. I'm sorry. I didn't mean to be ungrateful.' Tom flopped into a chair and stared into the fire.

'What's the matter, Tom?' Ellen crossed the room and put her hand on his shoulder, massaging it gently, as she so often did for her father when he complained about his rheumatics.

He continued to stare into the flames until his eyes began to smart with the heat. He was conscious of a small flicker of desire, almost imperceptible at first but strengthening as she ran her hand through his matted hair in an attempt to tidy it.

'Look at you,' she laughed. 'You look gey weather-beaten the day. You need to take a comb to... Oh, Tom, what are you doing?' For he had turned impulsively towards her as she stood there and grasped her legs within his strong arms, burying his face within her skirts and smelling the warm feminine scent of her. 'There, there,' she crooned, still smoothing his hair. 'Why don't you tell me what's the problem?'

It was Clara who was the problem... and at the thought, his mounting desire began to trickle away. What in heaven's name had come over him? He let go of Ellen suddenly so that she lost her balance and nearly fell into his lap.

'I'm sorry,' he muttered, taking her by the arms and righting her. 'There's nowt wrong that I can't sort out myself. Now I'm going to have a wash and get out of these dirty work clothes before supper.'

'Of course.' Ellen shrugged. 'I've left your supper here when you're ready.' She smoothed her apron and turned to go.

'Thanks, lass. You're a good girl.'

She gave him an uncertain smile, crossed quickly to the door and went out into the dusk.

*

He dreamed of Ellen that night. At least it was a strange combination of both Ellen and Clara. Over and over again, he heard Clara's voice telling him that he was a friend, nothing more... a special friend but only a friend. But the body he saw was Ellen's: the smooth brown skin of her arms as it had been in the summer months just gone, the long fair hair tied carelessly back with a ribbon that slipped slowly down so that strands escaped and shone like spun gold in the sun's rays, the glimpse of ankle and more, as she had lifted her skirts to climb a stile, her laugh as she teased him about his aloofness. The laugh rang in his ears and when he looked again it was Clara who was laughing, as her form retreated from him into the distance out of his reach.

He woke in a cold sweat. The covers had fallen from the bed and he had to get up and heave them into place. Feeling his way through to the kitchen, he filled a cup with cold water and drank. A flurry of sleet was thrown against the window and he shivered and returned to his bed, pulling the covers around his chin in an effort to keep warm.

In the following days the dream came again... and again... never quite the same but always containing these two women combined in one baffling, intangible, taunting body.

Ellen was, of course, desirable. If it weren't for Clara, he would have been quite drawn to the younger girl. Over the months since his arrival, she had matured unexpectedly from a lanky, ill-formed adolescent into a pleasing young woman. What was more, she was innocent of the effect that she had on him... and other men too, he suspected. Maybe it was the lack of a mother, but she seemed not to know where the line should be drawn between friendliness and what he saw as overfamiliarity.

Tom was thinking about this as he trudged heavily down the path to the barn. He was planning to fork fresh straw into the pens in readiness for any ewes and their lambs that might need more protection than that given by a night on the hill. He did not want to be caught unprepared. The black-faced sheep were a hardy breed but, even so, he occasionally needed to give nature a helping hand. A bitter wind, laced with sleet, hit him in the face and blew his hair this way and that. His eyes surveyed the horizon, skies hanging grey and sullen above the smooth outline of the hills. They could be in for another heavy fall of snow by the time the day was out. The lower valley sides were dotted thickly with sheep now, as they came lower to escape the worst of the early spring weather. Luck would need to be on their side if they were not to have to dig any out of the snowdrifts, as had happened the previous year.

The barn felt warm as he entered and pulled the heavy door closed behind him, shutting out the wind. It continued to whine around the corners of the building, but within there was quiet. Then he became aware of another sound mingling with that of the wind. It was a girl's voice and she was singing. He approached slowly and, rounding a corner, came upon Ellen. She was oblivious to his presence and was forking straw into the pens. He felt a twinge of irritation that she should be doing the job that he had set himself to do but, as he watched her, the irritation subsided, to be replaced by a stirring of the desire that had unintentionally surfaced the previous week. He stood unmoving, hidden by a wooden upright, watching her.

She had a liquid, flowing movement as she forked the hay and tossed it into the pen so that it scattered across the floor. She had lifted her skirt and tucked the hem into her waistband to keep it clean, so her petticoats were visible. She stopped for a minute and rested the fork against the side of the pen so that she could refasten her hair, which, as ever, had come loose from its restraint and was falling around her face. She raised her arms to catch it into the ribbon and he could see the rounded outline of her breasts above her slim waist. The sight caused an involuntary groan and she turned, suddenly aware that she was not alone, and saw him.

'Tom! You startled me. I was just putting out some

straw for the ewes.'

'So I see. I was planning to do that. That's why I'm here.'

She laughed. 'I was fed up with being indoors. I needed a bit of fresh air.'

'Did you now?' He walked up to the pen, lifted the door and came in.

'Are you going to help me then?'

'You look as though you are managing quite well without my help.'

She shrugged and held out a fork, laughing at him. 'The more the merrier is what I say.'

Tom took the fork that was offered and laid it against the bars of the pen. He stepped up to her, took her face in his hands and kissed it gently, first on the cheek and then on the lips. He drew back and looked at her.

'That won't get the straw bedded down,' she said with a mischievous look.

'Maybes! But it'll make a good enough bed for the two of us.' His face was unsmiling, his heart pumping violently, his voice gruff with desire. He took hold of her face again and this time the kiss was hard and insistent.

She pulled back breathless, doubtful.

'Come along, Ellen. Lay down here. I won't do owt to hurt you. You know this is what you want. I'm not daft, tha' knows. It's what tha's been after for a long time.'

He pulled her down slowly and steadily into the straw. And when she opened her mouth to say that she didn't know what he was talking about, he silenced her with another kiss, as he reached for the hem of her petticoats and drew them upwards in his trembling hand.

*

The panorama of interwoven hills was growing indistinct in the approaching dusk. Hilltops were dusted with snow and, at intervals, green reaches of trees divided one from the next. It was a raw, colourless end to a day devoid of sunshine. The snowflakes were thickening now, falling steadily from a leaden sky. At this rate the ground would soon be covered. He knew he ought to go back, but still he sat on, staring into the distance until his eyes watered with the cold.

What in heaven's name had got into him? Of course the girl had asked for it – the open, provocative way she had about her. But she was sixteen. Sixteen! He knew even as he thought about her, that she couldn't be blamed for the way she was. It was highly probable, he thought with a spasm of shame, that Duncan had never enlightened his daughter as to the ways of men and women. Of course, she could not be in ignorance, living on the sheep farm and witnessing the frenzied activities of the tups at each back end. But that was to lower the intimacies of men and women to the level of the animals... which was precisely what he had done. He had vented his frustrations over Clara on this innocent child. There! That was putting it plainly. He covered his face with his hands and massaged his aching eyes.

What if Ellen went home and told her father what had happened? He swallowed nervously and stared at the ground. He could lose his job over this. He might be forced to go back to Yorkshire in disgrace. Duncan might, heaven forbid, insist that he make a decent woman out of Ellen by marrying her.

Perhaps he should have stayed longer with her, he thought now... given her the attention that he supposed women craved... kissed her, sat with his arm around her, showed that he cared. The things that he would want to do if it had been Clara and not Ellen with whom he had lain in the straw.

Maybe she wouldn't say anything to her father. Maybe she didn't mind what he had done. Perhaps she had quite enjoyed it. Of course, it was obvious that it was her first time. She had found it painful... and there had been blood. But at the end she had seemed not to mind. When he had lifted his weight off her and sunk down in the straw at her side, she had said nothing... no word of rebuke... nothing. At the end, she had sat up cautiously and straightened her clothes, before rising unsteadily to her feet.

'I'm going now,' was her only remark, and he had

grunted by way of reply, as she made her way slowly and stiffly to the entrance. A flurry of snow blew in as she struggled with the door, and stalks of straw rose into the air and settled again as it slammed shut. And then there was silence. He had stayed there, numb, exhausted, for ten, maybe fifteen minutes, before spurring himself into action. He had grabbed the fork, still leaning where he had placed it against the wooden frame of the pen, and tossed the flattened straw until there was no evidence of its occupation. Then he began to scatter straw as though his life depended on it, plunging the fork deep into each sheaf and shaking it loose over the stone floor of the barn. For over an hour he worked, until his arms ached and sweat ran in rivulets down his face and the thick dark hair of his chest was matted and damp. Finally, he had rested the fork against the corner of a pen, grabbed his coat and gone out into the late afternoon.

Tom looked up suddenly. Night was closing in around him now. He knew the hill well but he knew too that he had only to take one awkward step to twist his ankle or send himself skidding over the wet snow. Besides, the hill sloped to a precipitous drop not far to the left of him and he did not wish to bring his short life to such an abrupt end. He rose reluctantly from the stones on which he had been sitting and began to descend.

As his path wound downwards, he could dimly make

out the whiteness of the cottages far below. As they came nearer, he could see that a light burned in Duncan's kitchen. It dimmed as someone passed in front of the flame, then flared again. He guessed it was Ellen clearing the pots after their tea. Again guilt coursed through his body, leaving him weak and miserable. He could see now that it was indeed Ellen in the room. His steps slowed and he came to a halt, watching her quick movements as she went about her work. How young and innocent she looked. She crossed to the window and stared out, his form invisible to her in the darkness. Her face was inscrutable, but he noticed that it seemed devoid of that spark of animation that so characterised her usual bearing. As he continued to stare, she moved her fingers quickly across her cheek, as though brushing away a tear. He was aware next of her father coming up behind her. She turned slowly and buried her head in his shoulder. He lifted a hand and stroked her hair. Then she reached out and picked up the candleholder and Tom watched the wavering light as father and daughter crossed into the parlour and disappeared from his sight.

Tom plodded across the sodden grass, stamped the snow off his boots and entered his cold, unlit cottage. With a forlorn thud, the door closed behind him.

7

Making the Most of the Good Weather

Tom strode across the hill with Nell in the early morning of a beautiful summer's day. He never ceased to be amazed by the shortness of the Scottish nights at this time of the year. Even at midnight the sky retained a luminous glow, and by three in the morning the oystercatchers, grouped along the sides of the water, were greeting the approach of dawn with shrill piping and the curlews nesting on the hills responding with their soft bubbling call.

Beneath his feet the grass was wet with a heavy dew. Opaque white mist gathered in the valley, wreathing itself between the hills and blotting out the view of the river as it meandered through its base. Slowly it dispersed as the sun cast its warming rays along the glen. Wisps of vapour, like the discarded wool of passing sheep, clung to hilltops and became trapped in the clefts between hills. From one of these clefts came the repeated song of an invisible cuckoo.

Tom began to call instructions to Nell, and the dog, responding immediately, ran up the hillside until she was above the highest of the grazing sheep. At a further command, she began to work the flock downwards in a solid group. If one sheep bolted, she outran it, encouraging it back to the main body as they approached the in-bye ground. Below, the shepherd could see Ellen standing by the open gate of the sheep pen. Nell raced on ahead to prevent the leaders from overshooting their destination and, as she encouraged them into the enclosure, the others followed without trouble. Ellen closed the gate and smiled at Tom.

'That was no' so bad. I have some breakfast prepared if you care to join Father before you start.'

'I'd like that.' Tom smiled and looked away again. He found it hard, after what had happened only a few months previously, to act normally with the girl. He knew what he had done was wrong, that he had acted in the aftermath of Clara's rejection. She too, he fancied, had changed. She had become quieter, at least when she was with him. Her girlishness had disappeared and been replaced with a calm composure that he took as evidence of her approaching womanhood.

'A warm day for this job, it's going to be,' she said, as they passed a wooden crate, on which were lined up several pairs of shears. Her words were all but lost in the loud bleats of complaint that came from the captured sheep.

Tom caught up with her and they walked side by side towards the cottages.

'I'd rather a day like this. At least we can get on without having to worry that the rain will call a halt. Leastwise, I hope not.' His eyes searched the distant hills, above which the sky was a uniform blue. He attempted a rough calculation of the time it would take them to shear this first batch of ewes. There were about a hundred and fifty that he had brought down from the hill. Providing the weather stayed dry, and he was as sure as possible that it would, they would get through them in six hours or so, though that didn't allow for meal breaks. Duncan and Kenneth would do turnabout in bringing the sheep out of the pen. This would give each a rest from the back-breaking work of shearing. He, being the youngest and fittest – and the fastest – of the three, would keep on with the shearing. Ellen would be employed in rolling the fleeces and she and Kenneth's wife could be relied upon to keep them well fed and supplied with mugs of tea.

Lifting the cast-iron pot from the warming oven, Ellen gave the porridge another stir before ladling out a generous helping each for her father and Tom and a smaller one for herself.

Och, lassie, you'll need to eat more than that if you're to spend the day at the shearing with us.'

'Oh, Feyther, don't make such a fuss. Sit yourselves

down and eat up while it's hot.'

Tom pulled out a chair and joined Duncan, and the two men ate in silence. Ellen joined them and made a start on her porridge, but then she was up again, removing warm potato scones from the oven, fetching butter and honey, filling the big teapot with boiling water. Tom was aware of her swift supple movements as she bustled round the kitchen. It felt good to be surrounded by this comforting domesticity. Most mornings he padded around in his own bare kitchen, not bothering to cook a breakfast, filling himself with whatever happened to be left over from the previous day, even if it were only a crust of bread, thick and solid and toughening round the edges. Duncan had invited him to join them regularly for breakfast but he declined. Today, though, was different, this first day of the shearing ritual.

Tom glanced at the clock. It was nearly seven. He rose abruptly.

'We better be making the most of the good weather, boss.'

'Aye, lad. You're right.' Duncan nodded. 'What I wouldn't give to be young again.' He scraped back his chair and followed Tom to the door.

They worked steadily over the first hour and a half, talking little. Ellen went between them, rolling each fleece as it fell discarded to the ground. They paused for a mug of tea, before continuing, for a further similar length of time. By their second break, Tom's back was already aching. He knew, though, that by the end of shearing he would have become hardened to the stoop of his back and the struggle of each sheep as it sought to free itself from between his legs.

By twelve o'clock, they had shorn seventy-five sheep between them, almost exactly a half of the number that Tom had brought off the hill that morning, he thought with satisfaction. It had been a good morning's work. Tom knew that Duncan was not as fast as he. He was not as fast with any of the jobs on the farm as he used to be. The younger man did not blame him. Over the years, he had seen the effect that the continual burden of heavy work had on farmers and shepherds... how once strong, upright men became bent with the rheumatics before their time, how their wrists and knuckles swelled and their fingers stiffened and ached. He put down the shears and stretched, pushing his strong hands into the small of his back to ease the aching.

The two shepherds walked side by side to the shade of the cottage and sat a while to ease their aching backs. Kenneth's wife brought out bread and cheese and made large mugs of strong tea. Ellen had baked an apple pie and the three men ate hungrily.

'She's a good lassie,' Duncan commented, when his daughter had taken their mugs into the cottage to refill them. 'Don't know how I'd have managed without her all these years.'

'Aye, I can see that. She certainly makes a grand apple pie', Tom smiled.

'What's that about my apple pie?' Ellen appeared around the corner of the cottage. 'Are you wanting more?'

'Well, now, if you're offering, I'm not one for refusing.'

Ellen laughed and cut another generous slice. They sat in silence while Tom ate. In the distance the river gurgled companionably, and the mew of a pair of buzzards came to them, their circling forms no more than dots in the blue sky.

*

When shearing resumed in the unaccustomed afternoon sunshine, Duncan began to dreamily recall the summer preceding Ellen's birth. Ellen was fascinated. She had never heard her father talk so freely about a time that must hold so many painful memories.

'Did you have only one summer together, Father?'

Duncan lay down the shears and helped the ewe to her feet. Ellen opened the gate of the pen and the ewe bounded away over the grass, to join the rest of the flock, similarly shorn, on the other side of the field.

'Aye, lassie.'

Kenneth fed another sheep through from the holding pen and Duncan took hold of the ewe by her horns, dragging her onto the clipping stool and twisting her onto her back. Ellen took the fleece that had been removed from the last sheep and began to roll it.

'Aye,' Duncan continued, holding his shears poised to start clipping. 'We had only the one summer together as man and wife.' He sighed. 'Of course, there were a few years before, when we were getting to know one another. But that's not the same as being married. I mean, there's certain things you cannae do.'

Tom, bent double over a particularly recalcitrant ewe, listened in silence. Was this Duncan's idea of talking to his daughter about the facts of life?

'Why did Mother die? Is it so hard to have a baby?'

'Aye, it can be. Look at the sheep. Think how many of them we lose each year, not to mention their lambs. Aye, it's a dangerous thing is childbirth. But it's getting safer all the time, thanks to doctors learning more about it.'

Tom's clipping never faltered, but, at this mention of the medical profession, he clenched his teeth tightly and silently buried his chin into the steaming flank of the sheep. Four month's silence from Clara had done nothing to diminish his feelings for her.

They were shearing more slowly now, a combination of tiredness and the telling of old stories lending an easygoing feel to the afternoon's activities.

Duncan glanced across at his daughter. She had gone quite pale and was sitting on the floor of the barn next to an unrolled fleece.

'Is there anything wrong, lassie?' Duncan asked quickly, hurrying to finish the half-shorn sheep.

'Just a wee bit tired, Father. Give me a minute and I'll be fine again.'

'Like I said this morning, you don't eat enough. This is heavy work and you have to have energy for this job. Tom, give the lass a hand, if you've finished that one.'

'Don't fuss, Father. I'll be all right.' Ellen said testily, but Tom had stepped over to her and, putting his arm round her waist, escorted her to the wooden seat outside the cottage.

'There, lass. Stay here for a bit. We can manage. I'll call Mrs Douglas to put t' kettle on.' His eyes lingered on her. 'We can't have you falling by the wayside on the very first day of shearing.' He leaned over and gave her shoulders a friendly squeeze, before straitening up and going off in search of the farmer's wife.

He found Elizabeth Douglas in the kitchen making bread, the regular slap and punch of the dough rekindling childhood days in the Yorkshire farmhouse.

'Gracious, Tom. Is it time for tea already? I was fair carried away with all my baking.'

'No, it's us, not you. Well, it's Ellen. She's in need of a cup of tea. We wondered if you could put the kettle on.'

'Aye, of course I can. She's growing up fast, that one, outgrowing her strength. She needs to eat more.'

Tom looked round the kitchen. 'Shall I get out the mugs? You look as though you've enough on with the bread.'

'Aye, that would be helpful.' Elizabeth divided the dough with a sharp knife, shaped each into a rough rectangle, gave them a final dusting with flour and slapped them into the loaf tins. The oven sent out a blast of hot air as she slotted them quickly onto the shelf and slammed shut the iron door. 'So what about you, Tom? Are you happy here? Are you missing home?'

Tom gave a short laugh. 'Yes to both! I like the work here. They're good to work with, the blackface. And I'm given plenty of responsibility. Aye, I do miss home though. I worry about my mother. She were never strong, you know. And it's hard, the job of a farmer's wife.'

'I can vouch for that! So what made you decide to come up here? Don't get me wrong... we're glad you did. But couldn't you have gained the knowledge you needed by staying in Yorkshire?'

'Aye, 'appen I could. The truth is... there's a girl. We were friends at home. She studies in Glasgow now and I thought, well, if I was nearer, I might be able to see her.' He paused, then went on. 'You see, I was hoping that one day we might get wed... but I'm not so sure she feels the same way.'

'Well, there's only one way to find out. Why don't you invite her over one weekend? It'll give you time together'

'I wanted to... in fact I asked her. But she was too busy with her studies. She did say she might come at the end of the year though.'

'Good! Then we'll have to make the end of the year one to remember, won't we!'

*

They finished shearing just over a week later. Amazingly there had been no rain during the whole of the week and their work had progressed without hindrance. Just over one thousand one hundred sheep had been through their hands at the end of this time. To celebrate a job well done, there came an invitation from Kenneth Douglas to eat with him and his wife that evening.

Tom locked the door and heaved the tin bath from where it lay on its side in the hall. He had heated enough water over the fire to give him an adequate, though not luxurious bath. Strong as he was, his back and limbs ached with the exertion of the last few days. He lay back in the bath, willing himself to relax in the tepid water, and gave himself over to thoughts of Clara.

In the four months since her letter had arrived his feelings had flicked uncontrollably from love to anger, to hate and rejection and now to a dull pain verging on acceptance. He would have to face the fact that he had lost her for good.

There was a knock at the door and he sat up abruptly, causing a tidal wave of scummy water to slosh over the side of the bath.

'Are you ready, Tom? Father's gone ahead. I said I'd call for you.'

'I'll be right in a minute or two. You go on and I'll join you.'

He lay down to rinse the soap off his complaining body and climbed out dripping into the puddle of water on the tiles. He dried and dressed quickly, searching for a hairbrush as he buttoned his shirt. He had not intended spending so long soaking himself and was anxious not to keep the farmer waiting.

Ellen was sitting on the grass outside his cottage when he emerged. She had on a long blue skirt and white blouse and her hair, newly washed and still damp, hung loose over her shoulders.

'I told you not to wait,' Tom said gruffly, closing the door with a bang.

She shrugged. 'I thought I might as well.'

'I'm glad you did,' he said. 'You look grand.'

Ellen smiled. 'It's good to feel clean again after all those smelly sheep. It's the best part of it, when it comes to an end.' She wrinkled her nose in disgust, then laughed. 'Farmer Douglas always gets in a jug of ale for the end of shearing, so we better hurry before Father drinks it all.'

'I've to go up the hill later to check that the ewes

know their way back to where they belong, so I'll have to go steady on the ale, any road.'

Duncan hadn't drunk all the ale and Tom didn't go particularly steady with it. By the time the mutton stew was placed in the middle of the table and the big bowls of potatoes and carrots joined it, the lad was beginning to relax. He looked at Ellen through a haze of goodwill and alcohol. She was turning into a beautiful woman. Her eyes, he noticed, matched the colour of her skirt, and her hair was the colour of spun silk. He shook his head, laughing to himself. Good heavens! Whatever was getting into him, all this waxing lyrical about a mere strip of a girl?

He gazed at the softness of Ellen's hair, and a picture of Clara's dark curls framing her serious face unexpectedly replaced the gentler one of the girl before him. His mind turned for the thousandth time to that letter...to the message it had contained and to the manner in which it had been written. Cold-hearted bitch, he thought now and scowled.

He looked at Ellen again and the memory of that time he had lain with her in the barn came back to him. Previously he had forced the scene away whenever it impinged on his consciousness, but now he resurrected it, savoured it even. *She* was no cold-hearted bitch, he was sure of that. His features softened. He lifted his head and regarded her across the table. She was smiling at him and didn't look away. He felt the familiar twinge of desire.

*

It was nine o'clock when Tom rose a little unsteadily and explained that he must check on the sheep. Those sheared latterly had been taken from the furthest reaches of the hirsel and could take several days to reach the hill on which they had been born and raised, so Tom was anxious that none should go astray and end up lost.

The evening air cleared his muzzy head and he strode over to the cottage to change into his stronger boots and then to the barn to release Nell.

She barked and scampered ahead. Looking up, Tom could see Ellen in the distance. He approached, watching as she fondled Nell's soft head, seeing the way her fair hair cascaded around her face as she bent forward., and the soft folds of her dress flowed over her supple body.

'What are you doing out here?' His voice was hoarse. 'Isn't it time you were tucked up in bed. You must be o'er tired after all your hard work. I'm off to check on the sheep. Do you fancy a walk because, if you do, I wouldn't mind some company?' His tone was casual, offhand even.

'Aye, that would be good.' She ran over and slipped her arm through his.

He glanced at her briefly and her eyes, looking back at him, held a challenge. It struck him that she might have drunk some of the ale, though he had seen none pass her lips.

Watching for rabbit holes or rocks over which they might trip, he started to traverse the rough ground of the lower slopes. His mind was racing. It was as if she were enticing him to repeat what had passed between them earlier in the year. He felt her arm tighten on his. There was no mistaking her intention. And what man was there who could resist such an invitation?

'Let's climb to the top of the hill,' Ellen said impulsively and, letting go of his arm, set off up the steep slope at a run.

He watched her climb, tripping at times over her skirt, stumbling over the tussocks of grass that were becoming indistinct in the dusk. She turned and laughed and her skin was a pink glow in the setting sun. Her hair was on fire. In a turmoil of longing he set off up the hill after her.

8

The Brightest Star

By the beginning of December there had already been two heavy falls of snow, the second lasting a week and causing considerable disruption to the smooth running of the farm. Tom struggled through the deep drifts, digging for sheep with his bare hands, finding them safely trapped in the pockets of air, which gave them temporary respite. Others of the flock he found sheltering in the stells, the circular, drystone structure which ensured that the snow was unable to build up a drift but instead was blown away by the prevailing wind. They lost none of the sheep, though Duncan acknowledged that if the snow had come later when the harsh winds of January could freeze the drifts into solid ice, they would have fared a lot worse.

When the snow cleared, Ellen resolved to shop for extra supplies in case of further inclement weather. Christmas was fast approaching and then Tom's friend would be with them. It was exciting, though somewhat daunting, to have someone so prestigious to visit. A doctor... or nearly so! And, what was more, a woman! Duncan had muttered something under his breath about women no longer knowing their place in society. He had not said this within Tom's hearing, but Ellen had caught his words and, turning away, given a secret smile. She admired Clara's bravery. She had never heard of a woman doctor before, much less come into contact with one. Ellen supposed that her head must be full of knowledge and her time full with her studies and her hospital work.

But it was strange, this friendship between a shepherd and a doctor. And although the opportunity of meeting such an important personage excited her, she was uncomfortably aware that Tom's full attention was focused on the forthcoming visitor. For the last year and a half Ellen had been his friend... his only friend, she had always considered. Now that this earlier alliance had been revealed, she felt a twinge of something previously alien to her... jealousy. Surely, what she and Tom had shared was special. She loved Tom and she thought he loved her – though he never said so. Now she wasn't so sure about his feelings. She suspected that Clara occupied the greater part of Tom's thoughts, for his behaviour could veer from distraction to excitement in the blink of an eye.

Ellen stood in front of the mirror fastening her hat, the face looking back at her from the mirror as pale and drawn as the landscape outside.

A knock came at the door and she hurried to open it. Tom's form was indistinct in the pre-dawn darkness.

'Are you ready, lass? We'll have to hurry or we'll miss the early train to market. And make sure you've got enough clothes. It's reet cold out here.'

Ellen grabbed a long woollen scarf off the peg and wrapped it round her neck and mouth before stepping out into the raw morning and slithering down the track at the side of Tom. She struggled to keep up with him on the frosty surface of the path, miserably considering that she might be any farm worker going along to assist the shepherd at market, and not the girl whom he had desired on that rare day of summer warmth.

'I'll have to leave you to travel back by yourself after you've finished buying what you need. I've some shopping to do in town. Is that all right with you, lass?'

'Aye, I suppose so. But I'll no be able to carry everything back to the farm myself.'

'That's all right,' he said more kindly. 'Leave it at the station and I'll pick it up on t' way back or when I fetch Clara.'

'When is she arriving?'

'Christmas Eve.'

Ellen glanced at him in time to see the look of pleasure that flitted across his face.

'I think she would have waited until Christmas Day itself until I told her that there were no trains. She's been very busy in the hospital, tha' knows.'

'Aye, I guess so. She must be very important. I'm surprised she finds time to come and visit the likes of us,' Ellen said forlornly.

'Oh, we're old friends. We've known each other since we were seven years old.' Tom laughed. 'It's grand that she's found time to come. Nine months is a long time to wait.'

Ellen frowned. 'Nine months? Have you seen her this year already then?'

There was a momentary pause. 'Aye. I visited her in the college. I wanted her to come in the summer but... but she was too busy.'

'Oh.' They walked on in silence until Ellen said, 'I suppose she better have my bed.'

'Well, I don't suppose she'll consider it right to stay with me.' There was a hint of embarrassment in his laugh.

'And shall we be together for the meal?'

'Of course! Everything will be the same as it's always been.'

'I hope you're right.'

*

The short winter day was already drawing to an end as Ellen wearily retraced her steps into the valley. Her feet and legs, painfully cold from sitting in the unheated carriage, grew numb and heavy and her shoulders ached

80

from carrying the heavy baskets. In the small of her back she felt a nagging pain.

Perhaps Clara's arrival would be a good thing. It would force her to put away the listlessness and heart-heaviness that were so unlike her usual sunny temperament. Duncan, whose daughter had been his sole companion for sixteen years, had put his finger unerringly on the reason for her dejection.

'Dinnae fret, lassie. He's bound to have his head full of the visit. After all, she'll be a very high and mighty lady one day, no doubt.' He sniffed. 'You've been a good friend to him since his arrival and he'd be daft if he didnae see that. But he's bound to have acquaintances from his younger days. After all, the lad's a grown man. We've only known him for such a short time.' He gave her a sideways look. 'And don't you go getting any fancy ideas about him. You're too young to be thinking about such things.'

She cheered up as she thought about her father. He would no doubt have the kettle simmering in readiness for her return. She could not imagine life without him. And if her father thought Tom too grown up for her, well, he would soon come to see how much Tom thought of her. She looked at the bulging packages in the baskets. She had bought him a new pipe and a couple of twists of his favourite tobacco for Christmas. Also in the basket, were a quarter-pound of Tom's favourite sweets and a small bottle of lavender water for Clara. There were provisions too – flour and oatmeal, sugar, tea, dried fruit. It was no good Tom saying he would pick them up later. He might well forget and then where would she be, especially if they had another spell of bad weather? She must bake the following day. Clara would expect seasonal delicacies on the table, and her father and Tom would need the usual bread and oatcakes and buns.

Ellen rested her baskets on the ground and stretched her arms to ease the aching in her shoulders. She could just make out the cottages at the other side of the valley. The sky had cleared since morning and a scattering of stars winked in the darkening blue. One of them was larger and brighter than the rest. She could smell frost on the air. Even now, the cold was sharp on her cheeks and her breath clouded in front of her face. As she watched, a light flared in the cottage. Her father must have finished his work. In a few minutes he would have stoked up the fire and put the kettle on to boil. Bending to her baskets, she picked them up slowly and went on again.

The brightest star seemed to bounce along on the horizon of the hills as Ellen walked. She felt like one of the wise men in the Christmas story. But they at least found what they wanted at the end of their journey, and they had each other's company on the road. Unlike her, she thought, left to struggle back to the farm alone. Tom's mind was full of the Christmas visitor and Ellen might as well not be there, for all the notice he took of her.

9

The Christmas Visitor

On the night before Clara's arrival, Ellen woke from a particularly troublesome dream. The bedcovers were this way and that and none of them covering her. She struggled to untangle her legs from her twisted nightdress and gingerly put her feet onto the cold floor. Striking a match, she held it to the candle and the flame flared and guttered in the draught. By its flickering light she could see that the hands of the clock showed half past two.

Tiptoeing through to the kitchen, Ellen poured herself a cup of water and sat down at the table with a shiver. She suspected that she had caught a chill during her trip to market at the start of the week. Her body ached all over and she was not comfortable either in bed or out of it. She stood up and pushed her hands into the small of her aching back. Quite unexpectedly a spasm of nausea overwhelmed her and she spun round to find the bucket that always stood on the floor at the side of the stone sink. She crouched over it, clinging onto its sides.

When the retching had stopped, she raised her head slowly and wiped the perspiration from her brow. She was shivering violently and a dull ache had started low in her abdomen. Dragging herself up from the floor, she sat at the table until the pain subsided. She took a tentative sip of water and then another. It tasted delicious. Through the bedroom door she could hear her father's regular snores. Her young sixteen-year-old self longed for his comfort, but she felt better than she had. Maybe she had eaten something that did not agree with her and the worst was now over. She would wake him up if it came again.

The bucket clanged as Ellen lifted it from the floor and rinsed it with water. Opening the door, she stepped outside and threw the contents onto the garden. The hill at the back of the house loomed dark, the clear skies that had characterised the last few days having given way to grey sheets of cloud that hid the stars, even the Bethlehem one that had guided her homeward footsteps on market day. As her eyes scanned the sky for any sign of brightness, a few desultory snowflakes fluttered slowly down in front of her face.

It was all going wrong, her friendship with Tom. She had been so looking forward to them spending time together. Clara might, of course, have trouble reaching them, if the snowfall was as heavy as earlier in the month. The thought brought her no joy though, for she knew how Tom would be if he were disappointed. She could picture him sitting in silent misery at the side of the fireplace and nothing she could say would make any difference. Or he would prefer to be on his own and take himself off up the hillside and she would be deprived completely of his company. With a last glance at the falling snowflakes, she stepped inside, closing the door as quietly as she could, as the aching in her abdomen started up again.

*

Tom heard the door of Duncan's cottage being opened, and the rattle of the bucket, and wondered what was happening. The noise had startled him, for though he was awake, his mind was miles away and he did not at first realise where the sound was coming from. He slipped out of bed and crossed to the kitchen window, craning his neck to see who was awake at this hour of the night.

Ellen stood on the grass at the back of the cottage. In the darkness, her nightgown billowed around her small figure. She looked like a ghost. He watched as she gazed into the sky, then he saw her turn and disappear from view. A second later the clunk of the kitchen door indicated that she had gone inside.

He stared at the spot where she had been standing. Guilt niggled at the back of his mind, as it did so often when they met. He suspected... in fact he was sure...

that her feelings for him were strong and genuine... as genuine as the feelings of a young girl of sixteen could be. That she would get over him he was certain, but he still felt that he had taken advantage of her innocence, even if, on that second occasion, she had given him ample encouragement. He had avoided being alone with her since that evening, not wanting to encourage her, when it was Clara he loved, and Clara who he hoped would eventually love him in return. He had to admit though, that Ellen was a desirable lass. Her body was filling out nicely... a bit too much for some men's liking perhaps, though he himself appreciated a woman who wasn't all skin and bone. Added to this, she had a pleasant way with her. In fact, her very kindness irritated him at times because it forced him to be less sullen and moody than he often felt.

He started and stared out into the darkness, sure that he had seen snowflakes. Yes, there they were again. He crossed the kitchen and wrenched open the door, searching the sky. Swearing softly under his breath, he slammed the door and made his way back to the bedroom. Throwing himself onto the bed, he pulled the covers up to his neck and gave an agonised groan. If it were to snow as it had at the beginning of the month, the trains would be disrupted and all his plans would come to nothing. He had written to Clara twice before she had agreed to spend Christmas with them. He felt sure that her agreement to come for the holiday meant that she had thought about his previous offer and relented. She would agree to their marriage, even if she insisted they wait until her course of study was at an end.

Perhaps he was worrying unnecessarily. The flurry of snowflakes might be nothing more than that. She would be here, as planned, the following afternoon. In his mind's eye he watched the train slowing and stopping at the station and Clara stepping down onto the platform, looking around in anticipation. He saw himself stepping up to her, kissing her cheek, taking her arm in his, feeling her closeness to him. He would seat her next to him in the wagon and they would drive into the valley together and there would be no need for words because they would understand one another, just as they always had.

He rolled onto his stomach, closed his eyes and endeavoured to sleep.

*

Ellen turned onto her side and sat up cautiously. She could hear her father's characteristic morning cough and his quiet movements around the bedroom, interspersed with grunts as he pulled on his clothes. She felt better than she had done three hours ago. The nausea had gone and she was no longer shivering. Her back still ached, but that too would ease as she busied herself with the day's preparations.

Her father knocked cautiously and put his head round the door. 'Is that you still in your bed, lassie? Could you no' sleep?'

'No' so well, Feyther. I was dreaming. And I took a pain in my stomach. But I'm a deal better this morning.'

'That's good, lassie. We can't have you sick when we've a guest to look after.'

At this reminder of the Christmas visitor, Ellen crossed to the window and peered through the curtains. It was still as dark as it had been when she stood outside the door in the early hours. A light covering of snow whitened the ground, but the air was clear. There would be no disruption to the railway as long as it got no worse than this.

She stooped to pick up her dress from the floor and was conscious that the nocturnal aching in her back was returning. Still, if it got no worse than this, she would cope, and all the preparations would be completed by the time their visitor arrived.

'Tom and me, we have to check on all the ewes today.' Her father raised his voice as she riddled the grate. 'I'm walking the far hills and he's walking those behind the cottage.'

'Well, be careful, Feyther. There's been snow in the night. It's Tom's job to walk the far hills.' She paused, guessing the reason for the change in their habitual routine. 'I heard him up in the night,' she went on. 'I don't know whether that was him up for good or if he just couldnae' sleep. Perhaps he's too excited about seeing Clara again.' She turned away abruptly and begun fiercely raking out the ashes.

'Let me do that, lassie. You look done in… and we've only just started the day.'

'I'm fine, Father,' she bit back. 'Let me come past, or I'll drop these all over the floor.' She ignored Duncan's look of concern and crossed to the kitchen door. A cold wind funnelled down off the hills and the ashes spiralled in a dense cloud off the top of the ash pan.

Once the fire was blazing she filled the kettle and hung it on the hook to warm. Duncan, who always fed the dogs and did other bits and pieces of work before returning for breakfast, left the cottage and she could hear him chatting amiably to Tom, as they set off down the hill together to the barn.

*

The snow had been falling for nearly an hour when Clara's train pulled in at the station. It was enough to give a chocolate-box prettiness to the village but not enough to inconvenience the final part of the journey into the hills. With any luck, Tom thought, it would continue to fall and might delay Clara's return to Glasgow at the end of her stay.

It was all that Tom's nocturnal imaginings had

predicted. She stepped from the train and stood on the platform smiling. She was less serene, perhaps, more animated than he remembered her. If her face registered embarrassment, it must be because of that unfortunate letter, now, doubtless, regretted. She stepped across the intervening space and kissed him before he had the chance to do so to her. Then she secured her arm through his and they left the platform and strolled jauntily to the wagon. He apologised that there was no proper carriage for her and she said that the wagon was what she had always been used to when she was young and she expected nothing different. He dusted the snow off the seat before she sat down.

'I'm looking forward to meeting Duncan and his daughter,' Clara began when they had left the station and were making their way through the village.

'They're all ready for you.' He gave her a grin. 'Duncan and me, we were out on t' hills this morning, checking that the sheep were all behaving for your visit.'

'Poor sheep... out in all this weather!'

'Nay. They don't think owt of it. They're a tough breed up here.'

'Ellen must be growing into quite a young lady now. How old is she... fifteen or sixteen?'

'Aye,' said Tom self-consciously. 'Summat like that. Aye, she's bonnie.'

'Thomas Fairclough, I do believe you're beginning to speak Scottish!'

'Nay, lass, I'll never do that. I'm as Yorkshire as Blind Jack of Knaresborough.'

They both laughed, swaying together as the horse crossed the railway bridge and descended the sharp hill to the river.

'It's good to be out here.' Clara sighed deeply and looked around. 'Glasgow is so full of people and incredibly dirty and smoky. Sometimes I feel I can't breathe.'

'You should come more often. It would do you good to get away. And you know how much I want to see you,' Tom added boldly.

Clara flashed him a look of warning. 'I can't, I really can't. We are expected to spend most of our time in the hospital now. There are so many things to learn about... and not enough time in which to learn them.'

'Not enough time to see your friends.' Tom's voice was sulky.

'Oh, Tom. I told you. You have your life here and I have mine there. Aren't you happy, doing what you've always wanted? You've all this land to roam around on, all those sheep to care for...'

'...And no one to share it with.' He looked ahead through the thickening snowflakes. 'Still, you can always come down this way to work when you've taken all those fine exams.'

'Perhaps, Tom. I don't know where I'll end up. I may get a job at the other end of the country.'

Tom didn't reply. She was here now, wasn't she? Not so long ago he had thought it was all over. Anything could happen in the future. Much against his nature, he refused to be despondent.

Duncan was at the door of his cottage as they drew up outside. Tom handed Clara down and reached into the wagon to retrieve her case. She walked to where Duncan was standing and introduced herself.

'How are you, Duncan? I'm Clara. It's lovely to meet you.'

'I'm fine. And yoursel'?'

'Very well. Glad to have a break from work.'

'Aye. Come away in then.'

She followed the shepherd slowly into the kitchen. It stood in disarray. Unwashed dishes filled the sink. On a floury table, oatcakes were heaped in small circles ready for baking. Dried fruit for a cake had been weighed and put to one side on the dresser. A smell of yeast emanated from two loaves of unbaked bread that were overflowing their tins and spilling onto the hearth.

'Where's Ellen? She looks as if she's gone somewhere in a hurry,' Tom said, following Clara into the room.

Duncan shook his head and frowned. 'I dunnae ken where the lassie is. I went oot this morning to check on the sheep and when I came back, she was away. I tried to find you, Tom, but you'd already gone to the station.'

'Didn't she tell you where she might be going?'

'No. I didn't even know she was away oot. She said

she had baking to do. She's maybe forgotten some messages and walked to the village, though if so, it's strange she didnae leave me a note.'

'I'd more than likely have passed her in the wagon, any road.'

A wave of irritation swept up and over Tom. He had planned to sit down with Clara and enjoy a good tea and an evening's relaxation after he had finished one or two necessary jobs. He glanced out of the window. The snow was heavier now and already its flakes were floating an unnatural silence over the valley. With this kind of weather, the daylight hours would be even shorter than usual. 'I'd best go and check the barns,' he said with ill grace.

'I'll come with you,' Clara said at once and Tom's mood lifted immediately.

'Aye, all right, if you don't mind.'

'She's quite well, is she, Duncan?' Clara asked, turning to him.

'Aye, quite well... though, now you mention it, she did tell me she'd took a pain in her stomach during the night... but she told me it was gone this morning.' Her father rubbed his chin thoughtfully.

'Don't fret, Duncan.' Tom decided to put a brave face on the problem. 'We'll soon sort it out. Why don't you go and check with Kenneth? She might have gone down there for summat and got delayed.'

Duncan brightened at once. 'Aye. Perhaps that's

where she is. I'll go directly.' He grabbed his coat from the back of the door and hurried out into the snow.

'Come along, Tom. Let's go too, before it starts to get dark.' Clara turned to the door and stepped out of the cottage. Tom grabbed an oil lamp from the entrance and followed her down the path. At the base of the hill stood a small barn. They entered its warmth and looked around. It was silent and empty.

'There's nowt here,' Tom said and they emerged into daylight. He scanned the fields, a ball of apprehension unravelling in his stomach now. There was something wrong. Ellen would never vanish like this unless something untoward had happened. 'We'll check the other barns,' he said, stepping into the snow, which now lay inches deep over the grass. Nothing disturbed the white evenness of the ground ahead.

The second barn was empty too and so was the third, which lay a good distance off across the other side of the farm. A pink sunset, forcing its way between the gathered clouds and through a window, illuminated the pens, where, in late spring, they brought the ewes and lambs that needed extra attention. Tom gazed around, thinking of the hours he had spent here earlier in the year, encouraging ailing lambs and tending ewes. With a pang he remembered that it was here that he had first had carnal knowledge of Ellen. His face burned as he recalled coming upon her that day... the rhythmical sway of her body as she spread the hay, his mounting desire as he watched her, fascinated, his words of encouragement as he seduced her... and his later remorse as he sat on the gathered stones at the top of the hill and thought about what he had done.

He glanced round at the pen and his eyes caught a movement in the straw. He blinked in the gloom and looked again.

'Are you coming, Tom? There's nothing here.' Clara's voice came from the doorway.

'Wait! There is summat.'

A prolonged moan made them both jump. Clara followed Tom's gaze. The moan came again, louder this time, building to a high-pitched scream that subsided in a sob. Tom felt the blood turn cold in his veins.

'Quick!' Clara pushed open the gate of the pen and fell at the side of the helpless girl. She threw a glance at Tom, questioning.

'Ellen.' Tom was by her side now. His voice was shaking. 'Ellen. It's me... Tom. Clara's here. Tell her what the trouble is. She'll 'appen be able to help.'

Ellen raised a moist hand and grabbed Clara's wrist. 'Aye. It's pain in my belly. I've had it all day. It started last night. I have sickness too. The pain's worse now. I don't know what to do.'

'Do nothing. Rest there. Tom! Light that lamp, will you? It's impossible to see anything in this corner.'

Tom, shaken out of the momentary inertia that the sight of Ellen had induced, felt in his pocket for matches and fumblingly struck one, holding it with a shaking hand to the mantel. The flame flared and lit the corner of the pen and he shrank back at the sight. Ellen's face was smeared with dirt and her tears had cut rivulets into the grime at each side of her eyes, which were wide with fright. Her hair was tangled with the straw in which she lay curled up on her side and was soiled with vomit. As he watched, she began to moan again. She rolled over until she lay on her back. Her moans grew louder and, without warning, she shrieked at Clara.

'Can't you do something? You're a doctor, aren't you? I cannae stand this pain anymore.' She lost all control and thrashed her head fiercely from side to side, her screams reverberating around the empty barn.

Tom stood up, infected by her panic and, turning abruptly away, put his hands over his ears. As the screaming subsided, he swung round to face Clara.

'Aye. Can't you do summat? Can you tell what the trouble is? Has she eaten owt that's upset her?'

Clara was studying the girl with a look of bewilderment. 'Tom, turn away a minute while I examine Ellen. Don't go right away though. I may need your help.'

Tom, grateful to be given the opportunity to put some distance between himself and the helpless girl, stepped out of the pen and stared through the unglazed window at the soft pink clouds on the horizon, the calm picture it presented at striking odds with the shambles within the pen. Its peace was shattered in an instant as Ellen's keening reached new heights. Among the screams came Clara's urgent voice calling his name.

Reluctantly he swung back the gate and dropped down on his knees. Clara's shocked face made his blood run cold.

'What is it? Do you know what's up with her?' he shouted above the din.

'Aye, I do now. She's having a baby.'

With a look of horror, Tom's eyes flicked to Ellen, then back to Clara. Colour drained from his face, as a tide of panic and disappointment in equal measure swept through his body, rendering him as limp and drained as the girl at his feet. He stared at Clara, all his plans avalanching about him. And then the moment was broken as Ellen reached out her hand and dug her fingers painfully into his trembling arm.

10

Another Small Avalanche

Ellen now knew with a certainty that she was going to die. At the sound of Tom's and Clara's voices she had been filled with an overwhelming relief. They would make her better. Tom would comfort her… and Clara, with all her learning, would take away the pain. But that wasn't happening. She had seen the frightened look on their faces, watched Tom turn away… and lastly and sickeningly seen his horrified reaction when Clara spoke those terrifying words.

She was having a baby. A baby! Never had the thought crossed her mind that this was the cause of her pain. Surrounded as she had been all her life by the birth of thousands of lambs, she had never once considered that she herself was about to give birth. In a moment of clarity between her pains she thought of the yearly ritual of lambing that went on all round her and with which she so often helped. It was never like this. The sheep often gave birth without a murmur or, at the very most, muttered a prolonged groan as the lamb slithered out onto the grass. If a sheep were noisy, her father or Tom would tell it in no uncertain terms to pipe down.

Occasionally they would do their rounds in the early morning and find a dead sheep, victim of the complications of labour. That was why she knew she was going to die. It was going to happen to her like it did with her mother. All this pain and for so long... it couldn't be normal. The baby must be stuck. And surely they couldn't start groping around to bring it out, like her father sometimes did with a difficult lambing. The pain was coming again now... waves of unendurable agony. Ellen let out a long wail of panic. By the time she was out of breath, the pain had gone.

It was suddenly very peaceful in the barn. She could see pink clouds through a square of window. The slanting rays of the sun hit the wall of the barn behind her, and below, evening wrapped the sheep pens in comforting darkness. Cobwebs festooned the roof over her head and the crumbling muddy nests of swallows clung to the rafters, their usefulness long past. She used to count the baby swallows, as they poked their heads over the edge of their home... maybe four of them, sometimes five. The adults had grown used to her as she lay unmoving on the straw, watching their industry. She came often to lie here in the straw after that time... that time when she had been working in the barn and Tom had disturbed her.

She remembered the pain. It had seemed bad at the

time, though it was nothing compared with what she was going through now. She had not known what was happening but she had put up with it because it was a sign that Tom loved her... at least she thought it was, although he hadn't seemed any different towards her afterwards – more distant if anything – and not in a hurry to repeat the experience. That was why she had tempted him that night when shearing was finished. She wanted to reassure herself that he really did love her. And the second time she too enjoyed what they did. But of course he didn't love her. He loved Clara. She was never going to change that. She knew that now. And now she would die and he and Clara would be married.

It came to her in a flash. That was when the baby had been made... that time here in the barn! She had seen it often enough when the tups were allowed to mix with the ewes at each back end. How had she not realised what had happened? Tom had given her a baby. It was his and hers. The thought brought her a fleeting shred of relief.

A lamp flashed in her face. She looked at them, startled.

'Now, Ellen.' It was Clara's voice. 'Listen to me. It will soon be over. Next time you get a pain, I want you to push. No screaming. Do you understand?'

She understood. She would push the baby out and then she would die. Her eyes swerved to Tom's and she whispered hoarsely, 'You will look after it, won't you,

Tom... look after it and love it? Promise me!' And as the pain started again, she had a picture of his white face, dotted with perspiration and lit in strange contours by the light of the lamp he was holding.

'Ellen, don't forget now. Do as I say. Do you understand?' Clara's voice came to her as if from a distance.

She nodded. She would do as she had been told for the baby's sake. Panic began to rise in her throat but, with a huge force of will, she bore down until she was certain her body would tear apart. Taking a deep breath, she pushed again, struggling, struggling against her desire to scream.

'Rest now, Ellen. Rest a minute. Tom, hold Ellen's hand, will you. Mop her brow. Do something to help.'

She was conscious of her hand in Tom's large and rough one, before a final tearing pain came and went, and she lay on the floor of the barn, staring at the swallows' nests. She was tranquil now.

In the distance, she could hear Clara and Tom talking, but it was nothing to do with her. And then a faltering wail split her tranquillity... followed by a loud insistent cry that none could ignore. And an awestruck father lay the clamouring infant in the crook of her arm.

'It's a little girl. You have a baby daughter.'

She turned her head to gaze in bewilderment at the child, who was nuzzling her mouth against her mother's clothes in an attempt to find her source of nourishment.

Clara was doing what she needed to do to ensure that Ellen was safe. Tom, meanwhile, divested himself of some of his layers of clothing to wrap round his tiny daughter.

*

'Tom, how could you let this happen? She's only a young girl?' Clara's voice shook with anger.

Resentment flared upwards through Tom's body and his face flushed. 'You've no right, no right at all, to accuse me of this. How do you know the babby is mine? It could be the bastard of any farm worker around these parts.' He lowered his eyes under the force of her gaze.

'I saw the way Ellen was with you. I heard what she said.'

'That happened because she wants someone to help her look after it.'

'Then tell me honestly that it isn't yours and I'll believe you.'

Tom raised his head and glared at her and then the fight went out of him as quickly as it had begun. His body sagged. What was the use of pretending? He had known from the start it would do no good. It was only a last impossible attempt to keep alive the hope of winning Clara's affection, but now she would despise him for his dishonesty as well as for his actions.

'It's mine... at least, I think it is. Though it's still

possible that she might have been with someone else,' he added lamely.

'What were you thinking of?' Clara shook her head sadly.

'What the hell do you suppose I was thinking of? There she was, a pretty young girl, constantly flaunting herself at me...'

'Flaunting herself?'

'Yes, I mean, there's only so much a man can stand. And you need not sound so prim and proper. If it weren't for you, this would never have happened.'

Clara gasped. 'Whatever do you mean? What have *I* done?' Her laugh held a hint of hysteria.

'You've put me off all the time. It's you I always wanted, no one else. You're the one I always loved.'

Clara's horrified face stared at Tom's and at the mounting colour that suffused his cheeks. 'Come on, Tom. You and I are old friends... but never anything else. I told you that in the letter. Surely you must realise that by now.'

'I realise nothing of the sort. We've always been close. Why shouldn't we be lovers? There's nowt to stop us.'

'There's everything to stop us. For a start, I don't love you... not like that. I love you as a sister loves a brother. I always have done and I always will, if you will let me. For another thing, there's my work. I've explained all that before.'

'But that needn't be a prob—'

'Tom! Don't be stupid. Look over there. You have a child… and its mother to care for.'

Tom was silent. There was nothing to say by way of reply, no wriggling out of his responsibility.

'You realise we will have to go and present Duncan with his new granddaughter.'

Tom groaned. He had not had time to think about this further inevitable consequence of his dalliance with Ellen. Another small avalanche crashed around him. Ellen was her father's pride and joy. He would lose his job over what he had done. Of that there was no doubt.

'We must get Ellen and the baby back to the cottage. It'll be bitter in here soon.' Clara stepped back into the pen where Ellen lay with the baby in her arms.

Tom followed reluctantly and Ellen looked up at him.

'Look, Tom, she's asleep. Isn't she beautiful? Do you want to hold her?'

'Not now.' Tom attempted to inject some levity into his voice. 'We need to get you and t' babby into the house before you get chilled to the bone. Give the babby to Clara and I'll carry you back.'

Ellen handed over the baby and Clara wrapped her coat around her and cradled her to the warmth of her body. Tom knelt down and lifted Ellen easily, wondering how he had never noticed her advancing pregnancy. True, he had seen that she had put on a bit of weight, but nothing more than that. Her figure was very firm and the baby small, so he supposed that a combination of these two things was enough to hide the changes that had gone on within her young body.

Duncan was standing at the door of the cottage as they came slowly up the track.

'Mercy! Mercy! Whatever's happened,' he cried, seeing only Ellen's prostrate form within Tom's arms.

'It's all right, Duncan. She's all right,' Tom said, stepping inside. Duncan fussed around his daughter's head, impeding their progress. 'Let's get her through to her bed, Duncan.'

The older man stood aside as Tom laid Ellen on the set-in bed and pulled the covers over her.

'Duncan, we'll need some hot water. Can you bring some for me?' It was Clara talking and Duncan seemed to register her presence for the first time.

He nodded towards the fire. 'There's a kettle of boiling water here. I put it on for your return.' He paused, frowning at the bundle wrapped in her coat. 'What have you got there, lassie?'

The baby, responding perhaps to the warmth of the room, stirred and let out a yell. Duncan came closer and gazed with a bemused expression at the bundle.

'What's that? I mean... where did it come from? Did you bring it?'

Clara took a deep breath and said, 'It's Ellen's baby... your granddaughter.'

Duncan stepped back as if she had slapped him,

paused as if gathering his thoughts, and veered unsteadily in the direction of Ellen's bed, the look of bewilderment on his face slowly giving way to one of outrage. He clasped the bedhead with a trembling hand.

'What does this mean?' he said slowly, as if having difficulty enunciating the words. 'Who did this to you, lassie. Tell me who did it and I'll kill him with my bare hands.'

Tom had stood to one side, watching the tableau unfold with awful inevitability. At the sound of the shepherd's voice with its barely controlled anger, he knew he could keep silent no longer.

'It was me, Duncan. Ellen and I, well, we... er... got together in t' spring.'

'You "got together" in the spring? We took you on as a good worker... and Ellen helped out in your cottage to keep you comfortable... and you did this to us? You betray my trust under my very nose.' Duncan's face was scarlet now and his voice shook. 'And to make matters worse, you don't have the common decency to come and tell me about the wain.'

'He didn't know about the wain, Father. *I* didn't know about the wain. It's as much of a shock to me as anyone.'

'But how come? There's changes happen in a woman's body to tell them a baby's on the way. Why, with your mother... with your mother...' He stopped abruptly, confronted with the even more dreadful events of his wife's birthing.

Clara came forward. 'Ellen's young. It may be that her body's natural rhythm had not yet established itself. It can happen, you know.'

Duncan wheeled round and brought his face close to the younger shepherd. 'So not only did you betray our trust… but you took a young girl, not even into womanhood, and defiled her with your lust. You ought to be horsewhipped.'

Tom made to object but thought better of it. He lowered his eyes and muttered, 'I'm sorry. I'm sorry for all the trouble I've caused. I'll pack my bags and go.'

'What's that? What's that you said?'

'I said I'll go. I'll go now.'

'You'll go nowhere,' Duncan roared so loudly that they all jumped and the baby began to scream. 'You've made your bed and now you'll have to lie in it. You'll marry the lassie.'

Why had he not realised that this consequence would be forced on him? He supposed that he had known all along but had not wanted to face the reality of it. After all, it happened often enough in farms around the valley. It was even considered by some to be quite within the man's rights to test his young lady's fertility before asking for her hand in marriage. He groaned. His offer to leave would now be seen as another ploy to absolve himself of his responsibilities to Ellen and the baby.

Tom looked at Ellen. She was lying with her head

partly turned away and he could see that she was weeping. He had fallen into a trap of his own making and there was no way out. His eyes came to rest on Clara and the fretful child, and he wished that the ground would open and swallow him up. Then, with a huge effort of will, he smiled at Duncan, before walking purposefully to the side of the bed and taking Ellen's hand between his.

'Will you marry me, Ellen? I promise to be as good a husband to you as I can be and to look after you and our baby. What do you say?'

Her pause was momentary. 'I say yes,' she replied, wiping a hand across her eyes, and his last glimmer of hope faded with the words.

Tom leaned over and kissed her forehead and she tilted her face up to his and kissed him on the mouth, as if to seal the promises they had made.

'And now,' said Clara, taking charge and forestalling any more discussion on the subject, 'I need to see to the patient and to the baby girl. Duncan, I would be glad of that hot water. And I suggest you refill the kettle and make us all a cup of tea... and then the patient needs to rest, so if you've any more discussing to be done, I suggest you go and do it next door.'

11

A Lucky Man

It was a relief to Tom that Clara was occupied in caring for Ellen and the baby. Now that the die had been cast and there was no way out of it, her continued presence was a torment to him. He did his best to avoid her whenever he could. This was not difficult, as she insisted on staying in Duncan's cottage, although the presence of a small baby meant that there was very little space.

What does she think I'm going to do to her, Tom thought bitterly, as he sat staring at an empty hearth. As things stood, the idea of making advances to her or anyone else could not have been further from his mind.

Clara busied herself caring for Ellen and the baby who had come through the ordeal unscathed. Ellen too, despite any lack of care during her pregnancy, rallied quickly and was soon taking to her maternal responsibilities with remarkable maturity. Duncan, despite his continuing anger with Tom, seemed besotted with his granddaughter, having been denied the opportunity of further children of his own by his wife's untimely death. Tom, uncertain what the older man's reaction would be, decided to stay away from the cottage as much as possible, but it would have been churlish to refuse the offer of dinner on the three days of Clara's stay. They were awkward occasions and he had no appetite for food and still less for celebration. Although he did not admit it to anyone, he was, however, anxious to hold his daughter and see for himself the miracle that was partly his. Still, that would have to come later, when he made sure there was no audience present.

Clara was due to catch the first train back to Glasgow on the Monday morning after Christmas. The snow of Christmas Eve had frosted over and for two days the land lay glittering in the slanting rays of the winter sun or the cold white of the moon. Now, though, it had turned warm and a thousand rivulets had sprung to life and were making their tinkling way down the hillsides to join the swelling river in the base of the valley.

Tom sat rigid, clasping the horse's reins and thinking about their ride to the farm less than four days earlier. It belonged to a different time, a bygone age... one that would never return.

'You're a lucky man to have Ellen,' Clara said, after several minutes' silence had elapsed. 'She's a lovely girl and a very good mother. And she will make you a wonderful wife.'

'Aye. Happen she will. Any road, I must make the best of it, mustn't I?' He looked at her sadly.

'Aye, you must. You know something? The baby has Ellen's eyes... and I'm sure she's going to have your hair.'

'I've not had much of a chance to see her for myself. If the truth were known, I'm more than a bit wary of Duncan and what he might say next.'

'Oh, I don't think you need worry about Duncan. He's delighted with his granddaughter. As long as you do the right thing by his daughter, I think he'll come round, given time.'

'It doesn't look as though I've got much choice, does it?' Tom said bitterly.

'No, Tom, you haven't. You've got responsibilities to fulfil.'

'I was hoping eventually that *you* would be my responsibility. Now that will never happen.'

'It never *would* have happened, Tom. It would never have worked, you and me, married.'

There was little else to say and the remainder of the journey was undertaken in silence. They stood unspeaking on the platform, until the train pulled into the small village station. Then Tom, suddenly fearful of losing her forever, stammered,' You will come and see us again, won't you, Clara? I couldn't bear it if you didn't come.'

'Of course I'll come. Why do you think I wouldn't?'

'Well, you seem so disapproving about my behaviour…'

'You're doing the right thing by Ellen and that's what matters. She's a lovely girl and you can't help but grow to love her. And don't think you can keep me away from the wee girl, when she was my very first unsupervised delivery!'

She climbed into the carriage and Tom stepped in after her and swung her suitcase onto the rack above her head. When he turned to go, she put a hand on his arm to detain him and they embraced.

'Look after them, Tom… and be happy.'

He stumbled onto the platform, unable to speak, and slammed the door shut as the guard blew his whistle and the train eased out of the station. Clara was carried slowly away from him and back to the life she had chosen.

He thought of their conversation as he turned his back on the village and steered the wagon across the bridge. He was never one to shirk his responsibilities and he would not do so now. Besides, Ellen *was* a lovely girl and she had borne his baby. Now was the time to establish his rights. And if what Clara had said was true, and Duncan did come round in time, there should be no problem in making it clear who was the head of the household.

The sun was climbing to the tops of the hills on the northern side of the valley. He watched the colour wash slowly downwards until the slopes were bathed in light as the sun reached the horizon. It had stirred him with its beauty when he had first arrived, and it did so now, setting a seal on his resolutions. And as the farm buildings became visible around the bend in the road, he flicked Archie's rump with the reins and they covered the remaining distance with enthusiasm.

*

Duncan put his foot down. No daughter of his was going to live in sin. There would be no alteration to their current living arrangements until a wedding had taken place.

'You need to make an appointment with the minister,' Duncan insisted to Tom, 'and the banns must be read for three Sundays in a row. Then there can be a wedding.'

Tom, whose early religious life had been at the hands of the Quakers and had failed to attend anywhere since completing his education, knew little of matters ecclesiastical, and bowed to Duncan's ultimatum. It seemed illogical to him, however, that Ellen and her baby could not be with him when there was incontrovertible evidence of their having been together already, and in a far more intimate way than he was at present proposing. Duncan, however, was adamant.

On the first available opportunity, the young

shepherd rode back to the village and called to see the minister of the kirk. It was a difficult meeting, for throughout the questioning Tom was uncomfortably aware of the unspoken and untimely fact of the baby girl's existence. It was only at the end of the interview that Tom admitted there was a baby and could they please arrange a time for his daughter to be christened. He waited with bated breath for the expected diatribe, but it never came. The minister smiled, congratulated him on the birth of a daughter and suggested that they combine the wedding and the christening in one service, adding that he hoped he would see the young couple in the congregation in the future and their daughter an enthusiastic member of the Sunday School.

A date having been set, the next problem was to decide on a name for the baby. Ellen said immediately that she should be called after Clara, in recognition of her help, without which neither of them might be here. But Tom shook his head and could not be persuaded. While they were arguing, Duncan announced that he would be very honoured if the baby were named after his wife.

'We'll call her Netta,' Ellen said.

'I thought your mother's name was Janet.'

'It was too. But Netta is short for Janet. It's a pretty name, don't you think?'

'Aye, happen it is.' At least it was better than Clara. Now that his friend had gone from his life, he could not bear constant reminders of the future he had hoped would be his.

From the first moment Tom was allowed to hold his daughter, he was entranced. The baby had the same dark hair as him. Her eyes were as blue as Ellen's and, if early appearances were anything to go by, Ellen's sunny temperament would be hers too.

As soon as the wedding service was over, Tom moved his wife and baby daughter into his own cottage, ignoring his father-in-law's mutterings of things being done with indecent haste. He considered that he was the one who had been made to suffer as a result of Duncan's insistence that Ellen stay where she was until after the wedding. He had no intention of waiting any longer.

Elizabeth Douglas, the farmer's wife, had given them a wooden cradle that had long sat gathering dust in the attic room of the old farmhouse. Tom carried it proudly into his cottage and placed it next to the bed. Ellen, in the time that had elapsed since the birth, had acquired items of baby clothing and had been stitching busily to make good any deficiency in her baby's wardrobe. There had also arrived a parcel from Glasgow containing a beautiful cream-coloured woollen cot cover with a message from Clara to say that she never again wanted to see the baby suffering from the cold.

Tom reached down and took the slumbering baby from Ellen. She had fallen asleep at her mother's breast and Tom could see that Ellen too was struggling to keep her eyes open. He had sat watching his daughter feed with a mixture of contentment and longing. It was many months since he had known the pleasures of a woman's body – the last time had been at the end of shearing, the previous July, when Ellen had tantalised him until he had been crazy with desire for her. And now it was the night of their wedding and there was nothing to stop a repetition of the wild passion of that evening on the hilltop.

Netta gave a small whimper of complaint as her father laid her in the cot and tucked the covers round her, and then she slept again. Tom turned to Ellen. She was still propped against the pillows, but her head was drooping and her eyes were closed.

'Ellen! Don't go to sleep. This is our wedding night, remember.'

Ellen did not so much as stir. Her husband went up to her and shook her arm gently. She opened her eyes and gave him a weary smile.

'Is that Netta asleep then?' she murmured.

'Yes, and you as well, by the looks of it. Come on, wake up!' He shook her arm again and, when she did not move, he set the candle down on the bedside table and climbed in beside her. He removed one of the pillows from behind her head and pulled her gently down the bed so she was lying flat. Then he began to kiss her, softly at first and then more urgently. Ellen moaned and half opened her eyes.

'I'm tired,' she murmured.

'And so am I... tired of waiting. Come on, lass. You weren't like this before we were married.' He reached down and took hold of her nightdress, pulling it slowly up to her waist.

'What are you doing, Tom? I told you... I'm too tired tonight.'

'Nonsense. It won't take long. I've waited months for this,' he muttered into her ear, as he lowered himself onto her and swiftly and painfully claimed his rights as a husband. When he had finished, he threw himself onto his back and stared at the ceiling, ashamed and dissatisfied. He had been looking forward to this evening and now he had ruined it. He cursed under his breath and turned to look at his wife. Her eyes were closed but a tear escaped and ran slowly down her face, followed by another... and another. He watched them fall and reached out to brush them gently away with the end of his fingers. Then he turned and extinguished the candle flame with a hiss, and the room was plunged into darkness, just as the baby took a deep breath and began to wail.

12

The Outsider

Spring was late in coming to the valley. The snow that had fallen to welcome the baby's birth returned and stayed, blanketing the valley thickly and softening the rough edges of barns and water troughs. In the distance it was difficult to see where hills ended and sky began. Sheep, customarily the brightest objects in that green backdrop, showed yellowish grey against the unsullied fields.

It had been snowing all night when Duncan knocked on the door of Tom and Ellen's cottage. Dawn was still an hour away. His daughter heard the rattle of the latch and the stamping of feet as Duncan attempted to dislodge the impacted snow from his boots. Ellen was pouring tea. She had dressed, but a dishevelled plait of hair still hung over one shoulder and puffy eyes hinted at another disturbed night. Duncan, nursing a cold, drew out a large handkerchief and blew his nose loudly. Then he sniffed the air, full of the aroma of frying potato cakes.

'Sit you down there, Feyther, by the fire and have some breakfast here with us. You need the warmth before you go out and work in this weather.'

The older man frowned. 'I'm no' looking forward to being out there with this chill. But I'm worried, I don't mind admitting.' He stared gloomily out of the window. 'There's nae chance of checking on the sheep when it's like this.'

'Happen I can get up the hill behind the cottage,' Tom said, coming quietly into the room and sitting down at the table. 'It's not so deep up there.'

'Nonsense, man. It's too risky. You've a wife and child to look after, ken. I'll no' have you taking unnecessary risks.'

'I'm well aware of my responsibilities.' Tom diverted his gaze to the fire. 'But I can't sit here all day doing nowt while the sheep may be suffocating up there under the snow. And them not so far off lambing an' all.'

Duncan shrugged. 'Do as you please, pal, only take care.'

The baby started to whimper and Ellen fetched her from her cot into the warmth of the kitchen.

'Here, let me have her for a minute before I go.' Tom held out his arms and cradled his daughter to him, but the crying only grew stronger.

'She's likely wanting fed again,' Ellen sighed, taking the baby back.

'There's no one like a woman when there's a baby to

be comforted.' Duncan said pedantically. 'Not that there was any choice in the matter when you were wee, Ellen.'

'Seems there's no choice in the matter now,' Tom sighed. 'I'm off then.' He scraped back his chair and rose quickly, snatching up his coat from the hook at the back of the door and checking in its pockets for gloves.

'Take care, Tom.' Ellen was behind him now with her hand on his shoulder. 'Kiss Netta before you go.'

Tom bent down and kissed his daughter gently on the forehead. He ran his finger down the softness of her cheek and reached for the door handle.

'Don't you have one for me?' Ellen turned her face up to his. Tom glanced back along the passage to where Duncan was still intent on his breakfast, and bent to give his wife a quick peck on the cheek. He turned the handle and a blast of snowflakes swirled in before the door closed behind him.

Ellen, chilled as much by the coolness of his manner as by the snowflakes, stared at her coat swaying to and fro on the back of the kitchen door. And then her daughter renewed her whimpering and she switched her thoughts to Netta.

*

Tom snatched up a spade and, whistling to Nell to follow him, trudged across the field behind the cottage, making for the gate. Before he had gone many yards, he realised that he had underestimated the depth of the snow. Common sense told him to turn back... but stubbornness drove him on. He felt himself excluded by that little scene in the kitchen and irritated that he should feel that way. After all, he knew well that he was unable to satisfy the physical needs of his baby daughter. But it was not just that. In some indefinable way, he felt himself to be the outsider. And his mind returned again and again to the cosy kitchen with Duncan eating the breakfast that Ellen had prepared, as she must have done ever since she was old enough to be allowed near the fire.

It was impossible to open the gate, the uprights barely visible above the snow. Tom felt for the bars and swung his leg over, jumping down into the softness on the other side. It stood waist high here and it was tiring work to plough a furrow across and upwards, where one group of sheep were hefted. With her light frame, Nell's progress was easier and she barely dented the white covering over which she bounded. Eventually a line of stones could be made out, indicating the wall between their land and that of the next farm. As they neared the wall, Nell began to bark and scrabble in the snow. He stopped her with a command and listened. Yes! He could hear the sound of bleating. His spirits rose. So, he had been proved right. There were sheep to be saved out here... sheep that would doubtless die if they were denied fresh air for much longer.

He and the dog started to dig. By the time the first of the sheep struggled panic-stricken out of the airless confines, Tom could feel the sweat trickling down his back. Only his feet remained cold, soaked by the snow that had fallen into his boots and melted there.

'There you go, ladies,' he said breathlessly, as the last of the ewes joined the rest of the freed sheep. He set about clearing as large a patch of grass as he was able, so that they would have at least a semblance of green on which to feed. Whether or not they survived would depend on further snowfall, but he congratulated himself on giving them a fighting chance.

Leaving the group to fend for themselves, he made his way next towards the stell, where more sheep were certain to be sheltering. It was a long way off and familiar landmarks were absent. Picking his way carefully across the hill, several times he found himself chest deep in drifted snow. His legs were shaking with exhaustion now and he was beginning to doubt the wisdom of his actions when, unexpectedly, he found himself up against the rounded walls of the shelter.

It was as he thought. Within the small haven, the area was crammed with sheep, huddling together for warmth. They were hungry but safe. He cleared a patch of grass for them, digging away the soft snow until his aching limbs could dig no more. Lifting his gaze eastward, he considered going further but he knew it would be reckless. If the weather were no worse tomorrow, then perhaps he would venture out again and check on more of the flock.

Tom began to retrace his footsteps. The wind was rising and flurries of loose snow were being blown across the tracks made by his boots on the outward journey. He was hungry now and looking forward to Ellen's warming vegetable broth. Not that he was cold… battling through the drifts saw to that… apart from his feet, which he could no longer feel. It would not do to find himself suffering from frostbite, although such an eventuality might lead to a spell in hospital, in the charge of a doctor… or even a caring medical student.

He had not allowed himself to think of Clara since his marriage, although at night he had no control over his dreams, in which she featured disturbingly often. Now though, with no other distraction, he allowed his imagination to roam, seeing her surprise if she should enter the room to find him her next patient. He felt her cool healing hands examining him, her calm voice giving instructions about his treatment, her frequent visits to assess his improvement. And the desolation when she informed him that he was healed and could return home. He had heard nothing from her since her return to Glasgow at the end of the old year. She had promised to write… but he had an uncomfortable feeling that she would not do so.

Without warning, his foot failed to hit solid ground. He felt himself plunging deep into the snow. He must have encountered an unseen drift.

'You wuzzock,' he muttered. 'That's what you get for not concentrating.' Expecting to feel solid ground beneath him at last, he was alarmed when none came. Only a lurching down and down through walls of snow, so white that they were almost blue. And then the drift through which he was falling came abruptly to an end and he was hurtling through space, legs and arms flailing as he attempted to grasp onto anything that might break his fall. With a grunt of pain, he hit the ground. He lay winded, distantly aware of the trickle of water. After a minute or two, he slowly raised his head. He was lying on a bank of wet grass. His eyes lighted on the stream that drained the hills around. If his fall had taken him three feet to the left, the channel of jagged rocks that carried the water downwards into the base of the valley would have dashed him to pieces. Painfully he rolled onto his back and gazed up through the white chimney created by his fall, to the small patch of blue sky, partly obscured by Nell's astonished face.

*

By three o'clock Ellen had attached the soup cauldron to the hook over the fire and removed it several times. She had not worried at first, for Tom knew the hills well, and if anyone could find his way around them, snow or not, it was he. But as the day wore on and he still had not returned, a nagging anxiety blossomed inside her.

'Why! Is the man no' back yet?' Duncan exclaimed, appearing on the doorstep. 'I told him it was foolishness to venture out on the high hills in this weather.'

Ellen looked fearfully out of the window. 'It'll be getting dark soon. What shall we do, Feyther?'

'I'll have to go and look for him, of course.'

'I wish I could come with you.'

'Och, no. I'm not having you risking life and limb out there, even if you didn't have Netta. No, I'll call at the farmhouse and ask Kenneth to come along with me.'

Ellen resumed her seat by the fireplace, absent-mindedly rocking the baby's cradle as she sat, glancing frequently at the hands of the clock on the mantelpiece. Dusk was falling now and although the snow lent brightness to the night, it would become more difficult to judge their bearings.

What on earth had possessed Tom to venture onto the high hills in this weather? It was foolhardy. Sometimes she couldn't understand her husband. He could be so silent, so distant from her. She thought he loved her, but sometimes he didn't behave as though he did. The nagging doubt returned to her as it had done on so many occasions, that perhaps he loved Clara. Ellen felt herself so simple, so uneducated, so uncultured... Clara's inferior in every way.

The door flew open without warning, letting in a

blast of cold air and filling the kitchen with noisy blustering men. They were there, all three of them – her father, Kenneth Douglas… and Tom.

'Tom! Are you all right? What's happened?' Ellen jumped up in alarm, as Tom limped to a chair, helped by the two older men, and sat down heavily.

'He was at the bottom of a drift, struggling to get out.' Kenneth shook his head. 'It's a good job we went in search of him. He'd never have managed it on his own.'

'It was Nell that led us to him,' added Duncan. 'If it wasn't for her barking, we'd never have found him. And we'd never have got him out if you hadn't thought to take that rope.' Duncan went over to his daughter and put an arm round her shoulders. 'He's all right, lassie. He's twisted his ankle by the looks of things, but nothing worse than that.'

'Let me take this wet coat off you… and those boots.' Ellen knelt to help her husband.

Tom was trying to undo his greatcoat but his cold fingers fumbled with the buttons.

'I'm away to my house.' Kenneth Douglas hesitated. 'No more hot-headed ideas, young Tom. I appreciate you going after the sheep, but I can't afford to be without a shepherd. I'm relying on you for the lambing in a week or so. Look after him, Ellen. Make sure he doesnae do anything daft.' And shaking his head and mumbling to himself, he stepped from the room.

Tom hobbled to the living room and eased himself into the fireside chair, his face creasing with pain.

'What is it? Are you hurt anywhere else?' Ellen hovered anxiously.

'Let me get these boots off and I'll look. Help me undo the laces, will you, lass, while I get the feeling back into my fingers.'

The bruising, when Ellen had eventually helped her husband to struggle out of his sodden clothes, was extensive. He had grazed his right elbow and lower arm and a developing area of blue-black disappeared beneath his undergarments.

'I'd best find the witch hazel for those bruises.' Ellen jumped up and ran to the cupboard.

'I'll be away to my cottage.' Duncan sighed dramatically and rose from his seat. Ellen, her head in the kitchen cupboard, missed the sight of his reluctant steps to the door.

'Aye. I'll see you tomorrow, Feyther.' Emerging successful from the gloom with the malodorous ointment, she was surprised to see that he had already disappeared.

'I thought for a minute he was going to stay and see me stripped.' Tom couldn't suppress a grin. 'Are you going to rub that on my bruises then, lass?'

'What else is a wife for?'

'This and a lot else besides.'

'Now, Tom, behave yourself. Turn round and let me

see your back.' She began to apply the ointment, wrinkling her nose at the pungent aroma. 'I don't know what you were thinking of, going right up the hill on a day like this.' Tom was silent. 'Well, what were you thinking of, up there in the snow?'

'I know what I'm thinking of now.'

'What, with all these bruises? You'll be too sore for anything but sitting by the fire, and that's a fact.'

'They'll be much worse tomorrow than they are today. So come here, now your father's gone, and before Netta wakes up. And I promise I'll take more care in the future.'

*

It was as well that they took advantage of the short interlude occasioned by the late snowfall. Within four days, the first sheep had begun to lamb. That same day Duncan failed to appear for his breakfast.

Tom threw open the door of his cottage and noisily entered the kitchen. Ellen looked up in alarm.

'He's got fever. Happen that cold has gone on his chest. Today of all days! We could do without this.'

'Poor Father. I must go and see to him.' Ellen glanced uneasily at her husband. 'Tom. We'll have to fetch him round here with us. I can't look after him there and you and Netta here... to say nothing of being nursemaid to however many motherless lambs you bring in. Come next door with me now, before you go onto the hill.'

She grabbed a shawl from the back of a chair and hurried out. Tom followed unsmiling. He knew as soon as he had seen his father-in-law that it would come to this. And while he was sorry for the man, he could see where it would lead. Duncan's normal reluctance to return home would be intensified a hundred-fold.

'You're coming to stay with us, Feyther,' Ellen said matter-of-factly, as she felt her father's brow and wrapped the woollen shawl around his shoulders. 'What's brought this on, I wonder?'

'It must be that day in the snow,' Duncan replied, his feverish eyes lighting up at his daughter's words, and his pointed reference to Tom's foolhardiness inducing in the lad a guilty silence. 'I cannae get out of my bed, lad,' Duncan moaned, as Tom stood over him. 'But I cannae leave you to the lambing. They're about to start.'

'They *have* started, Father. Tom's spotted one on yon hill this morning.' Ellen looked round the untidy bedroom. 'He'll manage... Kenneth will help him. To be sure, you won't be able to go in this state.'

Together they supported Duncan as he staggered from his home to his daughter and son-in-law's next door. And alone, Tom trudged away down the hill to alert Kenneth to the unfortunate timing of his father-in-law's illness.

13

The Uttermost Parts of the Sea

In the control room, claustrophobic with machinery and his fellow submariners, Josef Kessler stared through the periscope at the approaching destroyer. It was difficult to gauge its advance through the spray-lashed window and, in any case, he preferred to be in readiness for the commander's order to submerge.

'Stand by battle stations,' Commander Gunter Reinhart's voice rasped. 'Wait for my orders... wait.'

Josef Kessler held his breath. There would be men on the deck of the ship ahead of them, like ants going about their allotted tasks. Men who had left mothers and wives and children behind... like most of the thirty or so crew members at work behind him in the U-boat.

'Fire!' The command made him jump, even though he was poised to hear it. He felt the familiar tremor as one of the four forward torpedoes was released from its housing, and followed the stream of bubbles that it left in its wake. There was a long pause, uninterrupted by the sound of the torpedo striking home.

'Verdammt!' Gunter Reinhart roared. 'It has missed its target. Prepare to fire again.'

'Commander,' Josef Kessler shouted. 'There is no time. The destroyer is advancing fast. Look at how close it is.'

Reinhart swung the periscope towards him and gasped.

'Diving stations!' he barked. 'Close bow caps. Dive! Dive!' The chief wheeled round and flung himself into action in the enclosed space.

Josef grabbed the periscope again and stared, mesmerised. He was conscious of frantic activity behind him and could measure its result in the troubled boiling of the sea up the windows of the vessel. But the thing that dried his mouth and made his blood run cold was the speed with which the grey bow of the destroyer was bearing down on the sluggish submarine. Beneath his breath, he whispered, 'Schnell! Schnell!' but if the boat heard his plea, she ignored it. In the second before she was struck, a picture of his parents and his younger sister flashed before him. And then all thoughts of family were wrestled from his body, as the great bulk of the enemy destroyer tore in two the vessel that had been his home for nearly two years.

*

The taste and smell of oil were everywhere. He struggled

to open his eyes, but his heavy eyelids refused to cooperate. He took a deep breath and in the next second gagged and, lurching onto his side, vomited copiously.

'Here, Alf,' a man's voice shouted close by. 'This one's alive. Just don't strike a match or we'll all be up in flames.' There was a staccato laugh and then the voice continued, closer still, 'Poor devil. Would have been kinder to let him drown.'

Josef turned his head slowly towards the voice. He didn't understand the words, though he recognised the language as English.

'Keep still, Fritz. Let's clear off some of this mess.' He felt his cheeks being roughly wiped. 'Hey, Alf. Get us some water. Let's try and clean his eyes. And bring him a drink, will you. Poor chap's swallowed the muck as well, by the look of things.'

Josef struggled to sit up. The effort made him vomit a second time.

'That's right.' A second voice now, presumably Alf's. 'Get it off your chest. It won't do you no good if it stops there.'

He felt the cloth applied to his face again.

'Open your eyes now,' the voice said, and then louder. 'Open your eyes, mate... Augen... Öffnen!'

So surprised was the German to hear this approximation of his own language that he opened his eyes to see who had spoken... and immediately wished he hadn't. The intense pain caused a profuse watering and he shut them again, though not before noticing that his body, or at least the part of it that he could see, was covered in the blackest oil.

'Wo bin ich hier?'

'What's he saying, Alf? You seem to know the lingo. You want to be careful though. They'll have you up for a spy, if you don't watch out!' Again the cackling laugh.

'He's asking where he is.'

'You're with the enemy, mate... a POW... that's Prisoner of War to you. This is what you get for trying to do away with His Majesty's Navy. And make a note of this – you'll get treated a lot better with us than if it had been the other way round. So we don't want any grumbling. Do you hear me?'

Josef frowned. He had no idea what the man was saying. He lay back exhausted.

'Come on. Let's leave him to rest for a bit. He must be all in.'

The young German remained immobile. His eyes hurt too much to attempt to prise apart the lids a second time. Sounds came to him from a distance. He was aware of a slight rolling motion. A soft wind played about his face, and under the coarse blanket, with which he had been covered, he stopped shivering and began to grow warm.

With a spasm of shock, the horrifying events of those last few minutes came back to him. The colossal impact of the enemy boat on their submarine. The sound of rushing water and crushing metal that filled his ears. His body twisted and turned in the turbulence like so much flotsam. Lungs bursting with the need to breathe. And then nothing more… until this.

He must try again to make sense of his surroundings. With a huge effort, he slowly forced open his eyes, resisting the urge to close them against the pain. The sky above was blue and cloudless. For a while he lay looking up at it. Perhaps he had died and this was what the resurrection was like. It seemed peaceful enough. But eventually he turned his head… and knew instead that this was some kind of hell.

On the deck of the ship, for that is what formed his bed, were rows of bodies, some black like his own, a few recognisable as his fellow submariners… all of them unmoving. He looked at the body next to his own and recognised with a shock that it was Gunter Reinhart. Death, it seemed, was impartial to rank or length of service. At the end of the row, two of the enemy were bent over another seaman, like him, covered in oil. As he watched, the man's body contracted as he coughed. Someone else was alive then. Thank god! He would not have to face the coming ordeal alone. He tried to remember what they had been told about capture and treatment at the hands of the enemy… and could not.

He was tired… so tired. He lay back again, seeking oblivion. Above him the sky was still as blue and he tried to lose himself in it, forget the carnage that lay all around. Why could he not have died like his mates? Presumably God had some other plan for him. What was that passage from the Psalms of David that he had heard read so often?

If I take the wings of the morning, and dwell in the uttermost parts of the sea;
Even there shall your hand lead me, and your right hand shall hold me.

He closed his eyes and remembered nothing more.

14

The Comfort of Home

Pushing his way slowly through the crowd, Tom nodded to the barman and ordered a pint. The inside of The Shoulder of Mutton was hot and airless, the odour of stale sweat mingling with the sour smell of sheep's wool. But Tom was oblivious to the powerful stench. He ran his tongue round his dry lips and glanced from one to another of the weathered faces gathered along the counter. They were, without exception, elderly farmworkers, some of them shepherds, others unskilled labourers who had come into the area for lambing time and not yet returned to their homes.

'Here's another of them,' one of the men said, indicating Tom.

Tom looked behind him, thinking that someone else had followed him up to the bar, but there was no one there.

'Another of what?' He spoke politely enough but felt his hackles begin to rise.

'Another one who can't see where his duty lies, that's

what.'

'I don't know what you mean.'

'Oh, you ken well enough. You prefer not to see it.'

'If you mean the fighting... some of us need to make sure the farms keep running, and that there's food to fill t' bellies of our women and children.'

'So you would let their sons and fathers get mown down on the battlefields of France, while you walk the hills in safety.'

Tom saw this was an argument he was not going to win. He pushed his money across the counter, picked up his glass and took a long swallow.

'Look, pal.' The man did not intend to let the conversation drop. He indicated his own chest. 'We can look after the farms. It's what we've done all our lives. It's no' so difficult. The other... they'd no' take us. We're considered too old. You could go though... do your bit for king and country. There's men much younger than you volunteering.'

Tom looked round, but there was no one of his own age present.

'That's right, you'll no' find any of your pals in here today. They've gone outside to listen to the enrolling officer... which is where you should be.'

Picking up his glass, Tom took another gulp and turned to go outside. Rough elbows hastened his progress to the door.

In the warmth of the summer afternoon he breathed

more easily. On the far side of the market square a crowd of people had gathered. Their numbers waxed and waned as some left to continue their errands and others, curious, joined the throng. There were men and women there, some with children at their knees. He identified several of his acquaintance among them. He could not call them pals, for he wasn't someone who found it easy to make friends. Wandering slowly over, so as not to attract attention to himself, he caught the words of the army officer. He was explaining why all able-bodied young men, who had not already done so, were now required to join up forthwith, if the Hun were to be defeated.

'It's numbers that are important,' he went on. 'Let us show these bullies the overwhelming manpower that we have at our disposal. The tide is turning. Huge offensives are planned. We will soon have them on the run.' His piercing eyes bore through each of the young men in turn. 'Would you stay here in the comfort of your homes while others are fighting your battles for you? What would you say to your children in years to come? Would you be able to tell them that you did your part to keep your country free... or would you have to admit to your sons and daughters that you took the coward's way out?'

The comfort of home. There was little comfort to be had there any more, Tom thought with a cynical smile. His father-in-law's feet were well and truly under the table now and he was showing no inclination to return to his own cottage. He had known how it would be. Sympathetic to his father-in-law's illness and shouldering the extra work without complaint, he nevertheless chafed at the restrictions to his private life when Duncan, now fit and well again, continued to enjoy the comforts of domesticity that Ellen lavished on him.

Like a bad toothache, the sergeant's words nagged at him all the long journey home. It wasn't fair... he'd only been married four months. Hardly time to stamp his authority on the union. And then there was little Netta. He couldn't bear to be separated from her.

It was fortunate that he would be exempt from the new legislation by virtue of his work on the farm. But the words of the men around the bar nevertheless rankled. He knew that what they said was true. They were farm labourers through and through. They *would* be able to manage.

The horse rounded the last bend of the journey home and Tom felt his body relax. He had grown to love the wide barrenness of this land. With any luck, the plans of the Water Board to flood the valley eastward would come to nothing, for the money would surely all be needed for the war effort. He decided to stay away from the town if he could. Working quietly here on the farm, his presence would be hopefully forgotten.

Tom stabled the horse, unloaded his purchases and walked slowly up the slope to the cottage where Ellen was sitting outside in the evening sun. Her hair, long and loose, appeared to be on fire. It was a sight that never failed to arouse Tom. She was dangling the baby on her knee and laughing at her father and at a tall young man who was sitting next to him.

'Tom, you know Iain Murdie from along the valley. His dad needs to borrow a can of drench from us... and, no doubt, has told him to make sure he finds out how we've done with the lambing!'

Tom nodded in reply, but his face remained unsmiling. Lifting his daughter from Ellen's lap, he kissed the baby on the top of her head and cradled her in his arms.

'Iain's got some news of his own to tell us,' Ellen added. 'He's joining the army.'

Iain shrugged his shoulders. 'They've made it compulsory now for all of us, married or unmarried, unless we can claim exemption.'

'He reckons they can do without him on the farm for a bit, now that lambing's over,' Ellen added.

Tom stared at Iain. 'Lambing may be over but what about drenching, shearing, markets and suchlike? Dost tha' think they will run themselves then?'

'Nay. But the two old retainers who work for my father will manage until I come back.'

If you come back, Tom thought. Aloud he said, 'You've no family, have you?'

'None yet. We local lads don't stand a chance with

you all coming up from England and taking the pick of the girls!' The young man spoke light-heartedly enough but his eyes devoured Ellen.

'I better get yous some tea,' said Ellen, jumping up.

'What's the hurry, lassie? Stay for a bit.' Duncan put a hand on her shoulder and encouraged her to sit down again.

'Well, if that's the case I'll need summat to put me on until dinner time. Come on, Netta, thee and me'll go and see what we can find.' Tom lifted his daughter skywards, which elicited from her a deep chuckle and, holding her to his shoulder, disappeared around the side of the cottage and through the open door.

*

'How long have you been friendly with that Iain Murdie then?' Tom asked while they were preparing for bed. Ellen sat in front of the glass, brushing her hair.

She frowned. 'I've always known him. We've been friends since as long as I can remember... born and raised in the same valley. His mother brought him with her when she visited and we grew up playmates. I think she felt sorry for us, having no woman in the family to look after us. She used to bring us cakes and pies, and new-baked bread, before I learned to do it myself. And even then, she'd bake two loaves instead of one and Iain would drop one in on the way to school. He's a nice lad, don't you think?'

'I can see that's what you think.'

Ellen glanced inquiringly at her husband. 'I didn't mean anything like that. He's just a friend...'

'And he better stay just a friend. Come along now to bed, lass. I'm waiting for you.'

His wife lingered at the mirror so long that Tom, losing patience, crossed the room and swung her round towards him. In her eyes was the glint of tears.

'What's wrong, Ellen? What are you crying for?'

'Because of what you said. Iain and me, we've grown up together and I'll always be his friend.'

'And I'm your husband... and I can see he'll likely be carrying on as soon as my back's turned.'

'That's nonsense and you ken it well.' Ellen pulled her arm from Tom's grasp and turned back to the glass.

Anger rose through Tom's body in an unstoppable wave. Snatching the brush from her hand, he threw it into the corner of the room and grabbed hold of his wife, pulling her to her feet. When she still resisted, he lifted his hand and slapped her across the face, rage blinding him, until the sound of the slap echoing in the shadowy room brought him abruptly to his senses. He felt the fight go out of his body and his legs give way beneath him. Flopping down onto the side of the bed, he put his head in his hands.

Ellen stood in the middle of the bedroom, her body turned away from him, stiff with shock.

'I'm sorry,' he murmured at last. 'I'm sorry, Ellen. I don't know what got into me. Forgive me.'

His wife remained silent.

Tom let out an unsteady breath and said jerkily, 'I'm going away. That's why I was concerned for your safety. I don't want owt to happen to you while I'm not here.'

Ellen spun round, her face, apart from her burning cheek, pale. 'What do you mean? Where are you going? I don't understand.'

'I'm enlisting in the army. They were there at the market today, saying as how young men were needed to defeat the Hun. I decided it were the right thing to do,' he lied.

'But why didn't you say anything earlier when we were talking about it with Iain outside?'

'I wanted to tell you on your own, like, not in front of an audience.'

'But what about Netta? What about me? How long will you be gone?' Her voice rose in dismay.

'I'll be gone for as long as it takes. And as for you and t' babby... your father's here. You'll manage fine wi' out me.'

Ellen's reply was full of tears. 'Och, Tom. Don't go. I'll miss you so badly. We've only been married a few months.'

'Aye, but the same is true of a lot of the lads at the front. They've wives and bairns at home too. No, my mind is made up. The more of us enlist, the sooner the war will be over.' Tom threw back the sheets and climbed into bed. 'Come on now, lass. Let's talk no more about it tonight.'

Ellen pulled the bedclothes over them and, lying against his supine body, placed her arm protectively across his chest, his earlier attack seemingly forgotten.

Tom lay still and listened to her breathing. His own rest was long in coming. The effect of his sudden decision swept over him, but to change his mind now would be to lose face. In no more than a few days he could be leaving his wife and child and the landscape that he loved so much for the dubious glory of serving King and Country in a foreign land.

15

A Lot to Be Thankful For

As the line of men stepped out of the carriage into the slanting rain, each of them in turn lifted his eyes and scanned the panorama. A small huddle of villagers at the far end of the platform watched in silence. A child broke the spell by asking his mother whether they had come to stay and, if so, would any of them like to stay in their house because there was plenty of room, now that father had gone off to the war. His mother shushed him, took hold of his arm and pulled him, none too gently, towards her.

The crowd of visitors grew as the carriage disgorged its contents. Some, in the uniform of British soldiers, spilled from the same carriage and from the adjacent one and began to round up their fellow travellers, as though they were unruly cattle. In truth, they needed little coaxing. From the ticket office, the stationmaster emerged, followed by three dark-suited, self-important, bowler-hatted bureaucrats, who spoke in mumbled undertones with the army officials. A few clipped commands were given and the visitors marched up the steep path from the station. There, a further group of villagers were waiting to see the spectacle. They shrank back as the line approached, as though afraid of attack or contagion, or perhaps both.

They were a strange collection of men. Some wore uniform, though tattered and piecemeal now. Whatever they lacked was supplemented by rough jackets or jumpers. Most were bare-headed, though a few wore square navy berets, stiff with salt. Several of the men glanced at the onlookers. One or two of them smiled at the children gathered around their parents' knees and received a hesitant smile in return before the inevitable reprimand to 'pay nae heed to the enemy'.

One of the prisoners stopped when he reached the summit of the incline and surveyed the view. He was, like many of the others, a young man, not long out of teenage years, of slim build, with close-cut curly brown hair. He wore a bedraggled uniform of dark blue, stained white with salt, but his head was bare. His pale blue eyes scanned the rounded hills, whose contours made up the horizon and where the bareness was broken only by sheep dotted on the grass. From his mouth escaped a deep sigh.

'Yes,' an older prisoner at his shoulder muttered. 'It is a desolate place, is it not? I would rather we were back in the huts with our memories and our dreams... not in this harsh countryside... gottverlassen, is it not?' He laughed tonelessly.

The younger man regarded him with surprise. 'This land reminds me of my homeland. It is very like... Only at home, I think, we have more trees. The air is the same, clean and sweet.' He inhaled deeply but the sudden intake of breath caused a spasm of coughing and he failed to hear his fellow prisoner's reply.

'Move along! Keep in line! Stop talking!' An army officer had approached from behind and nudged the young man's shoulder with the butt of his gun. The prisoner began to walk again, keeping his eyes on the view ahead.

'That is a troublesome cough,' the older man resumed, when the soldier had dropped back again. 'How is it you were able to enlist? They should allow you to see a doctor.'

'I have been always in good health until now. This I got from being in the sea with oil spilled from the U-boat. I must have taken some into my lungs. I... I don't remember exactly.'

'Poor bastard,' the other murmured and then said more loudly, 'You were lucky to survive. Perhaps the fresh air of the countryside is what you need then. Though, for my part, I would rather have the city.'

The line of men had crossed a narrow bridge that spanned a river, and from the bridge a footpath led across a low-lying field of lush pasture to join a country road. This they followed as it took them away from the village and into the heart of the valley. The rain that had accompanied their journey thus far showed no sign of abating. At least they could be thankful that the westerly wind meant that it was behind them, rather than lashing their faces.

Josef Kessler, his spasm of coughing at an end, looked around him with increasing interest. The track ran along the valley side, and down below there was a chattering stream and a noisy collection of birds. Rounding a bend in the road, he could see in the distance a scattering of farm buildings. Behind them, pines clothed the deep channel between two hills and marked the path of a tributary that ran down to the valley floor and wound across to join the river near a small bridge. This, it appeared, was the single access to the farm beyond.

The party of men snaked its way into the valley, resisting attempts by their captors to hurry them along. The enfeebled state of several of their number in any case made this impossible. Eventually they drew level with the farm and Josef could see it more clearly now. A substantial grey building, almost certainly the farmhouse, stood, with its backdrop of dark pines, in a cleft in the hills. A short distance away two stone cottages hunkered down on the valley side, as if to escape the force of the elements. So engrossed was he in contemplation of the farm that he failed to hear the commands from the front of the line and collided with the man in front of him.

'Watch where you're going.' The prisoner swung round and two squinty eyes glared at him. 'Oh, it's you, Kessler. Don't you ever stop your daydreaming?' He gave a mirthless laugh. 'Once we have spent some time out here, you will not be dreaming, nicht war?'

'Are we to stay here? I see no accommodation,' Josef replied. 'Do you know then what they plan to do with us?'

'No, Dummkopf, but I see no signs that they are planning a picnic. More likely they intend to use our bodies, though what use yours will be I don't know.' His eyes ran slowly down Josef's thin figure before returning to his face, where they gave him an insolent stare. 'So, Music Boy, you better get used to it.'

The rain still slanted eastward through the valley and Josef shivered as he felt the dampness beginning to seep through to his undergarments. In better weather, he thought, they might be relaxing in the grassy meadow at the side of the road or sunning themselves on the lower slopes of the hill that ran down to the road on its other side. Instead, they stood like the sheep, their backs to the worst of the weather.

Presently, the sound of motors could be heard and the men turned their combined gaze to see a line of trucks approaching. Further orders were shouted for the men to unload the trucks and Josef's spirits fell as he helped to lift onto the grass the unwieldy boxes and canvas packages. Here in this beautiful but wild and wet place, they were to set up camp.

That night they shivered on their straw mattresses after taking several hours to erect the tents. They were large, each sleeping eight men. The acreage of suitable flat land not liable to turn to bog was small and the positioning of the camp needed careful planning. To a man they were soaked through and their uniforms now hung from lines draped above them, imparting a musty odour to the damp air.

Josef stared into the darkness above his head. He was thinking of his family. Had they received his letter, telling them of the sinking of their submarine and his subsequent rescue? He had written twice since but had no way of knowing whether the letters had reached their destination. Certainly, there had been no correspondence from any of the family since spring, when the boat was last docked. At that time, he had opened letters from his mother and his sister.

His sister Eva's letter had been full of news of her friends. She wrote of Marthe, the girl whom his parents hoped he would marry and with whom they had been carrying out hesitant negotiations in an attempt to interest Marthe's family in an alliance. And she described the concerts in which she herself had recently taken part. Her news made him yearn to be home, sharing with her their mutual love of music. Would his expertise on the piano still be as sought after when he eventually returned?

But how much worse things could be, he considered, and the thought dispersed some of the misery of the day. True, he was a prisoner of war. But how many of his countrymen now occupied a watery grave? How many more lay unburied and rotting in the French mud? He wasn't sure, but those of his fellow prisoners who knew a little English told him that their captors boasted of thousands of deaths at their hands. Yes, he had a lot to be thankful for. And the war could not last forever. Here, at least, he was safe.

*

When he emerged blinking and stiff in the early light, Josef gasped. It was beautiful. There was no trace of the rain of the previous day, save for wispy shreds of mist encircling the highest hills and snared on the pine branches behind the farm. The air was new-washed and full of the cry of birds, none of which he recognised. As he stood absorbing the scene across the valley, gold began to flow smoothly down from the summit of the hills. Slowly and silently it poured into the lower pastures, where it spread out to engulf the fields, the farmhouse and their occupants. Captivated, he continued to stare at the scene and strands of music came into his head... music that he had played so often on his piano in front of an appreciative audience.

'You there! Who gave you permission to leave your tent?'

Josef started at the harsh voice and turned, guessing that the words were a reprimand.

'I was doing no harm,' he replied in his own language, surmising that the man would not understand what he said. 'I have been admiring the wonders of creation. What a pity my enemy does not think to do the same.'

'Get back... back to your tent.' The guard indicated with the point of his rifle. 'Wait there until you are told to come out.'

Josef gave a last glance behind him but the magic had gone. Sighing, he lifted the tent flap and stepped into the frowsy atmosphere of sleep. He had been doing no harm. He would do the same tomorrow. Let them shoot him if they had a mind.

His fellow prisoners were dressing.

'Where have you been, Kessler? Dreaming again, no doubt... or maybe saying prayers to that God of yours.' It was the squinty-eyed prisoner whom Josef had accidentally collided into the previous day. He was small but stocky. His short hair, tousled from sleep, stuck out in all directions, giving his puffy face and thick neck a thuggish look.

'What is it to you, Vogel? I don't need your permission to go outside.'

Vogel stepped up to the younger man, and Josef

smelled the stale breath from the face only inches away from his own.

'You need my permission if your behaviour affects us all. Isn't that right, lads?' His eyes swept the remaining half-dressed occupants of the tent and there were murmurs of assent.

'There you are. Everyone is in agreement. I heard the enemy reprimanding you just now. I'm telling you, Music Boy, what affects one, affects us all. So don't go rocking the boat.' He broke into a cackle at his unintentional reference to their former maritime occupation and turned away to finish dressing.

Josef swallowed an indignant reply and bent down to tidy his bed. The man was a bully. Better to stay clear of him and avoid trouble in the future.

But this resolution, easily made, proved difficult to follow. Having breakfasted on a thin salty-flavoured gruel, the entire group of prisoners was lined up in front of their captors. The soldier in charge – at least that was what Josef assumed – stepped forward and began to talk. He was a tall man, slimly built, with a soft moustache. The prisoners looked at one another. Did this fellow expect them to understand? There was a long pause. He spoke again, briefly this time. Another pause... and then a German stepped forward and another... and then Vogel also left the line and joined the other two.

'They want English speakers,' the man in front of

Josef whispered to his neighbour. 'They need people to translate their orders. I suspect there will be something in it for them... extra food, a more comfortable bed, something of that kind.' His neighbour smiled ruefully. Josef groaned inwardly, imagining the superiority that Vogel would assume along with the responsibility of translation.

There were now six men who had admitted their knowledge of the English language. One of them, not Vogel, was given the task of translating what the English officer-in-charge was saying.

His name, the officer said, was Captain Cameron-Dyet. It was his job to knock the assembled company into shape. Prisoners were not to expect to be idle during their time in Great Britain. While the defeat of the enemy was being concluded, they were to be put to work. That work would be explained later. First though, rules must be put into force for the smooth running of the camp.

The captain's voice continued, quieter now and with frequent pauses so that the chosen man had time to interpret what he said and repeat it to the crowd. They were given instructions for collecting water (from the stream running through the valley) and the digging of latrines (a position a short distance from the encampment but within sight of it). A timetable was to be organised for the cooking of meals. Each man would be responsible for cleaning his own dishes and washing his clothes. Supplies would arrive by rail and were to be collected from the station in the village, prisoners chosen for this task were to be supervised by their captors.

Josef found himself listening to the captain's voice, rather than that of his translator. He sounded a reasonable man, fair-minded, as much as it was possible to judge. Perhaps it would not be so bad working here. But what on earth had their captors in mind for a workforce of what must be a hundred men or more? Apart from some essential help on the farms of the area – and he supposed the menfolk, like those of his own country, were away fighting – there was nothing else to do.

16

Unwanted Intrusion

Tom's first letter arrived a month after he had left for the borders to join his battalion. Ellen, pegging out washing, had half an eye on the goings-on at the other side of the valley. The prisoners had been camped there for two weeks now and she had taken to watching their activities after preparing breakfast for her father before he set off into the hills. Anxious at first, her mind was put at rest when they began to assemble each day at first light and march off along the track eastward. Wagons heaped with tools had followed them. Her father said that work on the reservoir was starting and the prisoners were there to do the jobs of the brave lads who had gone to fight. Ellen was glad that Tom was not there to see the work begin, knowing how unhappy he had been with the proposed plans and the loss of his peaceful life in the countryside.

In the distance she saw Iain Murdie's cart making its way towards the farm. She stood watching, one arm still raised, clutching the peg with which she had pinioned a sheet. The fabric flapped and slapped around her body and ballooned out as the wind caught it and pulled the line out of Ellen's grasp. Iain turned off the road and followed the track towards the cottages. Ellen smiled. It would be good to see him. She was lonely. Her father was busier than ever with Tom away, and she had not been able to leave the valley since her husband's departure.

'A letter,' he called, waving it above his head.

'Is it from Tom?' Ellen felt a rush of affection for her absent husband as she came towards the cart.

'How should I know, hen. I'm no' in the habit of reading other people's letters. Though judging by the look of it, it's been through a lot of army hands before it got here.' He handed it to Ellen.

Perusing the front of the envelope with a smile, she slipped it into the pocket of her pinafore.

'Are you no' going to read it?'

'Later,' she said. 'Are you in a hurry? Will you no' stop and have a cup of tea with us?'

'Aye. I'd like that,' Iain replied without hesitation. 'Though I must be back at the farm by one. The doctor's coming.' He swung his long legs over the side of the cart and climbed down.

'The doctor? Why, what's happened?'

'It's my father. He took a turn and my mother had to send for the doctor. He says it's his heart and he must rest. That's why I'm here and not making my way to

158

France.'

'Of course,' gasped Ellen. 'I'd forgotten you shouldn't be here at all.'

'They caught me just in time. We were about to embark. I've been given a fortnight and then I sail with the next contingent. So I thought I'd come and set eyes on my pretty neighbour!'

Ellen laughed dismissively. 'How is your father now?'

'Much better. I'm hoping the doctor will say he can work again. And then I will get off to do what I signed up for. Though at this moment I'm wishing I hadnae',' he concluded, giving her a wink.

'Aw, Iain. Get away wi' ye. There'll be plenty of pretty girls ready and willing when you get back.'

Netta started to whimper and Ellen turned to the perambulator, which stood in the shade against the back wall of the cottage.

While Ellen made a pot of tea, Iain nursed the baby, transferring her awkwardly from shoulder to lap, to knee and back to shoulder again, while Netta's cries rose to alarming proportions.

'She certainly talks more than her father,' he said with a grateful smile, as Ellen reached out to take her daughter, having placed a mug of tea on the table next to him. He leaned over to look at the baby as she quietened in her mother's arms. 'But she has a likeness to him, if I'm not mistaken... a very strong likeness.' He studied Netta's face – the dark hair, the stubbornness of

159

her tiny jaw. 'I could almost believe it's him looking at me. I better behave myself or she might put up a wee fist and punch me.'

Ellen laughed out loud, Iain's observation being so uncannily near the mark. It was as if he had known about Tom's reaction to his previous visit.

'What do you think about all these prisoners?' Ellen indicated with her head the collection of tents on the other side of the valley.

'Aye, it's certainly a big camp,' he replied impartially.

'I'm scared, I don't mind admitting,' she went on, 'having them staying so close to the farm. I've taken to locking the door at night. After all, you never know what they might do.'

'You mean if they see a pretty girl like you eyeing them up?' he joked. 'Seriously though, I wouldn't worry too much. Aside from the fact that they're guarded by our soldiers through the night, I hear they've been put to work digging foundations for the new road... and the railway too, if I'm not mistaken. They'll be too tired at the end of a day's work to get up to any mischief, that's for sure. I certainly wouldn't want to be in their shoes.'

'The railway is being started then?'

'Aye. The work is running well behind time. Dougie Strachan - he's from the Board of Agriculture - keeps us up-to-date, seeing as we will be more effected than most. He says there've been a lot of problems, mainly because of the fighting. Money that was promised for the reservoir is being used for the war instead.' He laughed. 'Sir Angus has had more headaches than he ever thought possible. He spends most of his time negotiating with the powers that be to get what's been promised him. I've heard he's been refused building materials and machinery because what's most important is the supply of arms for the forces. He's even finding it hard to get hold of second-hand railway materials.' He paused, taking a gulp of tea, and helped himself to a piece of shortbread. 'They've built several munitions factories north of here, so the demand for extra water is even more urgent. But now Sir Angus can't get the men to do the work because they're all going off to fight. That's why they've decided to use the prisoners. I suppose they would rather be busy than locked away doing nothing.'

'Tom'll no' like them being here and that's a fact. He's upset enough about the plans for the reservoir. Though it will be even worse for yous.'

'Aye. The farm is to be flooded eventually. It'll be in the path of the reservoir.'

'What will you do then?'

'Father's been having talks with the Waterworks. There's plenty of our land that's outwith the planned flooding, so a new house will have to be built alongside the water.' He shrugged. 'They're upset, my parents, naturally. I'm upset. But I try and tell them that it'll be a long time in the future, the way things are going. And who knows what will happen before then?' He looked at

Ellen fondly. 'There's no point you worrying your pretty head about it either. Though I suppose it might be best for now if you keep the door locked at night.' He sighed and rose to go. Putting his hands on her shoulders, he looked at her sadly. 'I'll miss you, Ellen... more than you think.'

And then he leaned across the baby and put his lips to Ellen's, causing Netta to thrash her arms and grumble in protest at the restriction. Turning abruptly, he walked to the door, which they had left open, took a few strides to where the horse was tethered, loosed the rope and jumped into the cart. He set off without a backward glance.

Ellen stood at the front of the cottage and watched him until he and his wagon were nothing but a speck in the distance. They rounded the bend in the road and were gone.

Flustered by his boldness, Ellen sat down and unbuttoned the front of her blouse to feed the baby. Once Netta was settled to the breast and suckling contentedly, she pulled out the letter and tore open the envelope. It was dated two weeks previously.

Dear Ellen,

I hope this finds you well. We are sailing tomorrow. I am not allowed to tell you our destination.

I miss you and Netta. Hopefully the war will soon be over and I will be back home with you again. Till then, I trust that you are remembering what I said. Stay on the farm. Don't do anything unwise. Keep away from other men. These are dangerous times.

Assuring you of my undying devotion,
Your husband, Tom.

The excitement that had accompanied the opening of her letter evaporated somewhat. She tossed the page onto the table in front of her and a breath of wind wafted it onto the stone floor.

'Goodness!' she addressed her feeding baby. 'Your father keeps me more of a prisoner than yon men.' She stared across at the camp and, maybe out of curiosity or maybe an unconscious inclination to flout her husband's wishes, she decided that she and her little girl would take a walk along the valley to see for themselves all the activity.

*

Along the far end of the rutted farm track where it joined the road, tents covered every available fragment of flat land. Canvas slapped noisily in the strengthening wind as Ellen struggled with the perambulator. Now that she was in the middle of the encampment, she felt uncomfortable, almost like an interloper, although she had every right to walk along the road and had done so innumerable times before. It was eerily deserted now. If there were men guarding the tents, they were not in evidence as Ellen and her daughter passed through into the heart of the valley.

Past the camp, Ellen breathed more easily. The land belonged to her again. Here the wide meanderings of the lethargic river dominated the view. A heron flapped lazily into the air and lumbered over the water in the hopes of a more advantageous fishing spot, while on the hill to her right an unseen curlew bubbled mournfully. They made her forget for a while the unwanted intrusion.

But not for long. Rounding a bend in the road, she saw in the distance a long string of men intent on their activity, though what that was she could not quite make out. She hesitated, wondering whether to turn back. But the thought of Tom's letter made her go on. She was not going to be prevented from living the innocent life she had always lived because of the mistaken fears of her husband.

It was back-breaking work that the prisoners were engaged in, she could see that now. About half of them were digging with shovels and picks at the side of the road. A short distance away and slightly down the slope, the rest were employed with similar implements. They were burrowing into the banking in order to create a wide swathe of flat land parallel to the existing road. Ellen stared with interest at the excavations. Presumably they were preparing for the railway line that Iain had told her about. She paused, afraid to walk through the men working on either side of the road. Her heart began to beat faster and a rising colour crept into her face.

'Just pass on through, miss.' The words were spoken by a tall uniformed man who appeared to be overseeing the activity of the workmen. 'They won't do you any harm. That's right. Come this way. We've no desire to disrupt the normal working of the community.'

'I... I often walk along here with the baby,' Ellen said, smiling uncertainly. 'She needs to be out in the afternoon, ken, else she gets bored.'

'Of course she does,' the tall man smiled. 'As I said, we don't want anything to be any different from how it has always been.'

Ellen nodded her thanks and proceeded to walk the length of the excavations, her face struggling to assume an indifferent expression in the presence of a hundred curious pairs of eyes fixed on her. She was struck by the look on their faces. Many were pale, some looked ill and one or two had troublesome coughs. Although they were curious, no one spoke as she passed. They merely gazed at her, before turning back to their digging.

Having gone this far, she was obliged to go further, for fear of looking ridiculous if she immediately turned back. So she walked briskly on until she neared the farm belonging to Iain Murdie's father. It was a long time since she had seen Iain's mother who, now that Ellen was married, presumably thought her no longer in need of oversight.

Margaret Murdie's welcome was a warm one when she saw that it was Ellen on the doorstep, and she lost no time in sharing her fears about the forthcoming changes to the valley.

'Progress? How can they call it progress when we farming families will be made homeless? It's all very well for Iain to tell me not to worry. How can I help but worry?' She took a large handkerchief from the pocket of her pinafore and wiped her eyes. 'This farmhouse has been in Robert's family for generations. I don't want to move into a new house, even if they agree to build it. I like this one. So does Robert. All the worry is making him ill, ken. It's a sad day when you see everything you've worked for disappearing under the water.' She blew her nose loudly, and abruptly continued, 'But look at me. I've not even offered you a seat. And you'll take a cup of tea? You've called on the right day because I did my baking today, so it's gey fresh.'

Ellen smiled. If she remembered rightly, Mrs. Murdie did her baking most days and could always be relied on to produce something mouth-wateringly good.

'Tell me, lassie,' she said, setting out cups and saucers on the table. 'Have you heard from your Tom since he went away? Your father must be busy without him. How is he, the poor man?'

'He's fine, though he is busy, and aye, I had a letter from Tom today. He's sailed for Europe.'

'The poor soul! I will pray that he returns to you safely, child.'

Mrs. Murdie's words brought to Ellen a tinge of guilt for her earlier annoyance. Tom was about to embark on an undertaking for which, she suspected, he had no inclination.

'Iain will be going soon as well,' Ellen said thoughtfully.

'Aye. He would be gone already if Robert hadn't taken ill. I suppose it's something to be thankful for that I have him here for a few extra days.'

They shared a pot of tea and Ellen had a second slice of cake to give her strength for the long walk back. She rose at last to leave.

'Come and see me again soon,' Margaret Murdie said. 'It'll be lonely without any young blood around the house. Iain's all we have, never having been blessed with a second... like your poor father, in fact.' She hugged Ellen warmly and the girl promised that she would pay her another visit.

The prisoners were still digging when she approached and one or two of them nodded in recognition as she walked along the track between them. A few more rested on their spades and watched her with vacant expressions, as if glad for the chance of a break from their arduous labour. She could not help but feel sorry for them. They looked sad and she thought that maybe the sight of her and Netta brought to mind their wives and families back home. Glancing at them at intervals, it occurred to her that they didn't really look any different from the men of the neighbourhood... those she had grown up with, the fathers and sons of the farming families all around her. Many of these men and boys – for some of them looked no older than boys – might come from farms themselves. This insight caused her to lift her eyes and smile tentatively at those who were looking in her direction... until she met the gaze of an older man who regarded her stonily with close-set eyes and lips pressed tight together. Then her smile disappeared and she turned her face homeward and quickened her step. No, she was wrong. They were the aggressors... and she would do well to remember it.

She wrote to Tom that evening, setting aside her earlier irritation and pouring her love and loneliness into the letter. She told him the news about the Murdie farmhouse and the planned flooding of the valley by the Municipal Waterworks. She didn't mention Iain Murdie's visit to their farm... and she thought it best not to worry him with news of the hundreds of prisoners of war camped no more than a few hundred yards away on the other side of the valley.

17

Her Enemy

At the brisk command to 'Down tools', Josef Kessler stood, leaning on his shovel, panting, a little light-headed. He slowly grew taller, stretching out the aching muscles along his back, took a deep breath and began to cough. After the spasm had passed, he walked slowly to the lorry and threw the shovel into the back. He turned, stumbled, righted himself. Looking along the road, he tried to gauge the time it would take to reach camp, where he could lie down and sleep.

At a further command, the men lined up and began to walk. Progress was slow. All had been labouring since first light, only allowed half an hour for a meal of bread and cheese. Josef had had no appetite for his and he was still not hungry. His legs were heavy... dead weights. He could hardly drag them along. Tomorrow he must eat, whether he wanted to or not.

He had noticed before that as soon as the sun sank behind the hills, the temperature in the valley dropped markedly. Tonight was no exception. The sky, darkening to purple, was cloudless and stars already glittered frostily. His hands felt rough as he rubbed them together for warmth. They would look incongruous over the keys of the grand piano at home. The opening bars of his favourite concerto ran through his head, but the music came to an abrupt stop. He had forgotten the next bar. In his mind he began again... but he could get no further than bar twenty. Tears blinded him and he stumbled, almost fell.

'Move along there. We all want to get back to our beds tonight,' came the gruff voice bringing up the rear.

'You heard what the gentleman said. Get a move on, Music Boy.' Josef recognised Vogel's voice but he did not have the energy to turn around and look at him, nor even to reply to his jibe. He screwed his eyes up to try and see the buildings that would indicate that they were approaching camp but could make out nothing in the encroaching darkness.

In his sleep that night he was transported to a nightmarish world of fiery colour and discordant music, always finishing at bar twenty, and himself carried weightlessly along a tunnel, dark and narrowing, until the brightness in the distance disappeared at a stroke and he was jolted into wakefulness with his pulse racing and sweat cooling on his brow. He hauled himself up, felt around for his boots, and staggered to the opening of the tent.

Outside, he stood, trying to reassemble his scattered

thoughts. From a distance came the sound of trickling water. It reminded him of why he had left the tent. He was thirsty. He would make his way down through the field and drink from the flowing stream... so much nicer than the stale water left over from their evening meal.

The boggy land bordering the small river anchored his boots and unexpectedly catapulted him forwards. Instinctively, he threw out his arms to break the fall. With a tremendous effort, he pulled himself up and sucked his feet out of the mud, staggering and almost falling again. It had been a foolhardy thing to do, coming down here to drink... but he had almost reached his goal now. Little point in turning back with his thirst unslaked.

The water was icy cold and tasted delicious. He drank his fill, scooping it in his cupped hands until his skin numbed. Hauling himself back from the water's edge, he lay on the stony bank and tried to ignore the trembling ache in the muscles of his legs. Overhead, a sky thick with stars a million miles away. Like his home. And just as unattainable.

*

When she answered the knock, Ellen was surprised to see the officer in charge of the prisoners standing tall and upright with Kenneth Douglas on the doorstep.

'Can we come in, lassie? There's something we

wanted to ask you,' Kenneth began.

'Aye. Come away in.' She stood back to make room for the two men to squeeze past and pushed the door firmly shut against the cold of early winter. For a few seconds she stood with her hand still on the latch, her mind racing as to the meaning of the visit. It was only when she heard her daughter's frightened cry at the appearance of these strangers that she stirred herself and hurried through to the room. 'Won't you sit down?' she said, rescuing Netta from the floor and settling herself with her daughter on her lap in her father's chair by the fire.

'This is Captain Cameron-Dyet,' Kenneth said, turning to the soldier.

'Aye. We've met... though I suppose we haven't been introduced,' Ellen replied, looking directly at the captain.

'This is Ellen, Captain... Ellen Fairclough.' The farmer turned back to Ellen. 'There's a wee problem in the camp, lassie, and the captain was wondering if you could help out.' Kenneth sat down heavily in the armchair, glancing at the soldier, who remained standing.

'Forgive my intrusion, miss. The thing is, we had no idea the weather would be this cold this early,' he said in a tone that made it uncertain whether the comment was an apology or an accusation.

'They've nae idea what a Scottish winter is like in

172

these parts,' Kenneth added smugly.

'We're putting the men on to building their own huts, so they have better shelter in the winter months.'

'Good. I was thinking that it was no' right for them to be in those tents all winter,' Ellen replied, glancing through the window to the encampment.

The captain cleared his throat. 'Precisely. The new camp is further up the valley, near to where the reservoir is to be. It will save the walk backwards and forwards each day and there's more space there for all the buildings needed for so many men.

'Anyway, the reason for my visit is, we've had one or two men take ill over the time we've been here. Some of them are... how shall I put it? ... Not used to hard physical labour.' He cleared his throat again. 'For the most part they've recovered quickly and are back to work in a few days. But there's one man giving us cause for concern... not pulling round as quickly as the others have done. He was picked up out of the sea originally. We know he must have swallowed some oil from the boat and it seems to have weakened his chest.'

'What he wants to know,' Kenneth interrupted, impatience seeming to get the better of him, 'is whether you would be willing to look after him.'

'Here?'

'Yes, here,' replied the soldier. 'It's such a long way to go for treatment elsewhere, you see.' Again the hint of accusation. 'We're building a hospital room alongside

173

the huts, but it's not started yet.'

'But... but isn't he dangerous?' Ellen looked scared.

'Well no, miss, not at the moment... in fact, not at all. The thing is...' He dropped his voice, as though fearing reprimand. 'Many of the prisoners are cultured, highly educated men... in all likelihood not dangerous at all. Naturally, when he begins to recover, we will take him back straight away. Oh, er, by the way, it goes without saying that we will pay you for his upkeep.' He paused. 'Would that be agreeable?'

Ellen hesitated. What would her father think of the request? But it was her cottage, not his. Hers and Tom's. Besides, she felt sure that her father would welcome the extra money that the arrangement would bring in. If the man was as ill as the captain said, he would pose no risk to Netta. She knew what Tom would say if he were here. He would certainly never agree to a strange man in his house in his absence. But he was absent and the winter months loomed long and dreary so, 'All right. I agree. I'll take him,' she replied.

*

There were two things she was not prepared for. The first was the age of the prisoner. The second was the state of his health.

She had expected an older man. Yet here was a young man, and he was very sick and she had no skill in

174

nursing. He was carried in on a stretcher, barely conscious.

She had lit the fire in the living room of her father's side of the cottage, the bedroom being the only room now regularly in use. Kenneth Douglas, with the help of her father, had carried a spare bed up from the farmhouse and Ellen had just time to make it up before her patient arrived.

The face of the prisoner, apart from a flush of pink high on each cheekbone, was almost as pale as the pillowcase on which they laid him. His eyes remained closed but she noticed how the long lashes curved onto the rim of each cheekbone. From time to time he muttered, strange phrases that she could not understand. She put a hand to his forehead and withdrew it rapidly. He had a high fever.

Ellen turned to one of the stretcher-bearers. 'I can't deal with this,' she whispered, appalled, though secretly drawn towards the vulnerability and helplessness of the suffering prisoner.

'Sorry, lassie. Captain's orders were to bring him here. Said you'd agreed to look after him.'

'Aye, but I'd no idea he was this ill.'

'We all have to do our best. Your country needs you, remember! Mind you, you don't have to try too hard with him. He's not one of our own lads.'

'No, but he's somebody's son,' Ellen retaliated, surprising herself.

She set about looking after the prisoner. Several times a day she bathed the burning skin of his face and chest with cool water. She held a cup of water to his lips, but he muttered his strange words and, in his delirium, tried to push her away. On the third evening he grew worse. She sat at the bedside until later into the night, watching helplessly. When at last he quietened, she was panic-stricken that he might die. But when she came close, his breathing was steady and beads of perspiration stood out on his forehead.

When Josef Kessler's eyes at last began to focus on his surroundings, he could not believe what his senses were telling him. Firelight flickered on the ceiling above his head and logs crackled in the hearth. Beneath him was a proper mattress and his hands traced the soft covering of blankets and silky eiderdown. Through an open door he could hear a woman's voice and the babble of a child. Better still, the aroma of fresh baking reached his nostrils. It was like being at home. He lay still, bathed in the luxury of the room, too tired to begin to wonder where he was and what he was doing there.

His sigh of pleasure induced a sharp spasm of coughing and within a couple of seconds a woman was by his side... No, not more than a girl really, though she had a baby on her hip. Taking a basin from the table at the side of his bed, she placed it on the pillow and lifted his head a little with her free hand so he could direct the evil-smelling phlegm into it. Exhausted, he lay back and she wiped his brow and lips with a cloth.

They regarded each other solemnly. His face creased in a questioning frown. She smiled and spoke to him. Still he looked at her, shrugged, shook his head slowly from side to side, as though not understanding. The baby whimpered. She straightened, turned to go back into the kitchen, but he caught her hand, felt the fingers soft in his roughened skin.

'Vielen Dank,' he whispered. 'Thank you.'

*

That evening, when she had put Netta to bed, Ellen came back and sat by the prisoner's side. Aware that they would not be able to communicate, she nevertheless thought that he might like her presence in the room.

'Have you no' done enough already, lassie?' Duncan argued. 'You cannae talk to him. You've nursed him back to life. You'll tire yourself with all this extra.'

Ellen grinned, aware that her father's anxiety lay more in a perceived neglect of himself than in the care lavished on their paying guest.

'Don't worry, Feyther. He'll be back with them soon enough. I only want to make him feel at home now that he's turned a corner and is mending. I might even be able to teach him how to speak like us before he goes!'

Duncan mumbled his doubts and shuffled back to his fireside chair. Ellen scanned the face of the sleeping man. It looked peaceful now and she felt herself begin to relax for the first time since his arrival.

She had been scared, armed with only a rudimentary knowledge of illnesses and their treatment. She knew better how to treat a sick sheep than she did an ailing person. A dog-eared box at the back of the kitchen cupboard contained all the medicines she used – a sticky bottle of syrup of figs and a tub of evil-smelling liniment, applied to her father's shoulders after the more gruelling days of wrestling with uncooperative sheep.

*

The sailor had been with them for a week and it was only now that he was looking around him with interest. His eyes were pale blue as though faded by constant contact with the salt air. It was impossible to look at them without pondering on the thoughts that lay behind their sad remoteness.

She had brought him a mug of thin soup and she helped him to sit forward while she banked up the pillows behind him. He sank back against them wearily and smiled.

'Mūde.' He closed his eyes, opened them again, as though illustrating what he meant.

'Tired,' Ellen said. 'You mean you're tired.' She

beamed at him, pleased. 'Here, I've brought you some soup. Let me help you. You need to get strong again.' She held the mug to his lips and he took a mouthful, swallowed.

'Es schmeckt mir gut.' He nodded slowly, took another sip and another, before lying back on the pillows. 'Danke. Genügt.' He closed his eyes, slept.

When he woke two hours later, she warmed some milk and he drank gratefully. Pointing to herself, she said, 'Ellen.'

'Ellen,' he repeated. 'Ellen.' He tapped his chest, 'Josef.'

Ellen mimed rocking a baby. 'Netta,' she said. 'Baby.'

'Baby. Ihr Kind... baby.' Josef smiled.

Over the coming days these scenes were repeated many times, and his strength began to return, although she could see it would be weeks before he was fit to restart hard physical work.

A week after he had 'turned the corner', as she later described it to the captain, she suggested he should try to sit out of bed for a while. She threw logs on the fire and pulled an easy chair up close. His legs buckled under him as his feet touched the ground but, with her arm around his waist, he made his way slowly to the fireside.

Late that morning, a second letter arrived from Tom. She sat across the hearth from Josef and, while he dozed, slit open the envelope and began to read.

Dear Ellen,

I am in Europe but must keep my whereabouts secret. There has been plenty of fighting and some of my colleagues have been killed, but I am keeping well and we are all in good spirits. The weather is closing in now. If you have nothing else to fill your time, will you knit me some more of those warm socks? The trenches are a bit muddy and it is difficult to keep anything dry.

Please give my regards to your father. I hope he is managing with all the extra work in my absence. We have been told that we will not be home for Christmas, but they promise that we are next in line for leave. I doubt it will be at the right time or long enough to help with the lambing, but we shall see.

Give our daughter a big kiss from me and tell her to be good for her daddy.

Assuring you of my fondest love,
Tom.

She folded the letter and sat back in the chair, staring at the sleeping form of Josef. It was incomprehensible that good men such as Tom and this prisoner here should be fighting one another. All the same, she felt a twinge of conscience that the enemy should be enjoying the warmth of her fire while her husband was immersed in the mud of the trenches. Why, it must be almost as bad as that day last winter, when he had gone out in the snow to rescue sheep from the drifts and finished up needing rescue himself. The memory of stripping off his soaked clothing as he warmed himself in front of the fire made her smile.

'Was gibt es denn zu lachen?' Josef's smile joined hers, but her face turned serious and she did not reply. He glanced at her letter. 'Ihr Mann?'

She nodded slowly. There was no doubting the meaning.

'Entschuldigung.'

She frowned, not understanding. 'Time you were back to bed.' She rose abruptly from the chair, plumped up the pillows of the bed and took his arm. When he was settled, she tossed more logs on the fire, replaced the guard and left the room, slamming the door behind her.

Throughout the afternoon, Ellen maintained her detachment. When evening came, she tiptoed in and crossed the room to close the curtains. The indifferent light of oil lamps from the encampment flickered across the valley. How cold and bare it must be, she thought, living in such conditions, though at least they were dry, unlike her poor husband. She drew the curtains with a swish.

Josef was still propped against the pillows where she had put him. His eyes were fixed on her, in his hand a folded pocket-sized piece of card. Ellen had seen this card protruding from a small book that he kept by his bed. He beckoned her over, opened the card. Inside were two pictures, crinkled, stained, indistinct. The one on the left was of a man and his wife, middle-aged, well-dressed, unsmiling… that on the right of a young girl with long dark hair in a plait, sitting at a piano, her hands on the keys. She was looking at the camera with the same faraway eyes as those that perused the picture and that now switched their gaze to Ellen. She saw the glint of tears.

'Schwester,' he said, pointing. 'Meine Schwester… Eva.'

'Your sister. Aye, I can see that she is. You are very alike.' She touched his cheek, then the photo, then closed the battered card carefully and folded his fingers over it, covering his hand gently with her own.

18

Quite Cosy

It soon became obvious that several more weeks would elapse before Josef was sufficiently recovered to rejoin his fellow prisoners. Ellen tempted him with nourishing dishes, but although he showed an initial relish for what she brought him, he tired after only a few spoonfuls.

'Sorry,' he would say with a contrite smile, as she came back into the room to collect his dishes. She eyed the half-finished bowl of soup or the meat pie, from which only a couple of bites were missing.

'You'll never grow fit and strong unless you eat,' Ellen scolded, taking the tray of food from his lap, knowing that he wouldn't understand what she said. He guessed though that her words were a reproach – she could tell this by the way he laid his hand over hers as she clutched the tray and gently squeezed her fingers by way of reply, making her heart skip a beat.

Despite her husband's absence and the general gloom that the dragging on of hostilities brought to the country and its people, Ellen could not help but be excited by the approach of Christmas and the welcoming in of the New Year. When she looked at her daughter, now nearly a year old, the memory of the momentous but frightening events of her birth came back to her. This Christmas, thankfully, there would be no such drama. They would spend their time quietly round the fire. Her father would do what was necessary to keep the sheep supplied with sufficient feed. She would write to Tom a week or two before Christmas, enclosing the letter with two pairs of warm socks. She would mourn his absence and she would grieve that Netta's first Christmas and Hogmanay would be spent apart from her father. But her own father would be there... and Josef too. They would be quite cosy.

But their visitor had no enthusiasm for the preparations. Listless but polite, he watched as Ellen decorated the rooms with ivy pulled from the trees behind the farm. He sat in the easy chair and stared into the fire as she wrapped a small wooden horse on wheels for her daughter, a small bag of favourite tobacco for her father. She glanced at his blank expression and thought how he must be missing his family back home.

She had bought him a present, a small tin of boiled sweets, thinking that these were something that might stimulate his jaded palate. She could not after all leave him out when everyone else was to receive a gift and, in any case, she did not want to. She enjoyed caring for him and his pleasure at her administrations was in contrast with the increasing irascibility of her father, which she could only put down to his receiving less of her attention.

For a full two minutes, Josef turned the small package round and round in his hands. When he looked up, his eyes were moist. He brushed his eyelids with his fingers and carefully removed the wrapping from his present.

'Thank you,' he said slowly. 'Thank you. I have not... I have not...'

'It doesn't matter.' She shrugged her shoulders to show that it was understood that he couldn't buy presents and that it was of no importance. 'You eat them... that's the best present. You eat!' she repeated, her voice choking with emotion, and miming what he must do. He laughed then and offered her one before taking one himself. Her father, observing the scene, gave a small grunt of disapproval and began to fill his pipe with a pinch of the tobacco that Ellen had given him.

Two days later the captain visited the cottage. With him was one of the prisoners, a man in middle age with a tall, well-defined forehead, wavy brown hair brushed straight back off his face and eyes a piercing blue. An aristocratic look, no less.

'A letter for you,' the captain said and drew from the inner pocket of his greatcoat an envelope dog-eared and creased. The aristocratic man smiled and spoke a few words as Josef took the letter with a grin. His grin widened as he looked at the writing.

'Meine Schwester,' he said, holding up the letter to Ellen.

'How did his family know where to find him?' Ellen addressed the captain.

'The prisoners were allowed to write to their families soon after they were taken captive. The letters have been sent on from where they were first held. A nice Christmas present for them!'

The captain's companion began to speak to Josef. The captain meanwhile turned to Ellen.

'This is Oliver Tauber. He is one of our interpreters. He has come with me to find out how Kessler is progressing and whether he will soon be fit enough to rejoin the other men.'

'He'll no' be fit for work for a few weeks, Captain,' Ellen replied, shocked that they might consider him ready to return to such hard labour. 'He is eating very little and has no energy.'

'Are you happy for him to stay here for a bit longer?'

'Of course he must stay here. He's no trouble,' she replied quickly, aware of a sudden flare of emotion at the captain's suggestion that her visitor must soon go, and surprised at her reaction. 'How is the work progressing?' she asked, to hide her confusion.

'At the moment, not at all. As I told you, the men are building more suitable accommodation and it will be a further month before it is finished. By then the weather should have improved and we can get back to what we should be doing, which is to widen and improve the existing road and to lay the foundation for the railway. When that has been finished we also have to lay the main pipeline through the valley and start excavating the embankment.'

'It sounds like a lot of hard work.'

'No more or less than our own men would do – and for the same wages. They don't labour for nothing, you know. The only difference is that the War Office refuses to allow them to work on the main road, in case they should attempt to escape, and, for obvious reasons, they are not allowed to handle explosives, so the blasting of the tunnel through the hillside at the western end of the valley will be done by our own men.'

He turned as Oliver Tauber returned from talking with the sick man.

'Kessler, he is not so good,' Oliver confirmed. 'With your permission, Herr Kapitän, I will again call. I think he is missing to talk with a fellow German.'

'Mm, perhaps next week.' The captain smiled. 'Come, Herr Tauber. We must get back. We will leave Kessler to read his letter in peace. Thank you for your help, Mrs Fairclough.'

Later that evening, when Netta was sleeping in her cot, Ellen knocked softly on the door of Josef's room. He was dozing but opened his eyes as she entered. His hand still held the letter from his family. He wafted it to and fro.

'They are good ... all good.' He gave her a broad smile.

'Then you must get better... you... good... also.' She pointed at him and he laughed, catching her drift.

'Yes... must get better,' he repeated slowly. 'I sleep now... get better. Thank you, Ellen.' He took her hand and held it against his chest and when her eyes lifted at last to his, he put her hand to his lips and kissed it tenderly. She stood at the side of his bed, allowing her hand to stay cradled within his, until he slept. The calloused skin had grown soft again with the weeks of illness. The gentle rise and fall of his chest mesmerised her, strangely at odds with her own rapid breathing. She studied his face... the long lashes, the cheeks a little sunken still and the chin devoid of hair now that he was well enough to shave. There came a desire in her to bend her head and kiss the pale lips. But while she considered it, her father's measured steps could be heard crossing the kitchen. Withdrawing her hand guiltily, she spun round with a racing heart, as he turned the door handle and entered the sickroom.

＊

When Josef suggested he should start going for walks, Ellen knew that his recovery was well underway and that it was only a matter of time before he returned to the camp and she would no longer see him.

The early weeks of January had seen a steady improvement in the young prisoner. His appetite picked up and he began to sit out of bed regularly... after dinner at first and, later, as soon as he had finished breakfast. One day he appeared in the kitchen, signalling that he wished to help, and dried the dishes stacked on the draining board. Netta was becoming used to his presence in the cottage and he began to show an interest in her play. She was at first cautious, but soon she was bringing him toys and insisting that he dress her dolls and build castles with her bricks, which Josef seemed more than happy to do.

Oliver Tauber had visited on two further occasions. The first time he called, he sat quietly at the side of Josef's bed and the two men conversed in their own language, Ellen catching strange-sounding phrases as she busied herself with supplying tea and griddle scones to her patient and his visitor.

Before he left, Oliver had explained to her how much work had been done to make their living quarters more comfortable. They all had proper sleeping accommodation now, which had been, of course, the priority. The prisoners were currently engaged on building a hut for cooking meals and one for eating and relaxation. There would be a washhouse, a bathhouse and also a hospital.

'So if one of us is sick, we will not a second time

trouble you.' He looked at her and added with a smile, 'But I am certain that when you want more work, the men would love for you to be their nurse!'

On Oliver's second visit he had sought her out in the kitchen, as she was getting Netta ready for bed.

'Josef asks that I thank you for what you do.'

'He's already done that himself.'

'Yes, but he cannot speak in your language. He says you show him great kindness.'

'It's only what I arranged with the captain.'

Oliver nodded slowly. 'Captain Cameron-Dyet. A good man, I think, and a fair one.'

'Will you ask the captain if Josef can go outside? I think the fresh air will do him good... help his chest. I will go with him, of course. And he's very weak, so there's no risk of him escaping.' She grinned at Oliver Tauber.

'Certainly I will speak to the captain.'

Ellen looked at the prisoner. 'You can speak English well. How did you learn it?'

'All my family... my generation and the one before... have learned your language. It is part of our education. What I do now is to teach others... in a university.'

'You must know so much,' Ellen said in admiration, wondering at the same time what Josef's job was before the war. 'My husband has a friend who is learning to be a doctor in the university in Glasgow.' Ellen paused, her mind immediately full of Clara's Christmas visit and the drama that surrounded it. 'Can I ask… how were you all taken prisoner? What were you doing? Only Josef can't tell me… or, at least, I can't understand him.'

'We are sailors. Many of us were submariners.' He saw the lack of understanding on Ellen's face and continued. 'You've heard of the submarine?'

She nodded slowly. 'I think so.'

'We call it the "Unterseeboot". There was much fighting off your north-eastern coast. There are many men and boats lost on both sides. We were the lucky ones. Our boats were fired on… but we… the men here… were saved. The English… and Scottish… take us out of the water. They show us goodwill.

'Josef here… he is not so lucky. They take him from the water, but he was in the oil from his boat and some has gone to… how do you say it? His lungs. I fear he will not be so strong again. But you help him to recover.'

'I think the letter from his family has helped him.'

'Indeed. His family. It is what we are all wanting. To hear that our families are safe and well. You too, I expect.'

Ellen nodded. 'My husband has been gone since August. He said in his last letter that he hopes he will be home in the spring.'

'That is good.' Oliver Tauber put a finger under the toddler's chin and smiled wryly. 'Strange, is it not, that we stand here to talk, when in Europe our armies kill one another.'

A sob escaped Ellen's lips.

'I'm sorry, my dear. I do not mean to say… I am sure no harm will come to your husband. I will pray for his safe return. Perhaps we see him when he comes to his home.'

*

The weather was mild when Josef stepped outside and took a deep breath.

Ellen was standing by his side, Netta in her arms, warmly wrapped against the January chill, and she took a similar deep breath of her beloved Scottish air. The aroma of damp earth and dry bracken invaded her nostrils and made her sneeze. He turned to her with a smile. His eyes sparkled above the warm scarf that Ellen had wrapped around the lower part of his face. His gaze turned upwards to the summit of the hills.

She laughed. 'You would never manage that climb. No, we'll take the path behind the farmhouse through the trees.'

It was unseasonably warm for winter. Pine trees stood dark and straight around them. One had fallen in the gales and leaned drunkenly on its neighbours, shallow roots upended from the soil in a ragged circle.

Breathless and sweating, they emerged from the trees onto the side of the hill. Josef nodded his head slowly and looked around him.

'Schön,' he murmured. 'Sehr schön.' He turned to Ellen, who was gazing into the sky. 'Du bist auch schön,' he repeated and laughed softly.

'Look,' Ellen pointed upwards. The sky was deep blue and cloudless. Far above them two black specks were circling slowly and, as they stared, their mewing call drifted down. 'Buzzards,' she explained.

He frowned. 'Buzzad?'

'Aye! Buzzards. See how free they are.' She stopped, realisation flooding over her. Standing next to this man who, any day, would be returning to the prison camp. There were huts now and the tents had been removed. But it was a grim alternative to the comfort of home and the love of family.

He had understood her and stared at the birds.

'Frei,' he whispered. 'Free... yes?'

'Yes,' she said in a small voice.

'It is good.' He lowered his gaze and looked at her, rested a gloved hand on her shoulder. 'You give to me free. I thank you.'

She held her breath, glanced at him, looked away, her heart hammering in her chest.

They returned, walking slowly past the farmhouse. Elizabeth Douglas was at the door and Ellen stopped to talk to her, Josef looking over Elizabeth's shoulder into the living room. Suddenly a smile lit his face and he pointed into the room.

'Ein Klavier! Das ist ein Klavier!' he said in

excitement.

Ellen followed his gaze. 'A piano. Mrs Douglas, his sister plays the piano. Would you let him see yours?'

'I suppose it can do no harm. Come in, won't you?'

Josef bowed his head in thanks and stepped into the room. The piano was out of tune and he wrinkled his nose as he ran his fingers up and down the keyboard. But then he started to play and Ellen held her breath at the beauty of it.

'For you,' Josef said when he had finished. 'How you say... a gift.'

Tears filled Ellen's eyes. She struggled to speak but could not.

Outside again, a movement caught her eye. Someone in a horse-drawn wagon was making their way towards the farm. It was the post, she was sure of it. And if she were right, it would no doubt be a letter from Tom.

'Far enough for one day!' she said brightly. 'We better get back. You'll be wanting your dinner.' Slowly they retraced their steps through the trees and emerged onto the rutted path that led up to the shepherd's cottage.

The letter lay on the mat. She tore it open.

Mon. 22nd January 1917.

Dear Ellen,

A quick note to let you know that we are being given

leave in two weeks' time. I should be home a few days after this, depending on the journey.

Give Netta a big kiss from me. I am looking forward to being with you both again.

Your loving husband,

Tom.

19

Nightmares

It was just like old times. Her father sitting at one side of the fireplace, her husband at the other. Netta, cautious now of this stranger, playing nearby but refusing to come to Tom when he addressed her.

'Give her time,' Ellen said. He nodded but she could see he was hurt.

Her daughter's reaction didn't surprise her, not in the least. She herself felt shy of her husband. After all, she reasoned, they had been married for little more than six months when he left for the front. And this silent morose man who sat warming himself at the fire seemed to her more of a visitor than the young man who, only a week ago, had been warming his feet at the same fireside and whose absence now sat like a weight on her heart.

'Tell us about it then, pal. They say that conditions are gey bad at the front.' Duncan, like many at home, who had heard only snatches of information about what was happening in Europe, was agog for news of the fighting.

Tom shrugged. 'Aye. It's muddy and noisy... and everything's more of a muddle than you ever think it will be. But that's war for you, I suppose. What else can you expect?'

'Were there many killed?' Duncan probed.

Tom stared into the fire until the heat brought tears to his eyes and he blinked wearily. 'Some... some... but, if it's all the same to you, I'd rather not talk about it.'

'Aye, pal. If that's what you want...'

'I'd rather hear about what's been happening on t' farm. Any problems? Are the flock all well?'

'Aye, as far as I can judge. We've had a bit of snow, but nothing too bad. We've missed you though. I hope you'll be back to stay before too long.'

'So do we all,' Tom replied grimly. 'I was hoping my leave might come at lambing time, but we'll be back in t' thick of it long before that.'

'How long is your leave, Tom?' Ellen lowered herself onto the hearthrug and put an elbow on her husband's knee. He reached out and began to stroke her hair.

'We have five days, that's all. So it'll be up to you to help your father and Kenneth with the lambing this year.'

'Same as I always do, then. Though it won't be easy with Netta into all sorts of mischief, as soon as my back is turned.'

'You've been busy this last month or two, haven't you, lass?' Duncan gave her an innocent smile. Her heart missed a beat. She knew she should have warned him to keep quiet... but then, if she had, it would have implied there was something she wanted to hide.

'Have you, lass? What have you been doing?'

'Oh... er, just helping the army captain along the valley.'

'The army captain? What army captain? What's an army captain doing in the valley?'

'Didn't you tell him, lass?' Duncan said, turning to his daughter. 'I thought you would have said. They were camped over there.' He nodded his head in the direction of the recent encampment.'

'Who were?'

'Prisoners... prisoners-of-war.'

Tom's hand paused on top of Ellen's head. He looked at her, bewildered.

She shrugged nonchalantly. 'I thought it would only upset you if you knew, so I didn't bother telling you.'

'What were they doing here?'

'Och, they're not gone yet... not for a long time, are they, lass? They've only moved further down the road a mile or so. They're laying the tracks for the railway and improving the road.'

'Why are they doing it and not our own lads?' Tom said angrily.

'Because all our own lads have gone off to fight them,' Ellen replied evenly.

'So how come you were helping the army captain?

How could he possibly want *your* help?'

Ellen's heart sank.

'She was looking after a sick prisoner, weren't you, lassie?' Duncan said, helpfully.

'You mean you went in, where there were captured Hun holed up... and actually looked after one?'

'Something like that.' Ellen squirmed her head away from his grasp and turned to face him. 'I was paid for it though. I thought you'd be pleased. It brought in a bit of money.'

'Pleased!' Tom's eyes flashed and his voice rose in anger. 'Pleased that you're here looking after the enemy when my comrades have been dropping like flies all around me at their hands.' He pushed her roughly away and dragged himself out of the chair. Crossing to the window, he stared across the pasture land to the other side of the valley.

Ellen shook her head in warning at her father, who looked as though he had been going to correct the finer details of the story. Duncan shut his mouth and examined his hands.

Abruptly Tom spun round. 'Don't you ever do anything like that again, do you hear me?' he shouted. 'I forbid you to have anything to do with any of them. As if it isn't bad enough them building on our land, spoiling our pasture, ruining our peace. I forbid you to go near them again... and that's an order.'

Flinging open the door, he strode into the hall,

wrenched his coat off the peg and left the house, banging the door so loud that Netta, already startled by his shouting, burst into tears.

*

Ellen was taking washing off the line when she saw him descending the hill in the distance. Nell bouncing by his side, full of energy despite the long climb. She eyed him with apprehension. The pleasure at his homecoming had evaporated and now she felt a gathering of fear in her stomach. She smiled cautiously at him.

'Well, the view hasn't changed, thank God,' he said, cheerily enough. 'And the sheep are in fair condition, aren't they, Nell?' He patted the dog's sleek coat and she gave him a lick of friendship.

Ellen let her breath out slowly. 'Like Father says, it's no' been such a bad winter. It should be a good lambing. I wish you could be here for it.'

'Me too. I miss the farm. I miss the peace and quiet. I... Well, it doesn't matter.'

Ellen dropped the clothes into the basket at her feet and, stepping quickly over to him, put her arms tightly round his waist. 'We've missed you too... Netta and me. I don't want you to go back.'

Tom said nothing but put his arms round her shoulders. They clung together in the fading light, Tom staring out across the valley.

'Who'd have thought it... I come home for a week's break from the enemy, to find they've set up home not a mile along the road.' He sighed heavily. 'Happen it's not such a bad idea, if the reservoir's got to be built, that their labour is used to build it. Better than them sitting around using all our resources till the war ends.'

'I suppose there are some of our own men in enemy hands?'

'Yes, I expect there are... though there's no way of knowing how many.' He shuddered. 'I don't know whether it's better to be blown to smithereens than captured by the Hun.' He broke off abruptly.

Ellen looked up at him. He was still staring into the distance, his face suggesting he saw pictures of war rather than the peaceful valley before him. 'Are there many getting killed?'

'What?' His eyes focused on her. 'What did you say?'

'Are many dying? Tell me about it... what's it like out there on the battlefield?'

Tom gave a short laugh and she caught the bitterness in it. 'Oh, you don't really want to know... like the farm on a bad day,' he said but his attempt to make light of what he had been going through didn't fool her. She felt aggrieved that he had been away all this time and yet what he had been doing remained a secret. She was his wife, wasn't she?

She slowly tried to draw away from him but, as though sensing it, he tightened his grip.

'What's the matter? Bored with me already?'

'Don't be silly.' She stood on tiptoe and kissed his cheek. 'It's only that there's tea to get and Netta to put to bed and Father's sore shoulders to rub.'

Tom gave a brief laugh. 'Well, I hope there'll be some time left for me after all that because there's one thing I've been dreaming about all the way home and I don't mind showing you what it is.' And he bent his head and began to kiss her mouth like a parched man stumbling upon an oasis in the desert.

*

It was not, of course, what he had been dreaming about all the way home. To begin with all he could think of were the pals he was leaving behind... those whose bodies lay rotting in the mud... and those who were still fighting and who would most likely not be there when he returned.

It was only later, when he had stepped off the boat and his churning stomach had begun to settle and the wish to die had receded to the back of his mind, that he began to think of home comforts. Naturally such thoughts had kept him going during the long months in the mud of the trenches. Time and again, he had drawn from the inner pocket of his greatcoat the picture, increasingly dog-eared, of his wife and child. He had stared at Netta seated on Ellen's lap, arms outstretched, laughing. Six months old. By the time he saw her again, she would be more than twice that age and he would hardly know her. And she would have no knowledge of him at all.

There were times as well, when he was alone, that he would delve into his pocket and withdraw another photograph, that of a girl with dark curly hair drawn back and intense eyes in a serious face. The eyes seemed always to be looking at him and every time he withdrew the picture from its envelope, his heart would turn over at their penetrating gaze. He did not look at her often, for the action was invariably followed by the despair of knowing that she would never be his.

Often his conscience smote him, not because she was there, in the place properly reserved only for his young wife and baby, but because of the possibility, nay, probability, of his death. If this should happen, his pockets would be searched by his commanding officer and photographs and other mementoes returned to the family. And he would not have Ellen suffer more than she would already do on receiving news of his death. But still he could not bring himself to dispose of this picture of his first love. So she remained, and when he replaced her photo, he always made sure that it was she, and not Ellen, who was closest to his heart.

*

Tom rolled off Ellen and lay back panting. His wife murmured and turned towards him and he put out an arm to cradle her head against his chest. He kissed her forehead and drew the sheet over the cooling sweat of his body. He was tired, an exhaustion that at that moment made him feel as though he could not raise himself off the bed, even if all the demons of hell were after him. But, above all, he felt an intense relief. He had been anxious that his efforts at lovemaking would result in failure. He had been so long away from Ellen that she had become almost a stranger to him. His head had been so full of the horrors he had witnessed that, for a while, all else had faded into insignificance. It was not until he kissed her that his need for her eclipsed all thoughts of what he had left and what he had lost.

He slept… and the nightmares returned to haunt him, as they always did. The mud and the water-filled shell holes and the tangles of barbed wire everywhere he looked. The nauseating smell of rotting flesh. The drift of smoke, disguising an insidious and deadly weapon. Men crouched vulnerable and helpless in the trenches while bullets whistled overhead. The silence of inaction, poised for the gunshot that never came, flinching and jerking and ducking, nerves strung so taut that he thought at times he would go mad. And just when it seemed that the enemy were really sleeping, some daft beggar put his head above the parapet and there was an explosion of fire. He could see the sightless stare of one of his pals as he lay sprawled in the stinking mud at his feet with a bullet through his forehead.

And now the order to advance had been given. And they were picking their way over rotting corpses and round craters and their nostrils were full of the stench. At first there was no retaliation and they thought they had not been spotted. And then a shell exploded to his right and another a little further away, and he and his pals veered to the left and ran on, blinded by smoke and the fog that, it had been hoped, would obscure their approach.

Without warning, three of the lads were thrown into the air as a shell landed mere feet in front of them. One second they were there, bayonets fixed, stumbling over the uneven terrain, cursing beneath their breath... and the next, the earth appeared to swallow them up. Tom fell to the ground. At his side another private flattened himself in the mud.

'It's hopeless,' Tom mouthed. 'Let's crawl back. There's no one else left. If we go on we're done for.'

'Wait a bit. Wait until they think they've got rid of us all.'

So for the next hour the two men lay motionless, feeling the chill of the autumn mud seeping into their bodies. Over them swirled the smoke, mingled with the dense fog. From time to time a distant moan of pain broke the silence.

'Bastards.' The word reverberated round and round

the inside of Tom's head.

'Let's go.' It was the soldier at his side. 'We'll crawl. Take it very slowly. Watch for any barbed wire.'

So they began. It was endless. And what Tom had seen at body's length as he had surged forward with the others in his company, he now saw only an inch or two from his face. His numbed fingers welded themselves to his rifle. Fear made him weak. When he thought he could go no further, he glanced up and saw that there was still further to go.

Not knowing if the direction they were taking was the correct one, Tom was amazed when he threw himself over the edge of the parapet and found himself back where he had started. He could almost have believed in a divine providence, if it had not been for the carnage all around him and the shot that, the next second, entered his friend's back, as he launched himself at the trench. His bloodied body was flung on top of Tom's, turning the whoop of triumph at their safe return into a scream of revulsion.

'Tom!' He was being shaken. 'Tom! Are you all right?'

He opened his eyes to darkness and screaming. Not the screaming of men but the screaming of a baby. The striking of a match and the sudden flare of a candle startled him and he sat up in panic and stared into Ellen's frightened face, unable to understand what was happening.

'Tom, it's me... Ellen. You were dreaming. You've woken Netta with your screams.'

Tom turned his head, staring in horror at his frightened daughter. Memory flooded through him and he pulled back the tangled bedclothes and swung his legs out of bed, cradling his head in his hands.

'I'm sorry,' he mumbled. 'I'm sorry.'

'It doesn't matter. Let me take Netta from her cot and calm her down. Then you can get back to sleep. You're overtired, that's all.'

He pulled the covers straight and climbed back into bed while Ellen walked up and down the room with the bewildered baby over her shoulder. The candlelight drew monstrous patterns on the wall and Tom stared at them and could not decide if this was the real world or a fanciful dream, and if the real world was the nightmare he had, until a few minutes ago, been living through, just as he had done every night since leaving the battlefields of Northern France.

20

Walking the Hills

At this quiet time in the shepherd's year, there was little to be done except to walk the hills and make sure none of the flock had got into difficulty.

At first, Tom stayed indoors, dozing in front of the fire. But he soon tired of doing nothing and, after two idle days, suggested that he would help Duncan by checking on the sheep. Ellen advised that he needed more rest, but he wouldn't listen. He rose early the following morning, ate a hasty meal of porridge and, whistling to Nell, set off briskly across the valley floor to the hills of its southern side.

The frosty ground crunched beneath Tom's feet as he climbed. Reaching the summit of the range, he surveyed the way he had come: the white cottage in the distance, glistening in the morning sun, the farm to its right and the dark stretch of pine trees that marked the line of the stream as it tumbled down the hillside to feed into the river at its base. Turning east, he made his way along the ridge of hills, checking on the sheep as he went.

As the valley unfolded, he saw the men far below. Strung out in a line, they were fashioning the course of the railway that would cut through the valley to its easternmost end. He watched fascinated, in spite of himself, as the men laboured, looking from this distance, like an army of ants. He resolved to walk back along the road so that he could take a closer look, once he had covered the four miles or so of hills over which the sheep grazed.

It was strange to be walking through the collection of prisoners, whose comrades he had been fighting and killing only a few weeks ago. They belonged to another world, those men in the trenches, but these too didn't belong. The thought ran again through his head that there was no longer any peace, not even here, in the place that he loved.

He and the men stared at each other in silence. They must know, he considered, that he was a soldier on leave. True, he was no longer wearing his uniform, but why else would he be strolling through the valley, when every other able-bodied man was away fighting for king and country? They looked, he had to confess, much like the soldiers of his own regiment... tired, thin, some of them to the point of emaciation, pale faces in which their eyes, ringed with shadow, appeared huge. His progression through the group had the effect of a wave, as the men ahead downed tools on his approach, watched him in frozen animosity as he passed them by and slowly resumed work as he receded into the distance.

One of the group called out and so unexpected was the sound that Tom started and stepped back in alarm.

'Why do you look at us like that?' the man snarled. A small man, heavily built, with close-set eyes and bristly hair.

'Because you're on our land, that's why. I've every right to look at you and there's nowt you can do about it.'

Another younger prisoner stepped up to the man who had spoken and murmured in an undertone, nodding in the direction of the farm. The older man laughed.

'So, you come to find out who your wife nursed back to health in your bed while you were away. How you say it... the cuckoo in the nest.' He cackled and turned away.

A pulse of anger and humiliation surged through Tom's body. In an instant he had crossed the rough ground between them and fastened his hand on the man's shoulder, swinging him round to face him. But before he knew it, arms restrained him. He struggled to get free, but the prisoners who had surrounded him refused to let go. The small mean eyes came close to his.

'I tell you only the truth,' he said. 'If you refuse to believe me, ask that boy who sits over there on the wagon... resting, is he not? Still not fully recovered, unless it is that he was made weak by the time spent with your wife.' The man looked at the assembled faces in order to share the joke, picked up his spade and swung it onto his shoulder before turning his back on Tom and strolling away.

Tom shrugged out of the grasp of those who had detained him and caught a fleeting glimpse of a younger man, a pale face that looked out of keeping in the excavations. He stepped towards him, then stopped, wheeled round and made for home.

Ellen was preparing dinner when the door was thrown back against the wall, and the smile of greeting was wiped from her face by the look of fury on her husband's.

'What's the matter? Whatever's happened?'

He crossed the kitchen, took hold of her arm and dragged her across the floor to the bedroom, where he flung her onto the bed.

'That's the matter! That!' With a shaking hand, he indicated the bed. Catching hold of her, he hauled her upwards with one hand and delivered the punch that had been intended for the prisoner who had apprehended him. She fell back on the covers and tried to claw her way out of his reach, but he took hold of her and dragged her off the bed. She collapsed on the floor.

'You whore! You filthy stinking lying whore!' He kicked her savagely. 'How could you humiliate me like that as soon as my back is turned... and with one of them? In my bed!' He kicked her again. She groaned and tried to reply, but he gave her no opportunity. Aiming a third kick at her ribs, he wheeled round and stumbled to the door. Panting, he paused and stared at her as she lay curled up and unmoving. Then the door slammed and he was gone.

*

For several minutes Ellen remained motionless. Her body hurt too much to move, but her mind was racing. Somehow Tom must have found out that she had nursed the prisoner in their cottage. But who had told him? Surely not her father, for she had indicated to him that he keep quiet. As she lay there, the guilt she had felt at hiding the truth from her husband was overtaken by a surge of anger. How dare he treat her like this, when she had merely been doing what the captain had asked of her?

There was a taste of blood on her lips. Gingerly, she put a hand to her jaw and felt the place where a bruise must be forming. Pain stabbed her chest as she rested an arm on the bed and struggled to rise. She held her ribs and limped to the mirror. The lower lip was swollen and the inside of it had a ragged tear, apparently pierced by a tooth. As she stared at her disfigured face, a cry fractured the stillness. It was Netta waking from her morning doze and eager for her dinner.

Moving as fast as her bruised ribs would allow, she

hurried to the kitchen, ran a bowl of water and bathed her face in an attempt to lessen the swelling. Her father must not see what had happened, but where was her father? He should have been in for his dinner by now. Taking a gulp of the cold water, she rinsed her mouth and spat pink froth into the bowl. Finally she urged her aching body in the direction of Netta's cot, to calm her distraught and hungry daughter.

*

Tom hadn't climbed far towards his favoured spot before he saw his father-in-law in the distance. The anger that was propelling him up the hillside without effort began rapidly to dissipate, as he saw the dilemma with which he was faced. Duncan was on his way home for dinner. When he arrived, he would find his one and only daughter bruised and bleeding. He stopped, indecisive. Duncan looked up, caught sight of his son-in-law and began to stroll across the field towards him.

Tom recalled the afternoon of his homecoming. It was Duncan who had told him that Ellen had been looking after a sick prisoner. He hadn't mentioned it as taking place in his own cottage. Was it possible that the prisoners had been inventing this story in order to provoke him? If so, they had more than succeeded. What an idiot he had been, if this was the case. He remained rooted to the spot.

'You all right, lad?'

He nodded his assent, shame relieving him of his voice.

'Are you no' coming for dinner?'

In silence he turned to accompany Duncan slowly down the hill. He must be clear in his mind what had gone on in his absence.

'Duncan. Tell me about this sick prisoner. Where did Ellen look after him?'

There was a pause. 'She told you, laddie, did she no'?'

'I want you to tell me.'

Duncan glanced at his son-in-law and away again. He sighed. 'Och, well. You'll find out one way or another. She looked after him in the house. The captain came to see her... He asked her if she could care for this man. He was in a bad state when he came. She didnae want to do it... but the captain said he would pay and she thought, well, it would bring in a bit of money in hard times.'

'And how long did he stay in my house?'

'A long time, right enough. Only went back last week.'

'When she knew I was coming home,' Tom added bitterly.

Duncan glanced sharply at him. 'He wasnae ready to go till then. He'd been out walking a time or two to get his strength up.'

'On his own?'

'No, with Ellen and the baby. They wouldn't have let him go alone, in case he got lost.'

'Of course not. And tell me, where did she do this nursing?'

'We put up a bed in front of the fire in my side of the cottage. It was cosy for him there.'

'It must have been... though a bit lonely away from his pals.'

'Oh Ellen kept him company in the evening. I told her she was doing more than she was paid for, but she wouldnae listen.'

'I bet she wouldn't!' Tom said vehemently, his face flaring red at this innocent explanation of his wife's infidelity. He stopped, staring moodily at the cottage below them. 'I've lost my appetite. Tell Ellen not to wait for me.' And without further explanation he turned on his heel and made off rapidly across the field, scattering sheep before him as he went.

21

Comings and Goings

As the days lengthened into spring, Ellen knew that she was carrying Tom's child. She longed to tell him, but she had no idea where he was. She had not set eyes on him since his rapid exit from the cottage as she lay on the bedroom floor nursing her broken ribs. She had rarely, if ever, seen her father as angry as he had been on his return from bumping into Tom on the hill behind the cottage.

'Wait till I lay my hands on him! How dare he do this to you! How dare he!'

'Someone must have told him that I looked after Josef here and he must have jumped to the wrong conclusion. I wish you hadn't mentioned me looking after him, Feyther. It would have saved a lot of trouble.'

'It would have been a lot less trouble if you hadnae agreed to take him in the first place.'

She couldn't help but agree with her father. She could understand Tom's anger; though, looking back on it, she would not have forgone the pleasure of looking after

Josef. What she couldn't understand was why Tom didn't return, even if it was to further berate her for not being honest.

She had thought then that he might have met with an accident, for mishaps did occur, even amongst those who knew the rough terrain of the hills well. She had set out to search for him, encouraging her reluctant father to do the same. Duncan had walked eastward into the valley and Ellen had climbed to the topmost peak, where Tom often went to sit and think and admire the view. But there was no sign of him. She had scanned the rough grass around the summit, tears stinging her eyes and running down her cheeks before they were whisked away in the biting wind.

It was only when she had put Netta in her cot that first evening after his disappearance that she noticed his uniform was missing. The wooden hanger swung empty on the back of the door. She had searched everywhere – in the wardrobe, in the chest of drawers, even under the bed, but the uniform was nowhere to be found. Neither were his other clothes nor his kitbag. It had all vanished, as though he had never been home. It was when she saw that the framed picture of Netta had also disappeared that she finally realised he had chosen to go.

She wrote to Tom at the same address to which her previous letters had been sent, but had received no reply. Neither did he write to her with any word of explanation for his sudden disappearance. At least, she had thought, writing again, he would respond to news of her pregnancy. But there was nothing.

She was wretched. Unable to eat and constantly nauseous, she nevertheless had to help with the lambing and the care of the orphans that were an inevitable result of this gruelling season in the shepherd's calendar. And, as the time for shearing approached, things got no better. Three months after Tom's disappearance, she began to be really ill.

She was channelling the sheep through from the holding pen to where her father and Kenneth Douglas were waiting for them when the pain struck. The two men, with the help of an old shepherd hired for the occasion, were intending to make the most of a fine day to get the shearing underway. Ellen bent double as the spasm gripped her. She clung to the wooden gate of the shedder, breathing hard until the pain subsided. Around her legs the sheep bleated in frustration at their imprisonment. She glanced at the shepherds but they hadn't noticed her discomfiture. Lifting her pinafore to wipe away the beads of sweat that were dotting her forehead, she breathed more slowly to steady herself. The pain had gone now but the intensity of it had left her weak and shaking.

She fumbled with the exit gate as a second pain began to build within her. The sheep, pushing impatiently, escaped in a rush and Kenneth Douglas looked up in surprise as they rampaged into the small field.

'Are you all right, hen?' he called anxiously, letting go of the ewe he was holding.

'Aye, I think so. Just a bit of pain. It must be that rabbit pie I made last night. I shouldnae have eaten such a large portion.' She attempted a smile, but the pain intensified and her face turned ashen.

'Let's get you inside, my lassie.' Duncan, realising his daughter's distress, laid down the shears he had that moment picked up, and abandoned a ewe to skitter unchecked across the pen until stopped by the fence, where she stood bleating loudly. He put a fatherly arm around Ellen and helped her into the cottage. She sank gratefully into the armchair. 'Nae, lassie. It's not like you to take ill. You're usually such a strong little thing. What can I get you… a drink of water, maybes?'

'Aye, that would be good. I'll rest for a bit.'

'Will you manage with Netta?'

'Aye. She's no trouble. She'll play here on the rug. You go and get on with the shearing.'

Duncan turned reluctantly to the door. 'I'll be back soon, ken, to check how you are.'

He disappeared and Ellen laid her head back and closed her eyes. The pain had eased now but she was frightened. She didn't want there to be something wrong that would harm the baby. Her pregnancy was unknown to anyone except herself… and her husband, if he had received the letter she had written. As things stood, she would rather it remained that way, until she knew what

Tom's intentions were.

It was with great relief that she heard footsteps in the passageway an hour later. There had been no recurrence of the severe cramp she had suffered in the field but it had left her with a nagging ache. She thought that she might ask her father to send for Margaret Murdie. Her neighbour's unofficial midwifery skills were well known and Margaret would be able to settle her mind about the baby. When there was a gentle knock on the door and Margaret herself popped her head into the room, Ellen could not contain her relief.

'I was passing and thought I'd call in with this.' She drew from her bag a knitted cardigan. 'It's for Netta. It'll fit her hopefully when the next winter comes. It's too big at the moment but she'll grow into it.'

Ellen was so glad to see her that she began to laugh and cry at the same time.

'Why, whatever's the matter, lassie? Is something ailing the wee girl?'

'No. She's fine. It's me. I've taken a pain in my stomach and... you see, I'm expecting another baby and I'm that worried...'

'Are you, hen? That's grand news. Does Tom know about it?'

'Yes. Well, I'm not sure whether he does or no'. I've written to him with the news, but I don't know whether he's got my letter.'

'Well now, what I suggest is that you go and get some

rest for an hour or two and let me look after the wain.'

'But the shearing…'

'…Is going on very well without you. Men can aye manage when they have to, believe me.'

'But Mr Murdie…? Have you no' got to get back to look after him?'

'Robert's a lot better than he was. He's insisting on getting back to the sheep and there's nothing I can do to stop him. He always was a stubborn man and has never listened to anything I said.' She shook her head and gave a small smile. 'He was trying my patience no end when he was cooped up in bed, I don't mind admitting.' Margaret took Ellen's arm and helped her from the chair.

It was cool in the bedroom and Ellen lay back gratefully and watched the curtains rise and fall in the breeze. The sounds of shearing wafted in on the air… the murmur of men's voices, a shouted oath, as a sheep struggled to escape her fate, a loud guffaw as a bawdy joke was shared between them. And then she slept.

Her pain returned to wake her in the night. She lay unmoving, as early light filtered through the thin curtains, and listened to the calls of waking birds and the bleating of the denuded sheep. She wanted to get up and walk around, but she didn't want to disturb Netta. Then she remembered that Netta wasn't there. Margaret Murdie had suggested that she take her for the night to allow Ellen to rest without interruption.

As Ellen put her feet to the floor, she felt her head begin to spin. A wave of nausea passed over her. She sat on the side of the bed, holding onto the headboard until she felt steadier. She stood up again and began to make her way to the door. The next moment, she was stepping through a black tunnel and the light up ahead was receding into the distance and, no matter how hard she tried to reach it, the brightness dimmed and dimmed and finally went out.

*

Margaret Murdie's face was the first thing Ellen saw when she opened her eyes. All she felt was an overwhelming weariness. Even to turn her head was an effort. Margaret's smile comforted her and she closed her eyes again. Sensing a drifting off into sleep, she pulled herself together and attempted to speak, surprised at the weakness of her voice.

'Is it you back with Netta? Has she been a good girl for you?'

'She's been a very good girl. Nae bother at all.'

'I must get up and see to her and let you get off to your farm.' Ellen struggled to lift her head from the pillows.

'Nae, lassie. You'll be going nowhere, so lie still.'

'But you had her last night. I can't let you...'

'Ellen, you've been ill. I've been here with Netta for a

few days.'

Ellen frowned, trying to rearrange the muddle that was swirling around in her head. She attempted to sit up but once more tiredness got the better of her and her head dropped back on the pillows.

'Ellen. Listen to me. I've something to tell you that you must hear.' She paused and took Ellen's hand in hers. 'You've lost the baby, Ellen. Do you understand? You've lost the baby you were carrying... and a lot of blood. That's why you're so weak. The danger is past now, but you must rest and get strong again.'

The girl lay unmoving, her eyes fixed on the ceiling, and silent tears began to track down the sides of her face into the tangle of hair that spread out over the pillow.

'Does Tom know?' she said at last.

'I don't know, hen. Your father wrote to the same address as you, but we've heard nothing yet. It's full early though. A letter may still get through to him and then they'll let him come home, rest upon it.'

'You told Father then?'

'Of course, hen. It was your father who found you in the night. You had collapsed on the floor. He sent Kenneth to fetch me. Netta had an early wakening that morning, to be sure. I had to bring her back with me. I couldn't very well leave her with Robert. She would have wondered what was happening... and, anyway, Robert was never very good at looking after wains. You should have seen him with Iain. All fingers and thumbs he was when I asked him to help. Not a bit like your father when you were little. Duncan always knew exactly what to do.'

'He had no choice really with Mother gone, did he?'

'No, hen, he didn't. So you must count your blessings. Things could have gone a lot worse. If your father hadn't heard you fall, I hate to think what might have happened. Little Netta might be without one of her parents.'

'She still might be. There's been no word at all from Tom. I have no idea whether he's alive or dead.'

'Come along now. You mustn't talk like that. We must keep hoping and praying for our sons' and husbands' safe return. He'll come back to you, and don't you doubt it. Meanwhile you must get well and strong again. I've agreed with your father that I will stay on for a wee while, to see how you improve. Robert is able to fend for himself but, in any case, his sister is coming to stay tomorrow, so he'll be able to rest again once she's installed. She never stays for less than three weeks, once she's arrived.'

*

On the night of Margaret's summons to the Douglas farmstead, Josef Kessler had been unable to sleep. Since the day of her husband's return from the battlefield in early February, Josef had not spoken to Ellen. He had often seen her walking with the baby, though always in the distance. She seemed bent on avoiding him, for she never came close to where the men were working and he suspected that Vogel's meddling might have prompted her husband to object to the help that she had given. He guessed also that her husband would have returned to his battalion long ago, for leave was never granted for longer than a few days, if the British treated their soldiers and sailors in a similar way to their own.

The sight of Netta being wheeled in her pram by the older woman was disconcerting, because it was so unusual. He had never seen the toddler in the company of anyone other than her mother. He looked at the woman as she hurried past. She must have been a similar age to his own mother. Her hair was greying, her cheeks weathered with the outdoors, her rough clothing, he supposed, that of the older farming women of the area. He longed to ask her if all was well with Ellen and the little girl, but he could not. Since the upset instigated by Vogel, there had been strict instructions that no contact was to take place with the villagers and farmers. And even if he had met her, how would she have understood his request?

The small incident reawoke in Josef the feelings he had attempted to suppress since his stay in the shepherd's cottage. Whichever way he looked at it, he knew that any hope of friendship with the lovely Ellen was impossible. She was 'the enemy' and he, a prisoner of war in an alien country. His parents had already looked out a suitable match for him on his return. Moreover, Ellen was married, though he doubted whether their union was a happy one, for she had said very little to him about her husband.

Eventually Josef gave up his attempt to sleep. Sliding noiselessly from between the sheets, he picked up his boots, and tiptoeing to the door of the hut, opened it quietly and stepped out into the night air. A near full moon lit his path as he picked his way to the barbed-wire perimeter fence and stared through it like a caged animal. From where the huts had been erected it was possible to see a mile or two up the road. Not a thing moved. He heard only the incessant piping call of the oystercatchers, which, alone among the birds in the valley, seemed not to recognise the need for peaceful sleep. Tipping his head back, he gazed into the velvet sky, its plentiful stars dimmed by the brilliance of the moon.

A crunch of heavy boots startled him and he lowered his eyes to see one of the guards making his way along the outside of the wire. He noted the red glow of the man's cigarette as he approached. He made no attempt to move, for it was not forbidden to step outside on these warm summer nights. In any case, he recognised the man as being one of the more friendly of the soldiers who guarded them. The soldier stopped at his side.

'You doing a spot of stargazing, pal?'

'Bitte?'

The man pointed upwards. 'Stars… moon.'

'Ja. Yes. Good, nicht wahr?'

'Very good. It would be a good night to escape, so it would!'

Josef looked at him blankly and the soldier chuckled.

'Just as well you don't understand what I'm saying.' He paused, drawing heavily on his cigarette so that it glowed fiercely. 'Not that you'd get very far if you did escape, with that cough of yours,' he muttered beneath his breath. 'Are you feeling better now?' he asked.

'Yes, better. Strong. Thank you.' Josef sensed the glimmer of an opportunity and struggled to string together the words he had learned into a sentence. 'The girl… she helps. She nurse me.'

'Och aye. The girl from the farm. A bonnie wee thing. It was good that she agreed to help when the captain asked. It could have been curtains for you.'

Josef frowned, not understanding. 'You see her? She is well?'

The soldier looked sharply into Josef's face, gave a last pull on his cigarette, tossed the stub onto the stones in front of him and ground it beneath his boot. 'You better get back to your bed. You've a hard day's work in front of you.' He indicated the sleeping quarters with a nod of his head.

'Yes. You see her, tell her "Thank you".' Josef turned away and stepped over to his hut. Inside, he groped his way to the camp bed and lay down, hands cradled behind his head, staring into the thick darkness. This was the time when he felt the restrictions of prison life most keenly. He could have spent the night out there under the stars in the moonlight. Even the wire fence could not take away completely the hint of freedom that such a night breathed on the land beneath.

Josef let out a long sigh of frustration. For just a moment he had thought he might glean a crumb of news about Ellen. He was desperate to see her, wretched that so much time had passed without so much as a glimpse of her. He had told himself a hundred times that such a friendship was impossible, but however much he recognised the futility of thinking of her, he could not stop. Each time he closed his eyes, he saw her own clear ones looking at him, her fair hair catching the sun's rays, her mouth with its irregular teeth smiling at him.

A distant sound alerted him. He lay, listening intently. It was the clip-clop of hooves and the rumble of a cart. Having no way of telling the time, he judged by the call of the birds and the pallor of the sky at the bare windows that dawn was approaching. It would be very early, for at this time of the year the hours of darkness were but two or three. Quickly he rose from the bed and crossed to the nearest window. He recognised the shadowy form of Farmer Douglas urging on his horse and, considering that the road still lay in semidarkness, making remarkably rapid progress.

A further half an hour elapsed, during which time the sky had lightened from dark grey to the promise of blue. The sound came again and once more Josef hurried to the window to observe. The cart was returning and this time its occupants could be clearly seen as the farmer and the older woman who had been pushing Netta along the road the previous afternoon. And if he wasn't mistaken, there was the toddler cradled in the woman's arms. He lay down again, his heart thudding. Something must be wrong. There could be no other reason for these unusual comings and goings at such an early hour.

Morning came. The huts were unlocked, the men released into the still air, where they did battle with a population of midges intent on covering every inch of exposed flesh. Josef scanned the valley to east and west, but no clue as to the night-time's activity was apparent.

The men washed, ate breakfast and departed for the day's excavations. Josef glanced up frequently from his digging but all remained quiet and he began to think that the whole episode had been a figment of his imagination.

22

The Embankment

Towards the end of August, a month after Ellen had lost the baby, a note arrived from Margaret Murdie, inviting Ellen to visit with Netta. She had enjoyed looking after the little girl and was missing her company, the note read.

'You should go and see her, lassie. She'll be lonely without Iain there. Robert was aye a man of few words...and never very good company. I could no' understand what she saw in him.' Duncan chuckled. 'She didnae get the best bargain when she picked him.'

'I don't know, Feyther. I don't think I've got the energy to walk right along there.'

'Nonsense! It's nae distance for you to go. It's time you were out and about again. You're losing all the colour from your cheeks. Get along with you now and see Margaret. It will make a nice change for Netta too.'

Ellen sighed. She felt so weary and so low that she had done little but what was necessary for the smooth running of the house. There had been no word of her husband and she tried to push thoughts of Josef from her mind, for fear that she would give in completely to her melancholy. She knew, though, that her father spoke the truth. And it *would* do Netta good to have a change of scenery.

She set off in the early afternoon, the air full of the sharp tang of heather blossom and the drowsy drone of bees as they made their shambling way from one purple patch to the next. They couldn't fool her of course, she considered, as her eyes scanned the distant hills. Margaret had invited her on purpose to get her out of the cottage. And it wouldn't have surprised her if Duncan had put her up to it. She didn't blame them. She must have been a drag to live with, moping round the cottage, snapping at her father over the least little thing.

Despite herself, her spirits started to rise. The cloud of disappointed hopes and lost dreams lifted a little. She held her head higher and her feet began to step more jauntily along the path. In her perambulator Netta chatted excitedly in the garbled language of a toddler.

Looking around her, Ellen was surprised to see how far the work had progressed since the last time she had walked this way. The road was wider now and resurfaced and, at its side, at a distance of fifteen to twenty feet, snaked the iron lines of the new railway. The sight caused a surge of excitement to run through Ellen's body. She tried to imagine the day when the first engine would make its sooty progress through the valley.

She had seen the great locomotives arrive and depart from the station in the village, and this was thrilling enough. But to have their very own railway was beyond her wildest dreams.

As she rounded a bend in the road, she came upon some of the prisoners and her heart leapt. Her eyes scanned the group of men but there was no sign of Josef. The surge of hope that the sight of the men had brought, evaporated as quickly as it had come. As she walked past, she looked at what was going on. Here the iron rails were not yet laid and the workmen were putting in place the foundations, upon which the wooden sleepers would rest. An unexpected voice made her stop. It was the captain.

'Excuse me, Mrs Fairclough.'

'What's the matter?' she said, alarmed. 'Shouldn't I be walking here?'

'Of course you should. No, I was wondering how you are. Only I haven't seen you out with the little girl for a long time and thought you might have been unwell.'

The man's thoughtful enquiry brought an unexpected flood of emotion and she choked on a reply.

'Oh, Mrs Fairclough, I'm sorry. I didn't mean to upset you. I wouldn't have said anything if…'

'No, no. It's kind of you to ask.' She smiled at him, her tears glistening in the afternoon sunshine. 'I *have* been ill. But I'm better now, much better.'

'Good.' The captain looked ahead down the road.

'May I walk with you? I have to go this way myself. There's plenty of digging up ahead.'

Ellen released the brake and the two continued along the road together.

'And your husband? May I ask how he is?'

She hesitated. 'I... he's safe... as far as I know.' She paused and sighed. 'Actually, Captain, I've no idea how my husband is because I haven't heard from him for months.' Her voice was half defiance, half despair.

'I'm sorry,' murmured the captain, clearly wishing he hadn't asked the question.

'Why is it that everybody hears from their husbands and sons except me? Can you tell me that, Captain? The soldiers at the front are given time to write, aren't they?'

'Well yes, they are.'

'Did you write to your wife when you were at the front?'

'Actually I'm not married, but certainly I wrote to my mother and sisters.'

'Och, I'm sorry, Captain. I ken I'm going on about it and it's none of your concern.'

The captain smiled at her by way of reply and they went on in silence. The river at her side, meandering its easy way along the valley floor, slowly calmed her thoughts. Then, abruptly she stopped in her tracks when the final bend in the road was gained.

'Goodness, Captain. What a change!'

'I said there was a lot of digging. The men are

excavating the earth where the embankment will be built. It needs to be extremely strong to hold back the planned volume of water. See how they're using the machinery to get the work done in as short a time as possible.'

'Yes, that's where we're going, Netta and me, where the water will be. We're going to visit Mrs Murdie at her farm.' She paused, looking in the direction of the digging. 'Can I ask, Captain, how Josef is, only I haven't seen him since he left the cottage? Is he well? Is he strong enough to be doing this work?

'He is working - maybe not as strong as the others but managing. You did a good job, Mrs. Fairclough.'

'Yes. Thank you, Captain for telling me. I'll say goodbye for now.'

'Good day to you, Mrs Fairclough.'

By means of a sharp incline and wide sweep of road, Ellen bypassed the activity at the base of the embankment and came at last to the Murdie farmstead, where Margaret awaited her with tea and cakes and a wide smile.

'Come away in, child. It's gud to see you looking yoursel' again. And Netta! See how she's growing.'

Ellen sat down gratefully in the kitchen. She had not walked this distance for a long time and was tired and pleasantly hungry. Margaret hurried to make the tea.

'Gud news! Gud news! We've had a letter from Iain. He's well. He sounds as though he's keeping his spirits up. There's no leave promised though, not until the end of the year. I suppose we will just have to be patient. Has there been any word from Tom?' She pushed a cup of tea across the table to Ellen.

'Nothing at all. That's four months now without a letter.'

'Well, look at it this way, hen. He must be alive or you would have had a telegram to say he was missing or worse. No news is good news when it comes to war, isn't that so?'

'But why doesn't he write?' Ellen almost shouted and her eyes flared in anger. 'He's no business to treat us like this. All these months when I've had to bear the loss of the wee one on my own and not a word of comfort from him. It's not fair, Margaret. It's really not fair,' she spluttered, and, laying her head on her arms, began to sob and sob, her shoulders shuddering under the effort of it.

Margaret rose from her chair and put her arm around the young woman but she made no attempt to stem the flow of tears, tears that had been held back since the loss of her baby.

At last, Ellen quietened and looked up, a twisted smile spreading over her face. 'I don't know where all that sprung from. I must have a wall inside me as big as yon embankment they're building down there!'

*

The following week Ellen went again to Margaret Murdie's cottage, as she had promised that she would. The beautiful late summer days of the previous week had given way to heavy rain and gales for the last three days, but today was quieter. The wind had dropped, and although rain still fell, it was of the gentle kind that nonetheless soaked through clothing and seeped into boots.

The work of excavation had, not surprisingly, progressed little since the previous week, but now the prisoners were out in force and Ellen could see them to and fro at the base of the huge embankment. She watched fascinated as she came alongside, wondering whether Josef would be one of the workers, but not seeing him. She skirted away from the site to climb the hill and walk the remaining distance to the farm. She remembered the pictures in her school history books of Egyptians and the pyramids and thought that this must be what it was like... the builders dwarfed by the immensity of what they were building.

On her homeward journey Ellen could see that the men were still working. She knew they didn't stop until daylight began to fade... and the sky had brightened in the last hour or two. There would be no early finish tonight.

Everywhere there was mud. Clods of it fell from the machinery. The land at the base of the excavations was a quagmire. An abrupt shout tore through the air and in the same moment a gurgling slurping rumble grew and grew. Another shout and several more and, as she watched in horror, a great slice of the embankment slithered down the steep incline and came to rest at its base. From the resulting mound of mud, the tops of pieces of machinery jutted out like comically shaped flowers. A momentary silence and several men rushed to the base of the mudslide. The guards shouted to stand back in case of further slips, but no one took any notice. They began digging with their hands, apprehensive about using spades, in case they should injure one of their colleagues trapped beneath the black blanket of wet earth.

Ellen stood transfixed as one man was pulled from a machine. He stumbled, fell, staggered to his feet and was led away from danger to the side of the embankment. Then she was running, pushing the perambulator ahead of her, down across the grass to the edge of the fall of mud, terrified that Josef could be one of the men caught in the mudslide.

'Stand back, Mrs Fairclough. Get out of the way. It's dangerous.' She stopped abruptly and turned to see the captain. His face was ashen.

'Can I do anything? If anyone's injured, I may be able to help.'

'Maybe you can... but we've got to get them out first. Just stand back for now. I don't want you or the little one in any danger.'

Another man was pulled clear. He was coughing and retching and they laid him on the grass by the first casualty, where he quickly recovered. All recognised that time was of the essence. A man covered in mud and deprived of oxygen would not last longer than a couple of minutes.

For a third time they burrowed in the mud, assisted frantically by the captain. Minutes ticked by. Then, a shout, as a hand was uncovered, and an arm. The prisoners themselves were by now clothed in mud and it was difficult to distinguish one man from the next. Ellen realised with a shock of relief that the man scrabbling to free the injured man's face was Josef. He was safe! She watched as he uncovered the head, ran a finger round the inside of the mouth and cleared the nostrils. The skin of the face showed pale where Josef had wiped the mud away. Josef looked up at the captain and said something that Ellen couldn't hear. She saw the captain's look of despair as he dropped to the mud again to help free the body and haul it from the machine to a place of safety.

Ellen ran quickly across the grass. The man was lifeless. Josef was attempting to revive him. But there was no hope. At last he looked up and stared into Ellen's face.

'It is Oliver,' he said. 'Oliver Tauber. My friend.'

With a gasp, Ellen looked down. She could see now that the dead man was indeed Oliver, the aristocratic prisoner who had been so kind to her while Josef was at the cottage. His face showed no sign of the horrific death to which he had been subjected. He looked as though he were asleep. The captain knelt beside him speechless.

'What will you do with him?' she said because she could think of nothing else to say.

'I do not know.' Josef's voice was bleak. She put a comforting hand on his shoulder and at the same moment they looked up and saw men bearing a stretcher. Carefully they laid the dead man onto it and retraced their steps, Josef supporting one corner. Ellen stood up slowly and watched the men stumble towards the hospital hut. The captain had risen from the mud and his eyes followed the stretcher.

Ellen turned from the edge of the mud slick to make her way back to her daughter. As she looked up, her heart gave a great lurch. The perambulator was empty.

She careered across the grass, stumbling in her haste. There was no mistake. Netta was not there. Ellen looked wildly about her, her eyes scanning the path, the grass slopes, the distant road, the river flowing crazily along the valley floor. She took a horrified glance at the sea of mud, but it gave no hint that the little girl had strayed in that direction.

A soldier emerged from the hut to which the dead man had been carried. She ran to him.

'Please, please! You must help me! It's my little girl. She was here a minute ago. Now she's gone.'

'Slow down, lassie. Are you sure about this?'

'Of course. The pram's empty. She was here. We were walking home when we saw the accident. I only left her there for a minute or two to see if I could help. Oh, please, will you help me look for her?'

'Of course. Give me a second. I'll get some more men.' He ran towards the hut and Ellen wheeled round and made off in the direction of the river, knowing that this and the mud slip held the greatest danger. Glancing behind her, she saw a clutch of men spreading out across the lower slopes of the valley.

There was no sign of Netta at the water's edge. Ellen did not think she could have gone far in the few minutes that she was occupied at Josef's side. She lurched from one uneven rock to the next, her boots full of water and her sodden skirt clinging around her legs. Pausing, she looked along the meandering riverbank as far as she could see. Nothing.

On the hillside she could just make out the figures of the other searchers. Ellen lowered her head and frantically renewed her slow progress along the side of the swollen river.

A shout made her pause and look behind her to the origin of the sound. It came again.

'Ellen! Come! Come here!'

Screwing up her eyes, she could just make out on the hillside the waving arms of a man. Only his top half was visible and she realised that he must be standing in one of the circular stells, in which sheep sheltered from the winter weather.

'Come here, Ellen,' the voice repeated. 'I find her.'

It was Josef. She raced up the hill towards him, her legs almost giving way beneath her. Would her daughter be all right... or had she come to some harm? How could she have been so stupid as to take her eyes off the toddler for even a second? Reaching the rough wall of the stell, she raised an agonised face to Josef's serious one.

He put a finger to his lips. 'She is safe. Come. Look at her.'

Ellen found the entry and staggered inside. Her daughter was curled up and sleeping peacefully beneath the protection of the stone wall. She sank to her knees, the weakness of relief getting the better of her, and lay a hand on her sleeping daughter. Then she leaned back, covering her face with her hands. Josef knelt beside her and gently pulled her towards him, resting her head against his shoulders and stroking her hair with slow, soothing movements. In the stillness, she could feel the excited beat of his heart, echoing her own.

Easing her trembling hands away from her face, he stared into her eyes.

'Liebling! It is a bad day, is it not? But now I see you, that is one good. You are well?'

Ellen shook her head slowly from side to side, her eyes locked on his. 'I was ill. I lost the baby I was carrying. I'm better now.' She felt the slight tensing of the arms that held her, as she started to cry, noisy sobs that convulsed her body.

Josef drew her towards him again and held her tight and she felt as if she could stay in his arms forever. 'Oh, Liebling. I am sorry. I always know something is not right. But your man, he is home to help you?'

'I haven't seen or heard from my husband for more than four months.'

'But he does not write?'

'I havenae heard anything.'

She watched the conflicting expressions cross his face... surprise, commiseration, hope. Lifting a hand, he softly brushed her cheek with his fingers. In the distance there was a shout and he seemed to recollect himself.

'Come, Herzchen. We must go. You and Netta both are cold. She is wet and you are... very wet. And I... if I stay away very long, they think I escape!' He took one of her hands to pull her up, but she didn't move.

Her face was so close to his that she could hear his rapid breathing and feel the shallow warm exhalations on her skin. And she wondered whether it was the after-effects of his illness that had caused the breathlessness or the nearness of her body to his. In the dusk she could see the faraway look in his eyes refocused on herself. She stared back, contradictory thoughts about her missing husband filling her mind, thoughts that disappeared as Josef's face slowly crossed the remaining distance between them. The kiss lingered on her mouth, loving, tender, and full of desire.

A shout came again and abruptly he stooped and picked up the still sleeping form of her daughter and began the climb through the rain-wet grass back to the encampment.

23

Devastation

In the thick layer of mud at the bottom of the trench, Tom's boots were invisible. He raised one foot slowly, the mud slurping and gurgling and trying to hold him down. When it was free of the stinking quagmire, he replaced it gingerly, for who knew what lay beneath the surface? Then he did the same with the other foot, anxious that if he didn't keep them moving, he would be held fast to the base of the trench when the order came to advance.

The mud didn't stop at his boots, of course. His puttees were thick with it. When they dried, which wasn't often, he scraped the mud off them in slabs. Above them, his trousers were similarly caked. He was lucky though. He could have fared much worse. Many did.

Lucky? He had ceased believing in luck, good or bad. He had given up hoping for an end to this hellish existence. It was foolish even to think beyond getting through the next hour. He raised his eyes to the slice of grey sky above the rim of the trench. The insistent drizzle had abruptly increased to a deluge. With his free hand, he raised the collar of his greatcoat in a vain attempt to prevent water running down his neck. On second thoughts, though, it might help to drown the lice that had invaded his skin. Thoughts of the infestation made him involuntarily reach his hand inside his collar and scratch.

What would his family say if they could see him now? His family. He had severed all contact with them. In his anger he had determined that he would teach Ellen a lesson. He had written no letters, although he had received them regularly from her. She had told him about the pregnancy, and about the subsequent loss of the baby. *Good riddance*, he thought. It was probably not his baby anyway. He had not even written a letter to console her, though he knew well enough how upset she would have been. It was he who was suffering now though, of course, but his pride would not let him go back on the decision he had made. It was all futile anyway. The chances of him living another day, let alone to the end of the conflict, should it ever end, were minute.

It had been bad enough here before his leave. Fighting had been going on in this part of France since the beginning of hostilities. For almost three years now, the allies had been bombarding the Germans with all the ammunition they could throw at them and receiving theirs in like measure. The low-lying basin, divided by streams that fed into the River Yser, had once been prosperous agricultural land, but the constant bombardment had reduced it to a swamp. Tom, arriving fresh from the upland hills and valleys of southern Scotland, had not been able to believe his eyes at the scene of devastation that had met him and he would not have believed that it could get any worse.

The abrupt shrilling of a whistle and the order to 'Advance' brought with them the habitual surge of adrenaline. Dragging his feet along the trench to the bottom of the ladder, Tom waited his turn to go up. Mud from the boots of the private above him slopped onto his head, but he didn't bother to wipe it away, knowing that there would be worse by the end of the day. And then he was climbing, hampered by rifle and bayonet, the gas respirator strapped to his chest, a bandolier of cartridges over his shoulder. Up and up and over the top of the ladder onto the duckboards. And then slipping and sliding forward along these arteries in the morass, more scared of falling off into the shell holes on either side than of the whistle of bullets all around. The explosions of shells getting closer as Tom and his comrades advanced.

In the line ahead, a soldier fell, a bullet ripping through his leg. The private behind him, slithering to a stop, lost his footing and the next second was off the duckboard and into the shell hole at its side. He floundered wildly, stepping on the bodies of dead soldiers, before being sucked beneath the surface. Tom stopped, staring in horror at where his colleague had been and seeing only the stinking mud with its cocktail of rotting flesh. He swallowed the urge to vomit as the man behind pushed him roughly onwards. He forced himself forward into the hail of bullets. A shell landed in a nearby crater of mud and its contents spewed out in all directions, stirring up the stench of rotting death and dissolved gas.

Ahead, Tom could see a German pillbox. If only he could reach it, he would be much safer. With one last effort, he covered the remaining yards and flung himself into the shelter. It was dark inside and already contained several soldiers and a foot of water. But its stinking interior was like heaven. Tom leaned against the thick wall, catching his breath. The man nearest to the door smiled at him.

'Welcome home,' he joked and handed Tom a cigarette.

For half an hour there was peace... not outside, where the shells continued to pound the battlefield... but here, within the protection of its thick walls, the soldiers could almost believe they were safe. More men joined them. They were packed together now. Suddenly, with an enormous thump, a shell hit the pillbox, almost lifting it into the air. The enemy had realised what was happening. If they could plant a shell in the correct position, they might tip the shelter over and the men would be drowned in the surrounding mud. What he had thought was a place of safety was no better than a trap. They were caught, the enemy's guns trained on them, ready to fire should any of them try to leave.

Relentlessly, the bombardment continued. Another shell fell nearby and Tom put his hands over his ears. He would go mad if this carried on.

'You OK, mate?' His neighbour nudged him in the ribs. Tom opened his eyes and studied the man's face in the gloom.

'What did you say?'

'I asked if you were all right. You look as though you've had more than enough.'

'Haven't we all? What a hellhole this is turning out to be.'

'Still, if we can hold our position here, we'll have made good progress.'

Tom snorted. 'You reckon so? There'll be none of us left at the end of this… if there ever is an end.'

'You've got to believe that we'll win in the end… to keep our country free and our wives and families safe.'

Tom said nothing.

'You got any family, pal,' the man asked.

'I've a little girl. Year and a half she'll be.'

'There you are then. You have to think about her… and, no doubt there's a pretty wife at home looking after her. Just imagine how it will be when you get…'

'Shut up, can't you! I don't want to think about owt like that.'

'Sorry, mate! Just trying to help. I can't wait to get back to mine. Just hope she's behaving herself while I'm away.'

Tom gritted his teeth. 'Look! I know you're only trying to help. But I happen to know mine's not behaving herself!'

There was a pause. 'Are you sure? The mind can do funny things when you're out here. Imagine all kinds of things that aren't true at all.'

'Aye, well, I happen to know I'm right, more's the pity.'

'Where will you go then?'

'What do you mean?'

'After the war's over. Will you go back to her?'

Tom's mind, clouded with anger as it was whenever he thought about Ellen, had not considered this eventuality. To avoid thinking about it now, he replied, 'Like I said, there is no end. And even if there were to be, I should go off my head just thinking about it.'

Outside, the shellfire had stopped and only sporadic gunfire could be heard. The men relaxed.

'Well, lads,' a lieutenant spoke up, taking charge. 'It looks as though we're here for the night. I suggest we all try to get some shut-eye, though we'll have to take shifts. Sorry about the supper.'

Tom struggled to make out the position of his

neighbours in the encroaching dark. *Better than a night in the trenches, I suppose*, he thought to himself. He was perched on a narrow ledge about two foot six off the ground and clear of the stinking water. It was so narrow that to fall asleep was to be in danger of rolling off into it. But to stay awake was to risk being too exhausted for the next day's forward push. And, anyway, it was only sleep that would bring the oblivion Tom craved.

24

The Happy Berry Tree

The grave of Janet Tonner, Duncan Simpson's young wife, could be found at the far side of the shady graveyard, a spot picked for its view over the distant hills that she had loved so much. In the years since her death, a rowan sapling, at first scarcely bigger than the headstone beside which it grew, had reached maturity and a proliferation of unripe berries promised a fine show in a few weeks' time. Duncan had told his daughter often about the ability of the tree to ward off evil spirits. He imagined it protecting her long-dead mother, he explained to Ellen, in a way that he had been unable to do during her life.

Ellen had visited the grave frequently, at first with her father but in later years on her own. She too loved the rowan, but less for its magical properties than for the smoothness of its grey trunk and its feathery leaves and profusion of orange fruit. 'The happy berry tree' she had called it as a child, and the name had stayed with her into adult life. Today, however, she gave the engraved stone and its protecting tree only a passing glance before joining the small group of men making their way towards a mound of freshly dug earth, a little removed from the other graves. *Did God take sides in this awful war that seemed to have no end,* she wondered, as she followed the procession. *Was Oliver Tauber the enemy in God's eyes, as well as in those of the people in whose land he had died.*

Her request to accompany the funeral procession had been greeted with surprise by Captain Cameron-Dyet, but there had been no objection. Her reasons for wishing to attend the short graveyard service were twofold. The tall aristocratic university teacher had been kind to her and Netta. She was sad that none of his family could be there to mourn his passing and felt that she at least was the nearest contact he had had to a proper family. But also she wished to give what support she was able to Josef, who had felt the loss of his friend so keenly. It was only when they stood in a semicircle around the deep hole that he looked up and realised she was there.

The service began. It was read in English but that, Ellen decided, would be entirely acceptable to Oliver, whose grasp of the language was so good. Josef stood, head bowed, between two prison guards. Next to them stood the captain, his erect bearing and serious expression giving no hint of his inner feelings.

It was soon over. The body was lowered into the ground, the piercing blue eyes never again to see his beloved Fatherland. The irony of his last resting place in the mud of the graveyard struck her as it must have the others.

She glanced at Josef, who still stood with bowed head, staring into the hole. Then they were leaving, making their way back along the path to where the truck was waiting to return them to the camp. Ellen watched them go, wondering whether to take the opportunity to visit her mother's grave. Deciding she would, she had taken only a couple of steps off the track when she heard the captain's voice.

'Would you like a lift with us, Mrs Fairclough? It's a long way to walk and there's plenty of room in the truck... unless you had something else to do, of course.'

She hesitated a moment and then smiled at the captain. 'Aye, I will, thank you. I was going to visit my mother's grave while I was here, but it will do another day. And I should be getting back to my daughter, so Father can get on with his work. I've been long enough away from her.'

'Take your time, Mrs Fairclough. We'll wait for you at the truck. You go and visit your mother. A few more minutes won't make any difference.'

The flowers that Ellen had placed in front of her mother's headstone at the last visit had withered and she spent a few minutes tidying the plot. Sitting back on her heels, she wiped tears from her eyes. The words of the funeral service had reawakened the deeply buried ache of longing to have a mother, whose advice she could seek and with whom she could have shared her thoughts and worries. But it was not to be – and she had to concentrate on her own daughter now. With a final glance, she rose to her feet and went over to the truck.

Ellen climbed up into the seat next to the captain and for a while they travelled in silence. At last she turned to look at Josef, seated between the two guards. It was the first time she had seen him since Oliver's death, though she had wrestled with contradictory feelings ever since that fateful day.

'How are you, Josef? Are you keeping well?'

'Thank you. I am well. I am very glad you come.'

'I wanted to be here. He was a good man.'

'Yes. He was a good man. I shall much miss him.'

'You speak English very well now, Josef. Have you been practising?'

'It is Oliver. He teach me to speak English. All I know I learn from him. No, that is not correct. My first words I learn from you.'

She gave a soft laugh. 'I'm no teacher... not like Oliver. But I could teach you more, if the captain would allow it.' She glanced over at the captain, but he was staring ahead and seemed not to notice their conversation.

'I would like. But I think there is no time now to learn. It is all work, work, work to finish the building. The towns, they need water to make the guns to kill the enemy, is it not true?'

She said nothing. What was there to be said?

*

In the weeks that followed, Ellen often saw Josef on her excursions to and from the Murdie farmhouse. Margaret Murdie was the next best thing to a mother that Ellen had. The older woman had heard little from her son, and Ellen nothing at all from her husband, so they felt themselves to be allies. Each week, and sometimes twice a week, Ellen would walk, pushing Netta in her perambulator, the mile and a half to Margaret's house and back again.

If the guards were not watching, Ellen stopped for a few words with Josef. She asked him whether he had managed to learn more English and, when he replied in the negative, next time she brought with her a book of Netta's, full of pictures and vocabulary, apologising for its babyish appearance. He smiled and told her that it was just what he needed and he would learn it from cover to cover. From then on, she always tucked a book into the end of the perambulator before each visit to the Murdie farm. Looking forward to these encounters, she was despondent on the occasions that he wasn't there. When the baby books ran out, she brought old farming magazines and he would laugh and say that she was trying to turn him into a farmer.

*

Margaret Murdie's friendship had a mothering quality which had been absent from Ellen's own life. She knew, because Duncan had told her, that her mother's favourite time of the year had been when the heather was in bloom, the last reminder of summer before the chill of autumn took hold. Therefore, on her latest walk through the valley, seeing the hillsides purple with the blossom, she stopped and picked a bunch to put on her mother's grave that evening. Then, on an impulse, she bent down a picked a second bunch of heather, intending to place one on Oliver's grave also. She knew that there was no one else to decorate it and she would not have it forgotten and overgrown.

The light was going and grey clouds were racing across the face of a three-quarters moon when she set off on her mission. She often chose an evening such as this to visit the graveyard, waiting until Netta was asleep and her father dozing in his chair. It was a long walk but one she knew well and moonlight brightened the path ahead. The iron gate of the graveyard creaked on its hinges as she opened it.

Ellen found Oliver's grave first. Josef had told her that the captain was arranging for the place to be marked with a headstone, but as yet there was nothing but bare earth and a small wooden cross bearing the name 'Oliver Tauber' scribbled in ink. She lay the bunch of heather reverently down and stood for a moment, reminded of the service she had attended with Josef and the soldiers.

Next she crossed to where her mother was buried. She placed the bouquet in a glass vase that decorated the front of the plot and then sat down at the side of it, as she always did if the weather was dry, to talk to her mother.

'Well, Mother. It's more than five months now since I heard from Tom. I don't know what to think. Margaret says no news is good news. What do you think, Mother? Is there any hope that he is still alive?'

She held her breath to listen, but the only answer was the leaves of the rowan sighing in the wind.

'I've lent Josef another of Netta's books.' She laughed. 'He tells me he will soon be able to find a job looking after children because he understands their language.'

The iron gate creaked and she glanced nervously over her shoulder. There was no-one there.

'I went to Oliver Tauber's funeral. He's buried in yon corner away from everyone else, though of course you know that. You were here.' She paused. 'I don't think this war will ever be over. I'm sick of it... all this waiting. It's much worse for the men who are fighting of course. Margaret Murdie has only heard once from Iain. That's her son. You ken Margaret, don't you? Father says you were all friendly when you were younger. She's a bit like a mother to me… though not as you would be, naturally. I ask her advice and…' She stopped abruptly, certain that she heard voices. There was nothing.

'Do you think it's wrong of me to be friendly with Josef, Mother? Father isn't happy about it. He says they're the enemy, even if they are doing the work of our young men. But I can't help it. I looked after him when he was so ill and we…' She spun round at the snap of a dry twig. Behind her a dark shadow moved, two dark shadows, blotting out the face of the moon. Ellen sprang up in alarm and whirled around to make her escape.

'Mrs Fairclough. Is it you?'

'Captain! What are you doing here?'

'We have come to check Oliver Tauber's grave. It's only right that the army should care for it. After all, he was in our charge when the accident happened. And Kessler here heard you, er… talking.'

Ellen stared into the near-darkness. 'Josef?'

Josef stepped closer and squatted down beside her. 'The captain let me visit Oliver's grave. I find flowers. I think you put them. You are very kind.' He hesitated, before continuing. 'You talk to your mother?'

'Aye. I come often. I never saw her. She died when I was born. But I feel as though I know her. I like to tell her things. I come here in the evening, when I can leave Netta with my father. It's easier on my own.'

'But you must allow us to give you a lift back, Mrs Fairclough… unless, of course, you prefer to walk.' The

258

captain had stepped up behind Josef and she could see his tall outline against the fading light.

'Thank you, Captain. I would like to have a lift back.' Ellen turned to her mother's plot. 'Goodnight, Mother. I'll be here next week.'

Catching up with the shadowy figures, who had turned away to afford Ellen some privacy, she followed them through the creaking gate, clanging it shut behind them with force enough to dislodge any ghosts that might be lurking within the crumbling walls of the old graveyard.

Josef turned to Ellen as the captain steered the horse and wagon up to the road and proceeded at a steady pace towards the valley. The rhythmic clip-clop of the horse's hooves and grate of the wheels on the road meant that the two could carry out a whispered conversation without fear of being overheard. Josef took hold of Ellen's hand within his own in a way he was sure was invisible to the captain. Ellen glanced at the captain uncertainly.

'Why does the captain come to the graveyard?' she whispered. 'Why not send one of the other officers?'

Josef shrugged. 'Maybe he thinks it is his fault that Oliver die.'

'But why does he come in the wagon? Why not drive a truck?'

'He says it is good to "take the air" in the evening.' He increased the pressure on the hand that lay within his. 'I think it is good for us, yes?'

She squeezed his hand by way of reply and looked into his eyes, her heart too full for words.

'So, you talk to your mother. You ask for her help?'

'She listens to me, I'm sure of that, but she never tells me what to do.'

'And you do not know what to do? You think to be friends it is wrong, you and me, because I am the enemy?'

She shrugged. 'I don't know.'

'If you say it is wrong, I understand. When you walk along the road, I go inside the hut... not talk.' His gaze dropped to their joined hands and he made to pull his away.

'No, you mustn't,' she gasped. 'I want to talk. Please be my friend.'

'I am your friend. You save my life. You understand me.'

'Will the captain be coming again?' Ellen asked, after the silence had stretched to minutes.

'I think yes, but not yet. Maybe one month, two.'

Ellen watched the clouds speeding across the face of the moon. She glanced at the captain's strained face, fixed on the road ahead, and thought that her own path was just as murky and uncertain as the road they followed back to the cottage. How was she to reconcile her life as a married woman with her increasing feelings for this man who sat at her side... her enemy, but in reality less so than the husband who had abandoned her?

25

Facing the Truth

The air breathed an uncanny silence. Tom lay on his back, his ears strained for gunfire. Daylight was fingering round the ill-fitting door. He stared at the roof of the barn, grey with cobwebs. A private began to shout in his sleep and Tom jumped nervously at the sound. Elsewhere there was gentle snoring. Earlier in the night it had been louder, helped, no doubt, by the generous rum ration, but the culprit's neighbour had quietened him with a none too gentle prod in the ribs and a colourful barrage of obscenities.

The men were exhausted, barely able to cope with the bathing and delousing and attention to their uniforms and equipment that had occupied them on their arrival. They had been relieved during the night before and sent down the tracks to the waiting lorry, which had taken them to a farm near the small village of Neubeuge. Both the farm and the village had, by some miracle, remained intact. A large barn filled with fresh straw was chosen for their billet. Here they were told to rest.

Rest! Tom turned slowly onto his side and removed a sharp stalk that was sticking into his neck. Rest was impossible. Every time he closed his eyes, he could see the bodies of men and horses; every time his mind began to drift off, it was jolted back to reality by imaginary gunfire. At last he sat up quietly and pulled on his boots.

'Where you off to, pal?' His neighbour on the bed of straw was watching him with unblinking eyes.

'Can't sleep. Going for a walk. Back later,' Tom whispered.

'Well remember how the saying goes – "If you can't be good, be careful,"' the man muttered and closed his eyes.

Tom forced his legs to step one in front of the other down the village street. His bones ached so much that he felt like a man of a hundred. The signs of normality – smoke curling from a chimney, chickens emerging from a garden gate to scratch in the road, late roses clustered over a kitchen door – all these served to create in Tom an overwhelming feeling of unreality. Ahead of him a young woman was encouraging a cow across the road and through an open gate into the field. Its engorged udders hung heavily, impeding progress. As the woman shut the gate, she glanced up and saw Tom. She smiled and spoke. Crossing slowly to where she stood, Tom studied her, too weary even to smile in return.

'Engleesh?' she asked.

'Aye. Resting... on the farm.' He pointed back the

way he had come.

The girl reached for a stool and bucket that had been left at the side of the gate and, sitting down, began to milk the cow. The rhythmic squeezing of her fingers on the cow's udders and melodious drumming of the milk as it hit the sides of the bucket were almost unbearably tender. Tom felt his eyes brim with tears. He brushed them away with the sleeve of his coat but they kept coming. The girl looked up and saw that he was crying. And she left off milking the cow, picked up the pail and came to where Tom stood. She took him gently by the arm and led him over the road and into a barn, where she sat down in the thick covering of hay that lay over the floor. She indicated for him to do the same. And she cradled his head in her lap while he sobbed without restraint. It was as if his tears carried the pent-up emotions of all the months he had fought in the war and in his stormy relationship with his wife. The sobbing slowed at last. Only then did the girl stand up slowly and, saying something he did not understand, disappear. A minute later she was back with an enamel jug of milk and a mug. She filled the mug and offered it him. Still warm from the cow, the milk was delicious.

'I'm sorry.' He fumbled in his trouser pocket for a handkerchief. 'I didn't mean to do that. It's the war you see. It's so... so...' He gave a convulsive sob and blew his nose hard.

The girl smiled and nodded. It wasn't difficult to

understand what had occasioned his outburst. She rose again, spoke a few words and once more disappeared.

Tom propped himself on his elbow and took another gulp of the milk. Then he lay back and closed his eyes.

When he came to, the sun's rays were piercing the warm air of the barn and landing at his feet. Dust motes danced languidly in the slanting beams and he lay watching them, poised between sleep and wakefulness, relaxed in body and mind. And then, with awful abruptness, he was precipitated into the hell of the front line by a sound as of shellfire. He rolled onto his side, shaking uncontrollably, curled embryo-like in the hay in an attempt to escape the onslaught.

'Ssh! Ssh!' Someone was stooping over him, arms outstretched, comforting. The shaking eased. Something was tickling his face. He opened his eyes slowly, scared of what he would encounter. The young woman was bending over him, her long dark curls, escaping from her head scarf, falling onto his cheek. She stepped back, lifted a bucket from the floor, shrugged in apology. He grinned and shrugged. Catching hold of the dark curls, he drew her face towards him and kissed her. She pulled back slowly and pointed to a plate of bread and cheese, the mug filled with fresh milk.

'Later,' he murmured, pulling her toward him.

*

He slept that night, better than he had in months, a deep dreamless sleep from which he woke refreshed. The captain arrived with the instruction that they were to be ready at four o'clock to return to their positions on the reserve line.

Amid the general groans of dismay, Tom made a silent exit and retraced his steps towards the farm with considerably more energy than the day before. She was in the field, her head buried in the flank of a nearly milked cow. The animal stood patiently until she had finished and removed the bucket. She rose, smiled a welcome, dipped a mug in the bucket and handed the warm milk to him. Drops ran down the side of the mug onto his uniform and she laughed and brushed them away. Still laughing, she led him across the road and into the barn.

*

Darkness was falling as the men stepped off the lorry and made their precarious way along the duckboards to take up position.

'Home, sweet home,' one of the group joked, as they hunkered down in the trench.

'Could hardly wait to get back,' came a reply. 'Hot and cold running water on demand, haute cuisine... and the sweet smell of success to boot! What more could a man want?'

'Shut up, Thomson. I'll tell you what I could do with... a bit of what Fairclough managed to find... am I no' right, Tom?'

Tom gave a small smile but kept his counsel. He wasn't going to have his two days of pleasure, bandied about in the trench, by those who had been unsuccessful in finding anyone willing to relieve them of the frustrations of several weeks in the mud.

The padre visited them that night.

'Perhaps he knows something that we don't,' a private said, in an attempt to make light of the man's appearance further down the mud-filled trench.

'He's probably here to tell us there's no room left up there.' The man jerked his head upwards, to where a couple of stars twinkled bravely in the distance.

'What makes you think you'd be going up there, anyway?' his companion replied. 'I've heard they've plenty of room left the other way.'

It was quiet in no man's land, eerily so, Tom thought. As though the enemy was hatching a plan to attack with renewed vigour. He felt a return of the anxiety that the last couple of days had lessened. Leaning back on the wall of the trench, he closed his eyes. The two days of relaxation, while they had served as an outlet for his long bottled-up emotions, had also raised other dilemmas.

When he had taken the young woman in his arms and buried his hand within her dark curls, he had imagined that it was Clara he was holding and that it was she who was responding to his kisses. And yet he knew, if he were honest with himself, that Clara would never do such a thing. Hadn't she told him often enough? She would never be his, however much she filled his thoughts. He slid his hand into the inside pocket of his greatcoat and felt the two photographs, dog-eared but intact.

The other, greater dilemma was the fact that he had been unfaithful to Ellen. True, he had accused her of being unfaithful to him... but, in his heart of hearts, he recognised it was unlikely. The baby had no doubt been his, and she had lost it and suffered the consequences without any consolation from him. It was the fact that she had nursed a German... and in his own home... that had really made him mad. And now he himself had done what he had charged her with doing. What an unholy mess.

'Can I help?'

Tom jerked his head up to see the padre standing there.

'Er, no. I don't think so, padre. This is summat I've to sort out myself.'

'It often helps to talk... sorts things out in your own mind, you know.'

'Aye, I suppose it does.' He looked round. 'I'd ask you to sit, but all the best seats seem to be taken. I was thinking about my wife.'

'Only natural, I would say,' smiled the padre. 'You must miss her a lot.'

'The thing is... last time I was on leave, I accused my wife of sleeping with the enemy. She were asked to look after a sick prisoner of war, you see. They... the Hun... had been put to helping build a road and railway near our farm. One of them were taken ill. I don't really think she would have done any more than look after him. I was angry, though, that she even agreed to do that. I suppose my anger got the better of me and I accused her of summat she would never do.'

'I suppose some would say nursing one of the enemy was a very brave act. After all, there were probably others who were willing to condemn her for what she did.'

'Aye. Happen there were.' He paused and took a deep breath. ' I was so mad, I hit her... more than once. But that's not all – I've slept with a woman in the village here. Now I'm the one who's at fault.

The padre put a hand on his arm. 'You know the Bible story of the woman taken in adultery?'

'Yes, I do.'

'Remember how Christ didn't condemn her. He told her not to do it again. She learned a valuable lesson. And it seems to me that you have too. You've realised how precious your wife is to you.'

'Aye. I suppose I have.' Tom looked up at the padre.

'We must hope and pray that this war ends soon so

that you can get back to her safely. It's not an easy job watching and waiting back home either, you know.'

The padre moved on down the line. Tom's heart broke as he thought of the months Ellen must have waited for the letter that never came. Hers came regularly. He read them and stashed them away in his kitbag unanswered. He hadn't even replied to her letters telling him about the baby. That was cruel, cruel to have left her like that without a word of comfort or any knowledge of what had happened to him.

He put his hand up to check in his pocket for pen and paper... and his fingers felt the package that contained his photographs. He drew it out and separated the two pictures. Even in the darkness he could identify his wife's by the rough edges of the folder that protected it. He replaced this in his inner pocket. Without stopping for further thought, he dropped the rest of the package into the deep mud at the bottom of the trench and trampled it beneath his boots.

*

There *was* no time to write. As dawn broke, the men were moved forward to the firing line. The fine spell of September weather, while it had given the soldiers some respite, was not long enough or hot enough to make any marked improvement on the condition of the battlefield. Ploughed up time and time again by the constant bombardment from the machine gunners, there was no solid ground left to walk on. Only the most recent shell holes, not yet filled with water, were safe to shelter in. And October brought the rain again. Mile after mile of land became nothing but a huge sea of mud.

Tom knew without a doubt that he was 'for it' this time. He could not go on and on seeing his pals die in their dozens all round him. By the law of averages, it must be his turn soon. He almost wished for it... as long as the wound was sufficient only to put him out of action and give him a pass for Blighty, where, in time, he would make a recovery; though hopefully not complete enough to send him back to action on the front line. He dreaded the thought of the loss of an arm or leg or getting blinded, all of which would mean he could no longer get back to shepherding. Better death than that. Above all, he dreaded death by drowning in one of the hundreds of filthy, flooded shell holes that lay like booby traps on either side of the disintegrating duckboards.

The surface of the battleground was so bad now that it was impossible to move the heavy guns. Their range was such that they barely reached the German front and, if the enemy were forced to retreat, the machine guns would then be rendered quite useless.

Tom shivered uncontrollably. He and two of his mates had been in a shell hole for three days and it was rapidly filling with water. The one redeeming feature was that there were only three dead bodies in it. Unfortunately, Tom thought, none of them were the enemy.

October had not only brought the rain. It had brought the cold too. Tom and his mates were soaked to the skin, covered in mud, their fingers and toes numb with exposure. Their emergency rations were all but used up. Not that he felt hungry. His nerves were too on edge for that. For the last three days they had been under constant bombardment. They did not dare to lift their heads above the rim of the shell hole for it would mean certain death. They were well within the enemies' sights now.

Tom stared at the yellowish oozing surface of the water, now filling the hole to half its depth. How much more could he stand of this? Should he shoot himself in the foot? That would get him out of the line of action. But would it? There were very few people left to rescue the injured... and, as time went on, the soldiers were concerned less with assisting their injured comrades and more with preserving their own lives. And who could blame them? No, if he gave himself a self-inflicted wound, he was most likely to finish up in the depths of the shell hole. Perhaps he would be better shooting himself through the heart... ending it all before one of the Hun did it for him.

One of his comrades was talking.

'The shelling's over, pal. Let's get out of this while

we're able to.'

Tom listened. His comrade was right. There was sporadic gunfire but the shelling had stopped. It was an effort to move. He had lain in the mud for so long that his legs and back were stiff.

He heaved himself out after the other two men, just in time to catch the blast of a huge shell that landed several yards in front of him and catapulted him back with a mass of lethal shrapnel into the stinking water of the crater he had just left.

26

Bitter Times to Come

Ellen had long since stopped worrying about the possibility of the graveyard being haunted with the ghosts of those who lay beneath its stone crosses and angels. Even the skulls and bones carved on the oldest tombstones no longer alarmed her. Accompanied by Josef and the captain, she had no fears.

It was a month before the captain knocked at the door of the shepherd's cottage and offered her a lift. Autumn was advancing and the air felt different now, an edge to it that told of bitter times to come. Already there had been one fall of snow, the remains of which still clung to the tops of the hills. Ellen thought often of how awful it must be for the soldiers serving at the front.

There had still been no word from Tom. She wrote often, letters that were full of news of the farm and of the antics of his young daughter. But his continued silence angered her and, when she thought about it, so did her treatment at his hands when he had last been at home. What made matters worse was the contrast with the polite and affectionate way she was treated by Josef. If only things had been different and they had met earlier.

'Is it very cold in the prison huts now?' Ellen began, once she had settled in the truck.

'It was more cold in the tents! Now it is, how you say, cosy.' He took her hand and squeezed it. 'I miss you, Ellen. I wish to speak with you... often. I do not sleep because I think about you.'

Ellen turned to him with a beaming smile, almost forgetting to keep her voice down. 'Then why don't I come and see you at night?'

'But, Liebling, it is snow now and the guards.'

'Are the guards there all the time?'

'No. They walk past our hut each half-hour.'

'Then I can come and talk to you. When the guard is due to come, I will hide and come out again when he is gone. Easy!'

*

It was, as Ellen said, easy. Easy but risky and, at times, uncomfortable, especially for Ellen. There were occasional nights when the air was unexpectedly mild. But more often, chilling winds tore through the valley, carrying Ellen along with them and whipping her dress round her ankles and her hair round her face. The homeward journey against the wintry gusts exhausted her. November brought a return of the snow, which lay a week and prevented Ellen's visits, telltale footprints likely to lead to discovery of what they were doing.

For Josef too, the assignations were accompanied by uncertain waits in freezing weather. He would listen for the steady tramp of the passing guard fading into the distance. Then he would leave the hut, closing the door silently behind him, and cross to the wire, attempting to stifle a bout of coughing brought on by the cold air. Ellen, crouched behind a distant bush, would emerge and hurry towards him. Difficult though the conditions were, neither of them would have forgone this opportunity to meet.

Their conversation was commonplace. Josef spoke of the day's activities; the progress of the building work, the friendships and petty rivalries between the prisoners, the animosity from Gunter Vogel.

'But why does he treat you like this?' Ellen asked. 'You are all alike as prisoners. What does he have against you?'

'In our country not all people live happy together. Here, I think, also.'

Ellen shrugged. 'Aye. I suppose so.'

'What you do, Ellen? How is your day?'

She smiled in the darkness. 'Oh, it was quite an exciting day. I helped Father put the tups out onto the hills. They're the male sheep. It's exciting for them, anyway! It's the only time they get to be with their ladies.'

Josef laughed softly. 'They have not a wire as we have.' He threaded his fingers through the barricade and gently shook it. Ellen brought her hands close and he took hold of her fingers and massaged the cold skin.

'If only there was no wire,' Ellen murmured.

'I still stay here. I do not wish to escape. I wish with you to stay.'

Ellen's heart gave a thud. 'You know my husband may come home at any time.'

'Yes? You have a letter?'

'No, no letter.' She shrugged. 'I don't know what's happening.'

'So we are friends now. Let us be happy now, yes?'

'Yes.'

'And we are close friends, yes?' Josef kissed the freezing fingers that were now entwined with his.

At other times, Ellen taught him new words of English or corrected mistakes made during the course of his reading. Occasionally he taught her some German. Mostly, though, he talked about his country and his family.

'Forgive,' he said one night. 'I talk much about my family. You are sad, no, that you have no mother, no brothers and sisters?'

'Sometimes I'm sad. I never knew my mother, so I don't know what it would have been like to have one. I would have liked brothers and sisters.' She looked at his face, so close to hers in the darkness. '*You* must be my brother.'

'Is that what you wish, that I am your brother?' His face fell.

'No.' In truth she wished for something else entirely but knew that it could never be.

'It is not what I wish too.'

'No?'

'No. This is what I wish.' He leaned towards her and kissed her lips through the wire. 'I wish this,' he whispered, 'And more.'

Ellen felt a wave of emotion flood through her. 'More?'

'Yes. More. I think you understand.' He raised his hand and once more pushed his fingers through the wire to touch the tears on her cheeks. 'And I think you also wish more.'

She ran that night back to the farm, an uneasy mix of elation, frustration and guilty despair swirling within her agile body.

*

At the end of November, the weather cleared. A near full moon appeared between scudding clouds, lending an almost daytime brightness to Ellen's walk and her meeting with Josef.

'Ha! I see you tonight, Liebling. That is good.'

'Is it?'

'Of course. You are very beautiful. Sehr schön, we say at home.'

'Sehr schön?'

'Ja! That is right.'

A sudden flurry of shouts and thumps came from the direction of one of the huts.

'What's that?' gasped Ellen nervously.

'Some men… they… er… not agree.'

'You mean they've had an argument?'

'Ja. I think they argue still.'

'But why? What is the matter?'

'Soon it is Weinachten…Christmas. The men, they wish to be with their families. They do not like to be here… prisoners.' Josef lifted his face to the moon and stared at it. 'You remember last Christmas?'

'Of course. You so ill and me looking after you.'

'And you give me sweets. I have the box still.'

'Have you?'

'Of course. When I to my home return, I have this to remember you. This year I have a gift for you and one for Netta.'

'Have you? Her heart lifted at this revelation but fell again as she thought of the Christmas to come. 'I wish you could be with us, like you were last year… only not ill, of course!'

'I wish it also.' He put his face to the wire and she kissed his lips. 'But in Germany we give gifts early – on

St Nicolas Day, the six of December. Next week I bring a gift for you. We must... how you say it? Make the most.'

Ellen shivered. 'I wish you didn't have to go back to Germany.'

The shouts came again, louder this time, and then a sudden flare of brightness. At the same time a whistle blew and the sound of running feet coming closer made them abruptly draw apart.

'Schnell! Hide!' Josef said hastily and Ellen sank into the long grass at the other side of the road and rolled into the safety of the bushes. She watched as the guard thudded into view, wrenching open the door of the hut. In the brightness, men tumbled out and the guard rounded them up at gunpoint. From the direction of the officer's hut, soldiers appeared, hurriedly pulling on jumpers and coats.

A sharp crack drew Ellen's eyes back to the hut. The windows had shattered. Flames licked around the open door. Officers were lining up the prisoners, handing out buckets, unlocking the gate. The line of men stretched towards the river, flanked by the guards. So absorbed was she by the unfolding spectacle that she didn't notice a slim figure dart out under cover of a passing cloud. When Josef crept up to her, she almost cried out with shock, forestalled by his lips pressed hard on hers.

'Josef! What are you doing? You'll be caught,' she gasped at last in a frightened chuckle.

'Like I say, Liebling, we must "make the most".' He stared at her face, pale in the moonlight, her hair wild, eyes startled as a rabbit's. 'You are very beautiful. Tonight you are the most beautiful.' He ran his fingers through the tangle of hair onto her shoulders and slowly sank with her onto the bed of dry bracken in the shelter of the bushes.

27

Something to Hide

Ellen was so shocked when the postman handed her the brown envelope that she had to sit down quickly on the old seat outside the cottage. This collision of events – the arrival of a letter from the War Office coming so soon after she had shown her feelings for Josef – took the wind out of her sails.

'Are you all right, hen?' The postman looked at her with a frown. 'It may not be as bad as you think. Your man may be injured, no more than that – and it may not be serious. Best to open it and see. I'll call Duncan to come and give you a wee bit of courage.'

By the time Duncan had been located and had hurried up to the cottage, Ellen was inside and had the open letter in her lap.

'What is it, lassie? What's happened?'

'He's coming home. He's been wounded. He's in hospital at the moment but they're sending him home to convalesce.'

'Does it say what his injuries are?'

'No.' She gave a frightened sob. 'Oh Feyther. Suppose he's lost an arm or a leg. What'll we do?' Her deceit over Josef was making her feel sick.

'We'll look after him, that's what. Anyway, lass, we've no idea what his injury is. It may be nothing much at all.' He took the letter from her and held it up to the light. 'Does it say when we're to expect him home?' He perused the writing, before taking up the envelope from the table and turning it over.

'Well, look at this. The letter's been a long time reaching us. It was written a month ago.'

Two days later a telegram was delivered. It stated that Tom would be arriving in the village at 4.04pm on Tuesday 4th December and would transport please be arranged as the soldier was in no condition to walk.

'That's tomorrow,' Ellen stammered.

'Aye, lass. You'll be excited about seeing him again. And home in time for Christmas too.'

*

As the Carlisle to Glasgow train drew into the station, Tom reached down to retrieve his crutch from under the seat. He was weary with travelling. The first train had left London at five in the morning and this one that he was now leaving was the third he had taken that day. He had heaved himself in and out of each and made his way between platforms until he felt he could do so no more.

Tucking his crutch under his arm, he made for the door. A nurse, who was accompanying another soldier into Glasgow, lifted his kitbag from the rack and Tom skilfully manoeuvred himself out of the carriage and onto the platform.

The train grumbled out of the station towards its final destination and he stood in the thinning smoke. A small group was clustered at the entrance to the platform and he watched as a woman hardly older than a girl step slowly towards him. She held the hand of a toddler and, with a shock, he realised that they were his wife and child. Ellen seemed taller and she had grown slim in his absence. Netta, only a baby when he had last seen her, had changed beyond recognition.

'Hello, Tom.' His wife's voice was quiet, subdued even. 'How are you? Here, let me help with your bag.'

'Don't I get a kiss then?' he asked.

'Aye. Of course you do. I thought maybe, after not hearing from you for such a long time...' Her voice trailed off.

'...That I didn't care for you anymore?' He finished her sentence.

'You didn't write.'

'No.' He looked over Ellen's shoulder and saw his father-in-law approaching. 'Duncan's coming. We'll talk about it later.' He bent and kissed his wife on the cheek, before holding out his hand to Duncan.

'Is that you back, lad?' His father-in-law's tone was

brusque. 'What have you done to yourself?'

'Nothing that will stop me looking after the sheep, thank goodness.' He let go of Duncan's hand and felt the soft curls of his daughter's head.

'She's grown.'

'She's nearly two.'

'I'm back just in time for her birthday.' He put a finger under her chin and tilted her head so he could scrutinise her.

Netta pulled away and looked at her mother uncertainly.

'It's a long time since she saw you. Give her time. She'll come round.'

'I've plenty of that, any road. I'll be convalescing for a couple of months, the doctor reckons.'

'What happened, Tom?'

'Shrapnel in my leg. They got it away, like, several pieces, and the wounds are healed. But one piece went into my knee and it's still very stiff. I've to use a crutch till the end of this week, the doctor says. Then I've to start walking on it to get rid of the stiffness. Any road, let's get home. We can talk about this some other time. I hope I haven't got to walk all the way!'

'Of course not. We've got the wagon.'

'Home in style then!'

Tom hobbled out of the station to the waiting wagon, pleased that he had managed to maintain the light-hearted mood he had decided upon. Archie stood patiently, hitched up to the wagon and when he saw Tom, he whinnied softly. At the sight of him, Tom's mind flew immediately to all those horses he had seen dead and maimed on the battlefield. His mouth contorted and he stepped up to the animal and buried his face in its mane to hide his emotion.

'Are you all right, Tom?' Ellen laid a hand on his arm.

'Of course I am. It's grand to see the horse again, that's all.'

He stepped into the wagon, swinging his bad leg in after him. In truth it was still a lot more painful than he was letting on, but he had had enough of the military hospital with its full complement of wounded men who would never make it back to normal life. The aura of sickness that surrounded him was dragging him down, back into the well of despair, out of which he was trying to lift himself.

How good it was to see the hills again. Even apart from the mud, the unremitting flatness of the land in which he had spent the last year and a half had been depressing. He covered his face with his hands and dug his fingers into his eye sockets, massaging the tiredness. He must stop dwelling on the scenes he had left. He was home now.

The touch of a hand on his arm made him jump and he spun round violently, almost knocking Netta off the seat. Ellen snatched back her hand and looked at him uncertainly.

He shook his head. 'I'm sorry. It's hard to get rid...
It's hard... to believe I'm home again.'

'You'll get used to it soon enough when we're back at
the cottage, won't he, Netta? We've left a special dinner
of rabbit stew and dumplings cooking in the oven, and
we've baked a cake in your honour.'

'Eh, lass. That sounds more like it. Better than the
restorative gruel we were fed in t' hospital!'

It was almost dark now but Tom could sense the
smoothness of the road along which they were
travelling. With a sickening jolt he remembered the work
that was going on in the valley. He focused his eyes on
the fields and could just make out the glint of metal
rails. He let out a bitter sigh. So, the Germans were still
here, contaminating the valley with their evil. Would he
never be free of them?

'Nearly home now.' Ellen's voice was cheerful.

'What?' he spoke sharply. 'What did you say?'

He heard her sharp intake of breath. 'Nothing,' she
muttered.

What a mistake he had made. He should never have
come home, he knew it now. Once again, he would be
face to face with the enemy, defacing and spoiling his
land. It made him sick!

He tried to push the thought to the back of his mind
when he entered the cottage. Ellen had gone to great
lengths to welcome him: stringing paper chains across

the ceiling, cooking his favourite meal, drawing his chair in front of a hearth full of crackling, pine-scented logs, fetching a stool on which to rest his injured leg. So solicitous to his every need, in fact, that he was beginning to wonder whether she had something to hide.

*

Putting his hands behind his head, Tom stared into the blackness. It was luxury to lie in a comfortable bed. Those in the hospital had been insufferably hard but, even so, they were the first beds he had known for many months. But to lie in his own was a pleasure he had thought would never again be his.

He listened to Ellen's breathing, sure she was not asleep, but he made no effort to approach her unmoving body. One failure was enough.

He had known how it would be. It was what he had feared all along. Although the manner of its failure he did not expect. Pictures constantly and unwittingly swam into his mind when he least expected or wanted. This time it had been that woman in the barn... that lovely dark-haired woman whose curls had tickled his face and who had been able to make him mad with desire, even in the midst of all that desolation and slaughter. He groaned. The lorry carrying him and his wounded colleagues away from the battlefield had passed through her village on its way to the coast. The farm and the other cottages lining the road were burned. Razed to the ground. He had stared in disbelief. How could it have happened?

Now, it was one more in a long parade of images to convince him that the world in which he was living was a sham. He was sleepwalking. But he no longer believed he would wake up.

By his side, he felt Ellen stir and get up. His eyes followed her, the pallor of her nightdress dimly visible in the darkness. He thought she had risen because of the need to relieve herself, but, no, she tiptoed softly to the window and, pulling up a chair, drew back the curtain and sat down. She rested her elbows on the windowsill and stared out at the night. The moon turned her nightdress to silver. It caught her dishevelled hair in its beams, giving her pale face a halo of light.

Tom lay watching her. There was no denying that she was lovely. In the time he had been away, she had matured from girl to woman. But there was something too that had not been there before. A distance. A secret self locked away in the inner recesses of her being. She had always been so open, so easy to read. But she was different now, remote, withdrawn. What was the reason for this? He looked at her again, so unmoving in the darkness. Could it be that the suspicions aroused during his last visit were real?

'Ellen! What are you doing there? Come back to bed.'

She spun round at his words. 'Tom! You made me

jump. I… I couldnae sleep, that's all. The moonlight is beautiful tonight. Look. Can you see it?' She pulled back the curtain and the light fell onto the bed.

'Why can't you sleep? Aren't you glad to have me home?'

'Of course I am. It's strange, that's all.' She pattered round the foot of the bed and climbed in beside him.

'You're frozen through,' he said, pulling her towards him.

'Tom. Why did you no' write to me? You don't ken how worried I was not to hear from you.'

'You know why. I were angry that you had taken that prisoner into our house when you know I would never have agreed to it.'

'And I explained why I'd done it. I don't think you believed me though.

He sighed heavily. 'I didn't … and I'm right sorry.' He kissed her forehead. 'So, there's been none of the Hun near this place since I was last home?'

'Of course not.'

'And you've not been near them, I take it?'

'Well, Netta and I have to walk past them when we visit Margaret Murdie. We've been a few times, with Iain being away, ken.'

'Well, just make sure it stays that way, do you hear me?'

He rolled away from her, staring through the uncurtained window at the distant moon.

*

He rose late, irritable and tired. He hadn't slept at all, even when Ellen had climbed out of bed to begin her day's work. He had lain listening to her as she raked the ashes of the fire and clattered the breakfast pots in the kitchen, smelled the aroma of tattie scones, newly baked. He heard the cheerful chatter of his daughter and the deeper, intermittent voice of his father-in-law, registered the slam of the door as Duncan left the cottage and strolled down the slope to the barn, his boots crunching on the frosty ground outside the bedroom window.

The sounds should have been comforting, welcoming. Instead they annoyed him, made him feel excluded. He lay there, wanting to be comforted but knowing that his irritation would spill over to wreck the homely atmosphere.

The door to the bedroom opened softly and Ellen came in with a tray of breakfast.

'You shouldn't have bothered. I were getting up,' Tom said grudgingly.

'Nothing but the best for the wounded soldier!'

'No need to remind me,' he replied, pulling himself up and watching as she settled the tray in his lap and turned to go.

Later, when she came back, he smiled at her.

'That was good.' He swung his injured leg over the side of the bed and his smile changed to a grimace.

'What's the matter?' Ellen put the tray down on the dressing table.

'Nowt. It's this knee. It feels stiffer. Happen I need to get going on it. Don't fuss though, woman. It'll be right.'

He sat in front of the fire that day while she worked, dozing but never properly falling asleep. He ate little. He tried to play with Netta, but she, still wary of him, toddled off into a corner and sat watching him from a distance, playing alone.

That night he slept... and dreamed. He was in the muddy water, up to his waist in it. He had dropped his rifle in the shell hole and, groping in the mire, he encountered body after body but no weapon. Suddenly they were under attack. 'Forward, men!' the order came from the captain. 'Forward!' But he couldn't go forward. He was sinking now; the water was up to his chest. All around his head bullets whistled and he flung himself backwards and forwards in an attempt to dodge them. He was caught like a rat in a trap, like the rats that were waiting for him to die...

'Tom! Wake up! You're dreaming again. Wake up!'

He struggled up from the depths of his nightmare and sat forward, eyes staring ahead, body quaking with fear. Ellen was kneeling on the eiderdown, her hands holding his arms, stilling him. His shirt was soaked with sweat.

Gradually it began to register that he was safe. The hammering in his chest slowly settled. He wiped his wet face on the sheet.

'I'm sorry, lass.' He looked at her, but his eyes were still glazed, unable to tear themselves away from the scene of the battlefield. 'It was the drowning, the drowning. That's what I feared. That's what happened.'

'But they pulled you out. You're safe. You're home.'

He looked round the familiar room. It felt as though he were seeing it for the first time.

'Here, help me to change into a clean shirt. I'll catch my death in this one.' He looked at his wife and said grimly, 'If not in battle, then out of it.'

*

'I'm going to get some fresh air,' Tom said the next morning, hobbling to the door where his coat had been hung.

'Do you want me to come with you?' Ellen asked.

'I can manage.'

'But what about your crutch?'

'I'm not taking it.'

'But the doctor said to use it till the end of this week.'

'It *is* nearly the end of the week, so stop nagging. Besides, all this resting isn't doing it any good. It's getting worse, not better. And I shall go mad sitting here'

Before he had gone many yards, Tom was sweating with the effort. By the time he had been out for fifteen minutes, the wounded leg was excruciatingly painful.

When he limped round the corner of the cottage, Ellen had on her coat and scarf and was pushing Netta through the doorway in the perambulator.

'Oh, Tom. You startled me.' Ellen flushed and then said quickly, 'That's you soon back.'

'Why, were you going somewhere special?'

'No, of course not. Just giving Netta some fresh air.'

'Well, go on then. I'm not stopping you.'

'Are you all right, Tom?'

'No, I'm not all right. It shouldn't be this painful. There's summat wrong wi' it, I know there is. Any road, get along with you. I'll sit here. The day's not the problem. It's me.' He eased himself painfully onto the wooden seat in front of the window and leaned back, eying Ellen and his daughter morosely.

'If you're sure, Tom. We won't be long.'

'Aye, I'm sure. I'm sorry, Ellen. I don't mean to grumble. It's that painful.' He stroked Netta's hair. 'Daddy will wave to you when you reach the road.'

That evening, Tom struggled to stay awake, though his eyes kept drifting shut. He wanted a good night's sleep, convinced that the lack of it was causing his pain, and didn't want to jeopardise his chances by retiring too early. Ellen seemed unsettled and jumpy.

'What's the matter, Ellen? You're making me nervous. Come and sit down.'

'Aye, I will. Let me put some more logs on the fire and I'll join you.'

He followed her actions as she went to the basket and carefully loaded the wood onto the embers.

'You've let it get too low.'

'Aye, I ken. But it'll soon catch.'

As if to confirm her words, a spark from the warming logs flew out with a loud crack... and then another. A sound from her husband made her turn in alarm. He was shaking and his hands were clamped over his ears.

'No! Not again! I can't stand any more. Let me get some peace. Just let me die!'

'Tom! Tom! Wake up. You're here on the farm with Netta and me. You're safe.' She shook him and abruptly he stared at her. Another spark flew upwards like a pistol shot and he gasped and stared into the fire.

'It's only the logs, Tom. Nothing more. You're safe now.'

Tom flopped back in his chair and let out a huge sigh. 'I'm sorry. I'm no good to you like this, am I?'

Ellen cradled him tightly in her arms. 'Of course you are. You've no' been well, that's all.' She kissed his cheek. 'You get to bed and I'll make you a drink of cocoa to help you sleep.'

When she carried the cocoa through, Tom was sitting on the edge of the bed.

'Look at this, lass.'

The knee of his right leg was even more swollen and an area of angry redness had developed around the scar caused by the entry of the shrapnel.

'It's nae wonder you don't feel right.' She looked up. 'I think you need to get to the hospital tomorrow and ask their help.'

'I'll not go back to one of those places again. I've had enough of hospitals to last a lifetime.'

'Then what do you suggest?' Ellen's eyes flashed. 'I can't deal with this, as well you know.'

'Oh? I thought you were the expert at nursing the wounded. Or does that skill only extend to the enemy?'

Ellen stood up quickly and walked from the room, slamming the door behind her. Tom put his head in his hands. He had done it again. He didn't intend to say that. The words just came out. He swung his throbbing leg onto the bed and lay back on the pillows. The cocoa chilled. He couldn't face it anyway.

The minutes ticked by... an hour passed. Still Ellen didn't return. Eventually he crossed the bedroom and opened the door. She was not in the room. A wave of panic swept over him. But, no, she would have gone to her father, like she always did. He had been keeping to his own side of the house, to give the two of them time alone together. He snorted. Much good it seemed to be doing!

A cold draught was coming from the corridor and, hobbling across the room, he found that the door was open. He could see her outside, motionless. She hadn't put on her coat or her hat but seemed oblivious to the cold. He came slowly towards her but she gave no indication that she had heard him, her eyes fixed on the distant road.

'Ellen!'

She wheeled round and faced him.

'I'm sorry. You're right.' His voice was contrite. 'I'll go to the hospital in the morning. Come in now. Come to bed. It's nearly twelve.'

She came slowly towards him. Her face was impassive. Tears glinted on her cheeks. He didn't know what to say.

She lifted the latch and gave a last drawn-out scrutiny of the dark valley. Then she shut the door and followed her husband into the bedroom.

28

No Change at All

The cottage hospital was entirely eclipsed by trees. Whether these had been planted to help the residents of the village forget the ill and suffering collected on their doorstep, or in an attempt to aid the patients to good health by an appreciation of nature, was not clear. But by the time of Tom's visit, the shade of the surrounding vegetation had lent a gloom to the place that no amount of optimistic words could dispel.

Ellen had brought Tom in the wagon. It was a distance of some fourteen miles and Netta, who had accompanied her parents, was weary with sitting still. Her restlessness increased as they found themselves in a slow-moving queue waiting to see the doctor.

'You take her into the village,' Tom said. 'Come back for me later.'

'Are you sure you don't want me with you?'

'Yes, yes! Quite sure.' He leaned back wearily in the chair. 'All her noise and fussing is getting on my nerves. I can't be doing with it.'

'I'll away and get some messages in that case. I'll be back to collect you in two hours or so.'

Tom watched his wife and small daughter walk to the end of the waiting room and turn to wave to him. He waved back, feeling miserable and mean-spirited. He had slept poorly, troubled with the pain in his bad leg but that was no excuse for his behaviour. Ellen, he knew, had had no more sleep than himself.

Eventually he heard his name called.

'Thomas Fairclough! Follow me, please, into the cubicle. You are to see Professor McAndrew.'

Tom rose painfully and made his way slowly across the room. In the cubicle a nurse took down particulars – date of birth, address, next of kin, and then asked him to wait. The murmur of voices carried along a corridor. He struggled to quash rising anxiety, wishing now that he had never agreed to this visit.

The curtain was flung back and a portly ageing gentleman, sporting a large white moustache and bow tie, blustered in, followed by the nurse.

'This is Thomas Fairclough, sir. He's having trouble with his leg.'

'What kind of trouble?' the professor asked, glaring at Tom.

'It's a war wound, sir. I'm convalescing. It were settling well but it's flared up again since I got home.'

'Not doing too much on it?'

'No, I'm not.'

'Let's see it then, nurse,' said the professor testily. 'We don't have all day.'

The nurse turned the sheet down to the foot of the couch and the professor stepped up, frowning when he saw the inflamed knee.

'It were shrapnel, sir,' Tom volunteered. 'They removed the pieces at the military hospital but this one has gone t' wrong way.'

'So I can see. So I can see. Interesting. Nurse! Fetch the house officer to look at this.'

'Yes, sir.'

He continued to examine the knee until the curtain was drawn back again and a woman entered. She was young and tall, with dark curly hair pulled back into a low bun at the back of her neck, and blue eyes that looked as astonished as Tom's.

'Clara! I didn't know you were working here!'

Clara threw a worried glance in the professor's direction, but he looked from one to the other in amusement.

'Ah! You know each other. Right, Miss Moxon. I would like you to tell me what we are going to do with this young man's leg.'

Clara stepped forward and looked at the damaged knee. Tom didn't take his eyes off her face. He felt his cheeks burning, at odds with her cool hands as they examined the swelling and it was only when she attempted to bend his leg that Tom yelled out with pain.

'Oh, Tom. I'm sorry. I didn't mean to hurt you.'

It was her voice, unchanged over the years, that convinced him that she was indeed real.

'That's all right, lass. You've got to do your job.' A slow blush spread up Clara's face. 'This here is the result of me doing mine.' He gave a nod in the direction of his wound.

'On the farm?' she asked.

'At Ypres.'

'You've been in the war?'

'Aye, since July last year.'

'I'd no idea.'

'So, Miss Moxon, when the two of you have finished exchanging pleasantries, what do you think?'

'There is obvious infection there, sir. I suggest we use a poultice to bring the infection out. It may need lancing if pus has formed.'

'Yes. Good. What else?'

'There is a possibility that there is a foreign body in there – a piece of shrapnel, maybe, that's been left behind. So it may need another operation to examine it and remove anything that's still there.'

'Very good. And what if nothing is done?'

'It may settle down by itself, if the body fights the infection successfully. But to do nothing would be risky. If the knee joint is involved, continuing inflammation could lead to arthrodesis.'

'Which is…?' the professor prompted.

'An inability to bend the knee, sir.'

'And... what else?'

'I'm sorry, sir. What do you mean?'

'What else may happen, woman, if we do nothing?'

Clara's voice dropped, though not enough to prevent Tom hearing her next words. 'He could lose his leg, sir.'

'Precisely! He could lose his leg,' the professor repeated in a louder voice. 'So I suggest to you, sir, that you do exactly what you are told. I want a hot poultice applied to the leg, nurse. We will see him tomorrow morning and reassess the knee. Come, Miss Moxon. There are plenty more patients waiting for us.'

Tom stared at the swinging curtain, still finding it hard to believe in the apparition that had, until a second ago, been standing in front of him. He smiled slowly, and when the nurse returned to do his dressing, he hardly felt it when the thin bandage was wrapped round his knee and a thick layer of steaming kaolin applied to it.

His blissful distraction continued as he sat in the room outside, waiting for his wife to return. He was sure that at any minute Clara would burst through the open door to greet him. But although the nurse went backwards and forwards about her business, there was no further sign of either doctor. It mattered little though. Tomorrow he would be back. And surely then Clara would find time to talk to him. Whatever happened, he would now have no qualms about returning to the hospital. Perhaps his wound was the best thing that could have happened to him.

*

The euphoria of the morning's visit stayed with him during the day. He dozed in the chair and none of the nightmarish dreams returned to trouble his sleep. He had said very little to Ellen, apart from the fact that they wished to see him the following day. He did not tell her who 'they' were, preferring to keep the delicious secret to himself.

There was no change at all in Clara – the dark curly hair, the quiet self-assurance that he had always loved about her, the steady, almost stern gaze. He thought guiltily of the photograph crushed beneath his boot into the mud. If anything, she was even more lovely than when that picture had been taken. When had he last seen her? It must have been nearly two years ago, the day he had driven her back to the village to catch her train. Before his marriage to Ellen.

He shivered. The weather was getting colder and he hoped it wouldn't snow.

Ellen brought him soup but he barely touched it. She tried to tempt him with cups of tea, but he could swallow no more than a couple of mouthfuls.

'You'll no' get better unless you eat,' she said, putting a hand to his forehead. You feel as though you are starting with a fever.'

'I'm all right, lass. Don't fuss.' He smiled at her and dozed again.

*

Tom retired to bed early, seeking to allay his restlessness in sleep, but sleep eluded him. If only Ellen would come, he would at least have company.

He dozed and suddenly woke, and still her side of the bed remained unoccupied. He listened but there was no sound, tried to rise but his head felt heavy and he was slightly nauseous. The candle was burning low now. It must be hours that he had been lying alone.

'Ellen! Are you there?' He heard the sound of footsteps and she entered the room.

'What's the matter? Do you feel bad?'

'I were wondering if you were going to stay up all night.'

'I'm sorry. I didnae realise how late it was.'

He watched her as she undressed.

'I would have thought you'd come to keep me company. They say I might have to stay in hospital.'

'You didn't tell me that.' Ellen stared at him, alarmed.

'I'm telling you now. They might even have to operate.' His voice was drowsy. 'They said I could lose my leg if I didn't do what they told me.'

'Then why did you say nothing?' Her voice broke.

'Because I didn't want you making all this fuss.'

'But I've a right to know. I'm your wife.'

'And I've a right to expect you by my side at night. Like you say, you're my wife.'

She opened her mouth to reply, but the words remained unspoken. She hesitated, just for a moment, then blew out the candle and climbed in beside him.

29

Changing the Face of the Valley

Ellen sat at Tom's side as the train made its meandering way towards the city. She was frightened. Frightened of what would happen to Tom. Frightened of the city, about which she had heard so much but never visited. She glanced at her husband, amazed at his composure.

'What are they going to do, Tom?'

'The consultant said he will have to operate. He says there may be shrapnel left and, in any case, he wants to drain the knee.'

'But why do you need to go to Glasgow? Can't he do the operation in the cottage hospital?'

'He doesn't do operations there. All his staff live and work in the Royal Infirmary and it's them who will look after me. Don't fret. I don't expect you to come and visit me every day.'

'I want to... but I can't very well, right enough. It's too far. I would be all day travelling, and we don't have the money. And, apart from all that, what would I do with Netta? I can't bring her with me and Father's too busy to look after her more than occasionally.'

'I've managed for the last year and a half. I'm sure I'll cope. And I'll be in good hands.' He looked out of the window and smiled. Ellen followed his gaze. With a pang of disquiet, she noticed the city buildings encroaching on the railway. In no time at all, the train was clanking and hissing to a stop in the cheerless echoing building that was Central Station.

On questioning, they discovered that it was a considerable distance to the Infirmary, and they made the rest of the journey in a horse-drawn cab, Ellen anxiously attempting to remember the landmarks, for she had insufficient money to make the return journey to the station in the same way.

At the gatehouse, Tom handed the professor's hastily scribbled note to the nurse and was directed to the surgical ward. By the time they had reached their destination, he was exhausted. He slumped down in a chair in the corridor and blew out his cheeks.

'I'm fair lathered,' he said, wiping his brow with a handkerchief. 'Get me a drink, lass, will you?'

Ellen knocked timidly on the door of the office and watched as an official-looking nurse stood up and bustled towards her.

'Yes, how can I help?'

'I have this note from the professor... and my husband would like a drink, please.'

'Certainly not.' The nurse scanned the piece of paper.

'Professor McAndrew will be operating on him. There's to be nil by mouth.' She called to a young nurse who was walking towards the ward. 'Nurse Thomson, put Mr Fairclough in bed 18 and take his particulars. The professor will be here directly.'

'Yes, Sister. Follow me, please,' Nurse Thomson said, smiling at Tom.

Tom struggled out of the chair and limped behind the nurse, leaving Ellen stranded in the middle of the corridor. She sat down again and waited for what seemed like hours. The immensity and strangeness of the hospital cowed her and she longed to be back in the countryside where she felt comfortable. But she didn't want to abandon her husband here with little chance of seeing him until he returned home. Right enough, he had been grumpy and disagreeable since his return but, given the infection in his leg, this was only to be expected. Maybe after treatment he would be easier to live with.

Just as she was beginning to think they had forgotten her, Nurse Thomson reappeared and beckoned Ellen.

'I'll give you two minutes to say goodbye to your husband. Bed 18, halfway down the right-hand side of the ward. Be quick though… the professor will be doing his round soon.'

Several pairs of eyes, belonging to those patients who were alert enough to show interest in their surroundings, followed her as she tiptoed self-consciously between the beds. Tom's high colour contrasted with the whiteness of the sheets between which he lay, their pristine neatness disrupted by the presence of a cradle over his bad knee to protect it from the weight of the bedclothes.

'I'll see you soon, Tom. We'll all miss you.'

'I know that, lass. Look after yourself and Netta, and don't fret. I'll be well cared for here.'

She gave him a quick peck on the cheek, conscious that the nearest patients were still watching, and turned to go. The swing doors were abruptly pushed back and a cluster of white-coated individuals entered. The ward sister immediately left her office and stepped up to a large man sporting a bow tie. This, thought Ellen, must be the professor. Surrounding him were two or three other men and a woman. She frowned, trying to think where she had seen the woman before. Flattening herself against the wall as the group swept past, she hurried out of the ward, along the endless corridor and down the wide sweep of steps that led to the ground floor and out of the hospital. It was later than she thought. If she didn't hurry, she would miss her train. She ran through the busy streets, weaving round afternoon shoppers, who seemed in no rush to make room for her, and recognised the station up ahead. She slowed, knowing that now she would be back in time to resume care of Netta so that her father could make a final round of the sheep before darkness fell.

At the thought of Netta, she came to an abrupt standstill, realisation flooding through her. The woman doctor accompanying the professor was none other than Tom's friend Clara. Clara, who had visited them on that snowy Christmas two years ago and helped to bring Netta into the world.

Showing her ticket to the guard, she hurried onto the platform, where the train was waiting to take her back to the peace and security of home. She chose a carriage and sank back gratefully in a window seat, catching her breath. How had she not realised at once that it was Clara amongst the group of doctors?

She felt vague stirrings of the earlier jealousy that had at times troubled her. She had never really known how close the friendship between her husband and Clara Moxon had been, but she recalled the relish with which he had anticipated Clara's visit to the farm, even if that visit had turned out somewhat different from what they had all expected.

Had Tom seen her on their first visit to the cottage hospital? Ellen considered. He had not mentioned it, but he had been very loath to tell her what had gone on and he had seemed much happier after the visit.

Her train of thought was interrupted by a small, bearded gentleman, dressed smartly in top hat and morning coat, who stepped into the carriage and sat down opposite her.

The train began to pull out of the station and Ellen stood up to remove her coat.

'Allow me to give you a hand.' The smartly dressed

gentleman rose to help.

'Thank you, sir,' Ellen smiled.

'May I introduce myself,' the man continued. 'My name is Angus MacPherson... Sir Angus MacPherson,' he said with an air of authority.

'And I'm Ellen Fairclough. I've just been to visit my husband in hospital.'

'I'm on my way to London to speak at a conference of civil engineers. Do you know what a civil engineer is, my child?'

'Er, yes, sir, I think so. You build bridges and roads and reservoirs, like the one that's being built in the valley. My father and my husband are both shepherds on the Douglas farm.'

'Ah yes. I know the one. Well, what a coincidence!' The engineer's eyes twinkled as he looked at Ellen. 'So, what do you think of my little undertaking.'

'You mean *you're* building the reservoir in our valley?' She stared at him in guarded admiration as he nodded. 'Well, I find it's interesting, right enough, though there's plenty of things I don't like. And my husband doesnae like it at all. He wishes the valley could be left in peace.'

'You can't stand in the way of progress, my dear. Tell me, why is your husband in hospital?'

'He has to have an operation on his knee... a war wound.'

'Ah, so he's been at the front. A brave man then. I

wonder if he realises that the towns for which this water is intended are making the guns and bullets that he has been firing at the enemy.'

'I'm not sure that he does.'

'Well, I hope he is soon fully recovered and back with you again.'

'If he recovers fully, I suppose he'll have to go back and fight.'

'I suppose he must.' Sir Angus leaned back and considered the view from the window for a minute or two. 'So tell me, Ellen, have you been to the head of the valley and seen the excavations there?'

Ellen looked at him sharply. 'Aye, I've been.'

'Magnificent, are they not?'

'I was there when the German prisoner was killed by the mud slide.' Her voice was low.

'Oh, I see. Yes, that was most regrettable. Still, these unfortunate things happen when big projects are undertaken. And at least he was not one of our men.'

Ellen's eyes widened angrily and she sat forward in her seat. 'You have no right to say that! He was a good man. He was very kind to me and my baby. And he was well educated. He used to teach at the university. So, no different from yourself really.'

'No indeed.' Sir Angus looked suitably humbled. 'However, you must agree that the men are paid a wage equal to that of our own men, were they free to work on the site. It's one of the dangers of such work.'

'But Oliver Tauber would not have been doing this work if he had been in his own country.'

'My dear Ellen, if Oliver Tauber and his like had been getting on with their work in their own country, none of this fighting would be going on, your husband would be at home tending the sheep and I would have my usual labouring workforce to carry out my plans.'

Ellen could see that he was right so she leaned back and sighed.

'How did you come to know this German? Have you been chatting to the men and hindering their work?' said Sir Angus, his twinkling eyes at odds with his stern questions.

'I looked after one of the men. He took ill with pneumonia soon after they arrived. Oliver came from time to time and interpreted for Josef.'

'And he recovered well? You were a good nursemaid?'

She laughed. 'He recovered, though he's no' so strong as the others. It has left him with a weakness of the chest.'

'They are good workers, the prisoners of war, I will say that. The project has progressed well with their help. And what does this man do in his own land, this Josef? Have you found that out too?'

'Aye. He's a musician. He plays the piano.'

'Well, let us hope that the war will soon be over and then everyone can get back to doing what they want to do. I only hope there are enough young men left to finish my reservoir at the end of it all.'

Josef! She hadn't been able to see him since the fight at the camp and he would have no idea that her husband had returned. He would assume she wanted nothing more to do with him and nothing could be further from the truth. She had been out every night, walking along the valley to the camp in the hopes of seeing him. With her husband home, that was no longer possible. With an end to the war, she would never be able to do what she most wanted to do.

'This is your station, I believe.' Sir Angus broke into her reverie and Ellen jumped out of her seat in alarm, afraid that the train would depart with her still aboard. 'Thank you for your company,' Sir Angus said. 'I shall look out for you next time I am in the valley.'

The whistle blew and the train pulled out of the station, taking Sir Angus with it. Ellen left the platform and walked down the slope and across the fields. She was thinking how strange it was that she had met, quite by accident, the man who was changing the face of the valley and had, by employing the prisoners of war, inadvertently influenced the whole focus of her life in the hills.

30

Different This Time

'I think I'm expecting another wee one,' Ellen confided in Margaret Murdie one day in mid-January. The weather had turned milder and she had taken the opportunity to walk with Netta to the Murdie farmhouse. She wondered whether she might see Josef during her walk, but the prisoners were at the far end of the embankment and failed to show any sign of having noticed her and she had completed her walk with a heavy heart.

'That's good news, lassie. I'm very pleased for you.'

'Are you? I'm frightened after last time. I would hate the same to happen again.'

'Then you must be more careful this time and rest a little every day.'

'No' so easy with Netta so energetic.'

'No, I ken that. But I'll help if you would like me to.'

'Aye, I would that.'

'When will the baby be due?'

'Oh... I don't know exactly... towards the end of

August I think.'

'Celebrating Tom's arrival home, were you?' The older woman gave her a sly wink.

Ellen gave an unconvincing smile.

'Does he know about it?'

'No. I havenae told him yet. I wanted to be sure first and I don't get to see him often. It's such a difficult journey to the hospital and more than I can easily afford. He didn't take the news of the last one well. In fact, he's no' said much about it at all, so I don't really ken what he thought.'

'That's all water under the bridge, hen. He'll be different this time.'

'Aye, well I hope so.'

Robert Murdie came in, pulling off his boots at the door. He sat down in his ancient armchair and rubbed cold hands together in front of the fire.

'How are you, Mr Murdie?'

'Mustn't grumble, hen. It's no' been such a bad winter, which is just as well with no Iain here to help us.'

'They say the war may soon be over.'

'Och! They say all sorts. I'll believe it when it comes.'

Margaret swung the kettle over the fire to make her husband a cup of tea.

It was cosy, Ellen thought... Iain's parents either side of the fire, Netta playing contentedly on the rug with a pile of wooden bricks that had once belonged to Iain.

Their conversation was interrupted by a knock at the door.

'Shall I go?' said Ellen, jumping up.

'Aye, lass. It'll be Richard from the farm at the end. He promised he'd drop by with some oatmeal.'

But it wasn't Richard. It was the postman. He nodded to Ellen and, without saying a word, passed her a brown envelope addressed to Mr and Mrs Robert Murdie. Ellen lingered at the door, fear clutching at her chest, watching the postman cross the rough ground back to the track.

'Is it Richard, hen? Tell him to come in. He'll need to be paid.' Robert's voice reached her, as if in a dream.

'It's a telegram.' Ellen walked slowly into the room, carrying the envelope as though it would burn her.

'Here! Give it to me,' Margaret said, intercepting her husband who had half-risen from his chair.

Ellen wished that she could wind back time. She handed the envelope to Margaret and turned to the window. Margaret tore open the envelope and began to read aloud:

Regret to inform you that Corporal Iain Murdie died of wounds on 10th January, 1918. He showed great bravery to the end. I can assure you that his death was immediate and that he did not suffer. May I offer you my sincere condolences on your loss. Yours sincerely, H. C. Morton-Clarke (Captain).

For a second no one said anything. Ellen was conscious of Netta's chattering and the clunk of building bricks one on another.

'H. C. Morton-Clarke (Captain),' Margaret repeated in a monotone. 'Poor man, to have to write such letters.'

Robert staggered out of his chair by the fire and came slowly across the room to put an arm round his wife. 'There, there, lassie. Come and sit down here by the fire.'

'Oh, Robert. Our lad. Our only lad.' Her body began to shake and tears overflowed down her cheeks. 'He was everything we had… everything,' she choked.

Robert was steering her towards a chair, when, without warning, he uttered a groan of pain and doubled over, clutching his chest. Margaret tried to hold him as he sunk slowly to the floor.

Ellen, until now transfixed by the impact of the news, came to and ran to help. Together, she and Margaret made him comfortable where he lay. He was only half conscious and his face was ashen.

'It's his heart again, like last time. The shock has brought on another attack.' Margaret, her own face drained of colour under the influence of this double blow, stared at Ellen.

'We need to get him to bed,' Ellen gasped.

'How can we? He's a big man and heavy.'

'Then I'll find someone to help us. And I'll fetch the doctor. Mind Ellen for me while I'm gone.'

Margaret lifted her head and there was bleakness in her eyes. 'Last time this happened it was Iain that was here to help,' she said slowly. 'What am I going to do without him?' Her voice rose in a wail.

*

The prisoners were still at work at the far end of the reservoir when Ellen approached. One of them saw her and she heard him shout towards his colleagues.

Several of them laughed at the man's words.

'It is Josef you are looking for, is it not? He will be very happy,' the prisoner sneered across the intervening mud. He turned towards his workmates. 'Music boy! Hier ist ihr Fräulein.' His eyes narrowed. 'Perhaps now we all get some sleep. Every night he wakes us when he goes outside to look for you.'

Ellen hesitated. She saw an officer approach and reprimand the prisoner, who returned sullenly to his place in the line.

'Mrs Fairclough. Is anything the matter?'

'It's Mr Murdie. He's taken a pain in the chest. I think it's his heart. And there's no one to help us.'

'Give me a few minutes to gather some help together and I'll be with you. You get back to the farm.'

She turned and sped back to the farmhouse.

'How is he?' she gasped, clattering into the parlour. Margaret was cradling her husband's head in her lap.

'He's rallied once or twice and complained of the pain. Have you found anyone to help?'

'Aye, one of the officers. He's fetching some others.'

'I have medicine left over from his last attack. I wonder if it's safe to use?'

Ellen stayed with Robert while his wife went in search of the bottle of medicine. Her thoughts turned to Iain and their conversation when she had last seen him. She remembered the compliments he had paid her, his lingering farewell kiss. They had been good friends but she had never thought of him as more than that. Perhaps if he had given her these compliments before she had met Tom it might have been different. Strange how things turned out. Strange and sad. Now Iain would never have the chance of a wife and family and Robert, if he pulled through, and Margaret would be forever bereft of not only a son but also grandchildren.

A hammering on the door made her start, and the officer entered with three others – a second army officer and two prisoners. She registered Josef's face as they came forward to help and the sight of him brought a degree of comfort.

'We need to get him to his bed and we can't manage on our own,' Ellen said immediately.

'You're not to do any lifting in your condition.'

Margaret bustled forward and took charge again. Ellen stood back and watched as the men picked up Robert between them and carried him from the room. Josef gave her a quizzical look as he passed and she stared back, unable to give the explanation that he must have been seeking.

After they had made Robert comfortable and Margaret had encouraged him to take a spoonful of the medicine, the men went to leave, promising that someone would drive to the village to get the doctor.

'Can we give you a lift home, Mrs Fairclough? After all, it's on our way,' one of the officers offered.

'Thank you, but I must stay with Mrs Murdie and make sure she's alright. She's just had news that her son has been killed in the war, you see.'

'Oh. I'm very sorry, ma'am. I'd not have brought the prisoners if I'd known.'

Margaret Murdie looked at the group dispassionately. 'No matter.' Tears flowed down her cheeks. 'I dare say the mothers sitting round their fires in Germany are grieving just as much for their sons as I am for mine.'

*

Ellen stayed until the doctor had driven away in his trap. Night had fallen when she and Netta left the Murdie farmhouse, promising Margaret that she would return the following morning.

Captain Cameron-Dyet was outside with a horse and wagon. Instinctively Ellen looked at the seat next to his, but it was empty.

'I insist on giving you a lift and won't listen to any refusal. It's been an exhausting day for you,' the captain called down.

'Thank you, Captain. I wouldn't refuse. I'm very glad to see you.'

The captain jumped from the wagon and manoeuvred the perambulator into the back. He helped her into the front seat and swung Netta up after her. Ellen gave him a weary smile.

'It's been a sad day's work, Mrs Fairclough. Iain Murdie will be a loss as a son and as someone to continue the family farm.'

'It'll no' be long before the family farm is under water,' Ellen muttered, clutching Netta close.

The captain said nothing.

'How is Josef, Captain?' Ellen continued after a few minutes' silence.

'He's working hard. They are all working hard. They are a good band of men... considering. Of course, there are a few disagreements. They would hardly be human if there were not.'

'They must wish they could have been with their families for Christmas.'

'Indeed.'

'And what of your husband, Mrs Fairclough?'

'He came home on sick leave in early December. But his wounded leg got worse instead of better, so he's back in hospital again at the moment.'

'I'm sorry to hear that. I do hope he's home again soon.'

'Yes, sir. Thank you.'

The captain glanced at her and then gave the reins a flick to hurry the horse.

'We haven't visited the graveyard for some time, Josef and I. Would you care to come with us next week, if the weather stays fine?'

'Oh aye, very much, Captain.'

If the captain noticed Ellen's sudden animation, he made no indication of having done so.

*

'It's good to see you, Josef. I was worried that you might have got into trouble.' She glanced at the captain but he was occupied with steering the horse and cart over the small bridge outside her cottage. She took Josef's hand in her own.

'No. No... all is good.' He turned down the corners of his mouth, as if to contradict what he had just said. I am not... found out... Is that how you say it? But you? Are you well? I... I am worrying about you. You are to bear a child. Am I right? Is this what Frau Murdie says?'

he whispered.

Ellen glanced at the captain, but his eyes were staring ahead through the gloom. 'Aye. Aye, that's right.' She was ill at ease, embarrassed by his questioning.

'I am sorry. You wish not to speak of these things?' There was a pause. 'Ellen, I think I do not please you.'

'Oh no. It's not that. It's only... my husband has come home.' Tears glinted in her eyes.

A long pause. 'I understand.'

Ellen heard the dejection in his voice and her heart missed a beat. 'That's why I couldn't meet you. He came back and he was ill and there was no chance for me to leave the farm.'

'And he is better now?'

'No. At least, I'm not sure. He's in the hospital in Glasgow. He's had an operation on his knee. I don't see him often because it's too far to go.'

'So.' He hesitated. 'You wish to meet again as we did? Or maybe you feel that this is wrong?'

'Yes, I do think it's wrong,' she said slowly but definitely. But almost immediately, a picture of Clara in her white coat sprang to mind. Drawing a rapid breath, she continued, 'No. No. Forget what I said. It isn't wrong... not really. I don't have many friends... and I have one less now that Iain is dead. Why shouldn't we talk... at least until my husband is home again?'

31

My Country and My People

Three weeks after receiving the news of his son, Robert Murdie's heart failed. Ellen was at Margaret's side when it happened.

'I was sure he was on the mend,' Margaret said several days later, dabbing her eyes with a handkerchief. 'He seemed so much better, did he no'?'

'But the doctor warned us that it would be touch-and-go for the first month.'

'Aye, he did that. I daresay the news of Iain was too much for his weak heart to cope with.'

'What will you do now, Margaret?' Ellen studied Margaret's weathered face across the kitchen table.

'Do? What can I do but stay here and run the farm. I've nowhere else to go. If I had other sons or daughters...' She left the sentence unfinished.

'How will you manage?'

Margaret shrugged. 'There are the farm workers. I hope they'll be able to do most things between them. We do have another shepherd, apart from Robert, and we take on extra at lambing time. Of course, we may have to sell off some of the flock in order to cope.' She sighed. 'It's only a matter of time anyway until the land is flooded and I have to move. At least Robert has been spared that… and Iain too. He would have taken over from his father eventually and I think it would have broken his heart to see the farm disappear under water.'

*

Robert Murdie's death meant yet another grave to visit when Ellen went with the captain and Josef to the village. Their visits were less now, for the captain had several times been called to Glasgow for meetings with his superiors and it was imperative that the prisoners continue to work hard on the reservoir for the duration of their stay.

On the days when the weather was no longer their accomplice, the captain drove the truck. The opportunity for conversation then was limited, for the journey took less time. But as the first hint of spring returned to the valley, he had the horse harnessed up to the wagon and resumed the evening drive.

'You sit here and rest, Liebling. I will tidy the graves.' Josef indicated the soft new grass that was carpeting the worn-out floor of the graveyard and Ellen sank down gratefully. She was not finding this pregnancy easy and preparations for lambing were taking up everyone's time and energy. In addition, she had only the day before paid Tom an exhausting visit. He, in contrast, had looked happy and rested.

'The army officers – they say that the war may soon be at an end.' Josef glanced behind him at the captain who was brushing dead leaves from Oliver's grave. 'They say that America help you to win.' He pulled a bunch of withered flowers from the vase on Janet Tonner's grave and replaced them with the ones Ellen had brought with her.

Ellen said nothing.

'There are many U-boats sink now. I think many of my colleagues die.'

'I hope it will soon be over. What's it all for anyway? So many people killed. Such a waste!'

'You know how it will be when the war ends?'

'What do you mean?' Ellen replied, knowing how it would be.

Josef glanced behind him again but the captain's attention was on the small stone recently placed on the grave in front of him.

OLIVER TAUBER 1877-1917. R.I.P.

Josef lifted Ellen's hand to his lips and kissed her fingers one by one.

'It will mean...' He raised his eyes to meet hers. 'That I return to my country and my people.'

Ellen turned her face away to hide the tears that were coursing down her cheeks.

*

Time was running out. There was nothing they could do about it. In desperation, Ellen resumed her midnight walks to the compound. She had news to tell Josef. She stood up against the wire, yearning to be closer to him, encircle him with a comforting arm. He rubbed her fingers softly.

'Josef.'

'Yes, Liebling. What is it?'

'I went to visit Tom.'

She felt his fingers tighten on hers.

'Yes? How is he?'

'Much better. They say he can come home soon.'

'And then we will no longer meet?'

Ellen was silent. Josef raised a hand and his fingers touched her cheek, feeling the tears that were making slow progress down her face.

'What can we do?' His voice was a murmur.

'I don't know,' she whispered. 'I don't know. I... I can't bear the thought of not seeing you.'

Josef stared upwards at the indifferent stars and his voice shook with passion. 'It is all impossible. You are married to a good man. I must return to Germany. My parents wait there with Marthe, the girl they wish me to marry. When this war ends, we will both still be prisoners.'

'Tom may return to the front if the war does not end soon,' Ellen said, the words making her feel sick with disloyalty, even as they left her mouth.

'Is he happy that you have the baby?' Josef asked in a matter-of-fact tone.

'I don't know. He hasn't said much about it.'

'And you? Are you happy?'

'About the baby? Yes, very happy.'

'That then is good.'

Ellen studied his shadowed face. 'Josef. There is something …'

'What is it?'

Again, a prolonged pause before she answered his questioning gaze with a sad smile. She put her face to the wire and kissed him. 'I will never forget you,' she said simply.

*

Tom looked up from the chair, where he was idly perusing the newspaper, to see his wife and child walking towards him. Children were not allowed on the ward but the sister in charge had no option but to let the little girl in with her mother, there being no one else to take care of her.

'Is that you ready for home, Tom?'

Tom looked his wife up and down. Her hair lacked its usual shining vigour and the skin of her face was colourless. Netta, on the other hand, was bouncing with energy.

'Aye. I was waiting on you bringing my clothes. And how's my little girl been keeping?' He snatched Netta up and balanced her on his good knee. 'There's someone here wants to meet you.'

'Less noise on the ward, please, Mr Fairclough. I suggest your wife and child wait outside while you get dressed.' The ward sister turned on her heel and made her way back to the office, shoes squeaking on the polished floor.

'That's us telled,' Ellen said with a laugh. 'I'll take Netta into the waiting room. You find us there when you're ready.'

Fifteen minutes later the door opened. He was not alone.

'Here she is. Here's my little girl.' Tom stooped down and picked up Netta.

'Hello, Ellen.' It was Clara who stood behind Tom. 'How lovely to see you again. And this is Netta. I would never have recognised her. She's grown a bit since I held her in my arms. She's got your looks, Tom – the same dark hair and determined mouth at any rate.'

Tom blushed with pride, and ruffled Netta's unruly hair.

'And how are you, Ellen? Are you keeping well?'

'Aye, well enough, thank you. And yoursel'? You're a proper doctor now then?'

'Yes, a proper doctor now. And I don't mind admitting you gave me quite a scare when I saw you last, but all's well that ends well,' she concluded, laying a hand on Netta's dark hair.

Ellen nodded but said nothing.

'Let's hope that, if you have another, it's less of a surprise.'

'But I am having another. And I lost one in between. I'm surprised Tom didn't tell you.'

Tom felt his anger rise. 'Clara's got more to do than listen to all our problems.' He turned to Clara. 'I were away at the front when she lost the babby. And this one, well, I've hardly been at home since I got back, so there's been no time to even think about it.'

'No, indeed. Still, you can go home now and have some time together. Hopefully there should be no further problems.'

'And what I said to you earlier?' Tom asked.

'What was that, Tom?'

'About you paying us a visit. You will come, won't you?'

'I promise… though it won't be for a while. I have to complete my house officer posts. At the moment I have very little time off, even to sleep.'

Clara opened the door and the family made their way to the exit. Tom held out his hand and shook Clara's, before pulling her towards him in order to plant a kiss on her cheek. The doctor jerked back and then, to cover any embarrassment, bent down and kissed the top of Netta's head.

'Goodbye, little one. I promise to come and see you one day. And perhaps then,' she concluded, looking at Ellen. 'you will have a second baby for me to coo over!'

Tom hid his frustration over the disappointing farewell by setting off along the street at a pace that his newly mended leg found difficult to sustain. He arrived at the station bad-tempered and ill-at-ease with his wife, his child and, most of all, himself.

Throughout the slow journey through the outskirts of Glasgow, Tom's temper did not improve. Although he had determined while in the hospital that he would give his wife every consideration on his return, her listlessness and down-at-heel appearance annoyed him. In his mind he still carried the attractive and intelligent image of Clara. Back in the cottage his irritation spilled over into angry words.

'What's the matter, woman? Aren't you glad to see me home?' he shouted at her when she silently got up from the table and began to clear the dishes.

Duncan looked up sharply. 'Dinnae shout at the lass. It's been hard for her too, ken. This war's taking its toll on us all, not just those at the front line.'

'Aye, but I think those of us who've been at the front line deserve a little more consideration than they're getting at the moment.' Tom stared at his wife's back as she poured water into the teapot. She said nothing, but when he saw her hand trembling as she placed his mug of tea on the table, he suddenly felt guilty and covered her hand with his own. She snatched it away.

'At least you're here. There's Iain Murdie dead and now his father has died too, of a broken heart.'

'I'm sorry, lass. I weren't thinking. Come and sit down a minute and drink your tea. I'll help you put Netta to bed.'

'Aye. That would be good. And she would like her daddy to read her a bedtime story. It'll give me time to wash the dishes and tidy up. Then I think we all need an early night after the day we've had.'

*

A letter for Tom arrived three weeks after his return home from the hospital. He was requested to attend a tribunal at Company Headquarters in two days' time to reassess his fitness for active service. He stared at the letter in dismay that quickly escalated into a sickening dread. He had hoped that the considerable disability he had suffered would render him unfit to be returned to the front and that he would be allowed to live out the rest of the war in the peace of the farm. He folded the letter quickly and stuffed it into his pocket.

His leg had healed well with the help of the staff of

the Royal Infirmary, and his daily walks were beginning to relieve the stiffness and pain. In a few days' time lambing would start and he had been hoping to do his share of the extra work. With rising anger, he trudged across the field behind the cottage and set off up the hill to his favourite vantage point. In his heart of hearts, he knew what the outcome of his interview would be. There was no escaping his duty. Men with worse injuries than his had been returned to the front.

His anger was made the greater by the knowledge of Clara's promise to visit, and the probability now of his not being there to see her. The thought of it had lessened the loneliness he had felt since his departure from the hospital. There, she had been a daily visitor to his bedside and no one knew how hard it was for him to live without her now.

He sat until dusk began to blur his vision. Thinking he ought to move, still he sat, until the dog let out a short bark and wagged her tail. Looking down the slope, he could see a figure slowly approaching. When it drew near, he recognised his wife.

'Thank goodness,' she said breathlessly. 'I was beginning to worry that you had took badly with your leg. What are you doing up here so late?'

'I've been walking. Getting strong again, as I'm meant to do.'

Ellen glanced at him warily. 'I only asked because I'm worried about you.'

'Well, don't be. I can look after myself. Any road, why are you up here. Aren't you supposed to be looking after our child?'

'Father's taken her to visit Margaret. They're not back yet.'

He followed her gaze along the valley. 'She'll be all alone then now, will Margaret Murdie'

'Aye.'

'Will she continue on her own?'

'I don't ken. The farm will be flooded when the reservoir is finished.'

'Oh aye, the reservoir,' he said bitterly. 'Nothing's going to stop the reservoir. Tell me, are those Hun still working on it?'

'Aye. They're still here.'

'It's disgraceful. They've no right.'

'It's no' easy for them.'

'Ah! You would know all about it, would you? I've told you before, you stay away from them or you'll have me to answer to.' He took hold of her hand and pulled her roughly down onto the grass. 'You're mine and don't you forget it.'

He could see her eyes widen with fright in the dusk and the thought that his wife might be cowed by him only inflamed him more. She had trapped him into this marriage against his will and he was going to show her what her duties as a wife should be. His hands began to fumble with the buttons of her jacket.

'What are you doing, Tom?' she uttered, as he forced her to lie down. 'Not here, Tom. Please!'

He stopped her pleading with a hand over her mouth. 'Lie still, woman. You'll do as I please, for a change. I've had more than enough of your excuses.'

He felt her body go limp beneath him and the gesture reminded him of his vow to treat his wife with consideration. Uttering a colourful curse beneath his breath, he rolled off her, snatched up his stick, let out a shrill whistle to the dog and strode off down the hill.

Ellen sat up and, for several minutes, remained motionless. Eventually she got to her feet and slowly followed in her husband's footsteps to the cottage.

32

Very Much Mistaken

The decision had come to her while she sat in the near-dark at the top of the hill. Now she waited until her husband's regular breathing indicated that he was asleep. Putting her feet to the floor, she slipped carefully out of bed and stepped soundlessly into the living room, where she had left her clothes. Dressing by the dwindling light of the fire, she paused to make sure there was no sound from either her husband or her daughter and slipped from the house. She tiptoed to the track by way of the grass, so her progress would be silent. It was only when she was free of the farm that she began to hurry. At the road, she turned towards the encampment and half ran, half walked the remaining distance. As she neared the dark outline of its huts, her heart was racing. Crouching behind a convenient bush, she waited.

She didn't have to wait for long. Josef was easily recognisable by his slim build and the intermittent cough that he made unsuccessful attempts to keep under control. She saw him leave the hut and close the door

337

quietly behind him. He walked over to the barbed wire and stood so still that he seemed almost to melt into the darkness. Looking to the right and left to make sure no one was coming, she softly called his name. Immediately he was alert.

'It is you, Liebling?' he whispered.

'Aye.' She stepped from her cover and crossed the intervening space.

'I miss you very much.'

'I had to see you. I can't stand it'

'How do you mean?'

'I can't stand not seeing you and… I can't stand the way my husband is with me.'

A distant footstep alerted Josef.

'Schnell! Go to the bush… quickly. The guard comes.'

Ellen regained her cover and crouched down, hardly daring to breathe.

Josef and the guard exchanged a few sentences. She couldn't catch what they said but their tone suggested a friendly enough conversation. The night watch must be used to Josef's habitual insomnia. She heard the guard's measured steps as he continued on his beat, and crept out from her hiding place.

'You tell me about your husband,' Josef said anxiously. 'What you mean, "how he is with you"?'

'He… he gets so angry. He is cruel to me.'

'What is this "cruel"?'

'He is rough with me.'

'He is rough with you?' Josef's voice was incredulous. 'But why?'

'I don't make him happy. I annoy him. I don't know what it is. I have never made him happy.' She shrugged.

'That is bad, Liebling. He has hurt you now?' Josef's voice rose in anger.

'No. But you… you are so different, so kind.'

'Ellen.' Josef's voice was strained, the words sounding as though they were wrung out of him. 'What can I say? We cannot be together… but I must tell you how I feel. I love you, Ellen. I always love you.'

'And I… I love you.' Ellen's voice broke and she began to sob.

'Liebling, please do not cry. I love you always.'

'Will I see you here tomorrow?' she murmured as the sobs subsided.

'Of course. I wait.'

There was a staccato shout and they turned to see a guard standing at the corner of the nearest hut.

'Run, Liebling. Go home. Hurry.'

'Who goes there? Stop!' The guard began to run towards the pair.

Ellen glanced briefly at Josef.

'Run. Schnell! Run.'

Ellen careered down the side of the valley. When she reached the river, she paused, looking back up the slope. From this distance it was impossible to see or hear anything. She stood still in the darkness, hearing only the rasping of her breath and the indifferent chatter of the water behind her. She wanted to go back but knew that she could not. Stumbling on towards home, her breath turned to sobs again. Without a doubt there was no possibility of seeing Josef the following day. The guards would be primed for her arrival. Either that or he would not be there to greet her because they would have locked him up for the night.

At the door of the cottage she paused to gather her breath. She wiped her eyes on her sleeve and entered the cottage. All was quiet. Silently she closed the door and began to unbutton her coat.

*

Tom bided his time. He didn't know what Ellen was up to but he was going to find out.

He had woken as she left the bed. After several minutes, during which he anticipated her return, he went to investigate. In the living room he found her nightclothes. He looked in the usual place for her shoes and they were missing. Outside all was quiet. He had expected to find her on the doorstep, contemplating the moon or the stars, but she was nowhere to be seen. When she wasn't there, he turned back to the cottage, but then paused. Maybe she had walked in the direction of the reservoir building and the imprisoned Germans.

After several minutes' walking he could see her up ahead, a dark shadow against the waning moon. Following at a distance, he realised that his wild guess was indeed correct. She was making for the encampment.

He followed at a safe distance, though she never once looked round. Outside the camp, she stopped, crouching behind a bush. After a minute he watched in disbelief as she furtively approached the wire and a shadowy figure imprisoned within it. It was impossible for him to make out any of the words that were spoken, but, from the grassy knoll behind which he was sheltering, he could see the two of them deep in conversation. They seemed as close together as it was possible for two people to be when separated by a wire fence. It took every ounce of willpower to stay in hiding, when his body was crying out to leap forward and snatch his property back from this foreign thief.

Suddenly a shout rang out. He ducked, as though the words were aimed at his own head. The next moment his wife was running down the hill directly towards him. He slithered sideways as she hurtled past, making for the river below. For a few minutes he waited, watching her blur into the darkness. She appeared to have stopped among the rocks.

Tom scrambled up the hillside towards the road so that he could take the easier way back to the cottage and be in his bed by the time she arrived back.

'Where have you been?'

Ellen was so startled she almost cried out.

'I went for a walk.'

'Liar!' Tom roared, letting go at last his pent-up rage. He jumped up from his chair in front of the dead fire and strode over to her, standing so close that she cowered beneath him. 'I saw you.'

'I went for a walk,' Ellen's voice faltered. 'You know me, Tom. I like walking at night.' She tried to turn away, to remove her coat, but he caught her shoulder and wheeled her round to face him.

'Yes, but where did you walk?' he said through gritted teeth.

'Only along the road.'

'To the prison camp. To keep an assignation with one of the Hun.' His voice rose. 'And before you open your mouth, don't try and deny it. I saw you with my own eyes. You were there at the wire with him. God knows what you would have been doing if the wire hadn't been there.' He raised a hand and slapped her across the cheek. She fell backwards into the chair but immediately tried to clamber out of it.

'Tom, please...'

Tom pushed her roughly back and slapped her again with the back of his hand. Blood began to seep from the corner of her mouth. Her husband stumbled on one of

Netta's toys and in an instant Ellen was flinging herself out of the chair and across the room. Tom ran after her and brought her heavily to the ground.

'Tom! The baby!' she screamed. 'Think of the baby!'

'The baby! What do I want with another baby when I've a wife who can't be faithful to me?'

Ellen's eyes flared. 'How dare you say that to me? I've seen you all these months, years even. Making eyes at Clara… in front of me as well. And what goes on behind my back with her?'

'Don't you dare bring Clara into this!' Tom shouted, clamping his hand across Ellen's mouth. But the next second he snatched back his hand with a roar as Ellen sunk her teeth hard into his fingers.

'I've tried to be a good wife to you, Tom.' Ellen, backing away from her husband, started to cry. 'I tried so hard at first. But she was always in the way. I saw how you looked at her and talked to her… and you never talked to me or looked at me like…' But her outpouring was silenced by a punch to her left cheekbone that knocked her senseless to the floor.

*

Ellen put her hand up to her face and winced. Her jaw felt swollen and she could hardly see out of her left eye. Her elbow and hip felt bruised and sore. She sat up slowly and swallowed, as a wave of nausea passed through her body.

For a while she sat unmoving and attempted to gather her thoughts. With a jolt she recalled her meeting with Josef and discovery by one of the guards. She recalled her homeward journey, and then her eyes fastened on the neglected toy. The trauma of discovery came back to her.

She looked round the room cautiously but there was no one else there. The clock on the mantelpiece showed five thirty. It was growing light. Painfully, she got to her feet and walked stiffly to the kitchen, where she poured herself a glass of water. There was an uncanny silence in the cottage. Slowly she walked to the bedroom to check on Netta, where her daughter was sleeping peacefully. Tom was nowhere to be seen. Their bed was dishevelled but empty.

When she re-entered the living room, Duncan was standing there. He stared at her.

'What has happened to your face, child?'

She put an involuntary hand up to her cheek, as he stepped closer.

His face contorted. 'Did Tom do this to you?'

'Of course not, Feyther. Why would he do a thing like that? I think I fainted and hit my face on the bedside table. I must have got out of my bed too quickly.'

'I don't believe you, Ellen. This has happened one time too many. Wait till I see that so-called husband of yours.' He moved towards her. 'Let me see your face.'

'Just leave me alone, Feyther,' Ellen barked, taking a step back.

Duncan took a breath, as though to reply, thought better of it and sat down heavily in the chair. Leaning over, he began to lace his boots, all the while muttering under his breath. 'Where *is* Tom anyway?' he said suddenly. 'He's meant to be helping me with the sheep. They'll no doubt start lambing today and I need him here.'

'I don't know where he is. Can *I* help with anything?'

'No you can't. You'll stay here and rest.' He regarded her suspiciously.

She crossed over to him as normally as she was able and kissed him on the cheek and sat back on her heels. 'I'm sorry I snapped.'

Duncan looked at her and shook his head. 'I hope you're telling me the truth, lassie, I really do.'

*

As dawn crept through the valley, Tom stretched the stiffness from his back. Peeping over the wall of the stell, he could see the stirrings of early morning in the camp below him. He watched for a while as columns of soldiers proceeded to and fro over the rough ground of the enclosure, entering and leaving wooden huts that were lined up neatly along one side of the camp. Tom snorted in disgust and spat on the ground.

His stomach groaned. He was hungry now, as well as cold. The clear sky had brought with it a sharp frost and the hills glistened white as the sun gained the horizon and broke over the unfolding scene before him. He thought briefly of home and hoped that the injuries he had inflicted on his wife weren't too visible. He had no desire to be the recipient of a tongue-lashing from her father.

Transferring his weight onto the other leg, he felt a spasm of pain in his knee, exacerbated by the pursuit of his wife the previous evening. As always, contemplation of his knee led him to think of Clara. How Ellen had guessed about his feelings for the young doctor, he had no idea. He had always, to the best of his knowledge, remained detached and merely friendly when Ellen was present. His wife was, of course, trying to make him feel guilty about his friendship, when it was she who was the guilty party.

He was about to turn away when he caught sight of the prisoner, a slightly built young man with brown curly hair. He had only seen him once before and then only a brief glimpse. But he would have recognised him anywhere. Tom's lip curled. What made her prefer this apology for a man to himself?

The young prisoner entered the canteen and Tom lost sight of him. But his anger was rekindled. He would wait until he re-emerged and follow him to his place of work.

It was Tom's lucky day. As he approached the workers at the base of the reservoir embankment, he could see Josef Kessler just ahead, in conversation with two men who were delivering supplies. Taking advantage of the element of surprise, he walked straight up to the group and levelled a punch into Josef's stomach. The young man doubled over and fell to the ground.

'Hey… what do you think you're doing?' one of the deliverymen shouted, at the same time stepping back well clear of the assailant.

'I'm giving him what he deserves,' Tom muttered, giving Josef a fierce kick in the ribs. 'And, if you'd any pride in your country, you wouldn't be bringing food to keep this scum alive.'

Tom bent low over Josef and hauled him to his feet.

'This is for carrying on with my wife while I were away.' He aimed a fist at Josef's nose and the prisoner crashed to the ground again. And then Tom was kicking him in the stomach, the chest, the face, anywhere that his boot could reach, his anger rendering him insensible to the hurt he was inflicting.

Arms gripped him tightly and he felt himself being hauled backwards.

'That's enough of that. What in heaven's name do you think you are doing?'

Tom stopped, gasping for breath. He looked up into

the face of a tall man of superior rank and sneered. 'I'm giving him what he deserves, that's what. And you can't stop me.'

'Oh, but I can. I'm in charge here. These prisoners are working for His Majesty's government and I will not see them ill-treated. And, may I ask, what is the reason for your grievance against this man?'

'He's been carrying on with my wife, that's what.'

'And your wife is who exactly?'

'My wife is Ellen Fairclough from the farm.'

'Ah! Well, Mr Fairclough, I can assure you you're very much mistaken. Any association between your wife and this prisoner has been completely above board. I can vouch for that.'

'And who, may I ask, are you?'

'I'm Captain Cameron-Dyet, in charge of these prisoners, and I assure you I've been keeping a close eye on them.'

Tom snorted. 'It was you that asked my wife to take him into my house and without my permission. Keeping a close eye on them! Have you any idea what they have been up to while your back was turned?'

'I can assure you, sir, that nothing untoward has gone on.'

'Oh aye? Well, I invite you to come and talk to my wife and ask her face to face while I'm there and let's hear what she has to say. Nothing untoward has gone on. Pah!' Tom wheeled round and set off at a fast limp along the road, leaving the captain staring after him until a groan from Josef brought him to his knees to care for the injured prisoner.

*

'I think Tom must be away to Army Headquarters,' Ellen said to her father at dinnertime. 'He came in earlier and washed and shaved and when he came out of the bedroom he was wearing his uniform. He didn't say a word to me though. It looks as though you'll have to make do without him today.'

'Damn the boy! The sheep have started to lamb now. Me and Douglas, we cannae do it all by ourselves.'

A loud knocking on the door made them both jump.

'I'll go, Father. You finish your dinner.'

Captain Cameron Dyet stood outside. He stared at Ellen's face before seeming to collect himself.

'May I come in, Mrs Fairclough?'

'Of course, Captain.' She frowned, hoping his visit wasn't anything to do with Josef. She stood back to allow him to enter.

'Good afternoon, Duncan.'

'Good afternoon, sir.' Duncan rose to his feet. 'How can we help?'

'Well, it's Mrs Fairclough that might be able to help... to throw some light on a problem that has occurred.'

'Do you want me to stay?' Duncan looked from the soldier to Ellen and back.

'No, Father, you go, if you've finished.'

Duncan lifted his coat from the back of the chair and heaved it over his shoulders. He turned to his daughter. 'You tell that husband of yours to get himself up the hill when he returns. There's work to be done.' He went out, slamming the door.

The captain raised his eyebrows. 'Your husband is missing then, Mrs Fairclough? And you look as if you have been in the wars.'

Ellen put her hand to her face and frowned. 'Aye, I fell.'

'You did all that with a fall?'

Ellen was silent.

'Maybe I can offer another explanation. Maybe you have been at the receiving end of your husband's fist.'

Ellen said nothing.

'I can see I'm right.' He paused. 'You see, Mrs Fairclough, you are not the only one to suffer as the result of your husband's anger.'

'What do you mean?'

'Prisoner Kessler has also had a beating.'

'Josef?' Ellen gasped.

'Precisely so.'

'Is he all right? Please, tell me he is all right.'

'He is much the same as you, I imagine. Bruised and battered but nothing that will not mend. What he went

350

through on the high seas was a lot more serious than what he received this morning at your husband's hands. May I sit down?'

'Of course. I'm sorry.' The captain sat but Ellen began to pace up and down the room in her agitation.

'And you have no idea where your husband is now?'

'No. He came in earlier but didnae say anything. When he went, he was wearing his uniform. I tried to ask him what he was doing but he pushed me away and left without a word. I can only think he must have to go to Company Headquarters, though why he didnae tell me I've no idea.' She hesitated and looked at the captain. 'Between you and me, Captain, me and Tom, well, we havenae been getting on so well recently.'

'That much is obvious, Mrs Fairclough. It's strange though. He asked me to meet him here. No doubt he didn't reckon with the incriminating evidence of your face.' The captain cleared his throat. 'Forgive me for asking, Mrs Fairclough, but is there more between you and the prisoner Kessler than there ought to be?'

The blush that rose over Ellen's face told her questioner all he needed to know. She looked at the captain with a heavy sigh and sat down opposite him. 'I know what it looks like, Captain. But you see... we... me and Josef... became good friends when I was looking after him. I know it seems strange when we don't even speak the same language... but somehow it didn't seem to matter. Did you know that Oliver was teaching him

English? Then Oliver was killed and you know how upset Josef was at the loss of his friend. After a while I started to teach him English.'

The captain swallowed. 'You taught him English?'

'Aye. Well, to start with I gave him books… children's books mostly and some of Father's old farming magazines. He said how I was trying to turn him into a farmer.' She smiled wistfully. 'But later on, I gave him lessons.'

'You gave him lessons?' The captain was obviously finding it difficult to believe what Ellen was saying.

'Aye. Through the wire. I've been going at night. There's nothing wrong in that, is there? Talking?'

The captain looked amazed. 'You mean you've been walking along to the camp every night?'

'Och, not every night. I couldnae go if the weather was bad. Though Josef was always there whatever the weather. He doesnae sleep so well, you see.'

Ellen stopped to draw breath and the captain allowed himself a small smile.

'And now your husband has found out about your meetings. His reaction, in the circumstances, is understandable, if a little extreme.'

'I know how it looks, Captain. But Tom and me…' She shrugged. 'Well, at first we tried. But the truth is… he's always loved someone else.'

The captain raised his eyebrows. 'I see.'

'But he's jealous of me being friends with other men.'

'I'm not surprised. You're a very attractive young lady.'

'There was no need for him to be jealous. But he kept accusing me of misbehaving. He… he hasn't been nice to me for a long time. And, in the end, I suppose it made me more friendly than I ought to have been with Josef. Josef's very kind and thoughtful. Of course we know that when the war ends…'

'He will be sent back to Germany.' The captain finished her sentence.

'Aye.' Ellen got up abruptly and walked to the window so that the captain was unable to see the emotion in her face.

He sighed. 'You realise, of course, that these night-time assignations will have to stop. I cannot allow a prisoner under my guard to…' The captain seemed lost for words.

'Fraternise with the locals?'

'Precisely. And I cannot run the risk of him being attacked by jealous husbands. The prisoners in my charge are meant to be under my protection.' The look he gave Ellen was not unkind. 'What of your husband, Mrs Fairclough? Does he return to active service?'

'I don't know. As I said, I've no idea where he is.'

'If I were you, Mrs Fairclough, I would try and keep on the right side of him from now on.'

'…If he returns,' Ellen added.

The captain gave an embarrassed cough.

'If there are any difficulties… with your husband, I mean… if he should hurt you again, you know where to find us.' He glanced toward the door. 'I must go, but just remember, Mrs Fairclough…' The captain paused, as though unwilling to say more. 'Just remember, that these men are our enemy. It doesn't do to get too friendly with them.'

Ellen spun round and faced him. Her eyes flashed defiance. 'And please remember, Captain, who it was brought Josef to me in the first place.'

33

Playing Games

Tom had known how it would be. Men had returned to the front with wounds less well mended than his own. Even if they were not fit enough for the front line, they could be usefully employed in the Divisional reserve lines further back. He explained to the officers how a recurrence of his knee problem had necessitated a further operation, followed by a period of convalescence. He wished bizarrely, and not for the first time, that his recovery had been less successful.

Regimental reinforcements would be sailing in twelve days' time, he was told, and he would be sailing with them.

The interview had been short, no more than a formality, and he had time to spare before his return train. He made his way up George Street and turned left towards the hospital.

'Mr Fairclough!' the ward sister exclaimed. 'Come in. This is an unexpected surprise. Are you having problems with your leg again?'

Tom felt a little foolish. 'No, Sister. I just hoped I might see Clara for a minute.'

'I assume you mean Dr Moxon? I'm sorry but that's quite impossible. She is assisting Dr Fraser in theatre and I don't expect her on the ward until late this afternoon. In any case, she is much too busy to indulge in cosy chit-chat when she's on duty. If I were you, Mr Fairclough, I would write to her if you have anything to say. That way she can reply to you as and when she wishes. Now I must get on. Good day to you.' The woman turned back to her desk and resumed writing.

Tom stared at the stiff white frill of the sister's cap before swivelling on his heel and marching abruptly out of the office, his resentment increased by being made to feel like a naughty schoolboy. He made his way swiftly down the flight of stairs, eager now to be out of the building. He cursed the ward sister for how she made him feel. He cursed the system that ensured Clara's never being available. Most of all he cursed Dr Fraser, whom he had never met, for being able to command Clara's undivided attention.

The day was sunny and unusually warm for late April. He walked slowly over to the huge edifice of St. Mungo's Cathedral and sat on a seat in the sunshine. As he watched the passers-by, his gloom deepened. Some appeared cheerful, as if forgetting that thousands – surely their own menfolk among them – were getting killed on the other side of the Channel this very minute.

Children skipped and cavorted around the legs of their mothers. A young couple approached slowly, the man's arm linked tightly with his wife's. As they drew near, Tom looked at them and quickly averted his gaze. The man bore the unmistakable scars of mustard gas on the skin of his face. And he was blind.

As they retreated slowly into the distance, Tom watched them. He had seen pals, many of them, afflicted in a similar way at the front. He had listened to their cries as they lay stranded in no man's land, until rescued by stretcher-bearers or by a well-aimed bullet. Away from the front, he had seen columns of soldiers blinded by the gas, shuffling in lines, hands on the shoulders of the man in front. But it was a shock to see the daily struggle that such wounds would inevitably bring to the returning soldiers and to their families.

He got up abruptly from the seat and began to walk rapidly towards the station.

In the carriage he sat back and closed his eyes. This time the picture that came and filled him with remorse was that of his wife's bruised and swollen face. He had left behind a child whom he adored and a wife who adored him. Or had done until his rough treatment had turned her away. There were eleven days before he needed to leave. Time to make it up with Ellen and pacify the old man by making a start with the lambing.

*

Ellen heard the click of the latch and quiet footsteps in the passage and she knew it must be her husband. Angry but frightened, she was unsure how to respond to his sudden reappearance. She looked up warily, a pile of dirty plates in her hands, as Tom entered the living room.

'Where have you been? I thought you'd left us, like you did last time.'

'I were called up to Regimental Headquarters so I could hear their verdict on my fitness for service.'

'And what have they decided?'

'I have to present myself on Sunday 5th May, for sailing the following day.'

Ellen put down the plates with a clatter. 'Sailing where?'

'Back to France. Back to the war.' He paused. Neither of them moved. 'You didn't think they'd let me live out the rest of the war tending sheep, did you?'

Ellen shrugged. 'I don't know. I thought they might.' She stared at the pile of dirty plates.

'I'm sorry, Ellen.'

Ellen's head jerked up at the unexpected words and her eyes filled with tears.

'I'm sorry that I hit you. I know that the way I've been has driven you away. I... I think the world of you... you and the babby. Surely you know that.'

Ellen's face registered doubt.

'I've only got just over a week. Let's try not to upset

one another and make the most of the time we've got.'

Ellen winced at his choice of words, echoing the phrase that Josef had used on that memorable evening outside the wire. She was about to reply when the door crashed back on its hinges and she heard her father's voice.

'Are you all right, lassie? I thought I'd call in as I was passing to see if you've heard anything of that no-good husband of yours.'

Ellen blushed to her roots. 'Feyther, he's here. He's come back. Like I said, he had to go and get signed up.'

Duncan's head appeared round the door frame. 'Not before time. You could at least have given us warning before you left.' He looked at his son-in-law shrewdly. 'And I don't suppose you know anything about how Ellen got these bruises?'

'I've told Tom that I fainted. He knows all about it. You don't need to say any more.'

Duncan grunted. 'If you're sure, hen.' He turned to Tom. 'Well then, pal, there's ewes out there giving birth, so I suggest you get out of that uniform and into some working clothes and come and give us a hand.'

*

When Ellen turned to the sink to peel potatoes for dinner, her face was grim. She could not help but feel that Tom was playing games with her.

But as the days progressed, he proved her wrong. He set about helping his father-in-law with enthusiasm. Lambing began in earnest and their time – and that of an extra shepherd who had been hired by Kenneth Douglas in anticipation of Tom's absence – was full. They took it in turns to do the evening rounds of the ewes on the in-bye land. The rest, scattered over several square miles, were visited twice a day, each shepherd taking his turn to do the longest of the walks.

The days were lengthening now and the hours of darkness receding. As night followed night, Ellen lay unmoving by Tom's side, her eyes fixed on the rectangle of window. She watched dawn's steady progress and heard the ewes answer the high-pitched cries of their youngsters with sonorous bleats. Within her the baby stirred and kicked, oblivious to the turmoil of emotions that prevented Ellen from sleeping.

She had tried her hardest to be a good wife to Tom and look after their little daughter. She had loved him, or at least she thought she had. But now she was not so sure. The sensation that had blossomed over the time of her friendship with Josef was threatening to overwhelm her. She could neither eat nor rest. And the worst of it was that, in her eyes, Tom was largely to blame. If it had not been for his treatment of her, his distrust of her every action, the occasions when he meted out his heavy-handed punishment for supposed wrongs, she would never have looked to another for comfort and friendship. And now, when the die was cast, he was treating her as he had in the first months of their marriage. Only now it was too late.

She must have dozed. Abruptly she was jerked into wakefulness by Tom's shouts. Recognising a return of his nightmares, she groped for the bedside table and, with trembling fingers, struck a match and held it to the candle. She turned to her husband and shook him gently but firmly.

'Tom! Wake up. You're having one of your bad dreams again. It's all right… I'm here.'

Tom sat up suddenly and stared ahead. She put her arms round him and rocked him to and fro. He quietened and stroked her hair, running his hand down its soft silkiness.

'Clara, don't leave me. Stay with me. I need you.'

Ellen pulled away from him appalled and he stared at her blankly for a few seconds. Then his chin fell forward onto his chest and he gave a great sob.

'Ellen, I'm sorry. It must have been a dream. I don't know what's happening to me. I don't want to go away again. I want to stay here on the farm… with Netta… and with you.'

Tom held out his arms and she let him hold her and kiss her cheeks and her hair and her lips. But her own lips were unresponsive and her eyes sought the window.

When he lay back and drew her over him, she obeyed. But the kisses she tasted were not his and it was another's body that she imagined beneath her own.

34

All Change

News of the progress of the war filtered into the prison camp, giving rise to a variety of opinions. Some reacted with patriotic fervour to the information that their aggressors were gaining the upper hand. Others, weary with hard labour and homesick to the core, were secretly relieved that hostilities might soon be at an end, whatever the outcome might be. These kept their opinions to themselves.

To Josef Kessler, the reports served to heighten the emotions that assailed him daily. He too longed to see his homeland again and longed even more to be reunited with his parents and his sister. But, above all, he craved news of Ellen. Since the morning her husband had attacked him, he had not seen her. He had been called before the captain, who, though severe and reprimanding, had at least had compassion enough to tell him that he had visited Ellen. She too had been beaten by her husband, he said, but was thankfully none the worse for her ordeal. He implied that both of them had got no more than they deserved. Josef did not try to argue with him. Their visits to the graveyard would stop. They were not to meet again. The captain's words were like a death sentence.

How was Ellen being treated now at the hands of her husband? His heart turned cold when he thought of what might be going on in the farm cottage and he raged at his impotence to protect her. How he longed to see her again.

The watch on Josef and his fellow prisoners was increased. 'Look what you've done now, Music Boy,' Vogel snarled at him. 'You and your amorous adventures!' Josef said nothing. There was nothing he could say that would not inflame an already hopeless situation.

Ellen never took her walks in the direction the men were working and, because they were still engaged on building up the embankment, there was no opportunity for Josef to see, even from a distance, the farmstead where Ellen and her family lived. Often, he glimpsed the farmer's wife and it comforted him to know that she was visiting Ellen and no doubt looking after her. Ellen must be near her time now and fearful of the outcome after what she had previously had to endure.

How he wished the baby was his.

But he must stop thinking like this or he would go mad.

Tom stared unseeing out of the carriage window, as the train grumbled towards Glasgow. At Motherwell a throng of workers boarded, but his eyes remained fixed on the grimy glass. The guard slammed the door of the carriage and gave a shrill blast on the whistle.

Tom's face contorted in horror. He felt his mouth go dry and he lifted trembling hands to wipe the sweat from his brow. A voice was screaming inside his head: *'Faster up that ladder. We haven't got all day! Keep in line, you untidy bunch of no-good layabouts. Now, over the top. Forward, men! Let them know what we're made of. Forward! Forward!'*

'You all right, pal? Calm down. It's only the Glasgow train you're on, not the German front.'

Tom stared at the man who had addressed him and then looked round with a dazed expression. The compartment was full. Sympathetic faces stared in his direction. He turned away in embarrassment as he awoke to his predicament. The train was out of the station now, picking up speed, the clanking of couplings and reluctant grind of wheels on iron relinquished in favour of the rhythmic sing-song of the rails.

'Here, pal, have one of these.'

Tom raised a shaking hand and took the proffered cigarette, dropping it immediately into his lap. He fumbled to retrieve it, anchored it with concentration in his mouth, as his benefactor struck a match and held it close. He drew deeply on the cigarette, sank back on the headrest and blew out a slow spiral of smoke.

'Thanks, pal.' He gave a shame-faced look at the man opposite, trying to blot out the curious looks of the remaining occupants of the carriage. 'Sorry about that. Must have been dreaming.'

'Aye. Och, there's no need for apologies. I'm Jimmy Beattie, by the way.' He held out his hand and Tom shook it. He was an elderly man, ready for retirement, a thin, wrinkled face, blue-grey lachrymose eyes. He nodded toward Tom's uniform. 'You on your way back to the battlefield, pal?'

'Aye. Rejoining my regiment. The name's Tom… Tom Fairclough.'

'You been on leave then?'

'Compulsory leave, more like. War wound.'

'Good luck then, pal. They say the war may soon be over.'

'Aye, that's what they say. I'll believe it when I'm back looking after my sheep.'

Jimmy Beattie drew deeply on his own cigarette and gazed out of the window. The train stopped and started, picking up more workers, bearing them on its relentless progress towards the city.

Too soon, they arrived. Amid a bustle of people, anxious not to be late for work, Tom rose slowly and retrieved his kitbag from the rack. When he turned,

Jimmy Beattie was waiting for him. He held out his hand again.

'Well, goodbye, pal. And good luck.' His voice cracked and Tom looked up anxiously. Tears were tracking unevenly down the ageing face. 'My turn to apologise now,' he said, wiping his eyes on his sleeve. 'I had two lads myself. Joined up almost as soon as war started, they did. They were tram drivers in Glasgow. Do ye ken how they enlisted in large numbers, the tram workers?'

'Aye.'

'The wife and I, we were so proud of them... not knowing what it would be like. They died within days of one another, just weeks after the start of hostilities. I wasnae going to tell you. But it's gey hard without them... and it doesnae get any easier.'

A porter put his head round the carriage door. 'All change here, pals. Hurry along now.'

Jimmy stepped onto the platform. 'That's me away then, Tom. Here's hoping it will soon be over.' He forced a smile and made off towards the exit.

Tom walked slowly along the platform, handed in his ticket and emerged into the damp streets of Glasgow, setting off in the direction of Brigade Headquarters, where he was to report for duty before going on to Queen Street Station and picking up the Edinburgh train. The meeting was brief, no more than a few minutes. Leaving the building, he stuffed his papers into the inside pocket of his greatcoat and set off along the pathway.

It had started to rain. Tom turned up the collar of his greatcoat as the downpour got heavier, but it was futile... as futile as when he had done so in the trenches. If it was raining like this at the front, he could well imagine the mud that would greet his arrival. It would soon cake his legs and make its way into his boots. Then his body would be invaded with lice. And so it would remain, until war came to an end... or he did.

His steps slowed. It struck him again, as it had done before in the heat of battle, that his time would surely come. He could not go on being so lucky. How would it end? Would he finish up in one of those flooded craters that he had dreaded so much, drowning in the stinking mud among the decomposing bodies?

At the station, he bought a cup of tea and a bun and sat down in a corner, well away from the other travellers. But he had no appetite for food, and after one bite, pushed the cake away. The tea was scalding hot and good. He took several gulps and replaced the cup unsteadily in its saucer. He thought of his family. Ellen had wept at his going, but he wondered, not for the first time, if his earlier behaviour had been such as to make their future together uncertain. In just over three months, she was to bear his baby and him not there to support her when she most needed it. Pulling out a postcard, ready stamped, that he had intended to send once embarkation was arranged, he wrote hastily,

My dearest Ellen,

I am here at the station waiting for my train to Edinburgh. I shall be thinking of you over the next few difficult months. I wish I could be there to see our new baby.

Assuring you of my fondest love,
Your husband, Tom.

'Another cup, sir? The waitress was at his elbow but he was so engrossed he hadn't seen her.

'Oh, aye. I don't mind if I do.'

The woman took his cup to the counter and returned with a second steaming cup of tea.

'On the house, sir. You're away to the front, I guess?'

Tom smiled. 'Aye, lass, I am.'

'Just writing to your sweetheart, are you, before you leave?'

'To my wife, actually. I've a wife and child back home.'

'I guessed you might be.'

'My daughter's two now. I've a photo of her somewhere.' He put his hand into his inside pocket, found his packet of photos and, with trembling hands, began to withdraw the picture of Netta seated on Ellen's knee. His hand continued to shake as he handed the photo to the waitress.

She took it from him, giving him a sympathetic glance as she did so.

'That there's my wife, Ellen,' he indicated, trying desperately to bring the shaking under control. 'My little girl's called Netta. I... I'm sorry. I'm not so good at the moment.' He took the photo back and, in attempting to replace it in the packet, sent the remaining pictures skidding in all directions across the floor of the cafe. With a curse, he leant down to gather them up.

'Och, man, let me give you a hand.' The waitress scooped up the last two photos and, straightening up, handed them to him. 'Well, good luck to you.' She paused. 'Come home safe. They say the end is in sight now.'

Tom looked at the waitress's departing figure. Everyone was wishing him well today, almost as if they knew his number was up. He picked up the cup and took a gulp. Some of the tea spilled onto his greatcoat. Replacing the cup on its saucer, he wiped the stain with his handkerchief. He must take more care or he would have to answer to his C.O. for being badly turned-out.

In the station he made his way slowly to the platform. His train was not yet in, but on the other side of his platform the line was occupied. A crackling voice overhead informed him that the train now standing at platform four was the eleven forty for Craigendoran Junction. He had never heard of the place but, wherever it was, there were very few people interested in travelling there. The engine let out a sudden hiss of steam, making him jump, and the carriages clanked and creaked as the train prepared to leave. Tom's pulse rose. From boyhood the sound had always evoked a sense of excitement. All around him the air began to reverberate with the clamour, as the engine slowly drew out of the station. And in a second the platform and its sole occupant were eclipsed in the billows of smoke that accompanied the train's slow departure to its destination.

35

A Modicum of Comfort

On the twenty-fourth of August 1918 Ellen gave birth to a baby girl. She was surprised at the comparative ease with which the labour progressed. Time and again over the past weeks she had found her mind going back to the nightmare of Netta's birth when she had been sure she was going to die. But this time Margaret had held her hand and told her how well she was doing and she had found, to her surprise, that she was in fact doing well.

When it was over and she was cradling the baby in the crook of her arm, Duncan and Netta were allowed in. Netta gave the baby a disinterested look and slithered off the bed to find her toys, but Duncan stayed to admire his new granddaughter.

'She's not a bit like Netta. Perhaps she's going to take after you, hen. Her hair is certainly the same colour as yours.'

'It would be unusual to have another baby looking as much like her daddy as Netta does,' Ellen replied. 'This one will have a look all of her own.'

'Have you and Tom decided what you will call her?'

Ellen shook her head. 'I asked Tom before he left but he didnae give me any ideas for a girl, so I suppose I must decide for myself.'

'But you will write and tell him?'

'Of course.'

Margaret Murdie, who had been busy in the kitchen, put her head round the door. 'There's a gentleman downstairs, wishing to talk to the lady of the house. I told him she was indisposed, so he said could he have a word with you, Duncan. Hurry back though. I've made us all a nice cup of tea.'

Margaret placed the tray carefully on the bedside table and took the baby from Ellen. She stood a minute, cradling the tiny bundle in her arms. The baby had woken and was staring at the older woman with unblinking blue eyes.

'I can't thank you enough, Margaret. I don't know how we'd have managed without you,' Ellen said softly.

Margaret smiled at Ellen and, turning away, placed the baby gently in her crib, tucking the sheet in firmly around her. As she straightened up, she dabbed both eyes with the corner of her apron. 'I'm sorry. I'm gey happy for you all, I really am. It's just that it puts me in mind of Iain and when I gave birth to him. I suppose we're all the same, remembering our own labour. I miss him so much… and his dad, of course.' She sniffed. 'Take no notice of me. I'm just a silly old fool.'

'You're no' silly… and you're certainly no' old.'

Duncan had come quietly into the room and, stepping up to her, put a comforting arm round her shoulders. 'But as for being a fool…' He hesitated and Margaret looked at him sternly.

'You take care who you're calling a fool, Duncan Simpson, or you could find yourself getting your own tea in future.'

'Who was it at the door, Father?'

'Och, it was someone from Brigade Headquarters, wanting to speak to Tom. I told him Tom had been gone three months or more, as he would have known if he kept his records in order.'

'I hope you didn't say that to him!' Margaret laughed.

'Well, it's no more than the truth,' Duncan replied with a smile.

Netta climbed untidily onto the bed and snuggled down beside her mother, while the baby surveyed the scene with her pale blue eyes and a slight frown, as if deciding whether this was a suitable family for her. And Ellen, looking at the tiny miracle, felt her heart give a lurch of thankfulness and longing.

Ellen wrote to Tom the following day. It was the last of several letters she had written since his departure. She had received none in return, apart from the postcard sent from Glasgow while he was waiting for the train. The postcard that had assured her of his fondest love.

She sighed. Here she was in the same position as before... not knowing whether Tom was dead or alive. Beneath the joy of her daughter's arrival, she was angry... angry that she had to go through this without the support of even a letter, and angry that all possibility of contact with Josef had been taken away. *I have called her Eva,* she wrote bluntly.

If he was not upset before, this letter might well make him so. She could imagine his comment. '*What kind of a name is that? It's not Scottish. It's not even English.*'

If, of course, he received this letter.

*

Anxious not to miss the heather purpling the hillsides around the farm, Ellen set off walking with her two daughters, as soon as she felt strong enough to do so. It was hard work, the baby wrapped securely in one end of the perambulator and Netta bouncing up and down in the other. September was nearing its end but the weather was warm and she had not gone far before she had removed her coat and hung it over the handle of the pram.

Although Margaret was a frequent visitor, it was a long time since Ellen had walked the road to the older woman's farm. Everywhere there was talk of an imminent end to the war, and, if this were so, the prisoners were not likely to be in the valley for much longer. Ellen was anxious to see Josef one more time and knowing that she may get no chance to speak to him, she had written him a letter.

The prisoners were working on the far side of the embankment. To have approached would have made it obvious that she wanted to talk to Josef and she had no wish to cause him trouble. She went on along the road, her eyes straining for any sign that he had seen her. But none stopped from his work and she plodded unhappily on to her destination.

It was the same when she returned. The workforce was still occupied on the far side of the valley. She was so engrossed looking at the prisoners that she failed to see Captain Cameron-Dyet emerge from one of the huts. He stood watching her approach and she started when he addressed her.

'So, Mrs Fairclough, you have a new baby. May I congratulate you! Is it a boy or a girl?'

'It's a girl. I'm calling her Eva.'

'A pretty name. And you, are you quite well?'

'Yes, thank you, sir.'

'Good. Well, don't let me keep you. The nights are drawing in now and you don't want the little ones out in the cold.' The captain nodded and stepped back to let her pass.

Ellen paused. 'Captain,' she began with some hesitation. 'Would you do something for me?'

'Of course, my dear. What is it?'

'If it's true what everyone is saying about the war ending soon, I suppose the prisoners will be returning to their homes. I very much wanted to see Josef Kessler again before he goes.' The captain made as if to interrupt, but Ellen continued. 'It's all right. I know that's not possible. But could you please give him this? It's only a letter thanking him for his friendship.'

The captain frowned. 'I don't know, Mrs Fairclough. Fraternising with the enemy is to be discouraged, as you well know.'

'You were happy enough to allow me to *fraternise with the enemy* when you needed my help,' Ellen snapped.

'I suppose you could see it that way.'

'What other way is there to see it?'

The captain gave a small smile. 'Very well. You win, Mrs Fairclough. I don't suppose it can do any harm. As you say, hostilities will soon be over, God willing.' He held out his hand and took the letter. 'Take care of yourself and your family, Mrs Fairclough. And I hope your husband returns to you safe and well.'

*

Tom did return safe and well a few days after the signing of the armistice. Gone was the haggard expression, the haunted look in his eyes that had accompanied his earlier returns. The skin of his face was brown. He had filled out his uniform.

Ellen was feeding the baby when the door opened and he walked in. She uttered a cry of surprise, raising a hand to her mouth. 'Tom! Why didn't you let us know you were coming?'

'Oh, you know how it is, lass.' He bent over and kissed her forehead. 'Everything is so mixed up at the end of the fighting… people coming and going. Transport full or likely to be. You just have to take the opportunity when it presents itself.' He put out his hand and touched the baby's downy hair. 'So this is our baby daughter. What have you called her?'

'Her name is Eva.'

'Eva? What kind of a name is that?'

'Well, you didn't suggest anything yourself. In fact, I havenae heard anything from you since that one postcard, six months ago. I've been worried sick.' In truth, she felt no inclination to care for her husband or even to humour him. Her previous feelings for him had declined to the extent that she wondered if she had ever really loved him.

'I told you before, lass. It's not always possible to write when you're in the thick of it. Any road, no need to worry now. I'm home to stay. Things can all get back to normal.' He sat down heavily in his chair and began to unlace his boots.

'I'll make you a cup of tea when I've finished feeding Eva. I don't suppose you've had any lunch?'

'No, I haven't. I intended to call in at the village shop and get something to eat on the way, but I was so distracted by what was going on at the station that I clean forgot.' He gave a broad grin.

'What was going on at the station?'

'The prisoners were there, them from along the valley, being herded onto the Glasgow train quick as you like. Pretty miserable they looked as well. And they were getting a fair bit of abuse from the villagers, I can tell you.'

Ellen glanced involuntarily out of the window where the view was empty of everything except sheep and hills. It was an age since the enemy had had their quarters opposite the farm. Yet that was the view she remembered now... the day when they had marched in to pitch their tents on the patch of flat land that she could see from the window. And now there was nothing.

'Perhaps all this disruption to the valley will stop now and we'll be able to live in peace.'

'Och no,' his wife replied miserably. 'Things have gone too far for that. They've made their mark on the valley and no mistake. There's no turning back.'

*

Josef Kessler fixed the picture in his mind as the train pulled out of the station... the rounded hills, bare of trees and, from this distance, seemingly bare of sheep.

From here it was impossible to see the farm, but he knew where it was by the contours of the hills that formed its backdrop.

All too soon the train picked up speed and left the Uplands behind to follow the path of the River Clyde as it rambled into larger and larger towns on its journey to the sea. Putting his hand into his coat pocket, he felt the crispness of the envelope that lay within. It gave him a modicum of comfort. He could not, of course, read it again here, surrounded as he was by his fellow countrymen. But he had memorised the words and, even if the letter were taken from him, he would never forget what was written.

Dear Josef,

I think it unlikely that I will see you before you leave. It means that we will never meet again. My heart is breaking. Although I maybe should not say this, you have been more like a husband to me than my own husband.

I shall try to be a good wife to Tom if and when he returns, and a good mother to his daughter. I shall also try to be a good mother to your daughter, for I feel sure that the new baby is yours. She has your hair and the same faraway eyes, full of the sea. Her smile is yours and, when she grows up, I have no doubt that she will have your sweet temper.

I have called her Eva after the auntie she will never

know. I will look after her well. I shall never forget you.
You live on in our daughter.
  From your loving friend, Ellen.

36

Clara's Companion

After so many months without a letter, it was strange to see the postman approach the cottage a few days before Christmas. With a fast-beating heart, Ellen almost snatched the envelope out of his hand hoping it might be from Josef. The address, however, was to Mr and Mrs T. Fairclough.

Tom was out on the hill and would not be back for several hours. Slowly she opened the letter and, as she scanned the page, felt a rising mixture of pleasure and apprehension.

Dear Tom and Ellen,

I do hope this letter finds you well. What a blessing that the war is ended at last but awful that it has been replaced by the scourge of influenza. There are so many cases in Glasgow that we have spent most of our days caring for them. Our routine work has been put to one side until the emergency is over.

The reason I am writing to you is to ask you a

favour. I have been given three days off at Christmas and told to get away and rest. There is not time for me to visit my home and I wonder if I might impose on you. You said I might, if I was free at any time.

I have another favour to ask. A colleague is in a similar predicament to myself. Could you possibly find room for the two of us? I think the country air would do us both good.

I look forward to hearing from you.
Your affectionate friend, Clara.

She studied Tom's face closely when she handed him the letter at teatime, noting how a darkening flush travelled up over the skin of his neck when he glimpsed the name at the bottom of the page. He paused, as if to collect his thoughts, before folding up the page.

'Well, lass, we better start making preparations.' He grinned at her. 'Shall you reply to the letter?'

'No, you do it, Tom. She's your friend.' She would keep up this charade for the sake of the children but it was clear where Tom's affections lay. And his obvious excitement over Clara's imminent visit only emphasised the emptiness in her heart caused by Josef's departure.

'It's a nuisance we've got to have one of her colleagues as well,' Tom continued. 'I wonder which one she's bringing. I hope it's not that stuck-up bitch she was studying with.' Tom's lip curled in distaste.

'How have you met the girls she was studying with?'

Ellen asked, ignoring his coarse choice of words.

'Oh, I called to see her once... not long after I came here... just to see how she were getting along. She were in the middle of lectures, so it weren't convenient to talk.' He looked round the room, cluttered with the paraphernalia of two small children. 'Happen they'll have to sleep in your father's side of the cottage. We've no room here, thanks to you, little one.' He picked Netta up and sat her on his lap. 'Just think, Netta, in a few days we'll have Auntie Clara here. What an exciting time it'll be.' And he began to tickle her until she shrieked and begged to be let down.

*

With an uncanny feeling of déjà vu, Tom tied Archie to the rail outside the station and walked briskly onto the platform. Glancing at the station clock, he saw that there were still ten minutes before the train was due in. He found an empty seat and sat down, willing himself to be calm.

He cursed again at the thought that his conversation with Clara would be modified by the presence of another. If he were lucky, though, her friend would wish to spend some time chatting with his wife and he could then take Clara walking on the hills. At least Clara's companion would make it unlikely that he would face further quizzing about his activities in the last months of the war.

He stood up and began to pace the platform. A brisk wind ruffled his hair and sent scraps of leaves flurrying across the lines. When the warning bell sounded, Tom stood still as the Glasgow train approached, waiting for the first glimpse of his childhood friend. Then disappointment flooded through him. She wasn't there. As the smoke cleared, the only people who alighted from the train were a young couple, smartly dressed, and an elderly farmer, to whom Tom returned a brief nod of recognition.

He turned slowly to the exit. She must have missed the train or perhaps the influenza outbreak had reached such proportions that she was unable to get away. Maybe… and he was gripped by a sudden panic… maybe she had succumbed to the influenza herself. What if she were one of the many who had not survived?

'Tom! Don't you recognise me?'

She was there! How could he have failed to see her? She must think him stupid. He spun round wildly and came face to face with a Clara he hardly knew. She looked taller than before, better dressed, in a dark green suit and ankle-length boots. But it was her hair that arrested his gaze. It was cut short. Gone were the dark curls that had filled his dreams on so many occasions. In their place was a dark swirl of cropped hair that framed her face and gave her an authoritative air.

She must have sensed his shock, for she put her hand

up to the side of her head and laughed. 'I'm sorry. I should have warned you about the hair. It's so much more sensible for when I'm on the wards and in operating theatres.' She gave a chuckle and half turned. 'Tom… may I introduce Dr Alex Fraser… my husband.'

The look of shock on Tom's face intensified. He stood as if turned to stone. A man came forward and shook his hand before stepping to Clara's side and putting an arm round her waist. He was slim and tall. His piercing eyes were very blue and his hair sandy-coloured and brushed straight back from his face. He looked considerably older than Clara.

Tom felt a hand on his arm and the touch broke his stupor. He looked down. Clara's gloved hand rested on the rough tweed of his jacket. He fought to bring his emotions under control.

'I… I'd no idea.' He looked into her eyes. 'You should have said.' His voice shook.

'It was meant to be a surprise.'

'It's certainly that.' He withdrew his arm.

'Blame me.' It was Alex Fraser speaking. He had the authoritative voice of the educated Highlander. 'It was all very sudden, at least the wedding was, although we have been engaged for some months. It was the opportunity of a new job and the certainty that it would take me away from Clara that forced our hands.' He looked at her fondly. 'You see, I couldn't bear to go without her. You're a married man yourself. You must know what I mean.'

'Some of us had very little choice until recently,' Tom said bitterly.

'Aye, I'm aware of that and can only be grateful that my work kept me fully occupied in this country.'

Clara gave an involuntary shiver. 'Are we going to stand here all day, Tom? I'm looking forward to seeing little Netta again, and Ellen too.'

'Of course. Archie and the wagon are waiting outside.' Tom turned to the exit, summoning up all his energy to lift one leaden step in front of the other and ride the wave of disappointment that was threatening to engulf him.

He said little to the pair as he steered the wagon through the valley. In truth, he felt as he must look, like a country cousin, uncouth and down-at-heel next to their elegance and education. He was angry, so angry, with Clara for putting him in this impossible position and without warning. But, above all, he was overwhelmed with despair at the knowledge that she was finally beyond his grasp... even if, in reality, his marriage to Ellen had already made her so years ago. What didn't help was the thought that he would have to dance attention on them for the next three days while they stayed under his roof and did all the things that newly married couples liked to do. The thought was intolerable.

Ellen was delighted with the news. Not only did it remove the threat of Clara that had hovered over her for so long, but it was exciting to be able to entertain a couple of similar age to themselves. She had lived for so long in the company of her father and Margaret Murdie that she had almost forgotten what it was like to be with people of her own age.

Alex Fraser was clearly enchanted with Netta. The eldest of five children, he had spent most of his holidays entertaining one or other of his growing number of nieces and nephews. So he said it was just like being at home. And Clara was enchanted by the new baby.

'They're beautiful children, both of them... and so placid. I hope, when my firstborn arrives, it will be like yours.' Clara looked at Alex fondly and laughed at the blush that spread rapidly up his neck and face. 'Yes, I am having a baby in the New Year. We are so excited about it.'

After Ellen had voiced her congratulations Tom turned to Clara. 'So where is the new job going to be, only you said that you were moving away. Are you staying in the big city or will it be a quiet cottage hospital?'

'Neither,' Alex replied enigmatically and looked at Clara.

'We're travelling abroad, if all goes according to

plan,' his wife said. 'Alex has applied to work in a mission hospital. In a few months' time we will be leaving for China.'

*

'You have a lovely family, Tom. Thank you for having us to stay. We've enjoyed being with you all.' Clara gave Tom a kiss on his cheek before turning to her husband, who lifted her down gently from the wagon.

Tom stepped down after her, fastening Archie loosely to the railings and retrieving their case. He followed them onto the platform and they stood in silence, Tom both eager for and dreading the arrival of the train. At last they heard its approach.

Tom turned to Alex. 'Look after her. She was always my favourite girl at school!' The words caught in his throat.

'I will, you can rest assured.' Alex gave Tom a firm handshake

The train slowed, stopped and Alex helped Clara into the carriage before taking the case from Tom.

'Well, goodbye… and thank you.' Alex slammed the door and sat down. Tom took a step back and looked at them as the engine drew jerkily away. He raised his hand slowly and waved, his heart constricting as he faced the prospect of never setting eyes on Clara again.

As soon as the train was out of sight, Tom spun

round and hurried from the platform, his head down. At the entrance. he almost collided with two men who were standing just outside the station. He murmured his apologies, glancing up as he did so. One looked vaguely familiar, a face glimpsed across a cluttered desk, stacked with papers. He turned away hurriedly, reached the waiting horse and wagon, unhooked the reins, jumped into the seat and made off as fast as he was able. His heart was beating nineteen to the dozen. He had just remembered where he had seen that face before.

37

Proud of Her

'I need to check on the sheep.' Tom put his head round the door. Ellen was preparing a meal.

'Won't you have some tea first?'

'No. I need to walk the hill before the snow gets too bad. Give me some cake. It'll keep me going until later.'

He pulled on a thicker coat and a pair of heavy boots, snatched up his stick and left the house, scanning the far side of the valley as he did so. Nothing moved. Overhead the sky was grey slate. The snowflakes were thickening.

By the time he had checked on the ewes, a thin pencil of light was all that marked the sunset. Entering the lower barn, he made his way to one of the pens and sank down in the reeking straw. He put his head on his knees and for a while no coherent thoughts came to him, and even when they did, they didn't help him plan the next few vital hours.

He glanced round the barn. It was the very one in which he had found Ellen that Christmas night three years ago. The night when all thoughts of a future with Clara were dashed. Not that he begrudged the birth of Netta. He loved her. He was as proud of her as any father could be.

'He's gey proud of her, isn't he, Catherine?' He remembered the remark of one of the sisters in the train, as she laughed over his gazing at the photograph that he had pulled from his pocket for the second time that day. He smiled as he recalled the sisters, their playful, faintly mocking but never hurtful banter.

'He's still alive then, Jeannie. I was beginning to wonder.' The voice that greeted his precipitate arrival in the carriage, the accents soft, so different from the harsher tones that he was used to.

Leaning against the wooden side of the pen in which he was sitting, Tom closed his eyes and heard again that crackling voice telling anyone who was interested that the train on platform four was about to depart for Craigendoran Junction.

And abruptly he was dashing across the smoky emptiness of the platform. The train was gathering speed now. He grabbed at the handle of the nearest door and it flew open. With a huge effort, he threw himself into the carriage and caught at the door, swinging it shut. Then he fell back in the seat and closed his eyes, gasping for breath. At last his pulse slowed and his lungs ceased to strain for air.

When he opened his eyes, they met the amused gaze

of two young women, the only occupants of the carriage. They looked at one another and smiled.

'He's still alive then, Jeannie. I was beginning to wonder.' The voice sounded playful and soft.

'I... I thought I was going to miss the train,' he muttered, by way of explanation.

'So we can see,' said the other woman. 'Where are you going to, all dressed up as you are?'

He paused, not knowing what to say. He could give no explanation for his sudden action. He did not know himself what had caused him to behave as he had.

'Er, I... I... I'm going to Craigendoran Junction.'

'Aye, we guessed that. But where afterwards?'

'Oh, a little way up the line. I... I forget the name... I'm a stranger to these parts. What about yourselves?'

'Fort William. That's where we're from... well, near there. It's our first time in Glasgow. We've enjoyed it, but we'll be glad to be back, will we no', Jeannie?'

'Oh aye, we're looking forward to the peace and quiet again.'

Peace and quiet. The description sounded good to Tom. That's what he needed, peace and quiet.

'What do you do there? I mean, do you work?' he asked.

'Oh aye. We work.' It was the other sister speaking now. 'Catherine and I... we're sisters... we run a small cafe. Mother's helping out while we've been away. We'll be back in time for the summer visitors. What about you? I mean, I can see what you do by your uniform. Are you on leave?'

'Aye, on leave.'

'Are you a family man then?'

'Aye. I've a wife and child.'

'Pity they can't be with you.'

'My wife's expecting another baby soon. It's not good for her to travel at the moment.'

'How old's the wee one?'

'She's two now. I've a photo of her somewhere.'

And he had put his hand into his inside pocket, where it encountered his army papers. It had struck him then just what he had done. He had run away. He would be labelled a deserter. Fumbling in the pocket, he found his packet of photos and, with trembling hands, began to withdraw the picture of Netta seated on Ellen's knee. His hand continued to shake as he gave the photo to one of the sisters… Jeannie, he thought it was.

'He's gey proud of her, isn't he, Catherine?' Jeannie said and the girls looked at one another and then at Tom, and burst out laughing. Tom stowed the photos in his pocket. He looked at the girls. 'Tell me about Fort William. Do you like it there?'

The two looked at one another again.

'Aye, it's well enough. There are plenty of visitors passing through for us to make a living. And bonnie places all around, the likes of which you'll never see in Glasgow!'

'I think I might stop off there for the night, just to see what it's like… if it's as nice as you say.'

'Aye.' Jeannie hesitated. 'Aye, you can follow us if you like and we'll put you on the right train.'

The route to Fort William was winding and slow. The sisters invited him to join them in their carriage and shared their meal of fish sandwiches, hard-boiled eggs and chocolate cake. Then they dozed and Tom looked out of the window at the wonderful scenery that was opening up before him.

He felt calmer now, as though this was the route that he was always meant to take. He closed his eyes and refused to think about the boat awaiting his arrival at the Edinburgh docks. Instead he slept, lulled by the rhythmic thrumming of the carriage wheels.

He came to with a start. It was very dark. His head against the wooden boards of the barn was uncomfortable, his hands cold. But he had no desire to move. He wished only to be back in that idyllic landscape through which the train had taken him. Settling himself into a corner of the pen and tucking his hands into his armpits for warmth, he closed his eyes again.

Great hills towered in the distance. Different from the smooth curves of those he had left behind in the south, these were rugged and dotted here and there with snow pockets. The railway followed the edge of lonely lochs, in which the mountains towering above were mirrored.

Gradually the scene changed to barren moorland, reedy grass, between which the brown sludge of peat bog glinted uninvitingly. And then there were mountains again, even higher and more dominating than previously, their tops invisible in the low cloud of a windless day.

Without thinking, he put his hand into the inside pocket of his coat and his fingers were reminded a second time of his supposed destination. His heart missed a beat. He looked across at the girls. Jeannie had woken and was examining his face. She smiled.

'Where will you stay in Fort William? Do you have friends there?'

'Er, no. Happen I'll find lodgings this evening and then move on tomorrow.'

'Well, Mother takes lodgers. I know for a fact that she has a spare room and she'd put you up for the night, wouldn't she, Catherine?'

'Aye, nae problem. You just come home with us and we'll sort you out for the night.'

The arrangement seemed a good one. It would be late by the time he arrived at Fort William. He would stay with Catherine and Jeannie and tomorrow he would decide what to do.

It came to him in the night that if he were caught here in the home of Catherine and Jeannie, they would be in trouble for harbouring a deserter. For, however much he tried to form an explanation for his recent actions, he

knew that the army would label him just that.
Accordingly he rose by first light, packed his kitbag and
waited until he heard signs of movement. Tiptoeing
down the stairs, he came upon Catherine in the kitchen.
She started at his sudden appearance and smiled.

'My, my! You're an early riser. Would you like a cup
of tea? It's a fresh pot.'

'Aye. That would be grand.' He sat down at the
table. 'Then I must be off.'

'What, now? So early?'

'Aye. I've imposed on your company for long enough.
I… I want to see as much of the countryside as I can
while I've time. You see, I haven't been this way before
and I've only a day or two.'

'Well, there's plenty of it to see.' She laughed. 'In fact,
if you plan on going west from here, you'll no' come
across anything else but countryside between here and
the Atlantic.'

'That suits me fine. The quieter the better.'

'You'll have some breakfast before you go? A soldier
can't go into battle on an empty stomach.'

Tom winced at the unintended barb. 'Aye… er… aye.
I'd like that, if I'm not overstaying my welcome.'

'Not at all. We've enjoyed your company, haven't we,
Jeannie?' She looked up at her sister, who was standing
quietly at the kitchen door.

'Aye, that we have. So you be sure and have a good
breakfast. The houses are few and far between west of

here.' She laughed and as quickly became serious again. 'And don't you forget, Tom, if you're in any trouble, you can always stay here.' She turned and left the room before Tom had time to reply.

It was a long journey to the Atlantic but it was here Tom determined to go. He begged lifts in a small boat to bypass a long journey around the sea loch, in carts that grumbled their way up steep roads, pulled by ageing nags that plodded uncomplaining over rough tracks. And wherever the road wound, there would be mountains and hills that towered to right and left and panoramic views that opened up at the top of every laborious ascent. At last he could go no further because there was no path to follow. Sea lochs wandered far into the hillsides, their margins patrolled by lone herons, hunched and grey, and seals lay indolent on the huge boulders that littered the shoreline. Primroses dotted the banks in bright clusters, and in the water, white clouds, blue sky and the mistier blue of the furthest mountains were reflected.

Tom had never seen anything more beautiful.

While he stood, leaning on a gate, a movement caught his eye. It was a man, dressed in the uniform of a gamekeeper. He was making his way off the lower slopes of the hill and across the flat land, through which a track ran towards a large turreted house. As he came closer, he nodded his head and Tom waved a hand in greeting.

'Excuse me,' Tom called, acting on a sudden impulse.

The man stopped and turned.

'Can I have a word?'

'Aye. Are you lost?'

'Not exactly. But I am new to these parts.' Tom swung open the gate and walked towards the gamekeeper, accentuating the limp in his bad leg. 'I was wondering if you had any work.'

'For you?' The man looked Tom up and down. 'You look to me as though you have a job.'

'Aye, I have. Leastwise, I did. I were invalided out with a war wound.'

'Oh, I see. Well, I'm afraid the only work I have here is shepherding and that would no suit you. There's a lot of walking in the hills, chasing after the sheep. They're scattered far and wide.'

'Oh, but that would suit me fine. I were a shepherd before the war. And I can manage walking, as long as I take my time.'

The man looked at Tom suspiciously. 'Then why did you no' return to your own farm to work?'

'Oh, you know what it's like. I fancied a change of scenery after the mess of the battlefield.'

The keeper considered for a minute. 'Aye, I can understand that, especially if you've no one waiting at home for your return. I suppose you'll be wanting somewhere to stay?'

'If you have a room, I'd be grateful.'

'It would be very plain. Only a bed and a cupboard and a chair or two. You'd have to get your meals with the servants up at the big house.'

'That's not a problem.'

'And I'll have to check with the laird that he's happy for you to join the workforce. Though I can't see that there'll be any doubt about that. We've lost a couple of our estate workers to the war.'

Tom followed the keeper towards the house, limping just enough to make it obvious that he was not fit for action at the front but not too much that they would doubt his ability to cope with a day on the hill.

And so began an idyllic six months, far away from the horrors of the trenches and the demands and frustrations of family life. Lambing was drawing to a close when he arrived, but there were some ewes still to give birth on the hills and plenty of work needed in caring for mothers and babies. Once the keeper saw that Tom was competent, he left him alone for the most part, which suited Tom fine. He had no wish to get over-friendly with anyone who might become too interested in his life at the front or his family back home.

Back in the barn, Tom opened his eyes and stared into the blackness. Guilt surged through him, as it had done several times since the signing of the armistice, guilt that he had left the estate workers so suddenly and without warning. He had worked hard there and gained the respect of the other workers, the keeper in particular, but he had found the absence of his daughter difficult to endure. And the realisation that he could now return to her obscured all else. He had walked away from his job within a couple of hours of hearing of the cessation of hostilities.

Having no idea of the time, he staggered to his freezing feet with a groan and hobbled painfully to the door. Several inches of snow had fallen but it had stopped now and a waning moon made an intermittent appearance between scudding clouds. He looked up at the cottage. A lamp was still burning in the living room. Either Ellen was waiting for him to come in or she had left the light for him to see his way. But he could not go back. Suppose the man whom he had passed at the station was still around. But neither could he bear losing his daughter again.

Snatching up his gloves and a sturdy stick that was propped in a corner by the door, Tom emerged into the brightness of the snowy night. A blast of freezing wind hit him head-on as he set off to cross the field behind the cottage. But again, the light drew him. He approached slowly, peering into the uncurtained room. Ellen lay asleep in front of a dead fire. On an impulse he opened the door, unlacing his boots and leaving them on the mat. Thick socks cushioned his steps as he made soundless progress to the bedroom, keeping his eyes fastened on his wife. She never stirred.

The children were both deeply asleep. He glanced at

Eva, the daughter he hardly knew. She had no look of her sister, nor even of her mother. Maybe, given time, things might change. He turned to Netta. Her little boots lay side by side on the floor in front of her bed. He picked these up and thrust them into a coat pocket. Next, he drew a thick blanket off the bed and wrapped it round his sleeping daughter, lifting her into his arms as he did so. Stealthily he made his way past his still sleeping wife and into the corridor. At the entrance, he stepped into his boots, closed the door quietly behind him and struggled back to the barn. There he lay Netta gently in the hay, laced his boots, enveloped his daughter tightly in the blanket and secured her within the folds of his greatcoat, buttoning it around her. She stirred as he fumbled with his coat but settled against him as he stepped from the barn into the night.

The wind was blowing the top off the thick covering of snow, whirling it into his face, where it hit like needles. Again he crossed behind the cottage, following the path that led up the hillside, sure of his step, for he had trodden this route many times before. The wind snatched his breath from him and left him panting and weak before he was halfway up. It would be worse at the top, for he would meet the full force of it. But he trudged on with determination, refusing even to rest for a minute.

On the top, he struggled to stand, leaning against the stone wall for balance. He turned his face into the wind.

It was cleansing, freeing his brain from all the hurts that had afflicted it. Here, on the edge of reality, he was safe. No one and nothing could touch him and his sleeping daughter.

How long he stood there, he had no idea, but when he turned at last, it was to see the hills of the southern side of the valley standing dark against the earliest light of dawn. It must be later than he thought. Should he go down? But what if the officer did come calling for him? And if he stayed where he was, Ellen might alert him to Tom's favourite hideaway before she knew the reason for the man's visit. Looking down at the route he had come, he could see that the wind had scoured away the prints of his feet. If he set off a different way, they would never know that he had been here.

To the left of his usual path dipped a huge ravine, carved out by an ancient river. He had once clambered down its steep side to rescue an injured sheep. If he descended the hill this way and cut off to the east, his footprints would never be noticed. Clasping Netta securely to him and covering her head with the lapel of his greatcoat, he stepped out into the whiteness.

38

A Safe Place to Be

When Ellen glimpsed the empty bed, she smiled. It was not unusual for Netta to wake in the night and wander over to her toys, play for a while and fall asleep again. So, with Eva over her shoulder, she began unhurriedly to investigate all of Netta's hiding places.

It was her younger daughter's hungry cries that had woken her. Drowsy with tiredness and with a crick in her neck from hours spent curled in an armchair, she stumbled to her feet. She glanced at the clock as she crossed the room. It was six fifteen. Tom must have come in late and not woken her.

By the light from the oil lamp, she explored the bedroom. Netta was in none of her usual places. Perhaps she had wandered out into the living room and fallen asleep there. Unperturbed, she turned towards her own bed. It was empty, unruffled. Tom had not returned then. Where on earth was he?

Ellen stepped back into the light, murmuring softly to her truculent baby. She hunted behind chairs, under tables, in boxes, even in cupboards, slowly at first, but with a steadily rising anxiety.

Maybe her grandfather had her. Of course, that must be it. Ellen burst open the separating door between the cottages without knocking and surprised Duncan in a half-dressed state.

'Whatever is the matter, lassie? Is someone ill?'

'Is Netta with you, Feyther? Only I've been looking everywhere for her and then I thought, she sometimes comes into…'

'Nay, lassie, she's not been here.' Duncan rose from the bed where he had been sitting to pull on his socks. 'Are you sure she's not curled up somewhere asleep? It wouldnae be the first time.'

'I've looked everywhere.' Ellen's voice rose on a sob. She turned to run from the room.

'Where's Tom?' Duncan called. 'We'll go and look for her together.'

'He didn't come home,' she called over her shoulder. 'He's been out all night.'

'Out all night? In this weather?' Duncan drew the curtain and put his face up to the window.

'I've no idea where he is,' Ellen spat. 'And I don't care anymore. He's done this to me one time too many. It's Netta I'm worried about.'

'Aye, but we could do with him to help us look,' her father muttered, before saying louder, 'Dinnae fret, lass. I'm sure there's a simple explanation.'

Duncan pulled on his trousers quickly and followed Ellen through into the living room, heaving his braces over his shoulders as he did so. Together they searched again. By now Eva was screaming with hunger.

'Look, lassie. You sit down and feed wee Eva. I'll carry on looking for Netta. Like I say, there must be a simple explanation.'

Ellen sat on the sofa, her heart racing, and attempted to feed her baby. She listened to her father's muffled footsteps passing the window as he negotiated the slope down to the barn. A while later, she heard him return, stamp the snow off his boots and slam the door. His worried face told her what she dreaded.

'I've checked the barn… not that it's likely she got that far. But she does like playing in there on a fine day. But she's no' there.' He frowned. 'There's footsteps in the snow around the entry to the barn though… big footsteps.'

'Aye, Tom said he had to see to the sheep before tea last night. They'll belong to him.'

'Maybe, though there are none anywhere else, unless the wind has flattened them.' Duncan sat down heavily, rubbing his brow in thought. 'Right, lassie, as soon as you've finished, you search the cottage again. I'll go down to Kenneth at the farm and ask him and Elizabeth to help us.'

Presently Ellen emerged, skidding on the snowy path after another unsuccessful indoor hunt for Netta. She had wrapped Eva warmly in a shawl and buried her deep within the safety of the perambulator. Expecting to see a small search party of two or three, she was amazed to see a group of men numbering twenty to thirty gathered outside the barn. Duncan, seeing her appear outside the cottage, trudged up the path to join her.

'A stroke of luck, lassie. The men were just arriving to take over the building of the reservoir. Kenneth waylaid them and they're only too keen to help. Kenneth's wife suggests you go and wait with her in the farmhouse while we go and look for the lassie.'

'Oh no, I couldn't do that… but I'll ask Elizabeth if she'll look after Eva for me and I'll come with yous.'

By the time Ellen had joined the men, they had spread out in a large fan shape and were making their way across the field behind the cottage. She watched appalled as two of them climbed through the freezing waters of the gill that tumbled down the hillside to join the river in the base of the valley. They were exploring behind stones and bending to examine beneath overhanging grasses. Reason told her they must look everywhere, but she couldn't prevent her panic-stricken brain from flying to the worst conclusion possible.

And all the while the clock was ticking the minutes and the hours away.

She forced herself to return to the farmhouse at dinnertime to feed Eva. There had been no sign, no small footprint, no soft toy discarded in the snow. Nothing that could give them a clue as to Netta's whereabouts. And no sign of her husband, whose intimate knowledge of the hills would have been invaluable in the search for their daughter. Where, in heaven's name could he have got to?

By the time she rejoined them, the crescent of men had made their way deep into the hill. Ellen's face was puffy with crying and her cheeks inflamed with the salt tears drying there. Never, never would they be able to find her little girl.

But then a sudden shout echoed round the hills. All faces were raised to the shout. It came again.

'Over here. She's here. Quickly.'

She saw a man's wave before he sank to the ground. Ellen stumbled over the uneven terrain, and could see several men converge on the place from which the shout had come. Then one of them was up, cradling a bundle in his arms, another covering the bundle with a coat, and they were running, all of them together, coming towards her across the field.

Ellen stood, bracing herself for the words that she dreaded to hear.

'I think she's alive... I think she's alive,' one of the men panted, repeating the words, as though unable to believe them.

A surge of elation and Ellen was running with the men towards her cottage. They burst into a room turned upside down with the search for her daughter, ashes cold in the grate, but warmer than the chill air of the late December day outside.

They lay the small body on the sofa. Her lips were blue, and her face and hands white as the snow in which they had found her. She made no response to their touch, but one of the men pointed out to Ellen a small pulse that beat at her daughter's neck. Ellen brought blankets from the bed and laid them over Netta. One of the rescuers massaged her cold hands, while Ellen removed the little girl's soaking socks and rubbed her feet to warm them. All the time, the man who had rescued her was talking, anxiously telling Ellen how he had found her.

'She was in with the sheep... in the sheep pen, curled up, ken. It must have been them that kept her warm... a woolly blanket, ken. How the sheep didn't suffocate her, I'll never know. She was lucky to find it though. She would have died out in the snow all this time.'

'Wisht now. Less of your wild talk, pal. The lassie doesn't want to hear all about what might have been.'

'I found her once before like that,' Ellen said suddenly.

'How do you mean, lassie?'

'Once before. We were up by the reservoir, visiting a friend. There had been a lot of rain. The banking collapsed.'

'Och Aye. We heard about that. Someone got killed, didn't they... one of the prisoners?'

'Aye. I went to see if I could help and when I got back to the pram, Netta had gone. I looked everywhere for her. And there she was, asleep in a stell. Maybe, somehow, she remembered and knew it was a safe place to be.' Ellen pictured the scene again in her mind. Netta fast asleep and unharmed in the stell. Josef calling to her across the meadow. Josef's hand brushing her cheek. Josef looking at her with his faraway eyes, the eyes of Netta's little sister.

Just then Netta turned her head, her eyelids fluttering, and coughed. And Ellen, laying her head down beside her daughter's, began to sob uncontrollably.

39

The Decisions We Make

Spring came late to the hills that first year after the ending of the war. Farmers struggled through the lingering snow. Sheep were found dead, suffocated beneath the frozen blanket. Life was hard, but at least they were safe from the scourge of influenza that was wreaking havoc up and down the country.

Duncan told his daughter that Margaret Murdie was finding it difficult to manage. He made the journey out to her farm whenever he had time. One day in mid-March he drove her back in the wagon to the cottage.

Ellen, hands white with flour as she mixed pastry, looked up at the rattle of the latch, feeling again the rush of apprehension that accompanied every unexpected visitor.

'Here's someone to see you,' Duncan announced, opening the door wide and stepping back to allow Margaret to enter. 'She's lonely out in the hills and fancied a bit of company.'

Ellen crossed the room quickly and gave Margaret a

hug. 'It's so good to see you, Margaret. Come and sit down here by the fire. I'll put the kettle on.'

'I'll be back in twenty minutes, lassie,' Duncan said. 'I have a couple of jobs to do. I'll take a cup of tea though, when I come in.' He smiled at his daughter, glanced at Margaret and left.

Ellen turned away to fill the kettle. The visit had all the appearance of having been arranged by Duncan so that Margaret could have 'a little talk' with his daughter about her missing husband, and Ellen had no wish to talk about him. As far as she was concerned, he could stay out of her life.

'How's little Netta?' Margaret began. 'No more running off into the snow?'

'No, though it's no' been easy keeping an eye on her all the time.'

'She's a very lucky little girl.' Margaret turned to Netta, who was playing on the rug in front of the fire. 'Out there like that in all that weather. It's a wonder you didn't suffer from frostbite.' She stroked Netta's hair and the little girl clambered on her lap. 'How long was she outside, Ellen?'

'I don't know. But I must have woken up soon after she went. Maybe she disturbed Eva as she left.' Ellen shivered. 'Every time I think about what might have happened, I can't believe that she was found safe and sound.'

'Your father says you've heard nothing at all from

Tom.'

'Nothing,' Ellen replied. She plunged her hands into the half-finished pastry, sending a puff of flour into the air.

'Have you any idea where he is?'

'None at all.' She hesitated, before deciding to continue. 'But I've a feeling he'll no' be back this time.'

'Surely he's no' got to return to the army now.'

Ellen shrugged and said nothing.

'But why would he go?' Margaret persisted. 'He thinks the world of little Netta. Just imagine if he had known what happened to her... he would be distraught.'

Ellen sighed and glanced behind her, as though she expected eavesdroppers. 'We weren't getting on too well, Tom and me,' Ellen confided. 'And there was someone else, another woman who he thought a lot about. They were friends at school. He used to talk about her, and I could see he was very taken with her whenever she came to see us.'

Margaret's face registered shock. 'You don't think he ran off with her?'

'No, not that. But she came to visit at Christmas and she brought a husband with her. I could see it came as a big surprise for Tom. I think it was all too much for him. He was very low. He wanted to be out of the house at every opportunity, although the weather was so bad. I think he may have gone away because of that.'

'You don't think' he might have gone off because of

the Germans?'

Ellen's fingers paused their activity in the mixing bowl. 'What do you mean?'

'I mean... it didn't escape my notice that you kept up a friendship with that prisoner you looked after.'

Ellen stared at Margaret, colour suffusing her face. Then her shoulders slumped and she looked down into the bowl of flour, kneading it aimlessly again. 'Aye, it's true,' she murmured. 'There's no point in saying otherwise. But maybe I wouldn't have been so drawn to him if Tom had shown me more consideration,' she added, lifting her head defiantly.

'I'm not criticising you, lassie, neither of you. I dare say you both tried your best. If it hadn't been for little Netta's arrival, maybe you wouldn't have wed.'

Ellen nodded slowly. 'I'm sure you're right.'

Margaret rose from the chair and, coming up behind Ellen, put her arm round the girl's shoulders. 'Aye, lass. But we all have to live with the decisions we make. It might interest you to know that it was no'...'

Duncan's abrupt entry interrupted her sentence and made them both jump. 'Busy gabbing, I can see,' he joked. 'I hope that tea's ready because I'm ready for it.' He sat down by the fire and lifted his granddaughter onto his knee. 'You'll be able to go out and play soon, wee one. The snow's melting fast now and it's much warmer.'

'Not until I've bought her some more boots,' Ellen

said, shaking her head. 'I still can't find her others anywhere.'

'You must go into town next week, if the snow's away,' Duncan said. 'Catch the train. It'll do yous good to have a day out. Margaret might like to go with you, help you with wee Eva.' He looked at their visitor. 'Have you said anything?'

'Of course not, Duncan.'

Duncan cleared his throat and met his daughter's enquiring eyes.

'Said anything about what?' Ellen asked, wishing they would all leave her alone with her troubles.

Duncan coughed again and then blurted out, 'About the fact that I've asked Margaret to marry me.'

So unexpected was the revelation that Ellen could only stare wide-eyed from one to the other of them.

'There, Duncan, I warned you it was too soon. The lass is too upset about Tom to even think about anything else.'

'No... no, not at all. I think it's a wonderful idea.' Ellen crossed to Margaret, enveloping her in floury arms. 'It's the best news I've heard in ages. It's just that I thought... well... it might be a bit early for you with Robert dying only a year ago. I know how close you were.'

'Nowhere near as close as your father and me. Shall I tell her, Duncan?'

'Aye, you better had.'

'Your father and me, we were childhood sweethearts. We were meant for one another. But then one day we quarrelled. I don't even ken now what it was about. But we fell out... and Robert saw his chance and asked me if I would go with him... and, before we knew it, there I was expecting a baby. So that was that. We had to get married. We were happy enough... we had to be... but it was never the love I had for your father.'

'But what about mother?' Ellen asked accusingly, the rosy image of her parents' short life together falling around her ears. 'Didn't you love her?'

'Of course I did. I loved her very much.' Duncan kissed the top of Netta's dark head. 'I was upset when I lost Margaret here... very upset. But eventually I got over it. I loved your mother... it was awful when I lost her.'

'He was heartbroken,' Margaret interrupted. 'It was only having you to look after that brought him round. I used to come over and help when you were small. And all the time I would think, if only things had been different. But, like I said, we all have to live with the decisions we make. And things have a habit of working themselves out.'

Ellen looked at Margaret doubtfully. 'I don't know that they have.' She brightened, 'But I'm so glad they have for yous.' She kissed Margaret warmly, before bending down to her father and doing the same to him.

'With all the upheaval going on down the valley and

Margaret soon to be out of her home, it seemed the right time to do it,' Duncan went on. 'She's struggling to keep the farm going... and for what? In a few years the farmhouse and in-bye fields will be under water.' He sighed. 'Are you sure you don't mind, lassie? Thee and me, we'll still be as close as we've always been. You ken that, don't you?'

'Of course I ken that, Feyther. And I'm very happy for you both.'

'Only we weren't sure whether it was a good idea, with Tom away.'

Ellen snorted. 'If you wait for Tom to come home and stay home, you'll never get married. You've been long enough on your own, Feyther. You mustn't let this chance of happiness escape you a second time.' She had seen her own chance of happiness escape with the departing prisoners. From now on she must forge a new life for herself and her two young daughters.

*

A week later, Duncan hitched Archie to the wagon and drove Margaret, Ellen and the two little ones out to the railway station. Over the last day or two the air had turned warmer and overhead, the determined trilling of a lark confirmed spring's arrival. Sheep, heavy with wool and pregnancy, shambled away from them on their thin legs. When Duncan had dropped them at the station, he planned to take the opportunity of this improvement in the weather to inspect the higher slopes. There was plenty to be done, he said, especially now that Ellen's wastrel of a husband had left them short-handed.

*

Duncan unhitched the horse and led him to the stable, leaving the wagon outside for later in the day. Whistling to Fleet, his latest dog, he set off across the fields to the lower slopes. His comment about Ellen's husband was one born of frustration. He and Kenneth had been pondering how they would cope with lambing when they were one man short.

Duncan had liked Tom well enough in the early days. The lad was a man of few words and with little sense of humour but he had been a good worker. His opinion had changed with the suspicion that Tom was ill-treating his wife, and although Ellen repeatedly denied that this was the case, her bruises and black eyes could surely not be put down to mere carelessness.

But now the lad had disappeared for no reason, when the war was over and there was every possibility of things getting back to normal.

Duncan followed the gill as it scrambled between the rocks scattered in its path, sending rainbow shards of water this way and that. Once through the curtain of trees that encircled the farm, he took a track away from the water and began to climb. With a patience born of many years tramping the hills, he made his way slowly up the unrelenting slope. Before many minutes had elapsed, he was sweating in the unaccustomed warmth and stopped to catch his breath. His keen eyes swept the land westward, where a trail of dispersing smoke indicated the position of the railway line. Ellen and Margaret would be on the train by now and he allowed himself a small smile and a rare quiver of excitement at the thought of what the year would bring. The sensation was a strange one for a man who had, for so many years, with dogged determination, faced all that the weather, the uneven terrain and life itself could throw at him.

Taking a deep breath, he recommenced his climb. The ground beneath his feet was boggy with melting snow. It sucked at his boots and more than once he skidded on the wetness. Ahead, the ewes scattered, sure-footed as ever. Seeking to gain firmer ground, he cut off to the right until he stood on the edge of a semicircle hewn out of the hills by the stream that sparkled so innocently far below. The greening hills trapped snow in deep pockets. It would be weeks before these cool reminders of winter disappeared, even if spring continued its advance, and they would all need to be checked for stranded sheep. His eye was caught by one of these snow pockets, near the base of the steep drop in front of him. Screwing up his eyes to see more clearly, he felt his blood run cold.

40

A Promise of Happiness

Ellen stowed a packet of sandwiches in the base of the pram, adding cake and orange squash before replacing the mattress and covers. Next, she sat Eva in one end, strapped securely so that she could enjoy the surroundings. Netta insisted on walking, but a space at the other end of the pram was ready, in case her legs began to tire. Waving goodbye to her father, Ellen carefully made her way to the base of the slope to join the muddy track that led away from the farm. At the railway line they paused, looking to left and right, before crossing to the road and turning eastward.

The hills were thick with sheep. In a week, shearing would begin and her presence would be needed on the farm. Today, though, she was making the most of the good weather to take her girls for a picnic. Netta ran along in front, excited by the freedom and in expectations of seeing the train on one of its many journeys to the building site or back to the village. As they neared the excavations, they left the road and chose a grassy field, littered with pansies in shades of yellow and blue.

From this vantage point, Ellen could enjoy the quiet while watching the activity in the base of the valley. Men, like ants, scuttled noiselessly from one spot to another. The embankment was nearing completion now, the erection of which had cost the life of Oliver Tauber. That sad day had also been the first occasion of her elder daughter's disappearance. Instinctively she glanced towards Netta, but she was harmlessly engaged in picking wild flowers. Below them Ellen could just see the rounded shelter, within which Josef had found her daughter sleeping on that dreadful day.

Refusing to let her mind dwell on the thought of Josef, she turned her gaze to the land soon to be filled with the water of the reservoir. There was Margaret's cottage, appearing unchanged from this distance, but in reality deserted and boarded up, since Margaret had come to live with her father. It had been at Ellen's insistence that the wedding had gone ahead. Both her father and Margaret said they would postpone it, considering it unseemly that their happiness should take precedence over mourning. But Ellen had insisted that life was too short to turn away from the chance of happiness.

It hadn't been easy though, adapting to another woman taking control and usurping her claim to her father's affections. She and her father had lived so long together that she didn't stop to think that her position in his heart was because of the death of her own mother, and his wife. Sometimes now she felt as though she were the interloper in her own home.

What *had* helped was the money that Margaret had brought to the family. For Robert, unlike most of the neighbouring farmers, had owned his farm. Margaret had been compensated by the Water Board and she had generously shared this with Duncan, his daughter and the two little girls. And although compensation never gave full redress, it was more money than any of them had ever seen. It made little difference to Duncan, set in his ways as he was, but Ellen was relieved to know that when his health began to fail, he could allow himself the rest he deserved after a lifetime of hard work.

She watched Netta race across the grass and struggle to climb onto a fallen tree trunk, her face etched with the stubborn determination that had passed down from her father. Tom! After the passage of a few months she was more able to think of him calmly, without the barrage of conflicting emotions that had assailed her in the early weeks after Duncan's dreadful discovery.

They had carried his body back and laid it in the barn. It had seemed callous and uncaring to leave him there, but the corpse was in no fit state to bring into the house and, in any case, there would have been the risk of Netta seeing her dead father. By the time Ellen and Margaret had been collected from the station and arrived back at the cottage, the doctor had been long gone. Such accidents, while dreadful for all concerned, were not uncommon in the harsh reality of winter in the upland hills. Shepherds grew exhausted and lay down to rest, never to get up again. Or they lost their bearings in the blinding whiteness of the blizzard and fell to their death. This, it was clear, was what had happened to Tom.

But Ellen thought she knew differently. She had long been aware of the confusion in Tom's mind, the desolation wrought by the years of war, the disappointment of finding Clara married.

And after the shock of finding that he was a deserter, she was even more convinced. They had come one morning, the officers, not long after he had gone missing. She and the babies were alone in the cottage and she had no warning that she must be careful what she said.

'Mrs Fairclough. Is your husband with you?'

'No. He isnae.'

'Will you tell us where we can find him?'

'I would if I knew. I haven't seen him for two days.'

'And you don't know where he's gone?'

'No. I wish I did.'

'Well, if he returns, please ask him to report to company headquarters immediately. We'll call back in a few days.'

They came a week later. There had been no sign of

Tom. And then their bombshell. He hadn't reported for duty since his interview the previous May. He was registered as a deserter.

'But... but I don't understand.' Ellen rubbed her brow in confusion. 'He left here to catch a train. He was to board a boat in Edinburgh.'

'Precisely, Madam.'

'But he went. I saw him off. He came back when war ended.'

'But he didn't get on the boat. He didn't return to the front. He's a deserter. It's a serious offence. You know the penalty.'

She didn't, but it didn't take her long to find out.

'If he should reappear, Madam,' the officer concluded, 'don't try covering up for him. We will track him down, make no mistake.'

It was her belief that he had thrown himself over the side of the hill to end a life without a promise of happiness or perhaps he had merely lain down in the snow and waited for death to take him.

That was until she had come across Netta's shoes. She was going through the pockets of his greatcoat to check for possible clues, when she had found them. At first, she was confused. How could they be in Tom's pocket? Gradually her mind cleared and she concluded that Tom must have come back for Netta. Maybe he was going to run away with her, maybe he intended bringing up Netta himself, planning to spite Ellen by taking away her daughter. Or perhaps, and this was an even more dreadful thought, he intended to do away with them both.

Others tried to persuade her that this could not be so. She would have heard Tom if he had come into the house to collect his daughter. He must have put the shoes into his pocket earlier without thinking. And, anyway, he loved Netta and wouldn't do anything to harm her.

But Ellen knew better. They weren't aware of Tom's state of mind, like she was. And she kept the news of his desertion from everyone, even her father. The certainty of what he had done enraged her. That Tom should choose to end his life was bad enough but to take that of his daughter was too much to bear. The discovery of the little boots changed her guilt and despair to fury and bitterness in an instant.

Now she was no longer certain. It was of little consequence, whatever she thought. She had her daughters, both of them, and for that she was more than thankful. Eva was awake and wanting to be fed. She called to Netta, unstrapped the baby and retrieved the picnic from the base of the pram.

When Ellen and her daughters were recrossing the wooden bridge on their way home, she saw, in the distance, a man waving. Assuming his actions were for the children's benefit, she pointed him out to Netta. They waved back and walked on. Again he tried to attract her attention. She hesitated, waiting, saw him turn and speak to a colleague who was standing nearby, and begin to cross the intervening space to where she was standing. There was something in the way he walked that jogged her memory. He was tall and had an upright bearing. In an instant she recognised him.

'Mrs Fairclough! I thought I would see you again sometime. Though I'm of the opinion that you're not doing as much walking as you were.'

'Captain! What are you doing here?'

'Oh, it's just for a few days, passing on information about the building work. In the clamour at the end of the war and the arrangements to give the prisoners safe passage home, there were a few loose ends remaining. I'm here to tie them up.' He smiled at Ellen. 'And how's your family?' He ruffled Netta's hair. 'This is the one who used to give you so much trouble, I think.'

'She still does, given the chance!'

'And this little one was born after I'd gone.'

'Aye. She'll soon be a year old.'

Eva stared at him with her faraway eyes.

'Strange how two sisters can be so different from one another. Your other little girl is so like her father.' He hesitated and lowered his voice. 'I was saddened to hear about your husband's conviction, Mrs Fairclough. Don't worry. If the folk in the valley don't know about it, they won't hear about it from me. You may not believe this, but I have more sympathy for deserters than you might think.'

'You haven't heard then? He's dead. He died on the hills last winter. He went out one afternoon, just after Christmas. We didn't find him till March. He'd been on the hill all that time, covered in snow. You ken how long it lay last winter?'

'Yes, I do.' The captain appeared lost for words. 'I… I'm sorry. I hadn't heard. You must be…' His sentence petered out and he looked away embarrassed.

'I must be very upset? Distraught? I have been all of those things… and a lot more besides, as you can maybe imagine. But there's no point going over it all again. It won't bring him back.'

'But how are you managing?'

'Same as I always did.'

'Just you and your father at the cottage?'

'Not exactly. My father's married again. His wife's Margaret Murdie from yon cottage that's to be flooded.'

'Oh yes.' He followed Ellen's glance. 'I know her. I talked to them a time or two when the men were building the embankment.'

'The embankment,' Ellen echoed. 'Whenever it is mentioned I think of Oliver and his awful death.'

The captain was silent, staring at the towering wall that had sprung up from the valley base.

'Such a lot has happened since that day,' Ellen went on. Still the captain remained silent. She glanced at him and thought she saw the hint of a tear in the corner of his eye.

'Mummy. Go now,' Netta said, impatience getting the better of her.

'Yes, darling, Mummy's going now.' Ellen released the brake and smiled at the captain. 'Can I ask you just one thing, Captain?'

'Of course you can.'

'Did you give Josef his letter?'

'Naturally. I said I would, didn't I?'

Ellen nodded. 'Good.' Taking a deep breath, she continued, 'Only I wanted him to know that he had a daughter.'

The captain stared at her. 'What do you mean, Mrs Fairclough?'

'Look at her, Captain. Is she no' the living image of Josef?'

'But how? I mean, when?'

'Och, Captain! You wouldn't expect me to tell you that, now would you? I know what you thought about fraternising with the enemy.'

Captain Cameron-Dyet shot her a glance and looked away. 'If I'm honest with you, Mrs Fairclough – and I should be because you have been with me – I did more fraternising with the enemy than you think. Oliver and I... well, we got on well. We shared common interests, we could talk about things. We even held the same beliefs about life, about what we would do after the war. He wasn't married, you know.' The captain sighed and appeared at a loss for words. 'I… we… as I said, we got on well. But this accident happened. There was no time, you see… only a few short months.' He was still staring at the embankment. An involuntary shiver ran through him, then he drew himself up tall. 'Well, I better let you get on. The children will be wanting their tea. I'm sorry, Mrs Fairclough, sorry that it all turned out this way.'

'Me too,' Ellen answered sadly. 'But at least I have the children, even if I have lost both my husband and Josef.'

He nodded slowly. 'Perhaps. Well, goodbye, Mrs Fairclough. I'm very glad to have seen you.'

When Ellen glanced back, the captain was still standing on the wooden bridge, looking in the direction of the embankment.

*

Three days after Ellen's conversation with the captain, a letter arrived in the post. It was written in an elegant flowing script. Enclosed within a single sheet of paper was another letter, its corners dog-eared and her name, the single word on the envelope, in a strange hand. Ellen read the single sheet first. It was from Captain Cameron-Dyet.

Dear Mrs. Fairclough,
   Following our conversation, I have pleasure in

sending you the enclosed, which is, after all, addressed to you and therefore your property. I have kept it safe since the departure of the prisoners. Josef Kessler asked me to pass it on to you. At the time, given all that had happened, I thought it best not to do so.

What you told me the other day about the sad death of your husband and the parentage of your younger daughter leads me to think that there is nothing to be gained by keeping the letter from you.

In these uncertain times I do trust that you and your family will find peace and happiness in the future.

With my sincere good wishes,

Montague Cameron-Dyet.

(Captain).

With shaking hands, Ellen ripped open the second envelope. The message within was brief.

Wednesday, 13th November, 1918.

Liebe Ellen,

Your news breaks my heart. I too never forget.
If you need me, please to write to this address:
Baumstrasse 7
34076 Freiburg im Breisgau.
Ewige Liebe,
Josef.

Margaret was cooking breakfast when Ellen put in an appearance.

'I'm sorry, Margaret. I should have been up long ago. I was awake in the night and then couldn't waken when I should have this morning.'

'No worries, lassie. It's my job to provide for my husband.'

Duncan was lacing his boots in preparation for a trip to the market. The autumn lamb sales were beginning and he was keen to see the competition and to catch up with the exploits of his fellow farmers.

Duncan and Margaret's happy domesticity was, at times, a source of envy for Ellen, reminding her that any hope of similar happiness between her and Josef was impossible. She was still feeling out-of-sorts when the postman found her later that morning. It was a day of rare warmth for the time of year. The sun had risen in a cloudless sky to burn the mist off the water. In a few hours it would be gone, setting the stage for a sharp frost, if the clear weather continued. Netta was running up and down the grassy slopes with energetic enthusiasm. Her younger sister, attempting to follow her, tumbled frequently but complained little, picking herself up with patient deliberation to carry on their game.

'Making the most of the good weather, are you,

Ellen?' greeted the postman.

'Aye. There'll no' be many more days like this, I don't suppose.'

'Well, there's a letter for you here.'

He handed her the letter and her pulse quickened when she saw the strange but familiar writing of the address.

Carefully she opened the envelope and unfolded the sheet of paper. Her heart beat faster as she made her way haltingly down the page.

Liebe Ellen,

At last I hear that you are safe and well. For this I am very thankful.

You tell me that your husband is dead. What can I say? It is a dreadful thing to finish the war alive and to die like this. I do not like this man and what he do to you, but I do not wish this for him. I am sad for you that this happens to him.

I keep your letters always by me. I think of my little daughter all the time. I am full of thanks that you tell me about her, but now I am sad because I do not see her. I regret always that I cannot help.

Here life is hard. Many people have no money and there is not enough food. People are hungry. I play my music again, but my concerts are not popular. My sister Eva plays also. She is well. She will marry next year to Daniel. They are very happy. For myself, I...

A cry from Eva brought Ellen abruptly back to her surroundings. Her small daughter had fallen onto her face and Netta, struggling to right her, had succeeded only in falling on top of her. The two lay in a heap, arms and legs flailing wildly in a fruitless effort to get up. Stuffing the letter into her pocket she ran to free them.

*

The letter was burning a hole in her pocket. One thing after another had filled her day. Now though, she had pleaded tiredness and, leaving her father and Margaret in companionable silence at the fireside, she retreated to her room. For several minutes, she sat unmoving on the side of the bed, her hand, in the pocket of her skirt, gripping the letter. Every beat of her heart told her that something of significance was written there. Slowly she withdrew the pages and began to read, her eyes retracing the last words she had read.

For myself, I do not marry. I displease very much my parents. They wish me to marry a nice Jewish girl. How I tell to my parents that the girl I love is Scottish? How I tell them that I have a daughter? If they meet you, I know they will understand. But this thing is not possible.

Please to write to me. Please to send a photograph. I am learning more English, so I send you another letter.

Please write. I wish to know if you are happy.
  From your loving friend,
  Josef.

Ellen folded the letter and replaced it carefully in her pocket. Then she leaned over and blew out the candle flame. Darkness closed in. Only the comforting rhythm of her children's soft breathing interrupted the silence. How long she sat on the side of the bed, she had no idea. The words of the letter raced through her brain. He was not married. He was sad that he could not see his daughter or help with her. He wanted Ellen to write... to send a photo. Through the jumble of her thoughts one sentence kept flashing: *This thing is not possible.*

The click of the latch on the kitchen door roused her from her thoughts. She rose from the bed and walked slowly to the window, pulling back the curtain and staring through the glass. The stars were glittering brightly in a frosty, new-moon sky. Across the valley was the field where the prisoners' tents had stood. She could see them now in her mind's eye as clearly as when the camp had been struck more than three years earlier. She pictured the weather closing in, the arrival of the captain on the doorstep to ask for her help. She saw Josef as he had looked when the men carried him in... the pale boyish face with its long lashes and curls of soft brown hair... and the sea-washed blue eyes that had fastened on her once he was well enough to take in his surroundings.

Ellen allowed herself a small smile when she remembered her body flattened against the wire in a futile attempt for closeness with the man she loved. She thought of that one and only occasion when the gate was opened, allowing Josef a temporary escape to 'make the most' of their impossible predicament. It was a memory against which she had, for many months, firmly closed the barriers, for to think about it would bring only sadness and longing.

Her thoughts were disturbed by the low murmur of voices. Looking to her right, she could see the dark outlines of her father and Margaret, as they turned the corner of the cottage and came slowly towards the bedroom window. Margaret's arm was through her husband's and her hand was enclosed in both of his. They stopped in front of the window, not noticing Ellen's silent presence. Ellen heard the rise and fall of her father's voice, more animated than she could ever remember it. Margaret laughed and Ellen heard Duncan's low chuckle in return. They turned and strolled back towards the door.

The surge of pleasure she felt came as a surprise to Ellen. Previously she had fought to stave off the jealousy that had accompanied the seeming transfer of his affections. Now though, she rejoiced in her father's happiness at being with the woman whom he had loved for so long, but who had been denied him until now.

It came to her then in a flash, that a sea crossing and the problems of making herself understood in a foreign land were all that stood between herself and happiness. Such a small difficulty, compared with what her father had faced all these years. Her father would, of course, object. She would need to explain. Even then she doubted that he would be happy with what she proposed to do.

Late that night, when her father and Margaret had retired to bed, she got out pen and paper and settled down to write.

My dear Josef,

I was overjoyed to get your letter and to hear your news.

Of course I have a photograph for you, but I will not send it. I have a better idea. I will bring it myself. I have enough money to book a place on the boat for all three of us. I will spend Christmas and Hogmanay with my father. Then I will come.

There is nothing now to stop us being together.

From your loving friend,

Ellen.

She wrote the envelope, enclosed the letter and placed it, for safekeeping, in the drawer of the bedside cabinet. She would go to the post office tomorrow.

Unable to sleep, she pulled on her coat, slipped her

feet into her boots and silently left the house. She made her way through the deep darkness and looked back at the cottage. Leaving her father would be a wrench. Forsaking the land she loved would be difficult – though hadn't Josef said that her hills reminded him of his own homeland? A tremor of excitement rippled through her body at the thought of what she was about to do. With the certainty of Josef's love awaiting her, she felt invincible. A lifetime of happiness awaited them.

She stood until the insidious creep of frosty air caused an involuntary shiver. Then she ran recklessly across the floor of the valley to her home, while, overhead, a million twinkling stars tried and failed to pierce the dark unknowing of her path.

Acknowledgements

My thanks go to:

Andrew and Heather Craig for their hospitality, for showing me the practicalities of sheep farming, answering my endless questions, giving me a copy of the 'Lanarkshire (Middle Ward District) Waterworks1919' and reading and commenting on the first draft of my book.

The Long Long Trail: The British Army 1914 – 1918. (Chris Baker 1996 - 2008) Internet Publication. http://www.1914-1918.net/recruitment.htm

U-boat attack 1916; Battle of the Atlantic 1914 – 1918 (EyeWitness to History 1997) Internet publication. http://www.eyewitnesstohistory.com

Jeremy Belk for advice on the German character and for correcting my 'O' level German vocabulary which had been in mothballs since 1961.

Thanks as always to my daughters, Rachel, Wendy and Liz, for their interest in and support of all my writing projects; particular thanks to Wendy for reading my first draft and enthusiastically giving suggestions.

A big thank you to my youngest sister Sarah who suggested to her publishers, Aria, that they might like to read my book. If it were not for her, this story would never have seen the light of day.

HELLO FROM ARIA

We hope you enjoyed this book! Let us know, we'd love to hear from you.

We are Aria, a dynamic digital-first fiction imprint from award-winning independent publishers Head of Zeus. At heart, we're avid readers committed to publishing exactly the kind of books we love to read — from romance and sagas to crime, thrillers and historical adventures. Visit us online and discover a community of like-minded fiction fans!

We're also on the look out for tomorrow's superstar authors. So, if you're a budding writer looking for a publisher, we'd love to hear from you. You can submit your book online at ariafiction.com/we-want-read-your-book

You can find us at:
Email: aria@headofzeus.com
Website: www.ariafiction.com
Submissions: www.ariafiction.com/we-want-read-your-book
Facebook: @ariafiction
Twitter: @Aria_Fiction
Instagram: @ariafiction

Printed in Great Britain
by Amazon

35371412R00243